Pipit's Song

A Love Story

Alene Roberts

Published and Distributed by:

Granite Publishing and Distribution, L.L.C.
868 North 1430 West • Orem, UT 84057
(801) 229-9023 • Toll Free (800) 574-5779
FAX (801) 229-1924

Cover Artwork by Jennett Chandler
Cover Design by Tamara Ingram
Page Layout by Brian Carter / SunRise Publishing, Orem, Utah

Library of Congress Control Number 2001094018
ISBN 1-930980-46-9

Dedication

To Elliott:
my husband
my sweetheart
heart of my heart

Chapter One

Her mind struggled up out of the darkness—deep, silent and hollow as a well. Like water drawn up from the well, she slowly ascended to conscious awareness. Finding herself standing in a world of white, her mind reeled with confusion. Where was she? Though it was night, a full moon reflected an unknown and frightening landscape. Paralyzed, disoriented, her eyes traveled a wide arc; white was everywhere, as far as her eyes could see. Ghostly white arms reached upward, gently swaying around her, accompanied by a soft moaning sound. They reminded her of seaweed on the ocean floor, bending to the will of the current. Then confusion receded momentarily. Her vision sharpened. The arms were tree branches covered with snow!

The first sensation she felt was pain, throbbing pain in her head. The question came out in a whisper. "What happened to me?" She shivered uncontrollably. Her feet felt numb. She looked down and saw herself knee deep in snow.

"Where am I?" She heard her voice, shaky and hoarse. Only an eerie whine through the pines answered her. A wave of unreasoning terror threatened to engulf her. "No!" she muttered. "Dear God, help me." As if in answer, some inner strength held the fear at bay. She looked around, searching for something by which to orient herself. She saw tracks in the snow behind, apparently hers...then nothing.

Shall I follow my tracks back to get my bearing? she asked her muddled mind, *or go on ahead? But where was I heading?* The pain made it hard to think. *Was there a reason I was walking in this direction?*

Startled at a new sound, she listened intently. "Am I dying and hearing heavenly music?" she whispered to the empty wind. "Where is it coming from?" Straining to hear the direction, she realized it was up ahead. Had I heard it before? Is that why I was going in this direction?

One thing she knew for certain, she would soon freeze to death if she didn't move—if she didn't find shelter. Lifting a foot she took one step, then another. She clutched her head in pain from the movement. Nevertheless, she kept moving, forcing herself forward. Maybe I'm delirious. Maybe the music isn't real. Suddenly, there was a male voice singing to the music.

Her numb legs moved faster. She grasped the sound as one would a lifeline. Turning a slight bend in the path, she saw narrow fingers of light filtering through the pines making golden streaks upon the snow ahead of her. With her breath coming hard and fast, her head pounding, she struggled on. A few yards further around another bend, stood a cabin! Light streamed from two large windows casting its glow upon the porch and the snow in front of it.

Apparently she'd been following a road hidden by the snow. With the last few convulsive steps she reached the porch. She stopped; the music, the voice, that led her to safety, now held her mesmerized. She knew the song, *Silver Bells*. The voice was mellow and heartwarming. A sadness from deep inside her burst out in a tearless sob. Steadying her head with one hand, she stumbled up the steps to the door. Raising her numb hand to knock, she noticed for the first time that she had on warm gloves. She knocked and waited, but no one came—the music continued. Seized by an irrational thought, she panicked. What if it was a radio or a television she was hearing, and no one was there! She pounded with both hands. The music stopped.

Soon, the door opened. A man stood in the doorway, a look of astonishment on his face. "Yes?"

"I'm lost...I need help," she murmured. The man's head bent down in her direction, but his eyes seemed to look past her. *Can't he see I need to get out of the cold?* her foggy mind asked.

"Please, come in." He stepped aside.

"I'm covered with snow..." She tried feebly to stamp it off, but grabbed her head in pain and fell against the door frame.

The man seemed confused. "That's all right, come in out of the cold."

She slumped to the floor of the porch, unable to move further.

"Arthur!" she heard the man yell. Barely aware, she was lifted by strong arms and carried to a chair by a fireplace.

A gruff voice asked, "Where in the hell did you come from, miss?"

"I don't know," she muttered.

"I can tell you this, young lady, you've been in some kind of an accident!"

"What is it, Arthur?"

"She has a lump the size of an egg on the left side of her forehead."

The man with the mellow voice, gently felt the lump.

"Ow," she protested weakly.

"I'm sorry, miss," he apologized. "I'm blind. I had to feel it to see it."

She began slipping in and out of consciousness, vaguely aware of them unlacing her boots and putting her feet in lukewarm water...rubbing them briskly with towels, then repeating the same procedure with her hands. A stinging ache replaced the numbness and cold. Someone held warm broth to her lips, encouraging her to drink. It tasted good and warmed her going down.

"Thank you," she heard herself say.

~~~~~~~~~~~~

Matthew waited while his uncle Arthur checked on the girl for the umpteenth time. They were like a couple of nervous, clucking hens trying to look after one ailing little chick.

It was midnight—five long hours since the young woman had collapsed on their doorstep, and she was all they could think about. Matthew ran a hand through his hair, contemplating the unexpected event which had taken his mind so completely off his own troubles, gargantuan as they were. He and his uncle had been terrified at the responsibility of caring for this wounded, almost frozen, and incoherent girl. They couldn't get her to a doctor. The road out was blocked by several fallen trees as a result of record breaking blizzards.

As soon as they had warmed the girl's cold limbs, they fed her hot broth. Changing her clothes to flannel pajamas, Matthew had ruminated on how convenient it was that he couldn't see. They put her to bed in the room just off the front living area. Immediately after, Arthur had called a doctor friend in Chandler via his wife, Mamie, on the shortwave radio. The doctor walked them through her care and told them what to watch for. He told them that for the first forty-eight hours it would be an around-the-clock vigil. In order to make sure she wasn't slipping into a coma, they had to wake her every couple of hours. He explained to them that even though she might wake up, talk with them, and swallow the soup, it didn't necessarily mean she was in a conscious state. They were not to leave her alone when she was moving about...to even stand outside the bathroom and listen through a partially opened door.

Arthur exited the bedroom, closing the door quietly behind him. "She seems fine, Matthew, but what do I know?"

Matthew could hear the exhaustion in his uncle's voice. "I pray she is. Neither of us are going to rest easy until she fully regains consciousness. Why don't you go on to bed, Uncle Arthur?"

"We both need to go to bed. I'll set the alarm and we'll get up together and check on her, but first I need to unwind a bit." Arthur studied the worried and strained face of his nephew, who was, in fact, more like a son.

Matthew had been orphaned at age fifteen. Arthur was Matthew's only relative, so he and his wife, Mamie, took him in. The tragic death of Matthew's parents turned out to be a terrible time for all of them. Even at that, it was much more devastating to young Matthew. He and his parents were as loving and close a family as Arthur had ever seen.

Adding Matthew to the family circle had brought much joy and companionship to their children. The cousins had always enjoyed each other. At the time, he and Mamie thought they were doing Matthew a favor, but as it turned out, Matthew had proven to be a blessing to the whole family. He hadn't allowed himself to burden any one of the family with his grief. Instead, he helped on the farm and became more than a cousin to Randy, who was eleven at the time and to Elaine, who was sixteen. He became their 'brother,' and was a constant and cheerful presence in their home.

Now as a man, tragedy had struck Matthew again, and this time he had succumbed to it. It took eight months, but finally, one day he slipped into a depression.

Arthur encouraged him to come up here to the cabin for a short time—away from the painful memories. After a couple of days joking with him, reading to him, and talking with him, he began to act more like himself. But Arthur knew that what was going to help him the most was caring for this strange young woman who had so miraculously dropped onto their doorstep, and who so desperately needed their assistance. Matthew, in his usual style, had already risen to the occasion by putting aside his own misfortunes and focusing his full attention on helping him save the young woman's life.

~~~~~~~~~~~~~

Two hours later, the alarm awakened Arthur. Before he could go in to get Matthew, he found him waiting in the hall. Together, they entered the sleeping girl's room, turning on the light.

"The light didn't wake her, Matthew. Hope she's all right." He gently touched the young woman's shoulder and shook her slightly. "Wake up, miss." She stirred and slowly opened her eyes. "Are you all right, miss?"

She was slow to respond. "I...think so."

Relief flooded through both men. "Would you like to get up for anything?" Matthew asked.

"No," she muttered sleepily.

"All right, then, go back to sleep."

"She's closed her eyes, Matthew. Let's turn out the light and wait a moment to see if she moves." Shortly, Arthur whispered, "She's asleep."

"I hope it's sleep, not unconsciousness," Matthew whispered back.

The two men went back to bed with the alarm set for two hours later.

Arthur was relieved when morning arrived. It felt less frightening to care for the girl in daylight. This brought his attention to the fact that it wouldn't be daylight for Matthew. His heart turned heavy as he went in to wake him. "It's morning, Matthew. I'll go put on some oatmeal to feed our girl."

Matthew dressed quickly, his breath coming fast, feeling anxious, hoping the young woman had improved. As he walked into the kitchen, Arthur told him the cereal was about ready, suggesting they go in and wake her. Together, they stopped at the door and knocked. There was no answer, so they entered. She was lying just as they'd left her two hours ago.

Arthur nudged her gently and she opened her eyes. Each time she woke, both men felt intense relief. "She's awake, Matthew. How are you young lady?"

She stared at them blankly. "Fine."

"Would you like some breakfast?"

"Yes." Her voice was thin.

"My name's Arthur. This is Matthew. What's your name?" They had tried this routine after they brought her in last night, but she had only stared at them just as she was now. Arthur spoke to her again. "Matthew here is going to hold you while we help you eat some oatmeal cereal. Is that all right?"

"Yes."

Arthur left for the kitchen while Matthew sat down on the bed and helped her sit up. She groaned and held her head. "You've been in an accident, miss," he said softly. "You'll be all right."

She started to tip slightly, so Matthew slipped his arm around her small waist and gently pulled her over to him, helping her lean against his chest, holding her in his arms. Arthur brought in the bowl of cereal and a glass of water on a tray, and sat down on the other side of the bed. "Here, young lady. Can you hold the bowl?"

"Yes," she said, not reaching for it.

"Let me help you," Arthur said, holding a spoon of cereal to her lips. "Open your mouth and eat this." She did as she was told. She chewed and swallowed. "Here's a drink of water," he said holding it to her lips. She drank.

When Arthur had spooned the last bite of cereal into her mouth, and after she'd swallowed the last of the water, he smiled. "She finished it, Matthew."

"Good! Surely—that's a good sign, Arthur."

"I hope so. Now, young lady, would you like to go into the bathroom?"

"Yes."

"I'll help you," Matthew said, easing her legs carefully off the bed, trying not to jostle her. Helping her to stand, he placed one arm around her waist. "Can you walk?"

"Yes." Together, they walked slowly across the hall to the bath-room.

Walking her back to bed, Matthew helped her in. Immediately, she seemed to fall asleep. Disappointed that she hadn't stayed awake, the two men left the room to eat their own breakfast.

~~~~~~~~~~~

The patient continued to sleep, and her nervous caretakers con-tinued to worry. Each time they woke her, their hearts were in their throats, fearing she wouldn't respond. They had awakened her mid-morning, and now it was time for lunch. Arthur went into the kitchen to warm some soup while Matthew got her prepared to eat. Matthew longed for sight, for the ability to *see* how she was. Instead, he had to depend on his other senses. Listening, he could hear her even breathing and felt that this must be a good sign.

Already, this lightweight slip of a woman had entwined herself around their hearts, and their curiosity about her had intensified. Matthew no longer wanted to call her 'Miss.' It seemed too imper-sonal now. It was important that she have a name. From the begin-ning, he had thought of her as their 'snow angel.' He acted on the thought.

"Miss Snow Angel, it's time for lunch." He listened intently, but there was no response. Finding a shoulder, he rubbed it gently. "Wake up, Angel." She turned over onto her back.

"She's opened her eyes, Matthew," Arthur said entering the room with soup and water on a tray.

Matthew smiled, relieved, then addressed the girl. "It's time for lunch. Can you sit up?"

"Yes."

"She isn't making a move to do so, Matthew."

"Let me help you again," Matthew said to the girl, once more assisting her to a sitting position in his arms while Arthur posi-tioned himself to feed her. Holding her this second time, he noted that her body seemed more rigid, so he caressed her short silky hair until he felt her relax. He stroked her arm, felt her small wrist and her long slim fingers. A tenderness welled up inside him for this helpless young woman, and he uttered another silent prayer, one of many he and Arthur had offered in her behalf.

~~~~~~~~~~~~~

The end of the day brought their patient no nearer to consciousness. The two men hovered over and cared for their ailing chick, getting more nervous as the time wore on. The around-the-clock vigil went on all that night, the next day and all of the third night. The only relief they experienced came when the forty-eight hour crisis period had passed.

On the morning of the third day, as the doctor had suggested, they let her sleep, and waited for nature to take its course. However, Matthew thought he'd give it a nudge. He sat down at the piano.

Chapter Two

The music drew her up and out of the darkness, reaching deep inside to a longing, a forgotten dream. A shuddering gasp of breath forced her lips apart, and like the shutter of a camera, her eyes flipped open. Flat on her back, she stared at the strange ceiling crossed by a huge log beam. Warmth and comfort enveloped her, bringing back the memory of her stumbling arrival at the cabin.

Light streamed from underneath the heavy drapes on her right. *What time is it?* she wondered. Pushing back the covers to look at her watch, she found it gone. It was then she saw the flannel pajamas. *How did I get into these?* She sat up abruptly. The room seemed to tilt; a sharp stab of pain shot through her left brow. Her hand flew up to her head. She was shocked to feel a lump the size of a golf ball!

"What happened to me?" she whispered.

Fighting a wave of dizziness, she gripped the bedsheets until it passed. Gingerly, she moved one leg at a time over the edge of the bed, finding that if she moved carefully, she could prevent the pain.

Looking around, she noted two doors opposite each other. From behind one she heard the music. She stood up and took the first step toward that one, surprised to find warm house slippers on her feet—probably because her feet had been so cold. Padding carefully over the carpeted floor, she reached the door and was about to open it when she stopped and looked down at her attire. Deciding the pajamas were modest enough, she opened the door a crack and peeked into the room. She could see a man seated at the piano. His back was to her. Questions swirled in her mind. *Where was the other man? Was there a woman here? Who undressed me?*

Opening the door wide, she stepped in and took a moment to look around. The room was bright and cheerful with a large window in the log wall to her right, and a large one in the front. It was carpeted in several shades of blue cut pile as was her bedroom. In front of the large sandstone fireplace was a brown leather couch. On either side of the fireplace were two large overstuffed chairs of blue, yellow and brown plaid. Against the left wall stood a tall bookcase. To the right of that in the left corner was the man at the piano.

The house slippers made no sound as she walked slowly around the couch and chairs to the piano. The man, looking straight ahead, continued playing and singing. She waited for him to notice her, but he gave no sign of recognition that she was standing there. Frowning, she tried to remember something he'd said last night. Oh yes, he said, 'I'm blind.' He's blind! How odd staring at some one who couldn't see you.

Sensing someone, the man stopped playing, cocking his head to one side.

"Hello," the girl said. Unprepared for the reaction she got, she watched the man freeze for a moment, as if he wasn't sure she had spoken, then he responded with such enthusiasm, she nearly took a step backwards.

"You're awake!" Profound relief washed over Matthew, bringing him alarmingly close to tears. Instead, it produced a smile that spread across the width of his face. "I was hoping my music might pull you back to us."

"What would it matter if I slept a little? After all," she responded testily. "I just had a nasty bump on the head."

Momentarily taken back, his smile left, but it soon returned.

"What's so amusing? I don't find a bump on the head amusing."

He laughed out loud. "You're a presumptuous little thing. After all, you fell on our doorstep for help. We didn't ask for the privilege."

"What makes you think I'm little? You're blind."

Matthew pivoted on the bench. "I could tell from the level of your voice that you were at least five or six inches shorter than my height of six feet. And Arthur said you were a little on the thin side."

Feeling shaky, she stepped back and held on to the back of a chair. "Who's Arthur?"

"My uncle."

"Is there a woman here?"

"No, just us two."

"Who undressed me last night?" she asked suspiciously.

"We did."

"Well, I don't think..." She stopped, frowning with concern. "Did you...."

"I assure you, miss, we were very careful. We covered you with a blanket while we removed your wet clothes and put on the pajamas. Besides, it wasn't last night, it was three nights and two days ago."

The girl was shocked. "I've been asleep for three nights and two days?"

"No, unconscious, or rather, in and out of consciousness."

The girl moved around the overstuffed chair she'd been holding onto and sat down carefully, feeling weak.

"So you're awake, young lady," said a raspy voice behind her.

She turned to the older man, and nodded.

"What is your name, miss?"

"Uh..."she began. "Uh..." She shook her head as if to clear the fog away. "I can't think, just a minute." She'd never forget her name! How stupid. When it didn't come, her breath came faster and panic set in. "I...I don't remember my name!" She stood up abruptly. Feeling a sharp pain, her hand flew to her head.

"Please sit down, miss," the older man said. "You've had a concussion."

"How do you know?" she retorted, backing away from both men. "Are you a doctor?"

"Hmm, feisty little thing, isn't she, Matthew?" He grinned.

"I would say that."

"How do you know?" she insisted.

"I have a shortwave radio in my bedroom here, and I contacted a doctor friend. He's been diagnosing you the best he could and telling us what to do for you."

"Don't you have a phone, or a cellular?"

"No phone. I didn't bring my cell phone because it doesn't always work up here, so I used my trusty old shortwave."

"Why didn't you take me to a doctor?"

"We couldn't get you out. We've had record breaking snowstorms and blizzards."

She was too agitated to sit down as the man had suggested. She moved carefully, but restlessly about the room, then looked hopefully at the older man. "Did I have any identification on me?"

"Nope. Right after you arrived another blizzard hit like I've never seen up here...creating twenty foot drifts in places. You were darn lucky to find us before it blew in. When the weather settled down a little, I got on my snowshoes and went searching to see if I could find a car. Couldn't find a trace of one. I suspect if you arrived here by car, you either hit one of those downed trees or went off the road trying to avoid one. In either case, it's probably buried somewhere under one of those drifts."

"Where's a mirror? Maybe if I see myself, I'll remember."

"Sit down, miss, and I'll get one. My daughter, whose pajamas you have on, keeps one up here."

"I don't want to sit down," she replied, noticing the man at the piano was listening in rapt attention.

"Either you do what I say, miss, or I won't get you a mirror...or breakfast for that matter."

"All right." She sat down, and he left the room to get the mirror. The man on the piano bench was smiling. "How can you smile so much when you're blind?" she asked bluntly.

He laughed. "I think I've smiled more since you walked in here this morning than I have for months."

Arthur returned. "Here's your mirror, miss," he said, placing it into her hand.

Holding her breath a moment—hoping, afraid, she lifted it slowly and stared at the image. She gasped in shock. It was a stranger who stared back at her! "I...I don't recognize myself." *This can't be!* she thought. Yet—there was a vague familiarity about the disfigured face. "I have a black eye as well as a lump. My haircut is horrible...and I'm certainly no beauty—in fact, I'm...I'm homely!"

In her anxiety she glanced at the blind man and saw compassion on his face. She closed her eyes a moment, hoping that when she looked into the mirror again, she would find that her lack of recognition had all been a terrible mistake. Breathing deeply, the panic receded. Lifting the mirror, she slowly opened her eyes and gazed into it once more. Her voice rose with hysteria, "It isn't a mistake!

I don't recognize myself!" Putting the mirror down, her chest heaved with short rapid breaths.

"Are you hungry?" Arthur asked quickly, knowing that the young woman was close to hyperventilating.

"What? Uh...I'm starved—but I can't remember myself—or anything. And...I'm homely!"

"Okay," he said calmly, soothingly, "I'll go fix our homely girl some breakfast, huh, Matthew?" he said easing toward the kitchen.

"Good idea. I'm starved too, Uncle Arthur. Get to work."

Holding up the mirror again, her heart still racing, the girl focused on her hair. It was short, straight, dirty blonde at the roots, and light blonde above. Was it peroxided or was it sun-bleached? It stuck out in several different directions. "I'm going to fire my barber," she muttered.

The man called Matthew laughed.

"Chow's on, you two. Come and get it."

Taking in a couple of breaths trying to ease her heart back to it's normal beat, the girl muttered, "That was fast."

"It's been ready for a while. We were waiting for our homely sleeping beauty to wake up. Matthew was sure it would be this morning. He was singing to you."

The man's unconcerned down-to-earth banter and humor stabilized her. Still a little breathless, she turned to Matthew and spoke somewhat dryly, "Thanks. I might have starved to death while sleeping."

The man, Arthur, disappeared into the kitchen, leaving her to follow. She started, then stopped. Stepping over to the sightless man, she asked, "May I call you Matthew?"

"Of course. And what shall I call you?"

Sucking in an uncertain breath, she said, "I wish I knew." Taking Matthew's hand, she walked carefully, leading him into the kitchen area.

"Thank you," he responded. "You're nicer than Arthur. He lets me fend for myself."

"Of course," Arthur said. "How else can you learn?"

The girl noticed that it was a small galley kitchen, but at the end of it was a nice sized bay window. Nestled within it was a round pine table, set with three plates. In the center was a large platter with scrambled eggs, bacon, and a pile of toast. Steaming cups of hot chocolate were set by each plate.

"Mmm, this looks wonderful, Mr...."

"Arthur. Call me Arthur."

"You must be getting well if you're so hungry," remarked Matthew, "but the doctor said you have to take it easy for a while."

She gently seated herself at the table and stared out the window. The wind had died down and the sun was out. Hills of drifts and tall snow-covered trees glistened in the sunlight. "This is a nice place in which to take it easy. It looks like a fairyland out there. Far different than that frightening night I intruded upon you."

"It must have been frightening," Arthur said, the eyes under his scraggly brows were sympathetic. "Matthew, will you say grace?"

"Yes. Thank you."

After they had eaten a while, Arthur asked, "What shall we call you, young lady?"

"I'm sure I have a 'homely' name, also, so call me anything."

"Snow Angel?" Matthew suggested, smiling.

The girl stopped eating and stared at him. "Why that?"

Matthew only smiled and continued to eat as fastidiously as possible.

"He thinks you dropped in out of the sky to cheer up a couple of lonely men."

"What do *you* think I should be called, Arthur?"

"Well...let's see. I think...Pipit! Yes, Pipit will do nicely."

"Why that?" she asked even more surprised.

"I'm an old bird watcher. I've traveled the country bird watching. One summer day while walking near the cabin here, I came across this injured little bird. The bird was a pipit. Three nights ago, you looked like a wounded little bird who had fallen on our doorstep."

"Perfect, Arthur!" exclaimed Matthew enthusiastically. "Pipit it will be."

The girl smiled for the first time. "Fine with me. Somehow, I don't think snow angel fits me." She paused for a moment. "Is it a homely little bird?"

"On the contrary," Matthew said, "it resembles the lark and its song is echoic of its name. It has a slender beak and it constantly wags its tail. Quite a unique little bird."

"We're alike in that. My beak is a little slender, too."

Matthew and Arthur laughed.

Chapter Three

The girl had bathed, washed her hair and changed into the clean underwear she found in the drawer. Arthur told her she was welcome to wear anything of his daughter's that fit her.

Deciding to wear the clothes she came with, she studied them. The jeans looked hardly worn. The sweatshirt was blue and felt soft and fleecy inside. The high top boots looked new and expensive, so did the blue down jacket, knit cap and lined gloves. She was puzzled that she knew these were expensive. It was logical that she would be wearing warm clothes up in the mountains, but why was she here? For some reason, snow felt unfamiliar to her. Where did she live? Taking several deep breaths to ward off the rising panic, she forced herself to calm down.

She felt in all the pockets for something that would give her a clue—any clue concerning her identity or where she'd come from. Nothing...that is, until she looked into the last pocket which happened to be in her jeans. She found a scrap of paper. There was writing! Excited, she read it: 'Meet Kirk 7:00 PM gazebo.' Disappointed, this only brought more questions. "Who is Kirk?"she asked, stuffing it back into her pocket.

She went into the bathroom to comb her hair, but just stood there staring into the mirror. Was she trying to look like a boy or was this the latest style? It seemed as though she remembered a movie star with this hairstyle. She couldn't think who. Combing it did nothing. She still looked like a waif. Large blue eyes were her only good feature, she decided. Her lips were thin, or at least the top one was, the bottom one was fuller. The ridge of her nose was straight. It was slender and pointed like a pipit, she was sure. Was it because her hair was so short that her forehead looked high? On the whole, her face looked long tapering down to her chin. She simulated a smile. It was wide and crinkled her eyes. "Why didn't I get my teeth straightened?" she asked her image. One front tooth slightly overlapped the other. "Did I wear makeup? Probably not if I wore my hair in this style!"

Feeling a little dizzy, she went back into the bedroom and lay down on the bed, pulling the coverlet over her. She closed her eyes. *Maybe I don't even have parents, maybe I'm an orphan*, she thought. Her face in the mirror looked young, but for some reason she knew she was older than she appeared. *What kind of a person am I?* Her brain felt overworked. Gripped by anxiety, she found herself taking short, shallow breaths. She had to think of something else—Matthew and Arthur and their kindness.

~~~~~~~~~~~~

She awoke to the raspy voice of Arthur from the front room. She looked at her watch. Arthur had returned it to her, explaining that they had taken it off while dipping her hands in tepid water that first night. It said 1:00. She had slept three hours! Rising from the bed, she freshened up and went into the front room.

Arthur, who had been reading to Matthew, stopped, looked up and smiled. "Welcome to the world, Miss Pipit."

"Is it normal to sleep like this?" she asked.

"Yes," Arthur replied. "So I understand from what the doctor said. He suggested that while you were unconscious, we should try to awaken you periodically to make sure you weren't slipping into a coma. We had to feed you and help you to the bathroom."

She frowned. "I don't remember *any* of that! I don't like the idea of strange men taking me to the bathroom."

"Don't worry. When we woke you up, you were able to manage yourself pretty well under the circumstances. Are you hungry? Matthew and I have already had lunch."

"No, thank you. I think I ate too much for breakfast." She walked to the window and looked out. It was starting to snow again. "It looks like we'll be snowed in for a while."

"'Fraid so," Arthur said.

"Don't mind me, go ahead with whatever you were doing."

"I was reading to Matthew, but my old voice needs a rest. Come and sit down here with us, we need to talk to you."

She went over and curled up in the chair opposite Matthew since Arthur was sitting on the leather sofa.

Matthew spoke first. "Have you remembered anything?"

"No. I don't even know where we are. We could be in Africa for all I know." Then glancing outside, she amended, "Well, anywhere *but* Africa."

"Arizona," he answered. "This cabin is located between Greer and Alpine. Does that mean anything to you?"

She shook her head, then remembered he couldn't see her. "No, it doesn't."

"It's not too many miles from the Sunrise Ski Resort. We thought you might have come up to ski. Do you ski?"

"I don't know. It's strange, some things I seem to know, and others I don't."

"The doctor said that happens,"Arthur said. "While you were asleep I contacted him again and told him about your amnesia. He said many puzzling things attend amnesia. The doctors don't have all the answers for it, and the varied manifestations.

"Now, Matthew and I want to update you with what we've done. I called my wife in Chandler." Noticing her puzzled expression, he added, "Chandler's just south of Phoenix. Anyway, I called her on the shortwave and asked her to call the ski resort to see if they had a reservation for someone who didn't show up. She radioed back and reported that the only ones who didn't show up were couples or men."

"I hope I was alone in the car," she stated suddenly. The worried expression left almost immediately. "I was...I think I was. No, I'm sure I was."

"I hope so. We'll just have to trust your feelings on that one," Matthew said. "Go on, Arthur, tell her what else you've done."

"I also asked Mamie to telephone the police in Phoenix and ask if someone of your description had been reported missing. She radioed back and said there hadn't. There isn't much else we can do until the highway department at Eager can get up here to this out-of-the-way area, and clear off the trees which were blown over onto the road during the blizzards. As I said before, you might have gone off into the ditch trying to dodge one."

"Let me think," she said, staring at the floor intently. Arthur watched her hopefully, and Matthew held his breath. "For some reason, what you just told me makes me feel like any minute I'll remember something. It's right there at the edge of my consciousness." After a few moments, she sighed in frustration. "It won't come."

~~~~~~~~~~~~

Ever since the conversation with the men, the girl, now called Pipit, felt totally frustrated and at loose ends. She stared out the window of her bedroom, trying to remember the event that left her on foot, alone, in these mountains three days ago. If her car had gone into a ditch to avoid a tree, she needed to find it! Feeling certain that she left her wallet behind in the car, she decided to go look for it immediately. The wallet would have her identification.

Retrieving her coat, hat and gloves from the closet, she put them on. Instinctively she knew that if Arthur and Matthew saw her, they wouldn't let her go. Her head still hurt when she moved too abruptly, but in spite of it she had to go look for the car.

Opening the door to the main room, she peeked in. No one was there at the moment. She quickly walked to the front door gritting her teeth at the discomfort her rapid movement caused. Closing the door quietly, she moved to the steps and went down. The snow was deeper than she'd expected.

Looking around, she noticed how the snow had been blown into towering drifts here and there. She tried to walk in the places that looked more shallow, but still it was above her knees. Determined, she trudged on, ignoring the pain the jostling caused. At least it wasn't nearly as bad as it was three nights ago. She could stand it.

Arthur and Matthew entered the main room after talking with family on the shortwave. Noticing Pipit's bedroom door ajar, Arthur peeked in. He frowned. "I don't think our Pipit is here, Matthew."

"What do you mean not here?"

"I think she's left the cabin," he said, quickly walking to the door and opening it. "She has! I see her." Stepping out on the porch, he hollered. "Pipit!"

She turned and waved at him. "I'm going to look for my car!" she yelled back, clasping a hand to her head at a spasm of pain.

"Come back!"

She shook her head and trudged on.

"Foolish, stubborn girl!"

"You have to go after her, Uncle Arthur!"

"No. She's just going to have to find out for herself."

"Then I'm going with her, Arthur."

Arthur smiled. "That will be the blind leading the blind."

Matthew didn't react; he was out on the porch hollering. "Pipit! Wait, I'm coming with you!"

Since she hadn't been able to make much progress, she heard him. Shocked that it was Matthew who was calling, she yelled, "No! You can't see where I am!"

"Stay there and I'll find you!"

Before she could refuse, he had disappeared into the cabin. "Doesn't he know that he'll just slow me down? Why is Arthur allowing this?" she murmured impatiently.

It wasn't long before she saw Matthew moving carefully down the steps. Amazed that a blind man would attempt to follow her, she watched for a moment, then trudged back toward the cabin to help *him*.

"I'm coming toward you, Matthew!"

"Thanks. I'll follow your voice."

At last Pipit reached Matthew before he strayed off the path. "Matthew! Why did Arthur send you?" she asked, shocked and irritated.

"He didn't," he said, smiling. "He called you foolish and stubborn and said he was going to let you find out for yourself. *I* decided to come and help you out of the fix you're going to get yourself in." His smile broadened.

""Oh? And what's so amusing?"

Matthew chuckled. Pipit, annoyed, felt like shoving him into the snow. "If you don't tell me what's so funny, I'll leave you to fend for yourself." This only made Matthew laugh.

Suddenly, she realized the ludicrousness of the situation—she didn't *know* where she was going, he couldn't *see* where he was going—and started laughing herself. It was as if something unwound inside her and she couldn't stop, leaving her weak. Unable to take a quick step in the deep snow to steady herself, she reached toward Matthew for support, but instead, fell against him, knocking him off balance and plunging them both into the snow. Their laughter escalated.

Arthur watched from the window of the cabin, chuckling. "Well, Miss Pipit, I think you *are* Matthew's 'snow angel.' You've made him laugh—the first real laughter since the accident."

When their amusement had exhausted itself, Matthew said, "That helped. It released all the tension and worry over you, Pipit."

"At least I'm glad for that," she said, managing to stand up. "Are you up to the trek?"

He got up, brushed himself off, and grinned. "I thought you had a pain in your head?"

"It's not as bad as it was three nights ago. Actually, I think it's a little better. Didn't somebody say a good laugh was better than medicine?"

"Nevertheless, Pipit, the doctor told Arthur that you should take it easy for a while."

"I'm fine...really. I have to go look for my car. I want to know who I *am*."

"Arthur's right. You *are* on the stubborn side. Overdoing today could cause a setback."

"I'm all right," she insisted.

Matthew couldn't see the set of her jaw, but he could hear it. "Okay. Let's go."

After wading a few more yards, Matthew said, "You know, we do have snow shoes. It might be a little easier."

"I guess it would, but we've come this far, let's go on."

When they finally reached the main road, Pipit looked around and saw only high drifts and mounds everywhere. "I don't know where to start digging, Matthew."

"Digging?" He laughed. "Digging with what? Did you bring a shovel?"

"I have two arms and hands!" she stated defensively, trudging off toward a drift next to what she thought was the road. Her next step plummeted her into snow up to her chin. "Help!"

"Where are you? Keep talking," Matthew said, walking toward her voice. The next thing he knew, he was in snow up to his chest. "Where are you, Pipit!"

"Right here. I think you stepped on my toe."

He burst out laughing so hard, he wondered if he'd have the strength to get them out.

"This isn't funny!" The exclamation was uttered just before her own bout of laughter.

The cold seeping into their feet and legs soon brought them back to reality.

"Start digging, Pipit. Your car could be right here," Matthew said, grinning.

"Really?" Her digging felt like she was trying to swim, except she didn't seem to be moving ahead. "You know, Matthew, I didn't have lunch. I feel a little weak."

"It's about time. You should have felt weak thirty minutes ago. Hold on to me, I'm going to try to crawl up and out about where we stepped off." It took a while for him to get a footing, but at last, he managed to crawl up with Pipit holding on to his jacket.

Pipit sighed with relief when they were safely back on the road, only *knee deep* in snow. She leaned heavily on Matthew's arm as she led them along their tracks back, surprised that she felt so tired. When they reached the cabin, Arthur opened the door.

"Hey, you two can't come in here covered with snow from head to toe. Go around the back."

"I don't think I can make it, Arthur," Pipit said, breathlessly.

"Oh? Why does that not surprise me? Stay on the porch. I'll brush you both off."

Back with the brush, Arthur started with Pipit first. He grinned. "Did you find your car?"

She gave him a withering glance. "You know we didn't."

Even from the porch, Pipit could smell meat cooking. "I'm starved."

"After you both change from your wet clothes, we'll have hamburger sandwiches."

"Thanks, Arthur. That sounds wonderful," Pipit said, then spoke to Matthew facetiously. "Thanks for coming with me on my adventure. I think you may have saved my life again."

~~~~~~~~~~~~

Arthur, watching Pipit eat like a farm hand, wondered how one so slight could eat so much. "Matthew, I think our girl worked up quite an appetite this afternoon."

"I guess the outing didn't hurt you after all," Matthew said, smiling.

"I told you I was all right."

"So you did."

After dinner, the two men told their insubordinate patient to go relax by the fireplace while they did the dishes. By the time they got through and went in to join her, she was curled up in one of the chairs asleep.

"Matthew, I guess we'll just have to carry Pipit to the bedroom and undress her for bed."

"I guess so, Uncle Arthur."

Her eyes popped open. "No you don't! I'm perfectly capable."

The two men laughed.

Chapter Four

The fourth morning, Pipit awakened feeling stronger, finding that abrupt movements brought much less pain. She smelled something good though it was still dark out. Arthur was a good cook. She tried to remember if she knew how.

She lay there contemplating her circumstances, buffeted by contradictory emotions: peace here with these two men, yet rootless and lost. Outside, the wind howled and moaned under the eaves like some lost soul, echoing her own feelings of lost self. She shivered. Stepping out of bed, she pulled the drapes open and saw snow swirling viciously against the window. Did Arthur and Matthew have enough wood and food until they could get out?

She dressed quickly in the chill of the room, then washed her face and brushed her teeth with the new toothbrush Arthur had given her. Looking at herself in the mirror, she saw that the lump was smaller and the black around her eye was diminishing, but her hair still looked ragged. It wasn't even long enough to curl. It was then she became aware of something she hadn't noticed before. She had the vestiges of a tan! Did this mean she lived where it was warm...or did she go to a tanning salon?

Weary with the questions, she went into the main room and found Matthew standing at the front window as if he could see out. It struck her as both sad, and absurd. "Are you enjoying the view?" she asked.

Startled, he turned and smiled, thinking of how others usually avoided any reference to his blindness. "Thank you for not feeling sorry for me."

"You don't look like someone I should feel sorry for."

He smiled. "Thanks. Let's sit down. I want to talk to you."

"Where's Arthur?"

"He's in his bedroom talking to his wife, Mamie, on the short-wave."

"How many bedrooms *are* there?"

"Three."

"I thought you had exhausted all the subjects you could possibly talk to me about considering my limited memory, but go on, what do you want to talk to me about?" She sat down on the couch and watched Matthew walk tentatively to one of the chairs.

"First of all, how are you feeling after our rigorous outing yesterday?

"A little stronger I believe."

"Good. Now, how are you feeling emotionally?"

"As good as can be expected."

"You may be a very private person, Pipit, but I need to know how you are feeling," he asked a little more insistently.

"Why do you want to know?"

"I think you can figure that out," he stated with an edge to his voice.

She wanted to call him nosy, but thought better of it since she was under his and Arthur's care. "I feel like I'm in limbo...floating in the air with nothing solid to put my feet on."

"Go on."

"Why?"

"Maybe if you express your feelings, it might help you regain your memory."

"Maybe I don't want to remember." Her answer sounded flippant.

Ignoring her tone, he replied, "I might have thought that if you hadn't had a concussion. As I said, tell me more...think about it...analyze..."

She was silent for quite a few moments while he waited. "I....I feel totally inward—focused inward, but there's nothing there." She sucked in a tremulous breath, then spoke hesitantly because suddenly she felt like crying. "I....I feel fear."

Matthew's voice was gentle as he prodded her. "Is the fear from something in your past or is it fear about your present condition?"

Her mind felt foggy and she still wanted to cry. *This man was good*, she thought. *Maybe he's a psychologist.*

"Why don't you let yourself cry?" He reached into his pocket and pulled out two folded tissues.

She took them, surprised at his intuitiveness. "Your music, your voice makes me want to cry."

Surprised, he said with a small smile, "Shall I play and sing so you can cry?"

She nodded, then again realized he couldn't see her. "Yes. Sing *Silver Bells*."

"All right." He got up and stepped carefully to the old upright and sat down.

"Is it Christmas?" she asked.

"No, it's January 15th."

"Why were you singing a Christmas song?"

"Because the words and melody of that particular song make me feel like all is well and life is good." He began to play and sing.

She listened to the beautiful melody, and the indefinable mellow and tender quality of his voice. The yearning she felt before, filled her chest with such pain a few tears spilled over. Though not knowing the cause of the pain, the tears relieved some of the tightness in her chest.

Next, Matthew sang the song, *Cry: "If your sweetheart sends a letter of goodbye, It's no secret you'll feel better if you cry."* This song brought a few more tears than the first. Arthur appeared at the door. He paused momentarily, then stepped back, leaving the scene. Matthew had worked his magic.

As the tears dried up, she found her voice. "Matthew..."

He stopped. "Yes, Pipit."

"Come and sit down. I'm through."

"Did it help?" he asked as he walked over to his chair and seated himself.

"I'm not sure. I'm a little surprised that the song, *Cry,* made me feel fearful."

"Fearful of what?"

"I don't know, but I think I...uh feel afraid of relationships."

Matthew was quiet for a moment. "What kind of relationships? With men, family, friends?"

"I have no idea, but I think right now I'm afraid of getting to know you and Arthur because I feel empty. You've both given to me, but I have nothing to give back."

"That's not true, Pipit. You have already given Arthur and me more than you'll ever realize. When people are thrown together like we've been, there are shared moments, brief, but ones we'll hold in our hearts forever. In my sightless condition, you made me feel useful when you showed up at our door needing help. You gave me joy when you quietly came over and stood beside the piano and said hello. I knew then that you would be all right. You've given me something to smile about. Even your desire to hear me sing and play has given me assurance that I have something to offer."

"I...I had no idea. If this is true...then thank you for telling me."

"It's true, Pipit. Just you sharing your fears with me has made me realize something *I'd* forgotten. We have to live in the present if we're going to live at all. Some of us live in the past too much, some of us too much in the future, not really living life as it should be lived. *You* have a chance, now, that most of us don't have. You have the opportunity to live totally in the present—if you will."

Matthew had touched a chord of truth in her. He was right. What he said not only gave her hope and eased her heart, but it seemed to pull her out of limbo, placing her feet squarely on solid ground. With it came a semblance of relief, allowing her to observe Matthew—to really see him for the first time. His sightless eyes were beautiful—moss green with earth tones. She couldn't tell how old he was. His face was boyish, yet mature looking.

"How old are you, Matthew?"

He blinked in surprise. "That a girl, 'Pip.' I'm thirty-four."

"You haven't always been blind or you wouldn't have to learn to fend for yourself."

"I've been blind for only eight months."

"Hey, you two," Arthur said from the doorway. "It's 7:30 and time for breakfast."

"Sounds good to me, how about you, Pipit?"

Her heart easier, she smiled. "Sounds good to me, too—and thank you, Matthew," she added quietly, taking his hand and walking him into the kitchen.

Matthew smiled. He knew this cabin inside out, but her hand felt comforting to his aching heart.

Chapter Five

Earlier that morning, Pipit tried to help with the breakfast dishes, but both Arthur and Matthew protested.

"Take it easy today and tomorrow, then you can start to help," Arthur had said.

She sat on the couch, staring into the fireplace thinking—almost wishing this cozy feeling, here in this warm cabin with the blizzard blowing furiously outside, could last.

Matthew was on the shortwave talking to someone, and Arthur was sitting in one of the chairs reading. She laid her head on the back of the chair and dozed. An hour and a half later, she awakened and looked at her watch, surprised that she'd slept the time away again.

Matthew had replaced Arthur in the chair. He was holding his head in his hands. She quietly watched him as he leaned back. His eyes were closed and tears were slipping out from under the lids and beginning to roll down his cheeks. Quickly, he wiped them away with his forefinger.

Focusing outside herself for a moment, she wondered what had caused his blindness. She noted the grief on his face, certain she'd much rather have amnesia than be blind. Almost imperceptibly, he sat up straighter—masking the grief, and she knew he sensed she was awake.

Silently, she took in his appearance. His earth-green eyes, which were now open, were stunningly attractive with his thick brown hair. She wished she could have seen the expression in them before they lost their sight. Though his nose was long and prominent, what stood out was his jaw line which fanned out from his chin, widening to just below his ears like a wide V. There was definitely room for the smile, she remembered, which spread across his face producing furrows of laugh lines around his eyes. His wide full-lipped mouth seemed always on the verge of smiling.

Internalizing for the first time how distinctive and strikingly good-looking he was, her heart danced a triple beat. A normal reaction for any woman who looked at him, she was sure.

The rest of him was just as attractive. The green flannel shirt, tucked into jeans, revealed broad shoulders and a full chest. His hands lay on his knees, his whole body alert. Though they were large, strong-looking hands, his fingers were artistically slender, and she was aware for the first time that he wasn't wearing a wedding band. He lifted a foot and rested it on his left knee, his right hand holding it.

"What are you doing, Pipit?" he asked quietly.

"I think you know."

"I wish I could study *you* without you knowing." He heard her laugh, and realized for the first time how infectious and pleasing it was.

"What happened to you, Matthew?"

He stiffened. "Do you mind if I don't talk about it?"

"Yes, I do mind. You made me voice my feelings. It goes both ways, Matthew."

"It isn't a happy story. You've been through a lot, Pipit; you don't need it."

"I want to know the two men who saved my life. As you said, I have to live in the present—that's all I have. There is no one else in my life right now—except you two."

His smile was grim. "You learn fast, Pipit." He exhaled heavily. "Eight months ago, my wife and I were driving home from a musical and we were involved in a multi-car accident. A drunk driver hit our car broadside, driving it into another vehicle. In all, eight cars were involved in the pile-up. Our car was struck several times. Diane, my wife, was killed."

"Oh no!" A long moment of silence passed before she asked, "What happened to *you, Matthew?*"

"I had a lot of bruises, two broken ribs and somehow an injury to the back of my head near the occipital lobe—apparently the cause of my blindness."

Pipit fell silent for a full minute before she could speak. "How have you been able to be so cheerful, Matthew?"

He gave her a small smile. "A wounded little bird flopped onto our doorstep and she's taken my mind off my own troubles."

"What do the doctors say? Will you ever see again?"

"Well—you know how doctors are when they aren't certain. It's hard to get a straight answer out of them They indicate that there's a chance I could regain my sight...someday."

"I hope so, Matthew," she replied softly.

"Thank you. But the hardest thing to bear at the moment is to see the way my children miss their mother."

She gasped. "You have children? How many and how old?"

"I have two, a four-year-old boy, Daniel, and a five-year-old girl, Meredith."

"Where are they?"

"Aunt Mamie, is taking care of them right now."

"Why didn't you bring them with you up here?"

"As I said, you learn fast, but I would rather not answer that question."

"All right." A sadness crept over her, making her wish she hadn't pried into Matthew's grief. She had felt peaceful until then.

"I'm afraid I've burdened you, Pipit."

"I asked for it. At least I can't feel sorry for myself now. My amnesia seems insignificant compared to what you've gone through and *are* going through. I imagine your children are missing you."

"I didn't want to leave them right now, but for a certain reason Arthur talked me into it. I do talk with them daily on the shortwave though. They get quite excited about talking to me that way. We had only intended to come up for a few days, but as you know, we got snowed in."

"Do you have enough food and fuel to last?"

"More than enough. We always prepare for events such as this."

"As an uninvited guest, I'm certainly glad to hear that." After a moment she asked, "Would you play and sing for me, Matthew?"

"I thought my playing and singing only made you want to cry," he responded, smiling.

"It also makes me happy, and I need cheering up right now."

~~~~~~~~~~~~

After a lunch of ham and cheese sandwiches and a bowl of home bottled peaches, which Pipit exclaimed over, she was ordered to go into the main room and relax. Arthur suggested that she take over reading to Matthew.

Standing in front of the bookcase, she studied the books. She had no idea what Matthew would want to hear or what Arthur had been reading to him. One shelf was devoted to Louis L'Amour paperback westerns, another one mysteries and adventure.

Before she could examine the other three shelves, Matthew walked in carrying a book, unaware of the request his uncle had made to Pipit.

Seating himself in one of the chairs, he sensed her presence. "Pipit?"

"I'm over here looking at the books in the bookcase wondering what you would want me to read to you."

"*You* are reading to me?" he asked, surprised.

"Your uncle suggested I do that rather than helping him with the dishes."

"I thought you might be in your room resting. Uh...please don't feel obligated."

"Obligated? I love to read...I think," she added parenthetically.

"But...you may not want to read this," he said, patting the book in his lap. "I'll wait for Arthur."

"All right, if you'd rather have Arthur read to you, I'll..."

"It isn't that. I'd much rather hear your musical voice than Arthur's scratchy tones, but..." his voice trailed off.

"You're reading something private or personal. I'll find a book and go in my bedroom and read," she said quickly.

"It isn't private or personal, Pipit. Only the *reason* I'm reading this particular book is personal."

"What is the book, Matthew?"

"The Bible."

"The Bible?" Walking slowly back, she sat down on the end of the couch nearest Matthew. Something deep down nudged at her heart. It felt like something from long ago. *What was it?* she asked her blank mind.

Sensing something, Matthew asked, "Are you remembering something?"

"I wish I was," she replied in a small faraway voice.

"Would you mind reading the Bible to me, then?"

"No."

He held it out for her. She took it and studied the large and very old book. Carefully, she opened it up. On the inside cover, in exquisite penmanship, was the name: *The Milner Melloy Family Bible*. "This is your family Bible?"

"Yes. My father's name was Milner."

"Was?"

"My parents aren't living. I'm named after my father. My full name is Matthew Milner Melloy."

"Oh. Where do you want me to start reading, Matthew Milner Melloy?"

He smiled. "Anywhere in the New Testament."

Gingerly she turned the pages and found a place and began reading in St Matthew, Chapter 7: *Judge not, that ye be not judged...* and continued through chapter 11 finishing with the last verses: *Come unto me, all* ye *that labor and are heavy laden, and I will give you rest. Take my yoke upon you, and learn of me; for I am meek and lowly in heart; and ye shall find rest unto your souls. For my yoke is easy and my burden is light.*

She stopped, unable to go on. She closed her eyes, searching for understanding of the feeling these verses had evoked.

Matthew waited patiently, wondering, then asked, "Have you remembered something?"

"No. I hope these verses were comforting to you. Were they?"

"They were once in my life. Right now, *I'm* getting in the way. Are they comforting to you?"

"I'm getting in the way, too. I feel a little confused."

"I'm sorry. I was hoping they would help."

"We're quite a pair aren't we? An amnesiac and a blind person."

"The odds of us getting together were rather great weren't they?"

"Yes, and very strange." A comfortable silence settled over them. Matthew got up, went to the piano and began playing and singing. After finishing a song, he turned to Pipit. "Do you have a request?" he asked.

"Can't remember a one. I'm impressed that you know so many pieces by heart. Can you play anything?"

"I play by ear as well as read music. I'm grateful for the ear part." He began playing *Anniversary Song*. Next, he played and sang *As Time Goes By*.

"Those are old songs," his listener murmured when he finished.

"Yes. Lately, I sing my mother's favorites for some reason."

"I don't want to bring up something painful, but I imagine your wife liked to hear you sing and play."

His brows creased, thinking—feeling vestiges of the sadness and guilt that had sent him into depression. He swallowed with difficulty. "She did a little in the beginning, but she was busy with her work the first years of our marriage. Though she quit work when our daughter was born, she was even busier being a devoted mother.

"Do your children like you to play for them?"

"I don't play for them very often."

"Why?" she asked, shocked.

Matthew didn't know, and he didn't want to think about it. "Maybe it's because...uh...." He left it hanging. "I just don't," he stated with finality.

Chapter Six

Matthew awakened to the sounds of another howling blizzard. He groaned as he thought of his aunt having to care for his children this long. She was getting older and the children were difficult at times. Four-and-a-half days was all she was supposed to have taken care of them, and now it had been nine!

When he and Arthur had talked to her yesterday, she had insisted that she was doing just fine.

"But," she had informed him, "Elinor called. She found out what happened, and that I had the children. She tried to talk me into letting Mrs. Danville come and help with them. I told her no thanks. She was very persistent, but I was more so."

Matthew smiled in spite of his concern over Elinor. "Good," he'd said, "but you could at least get a high school girl to help you for a couple of hours, Aunt Mamie."

"I promise I will if I need it. Surely, you won't be snowed in very much longer."

Matthew sat upright in bed. The way it sounded this morning it might be a good while longer. "I shouldn't have let Arthur and Mamie talk me into coming up here," he muttered under his breath. They had insisted he needed to get away from everything and everyone for a few days. He had allowed his grief to pull him down to the point he could barely interact with his own children, but still, he hadn't wanted to leave them. As he had suspected it might, it got back to his mother-in-law, Elinor, that Mamie and Arthur had to take over for him. This would give her more ammunition to get what she wanted—custody of the children.

Since his sight had not improved and his state of mind had deteriorated, Elinor was constantly on his doorstep, checking, watching. She reminded him of a vulture circling a still moving prey, waiting for it to give up its fight for life—and he had, almost, until Arthur and Mamie stepped in.

Up here in the peaceful atmosphere of the cabin, talking with Arthur, listening to him read and smiling at his wry jokes had pulled him out of the deepest dejection. But what had begun to turn his focus outward was worrying about and caring for the strange young woman who dropped into their lives five days ago, even though it had been with trepidation that he and Arthur had taken over the responsibility.

He pulled himself up short. What had he been thinking? Of course he and Arthur should have come up here! He shuddered. What if they had not been here when Pipit showed up? She surely would have frozen to death!

His brows drew together in troubled thought. His children needed him every bit as much as Pipit, and more. Why couldn't he pull out of himself for them? Why did it take a stranger? The answer was obvious. It was because she was far removed from Diane and his grief—the grief his children were part of.

Thinking of Pipit, he smiled. She was like a breath of fresh air in their lives. It was amazing how much a person could see when sight wasn't available. Other senses sharpened, improving clarity of feeling, sensing and hearing. With sight, he wouldn't have been able to hear the infinitesimal and almost intangible changes in Pipit's tone of voice. These gave him insight to what she was really feeling despite what she was saying.

His smile faded as reality set in. When they were able to leave, what were they going to do with her?

~~~~~~~~~~~~

Matthew arrived at the kitchen door just in time to hear an exchange between Arthur and Pipit.

While stirring a pot of oatmeal, Arthur said, "Okay, tomorrow morning Pip ol' girl, Matthew and I are going to sit back and put our feet up while you make breakfast."

She stood next to him staring at his bony, callused hand stirring until the mass bubbled. Turning the gas down, he let it simmer.

"I don't want to get breakfast," she stated abruptly.

"Why?" Arthur asked, surprised at her reaction as well as her tone of voice.

"I just don't." She turned, stepped over to the table and sat down.

"You some kind of spoiled rich kid?" he asked.

"Probably," she shot back.

"I guess we'll all just have to go without breakfast tomorrow morning then."

Her brows rose in surprise. "What are you, my father? I'm not a child you can teach by punishing."

"We're kind of testy this morning, I see, Pipit," Matthew said.

The two, realizing his presence for the first time, turned to him and saw the smile on his face.

"Good morning, Matthew," greeted Pipit petulantly.

"Good morning to you...if it is a good morning."

"It was until Arthur informed me that I have to make breakfast tomorrow morning. Do I look domestic or something?"

"Not hardly," Arthur grinned.

"Since I can't see you, I can only tell you how you sound."

"Oh? And how do I sound? Like a 'spoiled rich kid' perhaps?"

Matthew eased past Arthur and seated himself at his usual place at the table. "You sound scared."

Arthur smiled. Blind or not, Matthew could always see through people.

"Well, I'm not...well, maybe a little. I don't think I know how to cook and I...uh guess I don't want to find out."

"Why be afraid? I'll teach you how," Arthur said.

"Thanks, that will help. But, I guess it's a little more than that. I'm afraid of finding out what kind of a person I was...am. What if I'm...oh, never mind," she murmured.

~~~~~~~~~~~~

When Arthur contacted Mamie, she told him that the weather report indicated a clearing up today. She also told him she called Eager and again requested a snow plow to clear the roads to the cabin.

Afterwards, Matthew talked with Merri and Danny, assuring them that he'd be home soon. He hung up feeling grateful that he could focus on them again. They had responded eagerly, and he knew they had reacted to a new vibrancy and awareness in his voice. He realized once more how frighteningly intuitive children are.

When he was through, he turned to Arthur, lowering his voice. "The pressing question now is—what are we going to do with Pipit when we leave for Chandler?"

"That's what I've been wondering, Matthew. I'm concerned about her family, but what can we do? If we only knew which state she came from."

"While dressing this morning, I gave it some thought. Let me toss out an idea that came to me. What if I hire her to care for the children for a while, Uncle Arthur? It will give us time to locate her family, and in the meantime her memory may return."

Arthur's wiry brows knit together. "Do you trust her with the children?"

"Perhaps I shouldn't, but for some reason I do."

"Elinor won't. She'll have a major hissy over you bringing in a stranger to take care of her grandchildren, let alone one who has amnesia."

The anxiety his mother-in-law always engendered expanded his chest with an uneasy breath. "Maybe we can hide the fact that she has amnesia."

"If Pipit will go along with it. She's kind of a pistol."

Matthew smiled. "I know. But I've got to do *something*, Arthur, Elinor has been waiting for just the right moment to take me to court. Before I came up here I knew I had to find someone reliable to care for the children, someone with whom Elinor could find no fault."

"That's not possible," Arthur spit out.

"I guess I should have phrased it differently. I need to find someone with whom Child Protection Services can find no fault."

"And you think Pipit is that person?"

"I don't know, but I feel she's a capable person...a strong person, and..." Matthew turned silent, trying to think of another word that fit the way he felt about her.

"And?"

"And a special person."

"That's good enough for me, Matthew. I like Pipit, but I don't have the gift of insight that you do. There's one problem, however. Where will she stay?"

"In the quarters Elinor added on to our house for Mrs. Danville to use when she came to help Diane."

"Elinor could make something of a young woman sleeping under the same roof, Matthew."

"Maybe she won't if Pipit is as homely as she says she is."

Arthur was silent.

"Is she, Arthur?"

"Is she what?"

"As homely as she says she is?"

"How would I know what her criteria for judging is?"

"Uncle Arthur, is she homely?"

"Well, compared to Diane, maybe some people would think so, but I don't find her so."

"Would Elinor find her so?"

"I'm sure she would."

"Good."

~~~~~~~~~~~~

After lunch, the sun came out, reflecting so brightly from the white sparkling landscape Pipit had to blink a couple of times. She remained at the kitchen table staring out, wondering what was to become of her when they left the cabin. She felt so utterly dependent on Matthew and Arthur, it frightened her.

"What is it, Pipit?"

Startled, she looked across the table at Matthew. "What do you mean?"

"You had begun to breathe more rapidly than usual."

"It's a little scary to be around you, Matthew. I think I could hide things from you easier if you could see."

"I doubt that," Arthur said, shutting a cupboard door. "Matthew has the gift."

"Then he's doubly scary," she replied as she watched Arthur clean up. He was a slender, wiry man with a narrow face, thin lips and twinkling hazel eyes. Though his light brown hair had not grayed too much, there were only wisps left on top.

When Matthew could see that Pipit wasn't going to voice the fear he sensed in her, he said, "Would you do me a favor, Pipit?"

Her gaze shifted quickly back to Matthew. "A favor?" she asked surprised. "I would be glad to, Matthew, but I can't think of a favor I could possibly do for you...except maybe read to you."

"We're going to be able to leave here soon. I was wondering if you would consider coming with me to Cave Creek."

"What in the world is a cave creek?" she asked apprehensively.

"It's a town. You must not be from Phoenix if you've never heard of it. It's about a thirty minute drive north of Phoenix. Cave Creek is where my children and I live. Would you consider coming home with me and caring for my children for a while...at least until we can find out who you are and let your family know, or until you regain your memory?"

Her surprise was so complete, she could only stare at Matthew, her mouth ajar.

"Pipit?"

"I...uh don't know what to say except that you don't know me. How can you trust me with your children?"

"I don't know. I just do."

"Thank you," she whispered, a little speechless. After a moment of silence, she added, "I don't know if I *can* care for children."

Arthur spoke up. "I have a feeling you can do anything you put your mind to, Pip."

"You both have more confidence in me than I do."

"There's one problem, however," Matthew began, "my mother-in-law, Elinor Halstrom. She didn't want Diane to marry me. They are a wealthy, influential family and they had plans for their daughter, and that didn't include marrying a farm boy from outside their social circle. Now that Diane is gone, they would like to have custody of the children, especially since I have this handicap. How would you feel about hiding several things from her? For instance—the way we became acquainted and the fact you have amnesia?"

"Then you are concerned about having me in your home."

"No. I'm concerned about the influence my in-laws have. Hiring someone capable to care for the children will help the situation immensely."

Pipit felt even more apprehensive about the offer. Still, this was a temporary solution for her, and would, at the same time, help Matthew. "May I think about it for a while, Matthew?"

"Of course, as long as you decide by tomorrow."

~~~~~~~~~~~~~

Curled up in a chair, paging absently through a magazine, Pipit listened to Matthew play old, heart-tugging love songs from another era.

Feeling grateful that her immediate future was not so bleak, she still felt uneasy over her ability to do as Matthew asked. What if she said or did something that would give his mother-in-law more ammunition to take his children away? Had she ever had any experience with children? She'd have to concoct a mythical past of sorts.

She had the choice of accepting Matthew's offer or be dropped off at some police station, or placed into some hospital for the penniless.

"Matthew," she said as he ended a song.

"Yes?"

"May I talk with you?"

"Of course." He left the piano bench and sat down across from her.

"The alternative to accepting your kind offer is rather unnerving, so I'll give it a try. But if I cause you any problem, any problem at all, I'll leave."

"Thank you, Pipit," he answered honestly.

"We'll have to come up with a last name and a past."

"I know. Any ideas?"

"I was a nanny to a wealthy family in Paris. *Je prendrai soin de vos enfants.*" She stopped, totally surprised at herself.

Matthew's jaw dropped. "Were you really? Did you just remember that you were a..."

"No," she said in awe. "I just made it up...the occupation, that is, not the French. I'm just as shocked at that as you are."

"You were very convincing. You fooled me. Maybe you really were a nanny. What did you just say?"

She was exuberant. "I said: 'I will take care of your children.' At least I know that I'm somewhat educated, either that or my family lived in France."

"That's wonderful! One more thing we've learned about you. Now, how about a French last name to go with Pipit?"

She thought a moment, then said, "How about Pipit Bordeau?"

Matthew repeated it. "Sounds just right."

Arthur entered the room smiling. "I just talked to Mamie. The snow plow is beginning to clear the road as we speak. They told her they would be able to reach here tomorrow morning. We'll leave right after they finish."

"Great," Matthew said. "I'm sure Aunt Mamie is relieved. He then announced with a smug grin, "Uncle Arthur, I want you to meet Miss Pipit Bordeau, my children's new nanny."

"Comment allez vous monsieur? Enchantez de faire votre connaisance. Or, in other words," she said happily, "How do you do, sir. I'm glad to meet you."

Arthur's brows rose in surprise."Sounds like you could be from France," he said.

"I am French," she grinned. "I was a nanny to a wealthy family in Paris."

Arthur studied her quizzically. "For real?"

She smiled. "No, not that I remember, anyway."

"You sounded darn convincing. Maybe you're an actress."

"In that case, I hope I'm a good enough actress to fool Elinor."

Chapter Seven

The low rumble of the snow plow was a welcome sound to Matthew, but it brought fear to Pipit. She knew her world here—the safe little cabin with Matthew and Arthur. The world outside was unknown. Her imagination took flight. *What if I was running away from something frightening? What if I was running from the law?* Taking a couple of deep breaths, she calmed down and tried to think more rationally. Deep down, she didn't really believe either one of those scenarios, and she fervently hoped she was right.

This much she knew for certain—her life inside this cabin was familiar and comforting. She didn't want to leave it, and face the strange new situation to which Matthew was taking her!

She studied her face in the bathroom mirror. The black around her left eye had turned to a ghastly yellow, and though the lump was down, it was still noticeable. "How am I going to explain this to Matthew's mother-in-law?" she asked her reflection. "I'll just tell her the truth. I was in a car accident," she answered herself. "But how shall I say I met Matthew and..." Her chest heaved with anxiety and her heart pounded. Quickly, she stepped across the hall and sat down on the bed almost choking with panic.

A knock on the bedroom door startled her. Through tight vocal cords, she responded with a hoarse, "Come in."

Matthew opened the door. "The snow plow has just finished. We'll be leaving in about thirty minutes, Pipit."

"I...I don't think I can do it, Matthew," she whispered.

Thoughtful for a moment, Matthew held out his hand to her.

Frozen with fear, she couldn't get up. Matthew stepped in and felt his way to a place beside her on the bed. "I can only guess what you must be feeling now, Pipit, leaving your safe little cocoon here and going into a strange new situation."

She couldn't answer. Matthew's empathy and understanding had constricted her throat.

Slipping his arm around her slender shoulders, he felt her trembling. He pulled her firmly against his chest and held her until the shaking stopped, then he asked, "Tell me, Pipit, what in particular is frightening you?"

"Explaining things to Elinor in a believable manner. There are too many questions we can't answer, such as—how you met me. It's just too big a responsibility for me, Matthew. I may make it worse for you."

"It's my responsibility, Pipit, not yours. Don't try to carry it. I know Elinor, you don't, so I'll be the one to answer any question she asks. It if doesn't work out, it won't be your fault. We'll just do the best we can and that's all we can do. Whatever help you can give will be much better than none at all. Right now, I can use all the help I can get."

"How will you say we met?"

"I was going to go over all this on our way to Chandler, but I see we need to do it now. Elinor has some kind of radar," he said, grimacing, "so our best bet is to sneak into town, so to speak. You'll have a little time to adjust before she gets wind of it. Of course, the moment she does, she'll be up there like a bird dog after quail. If she shows up when I'm not there and asks you questions, just tell her to ask *me*, but call me Mr. Melloy around her. I've already decided to tell her you came to see me and I interviewed you. Another thing I'll tell her is that I have references concerning you from two very reliable people."

"Who?"

He grinned. "Me and Arthur. But I won't give her the names of course. I've learned how to sidestep Elinor. She doesn't need to know everything, even if she thinks she does."

Breathing easier, Pipit got into the spirit of it. "I did come to see you—in a rather bizarre way...and you certainly have made me answer questions which could be construed as an interview."

"Right," he grinned. "You have the picture."

"I...I'll need more clothes and as you know I have no money."

"I've already talked to Mamie about this. She said she'd take you to a store and help you shop for a few things to get you started before we leave for Cave Creek. I'll take it out of your salary," he said, smiling.

"Salary?"she asked, surprised.

"I would have to pay someone else, so naturally, I don't expect you to work for nothing."

"All right, Matthew, I'll give it a try. Thank you for lending me a comforting arm. I feel better."

"You're welcome," he said giving her a quick squeeze before standing up. "And thank you for having the courage to take on my two children under the circumstances."

~~~~~~~~~~~~

As soon as Arthur had finished loading the suitcases and food, Pipit, dressed in the clothes she'd come with, stepped up into the second seat of the SUV. She watched Arthur go inside once more and this time, Matthew came out with him, waiting while he locked the cabin securely. Holding Matthew's arm, Arthur guided him to the car, opened the door for him to sit next to Pipit, then went around and got into the driver's seat. They were on their way.

Though feeling calmer, the thoughts of leaving this safe refuge left Pipit mute with uneasiness. Reminding herself that what made it safe was the presence of Arthur and Matthew, and she was going *with* them. This eased some of the fear, but not all. She would now have to interact with people other than these two, and it left her feeling insecure. All she knew about herself was what she'd learned in the small world of the mountain cabin. Would this little bit of knowledge be enough to start facing real life?

Matthew was silent and she wondered what he was thinking. Was he also nervous about her ability to face the life ahead of her? She looked over at him trying to see some sign of how he was feeling and noted that one hand lay relaxed over the wrist of the other. Letting out a small sigh of relief, she asked, "We're going to Arthur's place in Chandler to pick up the children?"

"Yes."

"What does Arthur do for a living?"

"He's a cotton farmer, but his son, Randy, has taken it over almost completely now, so Arthur is semi-retired."

"You called yourself a farm boy. Did you work for him on his cotton farm?"

"Yes."

The next question was asked with trepidation because of his blindness. "What do you...did you do for a living, Matthew?"

He smiled reassuringly at her. "I still do make a living in spite of my handicap. I have good help and I'm training a young man who will soon take over as manager of one of the stores."

"What kind of stores?"

"I own a piano store in Scottsdale called Melloy Piano Center, and another one in Phoenix called Melloy Music Center. In the Phoenix store I sell music books, sheet music and all kinds of instruments, except pianos."

"That fits you."

Arthur entered the conversation. "It does at that, Pipit." He grinned at her through the mirror. "Matthew can play almost any instrument. You might say he has a following of parents and children at the Phoenix store. When they go in and are indecisive over which instrument they want, Matthew plays a few bars on each. At this point both child and parent usually beg to hear the whole piece. By the time they leave the store, the child is already an eager student."

"I'm impressed," Pipit stated.

Matthew chuckled. "Arthur's just acting like a proud parent, Pipit. Don't take him too seriously."

"Oh yeah?" retorted his uncle. "Just walk into the store sometime and watch, Pipit." He winked at her through the mirror. "Not only that, he has a following of women. They like to hear him sing, and will use any excuse to get him to." Imitating one of them, Arthur's voice rose to a squeaky falsetto. "Would you please sing this piece of music for me? I'm not sure if it's the one I'm looking for."

Pipit and Matthew laughed, then Matthew protested. "All right, Arthur, enough is enough. How about we change the subject?"

Pipit smiled and changed it. "Did you attend college, Matthew?"

"Yes. I attended Arizona State University. I decided long ago that I didn't like farming. I studied music and graduated with an MBA in business."

Pipit frowned and shook her head. "I don't understand why your wife's parents were against you marrying her."

"I met Diane at ASU during her junior year when I was a senior. My parents were Texas peach growers, and I also worked for Arthur on his cotton farm to earn money for college. Mr. and Mrs. Halstom were not impressed with my background at all."

"But your education is impressive. I don't understand."

"The Halstroms are from an old and wealthy family that has been in the jewelry business for several generations, so it would be difficult to reach their social strata."

Something inside Pipit recoiled. It surprised her and it seemed that any moment she'd remember why. She tried to relax, hoping this would help the memory break through, but nothing came. Rubbing her forehead, she blinked back tears of frustration. Her memory loss would be easier to live with, she decided, if these incessant emotions didn't continually assail and torment her!

Matthew turned his head toward her. "What's happening, Pipit?"

"Nothing. That's the trouble." Her thoughts finished the rest— just an obscure, unidentifiable emotion with the memory lurking elusively behind it!

"I wish I could help."

"You already have and are. You're giving me a place to go."

Arthur drove silently, listening to snatches of their conversation, wondering what was ahead for these two, with their respective and unique challenges. He had told Mamie all about Pipit, and his wife's big loving heart was ready to take her in. Also, Mamie had prepared the children, explaining that their father was bringing a nice lady to help take care of them. Mamie reported that they were excited. More so, probably, because they chafed under the strict care of Mrs. Danville whom Elinor had sent to help Diane, and was now trying to foist on Matthew.

They had driven through Eager on highway 60 and were now passing through Show Low, which was nestled in that part of Arizona called the Mogollon Rim. It had snowed heavily through here, but the roads had been cleared.

Pipit looked out the window at the snow covered hills. "Snow feels unfamiliar to me, Matthew."

"It does? That's surprising to hear since you arrived on our doorstep all outfitted for the snow country. Arthur did say you had a tan which might indicate a warmer climate. Maybe you're from Tucson."

"Maybe," she muttered sleepily. Trying to remember was taxing. Leaning her head back, she dozed.

Chapter Eight

Pipit awakened just as Arthur turned into the driveway of his home in Chandler. It was an old cream-painted rambler of concrete block construction. An aged palm tree with a thick trunk and low fronds stood in the center of the wide front yard. Several citrus trees dotted the green lawn on both sides.

"Where are we?" she asked, suddenly wide awake.

"We're at Uncle Arthur's place."

"I thought he might live on his cotton farm."

"He did, but home developers bought the land. They paid him an obscene amount of money. He moved his farm, so to speak, to land he owned south of Chandler."

Arthur had driven on into the garage. "Well, here we are folks. Let's go in."

Pipit's nervousness at meeting Matthew's children escalated as they entered the hallway. Suddenly squeals reached their ears.

"Daddy's here! Daddy's here!" The two children left their aunt Mamie and ran past Arthur and Pipit to their father who had hunkered down. His arms reached out and encircled both children at once.

"You were gone so long, Daddy," complained the little girl.

"I know, but I'm back now." He kissed them both, then asked. "Have you helped your aunt Mamie while I was gone?"

The little boy whose wide smile reflected his happiness, spoke up, "Merri did all the breafuss' dishes this morning!"

"She did? And what did you do to help Aunt Mamie, Danny?"

"I picked up all our toys."

"Good!" Matthew hugged them again and stood up. "Now, go give your uncle Arthur a big hug while I give one to Aunt Mamie." His arms reached out and Mamie went into them, returning his hug with exuberant affection.

Mamie studied his face. "You look better, Matthew."

"I wish I could see how you look. I'm afraid you're worn out."

"The children and I had a good time, didn't we?" Both children nodded vigorously.

"Let's all go into the kitchen," Matthew said, "I want you three to meet someone special."

The children's gaze settled on Pipit, their eyes wide.

As they entered the large kitchen, their father said, "Merri and Danny, I want you to meet Pipit. Pipit, meet Merri and Danny."

Pipit smiled at each, "Hello, I'm very glad to meet you both."

They just stared at her, still clinging to their father. Once excited over the prospect of someone new coming to take care of them, they were now unsure of this strange person.

Arthur spoke up. "Well, you two, cat got your tongues? Aren't you going to say hello to Pipit?"

"Hello," Merri said.

"Hello," echoed Danny.

"I'm Mamie, Pipit," she said holding out her arms.

Pipit couldn't help herself. She went into Mamie's open arms and accepted the warm hug, soaking up the comfort it gave her.

Releasing Pipit, Mamie studied her face. "My goodness, dear, you did have an awful time didn't you? I'm so grateful Arthur and Matthew were still there when it happened." A slight shudder went through her, then she smiled and spoke to the group. "Everyone go freshen up, I have a pot of chili beans and fried bread waiting."

Arthur was the last to give her a kiss and a hug. "How are you, dear?"

"I'm much better now that you're here."

~~~~~~~~~~~~

Seated around the large round table, everyone silently enjoyed the meal. Merri was seated on the right side of Matthew and Danny was perched on a stool to his left.

Pipit, relieved to find that she felt as much at home here as she had in the cabin, studied Mamie. Slightly plump and round-faced, Mamie sparkled with cheerfulness and perpetual optimism.

Every chance Pipit could get, she studied the children, and smiled at them when they stole shy glances at her. Merri was a beautiful child with long dark lashes and mahogany-brown hair that fell below the shoulders. Her eyes were the color of a gray sky just before dawn, matching her finely chiseled, china doll features.

Danny, a brown-haired, freckle-faced replica of Matthew, had his father's wide, infectious and heart-stopping smile. Pipit had a hard time keeping her eyes off them. *Did Merri look like her mother?* she wondered. If so, her mother had been beautiful.

".....so why don't we run down there and get you a few clothes in the morning before you leave for Cave Creek?"

Mamie had been speaking to her. "Oh, I'm sorry, Mrs. Melloy, I'm afraid I wasn't listening...I..."

"Oh, call me Mamie. I was saying that there is a nice department store in the mall not far from here where we could get you a few things this afternoon to start your new wardrobe."

"I would appreciate that, Mamie. I'm afraid the clothes I have on will be a little warm in Cave Creek. They certainly are here. But I don't even know what size I wear...or how tall I am."

"Uncle Arthur can measure you," Danny said. "He's got a long measuring thing." He jumped off his stool and ran over to a broom closet and pulled out a yardstick. "See?"

"I see. Thank you, Danny."

"Here's where we're measured." He ran over to a wall and pointed to pencil marks. "This is how tall I am," he said, pointing to a mark. Pipit got up and went over to Danny and looked at the mark he was pointing to. "And this is how tall Randy used to be, and this is how tall my daddy used to be, and that," pointing even higher, "is how tall my daddy is now."

"Wow. He's tall. How tall is that?"

"Six feet!" he replied wide-eyed.

Arthur, got up and went over to them. "Here, Danny boy, how about we measure Pipit?"

"Yeah, let's do," he responded eagerly, handing him the yardstick.

"Step over here, Pip, and let's see where you fit in with all these marks."

Pipit shook her head. "Oh no, Arthur. That's a family record. Measure me somewhere else."

"Get over here," he insisted. She did as he directed. "Now stand straight up against the wall." He made a mark with the pencil just above her head. "There, now let's measure. It looks like you are uh...five feet five."

"Thank you, Arthur. That's nice to know, and thank you, Danny," she said smiling at him.

He grinned shyly, "You're welcome."

When they were seated, Pipit turned her full attention to the chili beans and fried bread. "Mm, this food is so good, Mamie."

"Thank you, Pipit. Would you like the recipes?"

"The recipes?" It hadn't even occurred to her to ask such a question. An awful thought struck her. She would have to cook! "Uh...yes, Mamie. I would like the recipes...I think."

Arthur laughed. "Atta a girl, Pip."

~~~~~~~~~~~~

"Here, try this on, Pipit, it kind of looks like you," Mamie said, "and it's a size four."

Pipit took the shirt and pants from Mamie and added it to the pile of clothes already on her arm. "That's cute. I think we have enough to try on for starters don't you?"

"Yes. I'll sit on this chair by the dressing rooms and when you find one that you like, come out and show it to me."

Pipit smiled. "All right," she said, disappearing into one of the cubicles. Relieved to be rid of the hot sweatshirt, she tried on the cooler clothes. So far, the trip to the department store hadn't been as unnerving as she had expected, but then, Mamie knew how to make anyone feel at ease.

After a parade of pants, shirts, shorts, skirts and sheaths and one nice dress, she and Mamie found they liked the same things, and chose one in each category. In another department, Pipit picked up a small purse. And after Mamie told her Matthew had a swimming pool, she purchased a swimsuit. At the shoe department, she picked out tennis shoes, sandals and dress shoes. After each purchase, Mamie pulled out a credit card that Matthew had given her and paid for everything.

As they left the store, Pipit asked, "Could we stop by a drugstore so I can get some makeup, deodorant, a comb and a few other things?"

"Of course we can."

When all the shopping had been completed, they headed for home. Wearing a couple of the new purchases—jeans and a knit shirt, Pipit felt much cooler. She also felt something else the shopping trip had accomplished. She felt she knew herself incrementally better than when they had started out. She learned a little of what her tastes were, and more importantly, that she was a decisive person.

Chapter Nine

The next morning, after the children had hugged their Aunt Mamie goodbye, they clambered up into the second seat with their father, one on each side of him. Pipit thanked Mamie and got into the front seat with Arthur.

After they'd driven for a while, Pipit's emotions began seesawing as she listened to the children's chatter. They were competing for their father's attention, and it was making her feel edgy. Before long, Merri was crying. She heard Matthew explain that it was Danny's turn to talk. The panic she'd felt just before leaving the cabin, came back. It seemed that she didn't have any emotional reserve at all! *Is this my nature, or did the head injury cause it?*

Clasping her hands together she tried to focus on the scenery and tune out the noise coming from the back seat. Staring mainly at trees and foliage, it struck her that something about Arizona seemed familiar to her...yet at the same time unfamiliar.

Turning west on Superstition freeway, Arthur said, "We're now in Mesa. Anything look familiar?"

"Palm trees feel more familiar than snow. Maybe I live in an area similar to this one."

"Well now, that's what I call a clue. That and a tan. I think we'd better alert the police in Florida...maybe Nevada."

"Maybe," she murmured, deciding to watch how Arthur drove to Matthew's. Eventually, he turned north on the Pima Freeway. For a while, the highway was enclosed by pinkish brown gravel and desert foliage, neatly kept. Passing that, Arthur pointed east to the now empty cotton fields on the Pima Indian reservation, and to the McDowell mountains beyond. North of the reservation, home developments sprouted up between desert stretches.

Laughter from the children and Matthew compelled her to turn around and look at them.

"Daddy's telling us funny stories," Danny said, giggling.

Pipit smiled at him and turned back. As yet, Merri had proven to be more reticent with her than her little brother. Another burst of laughter wafted to the front. "Tell me about *your* children, Arthur."

"I only have two. We wanted more, but it didn't work out that way. My oldest is Elaine whose clothes you wore at the cabin. She's married and has four children. Her husband's name is Richard and they live in Seattle. Randy is married to Joan. They have two children, a boy and girl about Danny and Merri's ages. Though Randy is four years younger than Matthew, he married at an earlier age than did Matthew. We wondered if Matthew would ever get married, but it's nice that the cousins are near the same age."

"Do all of you get together often?"

"Elinor is rather possessive of the children on holidays and on many weekends, so it isn't easy to get together, but we manage once in a while."

This disclosure distressed Pipit. Leaning her head back, she closed her eyes and tried to put it out of her mind. It wasn't long before Arthur informed her they were nearing the desert country of the Cave Creek area. "We'll pass through a town called Carefree just before we enter Cave Creek."

Sitting up, she looked around. Flanked on the east by gray-brown, barren mountains, the desert's yellow, sandy soil was covered with palo verde trees, saguaros, junipers and cholla cactus. *How*, she asked herself with a start, *did she know the names of desert flora?* Passing a small airport called Sky Ranch Airport, she noticed a greater abundance of saguaros.

The homes were spread out with at least an acre or more surrounding each. The terrain was rockier than the desert they'd passed coming up. Some of the front yards were landscaped with desert trees and flora, but most were left in their natural desert state. As far as she could see from the road, there were no green lawns.

The names of some of the streets intrigued her: Never Mind Rd., School House Dr., Stagecoach Pass. Arthur broke into her musings.

"We're almost at Matthew's, Pip."

She glanced in the back and saw all three asleep. "I hope I can do it, Arthur," she murmured.

"Sure you can. You're a strong person. Both Matthew and I can see it."

"I hope you're right."

Though his eyes were closed, Matthew was not asleep. He had heard Pipit's doubts, but was unable to focus on them. His mind was wrestling with thoughts of his own; doubting his ability to cope with what was ahead.

As they neared the house where he and Diane had lived together, he tried to quell the emotions which were rising up inside him. He dreaded walking into it and feeling its bleak emptiness. Diane had filled it with her many enthusiasms, and with her love for their children. The whole house was filled with beautiful things, reflecting her own delicate and graceful beauty—which never failed to enchant him. Even without sight, he could see her touch throughout the house and always he kept seeing the way she looked that last night as they left for the musical.

"Hey, gang!" Arthur's exuberant voice startled Matthew, interrupting his thoughts. "We're home." Glancing in the mirror, Arthur saw the children open their sleepy eyes. "I hope Pipit can swim don't you?" he asked as he drove into Matthew's driveway. He parked behind a two-car garage.

The house, Pipit noticed, was a mauve stucco with the same color tiles on the roof. The front yard was beautifully landscaped desert style with a couple of desert willows, thread-leaf sage and apache plume; prickly pear, desert zinnia and chamisa added color and texture.

How did I know these names? she asked herself. *Maybe I was a horticulturist, maybe...* Her life was consumed with maybes!

With feelings of anxiety just below the surface, she studied the house. A large square bay window on the left balanced the garages on the right. In between, a wide arched entry led to a nice sized porch.

"Is Mommy here?" Danny asked tentatively.

Matthew caught his breath. He'd explained and explained to Danny and Merri, but he realized Danny still couldn't quite internalize life without his mother. "Danny," he began, hoping that this would be the last time, "we talked about where Mommy went. Remember, I told you that she didn't want to leave us, but that she was happy and well and wants you to be happy and well."

"Oh, I 'member," he sighed, looking forlornly at his lap.

Undoing Danny's seat belt, Matthew scooped him up into his arms and held him tightly against his chest. *Dear God*, he prayed, *I need my eyes to see my little boy's face; I heard in his voice the expression, but I need to see it!* Would his heart ever stop breaking?

Arthur just sat still, waiting for the moment to pass, but saw Pipit turn around and watch the whole episode. He was certain she hadn't missed the anguish on Matthew's face that he himself had seen when he glanced in the mirror.

"Will you show me your house, Danny and Merri?" Pipit asked finally.

Danny nodded solemnly, but Merri nodded hesitantly. Arthur could tell that Merri was still not sure what to think of the woman who had come to take care of them. Pipit got out and opened up the door on Merri's side and Arthur did the same for Danny on the other.

"You lead your Dad inside, Merri, while Pipit, Danny and I carry everything in."

"All right, Uncle Arthur," Merri said, taking her dad's hand and walking toward the front door.

With a heavy heart Matthew unlocked the door, holding it open as all the things were brought in. Arthur carried the suitcases to the proper rooms and came back for the sacks which contained Pipit's clothes and purchases.

"Come on, Pip, and I'll show you your quarters. Did you notice on the other side of the garage that there was a window?" She nodded. "That was to be an additional one-car garage, but Elinor insisted that Matthew have that made into quarters for a woman called Mrs. Danville when she came to help." Opening the door, he added, "Now it's your place for the time being."

Pipit looked around. Noticing first the double bed with a small lamp table beside it, she was grateful to see that it held a phone as well as a lamp. In addition, the room consisted of a small couch, a television, a chest of drawers with a small private connecting bath. It looked like it had been decorated with discarded furniture, but to Pipit it looked pleasant. "This will be very comfortable, Arthur."

"Since it's on the opposite side of where the family is, it will be more private for you. Well, Pip, good luck. I need to get back to Mamie. I've been away from her far too long."

"Thank you, Arthur—for everything. I know that is an inadequate thanks to someone who has saved my life, but maybe I can do something for *you*, sometime."

"You're already doing something for me by helping Matthew out." He smiled as he left the room to say goodbye to Matthew and the children.

Pipit shut the door, feeling glad to be alone for a moment. She began putting her new purchases in the closet and chest of drawers. The skin care and makeup were neatly placed in the bathroom drawers. Sitting down on the couch, she felt a semblance of satisfaction at having things of her own. Thoughtfully, she contemplated her situation. Hearing a gentle knock on her door, she said, "Come in."

Matthew entered, and the children followed. "How do you like your room?"

"It's very comfortable, thank you," she answered in a stilted manner for she felt something different in Matthew.

"Well, the children and I have been looking in the kitchen, and we found the cupboards bare. We three decided that we'd like to go out to eat for lunch, run to the grocery store and pick up a few things to last a couple of days, then tonight, call in an order of pizza to eat while we watch a video." All this had been said in a light, but brisk, business-like manner.

Pipit smiled at the two eager little faces, then she remembered. "I...uh don't have a driver's license, Matthew." His face looked like she'd struck him.

Damn! he thought. Already, one of the feelings which had brought on his despondency—that of a prisoner whose independence had been ripped away—descended upon him unmercifully. He felt helpless. Managing a smile, he said, "Of course. Let me think..." He thought of the different neighbors...all of Diane's colorful friends, certain each would be glad to help out, but the last thing he wanted to do was visit with any of them at the moment.

Pipit watched, feeling his helplessness as well as her own.

The doorbell rang. "I'll get it, Daddy," Merri said.

"Me too," Danny said, running after her.

Matthew held out his hand to Pipit. "Come with us, it might be Elinor."

Her heart raced with anxiety as she stepped over to him.

Matthew took hold of her upper arm, feeling the firmness of it. He thought how different it felt than Diane's soft, supple flesh. *Why am I comparing?* he asked himself as he turned the knob of the front door.

"Hello, Matt," Margo Stillman, greeted, standing in the doorway with a large basket in her hand. "I saw you and your uncle and children drive in. I was sure you didn't have a stick of food in the house so I brought you over lunch. If you've had lunch, eat it later."

Matthew could have kissed her. Why hadn't he thought of Margo? A grateful smile spread across his face. "You're a lifesaver, Margo. Come on in. I would like you to meet Miss Pipit Bordeau. Pipit, this is our closest neighbor and the nicest one anyone could have."

"I'm happy to meet you, Pipit. I like your name."

"Thank you. I'm happy to meet you," she said, to the smiling, warm face of the woman in front of her. Pipit liked her immediately, and for some reason, having her as a neighbor gave her great comfort.

The children tagged along beside Margo, curious. "What's in your basket, Mrs. Stillman?" asked Merri.

"Yeah, what?" echoed Danny.

Everyone gathered around as Margo set the basket down on the bar.

"All right," she said, looking down at the two eager faces. "Let's see what we have here." She pulled out a bag of washed green grapes, some steamy hot dogs, a package of buns and a sack of her special homemade chocolate chip cookies. The children jumped up and down and clapped their hands.

"You see, Pipit, I've been over here often. I know what they like. Hope you like it."

"I'm starved. It looks wonderful."

Margo invaded the cupboards, pulling out paper plates, cups and napkins. "Matt Melloy, don't just stand there, sit down. All of you sit down here at the bar." Opening the refrigerator, she grabbed mustard, catsup and sweet relish and placed them on the table. "Okay, dig in folks while I get a pitcher of ice water."

Pipit began helping herself, then realized she was here to help. She prepared a plate for Matthew first. "What do you like on your hot dog, Matthew?"

"I know. I'll do it," Merri said, looking at her as if she were an intruder.

"That's nice of you, Merri," she said, trying to keep from feeling like one. "May I help you, Danny?"

He nodded smiling at her, making her feel better.

"Matt, what can I do to help today?" asked Margo.

"Margo, you're an angel of mercy. We were going grocery shopping to get a few things and remembered that Pipit has lost her driver's license."

"I'll take her."

"Thank you, Margo."

"You're welcome, Matt. Any change in the vision department?"

"Not yet, but I have high hopes. The little vacation was good for me, but we got snowed in, so Mamie had the children longer than she'd bargained for."

"I'll drive Pipit down to get her license whenever she wants to go, Matt."

Pipit shot a glance at Matthew. *Already we're in trouble,* she thought. His silence told her that he was analyzing what he could tell Margo.

"Margo, when Merri and Danny are through eating they need to unpack their suitcases. While they're doing that Pipit and I would like to talk to you."

"Okay. Let me go over and tell Phil. I'll be back in about thirty minutes."

~~~~~~~~~~~~

Seating herself in Diane's front room, for Pipit felt it was Diane's taste and not Matthew's, she looked around. It was a striking and beautiful room. The carpet, the two couches across from each other, the two smaller chairs, the coffee table and even the grand piano which stood in the bay window, were all white. Throw pillows on the couches and the silk flower arrangement on the coffee table were blue and rose, giving delicate color to the room.

Then it caught her eye. It was meant to catch everyone's eye the minute they walked into the room. Slowly, she got up and stood before the tall gold-framed painting above the marble fireplace. She knew it was Diane—for she looked like Merri. Mesmerized by her beauty, Pipit gazed at the ethereal looking woman with ivory skin, dark, shoulder length hair and large gray eyes. Her gown of white was a filmy, off the shoulder creation. A sheer swath of material haloed her shoulders. One graceful hand lay upon the other. Her regal expression would have been solemn if there hadn't been the slight upward tilt of her lips.

"Pipit?"

Startled, she turned. "I'm here."

"I thought so," he smiled. "I have the children busily unpacking and putting away. I'm sure Margo will be here momentarily. I told her to just walk in."

Pipit reseated herself and asked, "Are you going to tell her all about me?"

"Yes. I decided to when she came over with the food. She's a good friend and I think we could use someone on our side who knows the whole story. I especially think that would be helpful to you to have someone you don't have to be careful around."

"That would be nice, Matthew, thank you."

"Why are you so stiff with me, Pipit?"

"Because you're different here than you were in the cabin."

"Oh." He couldn't refute that. He *felt* different here.

"I've been looking at the painting of Diane. She's breathtakingly beautiful. Is that a good likeness of her?"

"It is."

"Did you have it painted?"

"No. That painter is far too expensive for my budget. Her mother had it painted a couple of years after we were married."

"Is it hard to be here where everything reminds you of Diane?"

Margo walked in before he could answer. "Well, I see you're waiting for me," she said sitting down. "I always feel like I should take off my shoes when entering this room."

"I think," said Matthew, "if Diane could have enforced it, we all would have had to."

"Okay, Matt, tell your aunt Margo all about it."

He smiled at her. "It's a most unusual story and a very private one. You can only tell Phil. I don't want any of Diane's friends in the neighborhood to know. I particularly don't want Elinor to know, so of course we can't tell the children."

"This sounds intriguing. Phil and I are the best secret keepers I know. Go on."

When Matthew had related everything, Margo was silent for a few moments. Finally she said, "This is right out of the movies, Matt. If I didn't know you better, I'd say you were pulling my leg."

"It's a little incredible isn't it? I shudder to think what would have happened to Pipit if we had been able to leave as we planned."

Margo gazed at Pipit. "You poor baby. How terrible you must feel not to remember. So Pipit is Arthur's name for you. It fits you, but I'm curious to know your real name. In fact, I'm a mystery addict. I read every one I can get my hands on, and here we have a real live mystery sitting right here in your antiseptic parlor, Matthew."

Matthew chuckled at the reference to the parlor. "I'm sure Pipit wishes you could solve the mystery for us."

"One thing for sure, when you regain your sight, and Pipit has regained her memory, we should throw one big rousing party. Now, how about we go grocery shopping, Pipit?"

"All right," she said not too eagerly, "but I don't think I know how to cook, Margo."

"Ah that's easy, just throw on hotdogs, open a can of Spaghetti-O's, broil hamburgers, have cold cereal for breakfast, and the children will think you're a great cook. Matthew, of course, is another story. Come on, we'll start with the easy things first."

Pipit smiled, feeling as though this practical, no nonsense-lady, with a great sense of humor, had just saved her life.

~~~~~~~~~~~~

The children were snuggled against Matthew on the couch in the family room and Pipit was sitting on the overstuffed chair, her legs curled up. They had just finished their pizza and were watching a video, *Toy Story*. Pipit remembered it. She had seen it! *I can remember a movie, but not my name?* she questioned, thoroughly puzzled. At least, she felt more confident since Margo had taken her shopping and helped her buy easy things to fix for meals.

Keeping her mind on the movie was difficult. She studied the family room, which was an extension of the kitchen. A hallway from the kitchen on the same side as the living room, led to the bedrooms. Kittycorner at the other end of the room, a hallway led to the garage and Pipit's quarters. The family room consisted of one overstuffed chair with lamp table and lamp beside it, a couch and a bleached wood entertainment center with bookcases on each side. A spinet piano stood against the upper right wall.

Diane had decorated her home with perfection. Even in the family room the colors were delicate—blues, rose and ivory. Everything was lovely and coordinated down to the last detail. She wondered if Matthew's income had paid for it all, or had Elinor?

Her eyes turned back to the small family on the couch. A feeling came over her that she hadn't experienced at the cabin. Up there, Matthew and Arthur had hovered over her, giving her their full attention. Now, Matthew and the children were wrapped up in each other, and Matthew had distanced himself from her. She felt left out and totally alone. Tears silently rolled down her cheeks unchecked because Matthew couldn't see them, and the children were engrossed in the movie.

Chapter Ten

A knock on the door awakened her. "Come in," she answered sleepily.

Matthew stuck his head in. "I'm leaving for work, Pipit, so you'll have to get up and look after the children. They've had a bowl of cold cereal so you needn't fix them breakfast."

She sat bolt upright. "What time is it?"

It's late, I should have left for work an hour ago. It's 8:30."

"You need to tell me when to get up, Matthew. I'll probably need an alarm clock."

"We'll sit down and go over my schedule tonight."

"Who's driving you?"

"My employee, Mike. He works at the Scottsdale store. He's added chauffeur to his resume," he stated with a touch of bitterness to his voice "He also drives me to the Phoenix store when necessary." All this was explained abruptly and without a smile.

"Have a good day, Matthew. I'll do my best to take care of the children." Where was the smiling Matthew she'd known up at the cabin? She missed him.

"Thanks. See you tonight."

Pipit threw off her new night gown, dressed hurriedly and went out to find the children. They were watching cartoons. "Good morning, kids."

No answer. She stood in front of them and blocked their view and repeated her greeting. Danny looked at her, his eyes lighting up, he said, "G'morning, Pipit."

Merri's eyes darted around the room. "Where's Daddy?"

"He's gone to work."

"I want my daddy," she said, her eyes filling with tears.

"He had to go to work, Merri. I'm here to look after you while he's gone."

"I don't want you to look after me! I want my daddy!" she screamed.

"It's okay, Merri, Pipit will take good care of us," Danny said, trying to comfort her.

"Shut up!" she screamed at her little brother.

Pipit turned and walked quickly into the kitchen area trying to get control of herself.

She had to open several cupboards before she found a bowl for her cold cereal, each time slamming the doors shut to vent her anger. The bar was cluttered with empty bowls, sugar and a carton of milk. Glancing at the children, she saw Danny huddled up in a ball, crying softly. Her heart went out to him.

Stepping quickly into the family room, she gathered him up into her lap, rocking him back and forth. "It's all right, Danny, Merri really didn't mean to yell at you, she just wants your daddy."

"I did too mean it," she said, giving Pipit a hateful look.

"Don't you go to kindergarten, Merri?" she asked hopefully.

"No," she answered sulkily.

"Aren't you five?"

She nodded. "Daddy said I didn't need to go to kindergarten. I can already read."

"Oh?" Pipit, recognizing there must be more to it than that, changed the subject. "Know what? Maybe if it's warm enough, we can go swimming. But first, have you both made your beds?"

"I didn't," Danny said.

Merri ignored her. "After I eat and clean up the kitchen and after you make your beds, we'll see how warm it is this morning. If it is, would you like to go swimming?""Yes!" exclaimed Danny, smiling now.

"I can't swim until the sun is almost down," Merri stated peevishly, " 'cause it will burn my ivory skin."

Pipit was speechless for a moment. "Who said you had ivory skin?"

"My mommy. She has ivory skin, too. She has to cover her arms and wear a hat when she goes out in the sun so her skin will stay beautiful."

"We can put sun block on your pretty ivory skin."

"Yeah, Merri," Danny agreed eagerly. "We can do that then we can swim together!"

"Mommy doesn't want me to do that. She wants me to swim only at night."

"When do you swim, Danny?"

His face fell. "I always have to wait until night to swim when Merri swims."

Pipit lifted Danny from her lap and told him to stay there while she went outside to check the weather. She looked around. The covered porch with its patio furniture and glass-topped table and chairs looked inviting. The backyard portion of the acreage was enclosed by a stucco wall. Instead of desert landscaping, green grass covered a small area, accented by flowers, bushes and palm trees. To the right of the yard the swimming pool, surrounded by a white wrought-iron fence, glistened in the sun.

Pipit walked back and sat down beside Danny. "I think it might warm up enough. I have an idea, Danny. Merri can sit on the porch and color or draw so her ivory skin can be protected and you and I can go swimming."

"Yay!" He clapped his hands, grinning from ear to ear.

"That's not fair! He shouldn't get to swim when I can't."

"Merri, we'll talk to your dad tonight about your skin. Maybe he'll give you permission to swim with sun block on."

She sulked, refusing to acknowledge what Pipit said.

Feeling more than irritated with Merri, she got up and began cleaning up the kitchen, reminding herself that the child had lost her mother, and that patience was in order here. Pipit felt certain she'd never taken care of children because she didn't have a clue how to handle her.

~~~~~~~~~~~~

When Matthew and Mike entered the Scottsdale store, the employees exuberantly greeted Matthew, teasing him about planning to be snowed in so he could have a longer vacation. He joked back, feeling more like himself here at work.

Known by most in the Scottsdale and Phoenix area as Matt Melloy, his wide infectious grin and easy approachable personality made people feel comfortable. He liked people, and wanted to be out on the floor as much as time permitted. Not only was he a good salesman, selling more pianos than most of his competitors, he became known as an expert on all brands.

Because of his clerks, he gained another reputation. If he was in the back room and someone wanted to hear how a piano sounded, the clerks would insist that Matt play a piece on it to make their sale. His reputation spread, so quite often a customer would ask him to play. The female customers who knew him, would also ask him to sing as well as play—a special perk for coming in, they felt.

Because of the time spent on the floor, Matthew had hired a good manager for the Phoenix store, and it wouldn't be long before he promoted Mike to manager of the Scottsdale store.

After the accident, it was only a short time before Matthew ventured back to work, still weighed down by grief over the loss of his wife, and despair at losing his independence. From then on, he had to have help getting to places around the stores; too many variables with customers coming in and out made it impossible for his path to be consistently free of human obstacles. Believing that his sight would return as the doctors said was possible, he refused to use a cane, or even entertain using a Seeing Eye Dog.

Putting on a smile, and listening carefully to the sound of voices, he had begun, once again, to function almost as he did before.

For the first time, he truly appreciated his ability to play by ear. He could still play a piece for a customer if they hummed a bar or two. He had been told that he had an outstanding memory for words of songs, and now he was grateful for that gift, also.

It felt good to get back to work, to be away from the house where Diane's clothes still remained, where the subtle fragrance of her lingered, and where the children still cried for her.

He thought of Pipit. Knowing he'd spoken abruptly to her, he felt remorse. She'd gone through enough, but he needed her there to stabilize the family and this morning, for some reason, he'd doubted she could do it. Realizing it was because of his own inner turmoil that he doubted, he vowed to be more patient with her.

~~~~~~~~~~~~

On this January morning, as it sometimes did, the sun warmed up by 10:30. "What towels do you use when you go swimming, Danny?" Pipit asked. He ran into the laundry room and she followed. He pointed to some colorful towels hanging on hooks. Searching through a couple of laundry room cupboards, she found both suntan lotion and sun block. "Go get your bathing suit on, Danny, then let's go out on the porch and put suntan lotion on you."

Merri, with pencil, paper and crayons, settled herself at the patio table and tried to look totally uninterested in what the other two were doing.

As Pipit and Danny walked down the path to the pool, towels in their arms, she wondered if she could even swim. "Do you know how to swim, Danny?"

"A little bit."

Stepping into the shallow end, Pipit found that the pool was heated and was pleasantly warm. "Sit here on the side for a moment, Danny, let me try the pool" What she meant was, I want to see if I know how to swim. Leaning into the water, smooth automatic strokes and rhythmical kicking of her feet took her across the pool and back quickly. Breathing heavily, she smiled at Danny. "I know how to swim."

"I know. I saw you. I wish I could swim like that."

"I'll teach you. Come here."

After the swimming lesson, Pipit and Danny just played, splashing each other and laughing. Every now and then, Pipit glanced over at Merri. When she saw Pipit look in her direction, she quickly looked down and pretended to enjoy coloring.

~~~~~~~~~~~~

After a swim, and a lunch of peanut butter sandwiches, Pipit felt extremely tired. The only way she dared close her eyes was curling up in the chair right here with them while they watched a movie from their video collection.

After she awakened from the short nap, she wandered through the house, acquainting herself with her new environment. Still in awe over Diane's ability to decorate, she wondered about her own in this area.

Curiosity got the better of her. She snooped in Matthew's bedroom, bathroom and closet. Looking in the second walk-in closet, she saw all of Diane's clothes still hanging. An exquisite fragrance hovered in the air. "How can he get on with his life if he doesn't give these clothes away?" she muttered. Looking at the clothes, one after the other, she saw that Diane also had wonderful taste in clothes. She left the master suite, feeling depressed.

Back in the kitchen, she searched the cupboards and drawers for the right pan and utensils to start dinner. Feeling it safer to fry the hamburgers instead of broil them as Margo had suggested, she made the patties and placed them in a large frying pan.

Merri wandered over, sat up on one of the stools at the bar and watched her. "My mommy doesn't cook hamburgers like that."

Since Merri had sulked all afternoon, Pipit wasn't inclined to respond to the remark. While the meat was cooking, she pulled out the catsup and mustard. "Does your daddy like pickles, Merri?"

"Yes. He likes dill pickles."

Pipit found the pickles and placed all three of the ingredients on the light wood rectangular table in the eating area which stood in front of a large window. This would be the first time to eat at the table. So far they all had eaten at the bar.

Merri watched her search for the lettuce and tomatoes and begin to wash them. "Would you like to set the table, Merri?"

"No."

All of a sudden, Pipit realized that the hamburgers were frying hard, splattering grease on the stove top. Grabbing the spatula, she turned one and discovered it was too dark. "Ouch!" She grabbed her hand, burned by the splattering grease.

"Mommy turns down the heat when she cooks."

Of course, she thought. *I should have known that*. Chagrined, she reached over she turned the heat down.

"Not that knob, the other one," stated Merri with disgust.

Pipit looked at the knobs. Merri was right. By the time she turned the heat down, and turned over the other four burgers , they were almost burned.

"My mommy never burned things."

Pipit stepped over to the bar and glared at her. "Listen, little Miss 'know-it-all,' I'm trying to get used to working in a strange kitchen. I could use a little help."

Just then, Matthew walked into the kitchen from the front door. He'd heard Pipit's remark and knew Merri had been giving her a bad time. "Hey, what's going on here?"

Pipit's face turned hot with embarrassment.

"Pipit burned the hamburgers," Merri stated gleefully.

"Did you help Pipit?"

"No."

"Well then, I guess we'll all just have to eat burned hamburgers."

"Daddy!" exclaimed Danny running up to him and hugging his legs.

Matthew bent down and lifted him up into his arms. "Hi there, Danny boy, how was it today?"

"It was great! I got to go swimming and Pipit is teaching me how to swim like her!"

"It wasn't fair for Pipit to let Danny go swimming when I couldn't go!" Merri added indignantly.

Matthew's face turned grave. "We'll discuss it later after we've eaten, and after we help clean up the kitchen."

"I'm not going to eat those burned hamburgers!"

"We're not fixing anything else, Merri," Matthew stated firmly, "so eat them or go without. Now both of you go wash your hands."

As it turned out, the hamburgers were only a little over-brown, not burned. However, after Pipit had taken one bite, she frowned and muttered, "I forgot to salt the meat."

Matthew chuckled. "As the saying goes, we all have to learn the hard way and it looks like that's your road, Pipit, as well as ours."

Pipit didn't find it amusing at all so she didn't respond.

After dinner, Matthew instructed the children that they were to help clean up the kitchen, for which Pipit was grateful. He also announced that he would have a chore list ready for the next day.

When they were through cleaning up, they all seated themselves in the family room to discuss Merri's grievances. After Merri had indignantly told her story, Matthew heard Danny's side.

Matthew was silent a moment, then said, "Pipit, Diane felt that Merri's skin was as delicate as hers and she preferred that Merri didn't swim until evening. Diane also didn't want her playing in the sun unless she had long sleeves on and wore a hat."

"Does she have a skin disease?"

"No."

"Does Danny have a skin problem?"

"No. His complexion is like mine."

"Why can't we put sun block on Merri?"

"Diane said that sun block didn't work well on her skin, and that it was difficult to spread it evenly."

"I think it would be good for Merri to get a little sun, Matthew."

"This is the way Diane wanted it and that is the way it will be, Pipit."

Danny set up a howl. "I want to go swimming in the daytime."

"Danny! Stop it right now," Matthew demanded.

Danny's howling quieted down to a soft sob, and Pipit gritted her teeth, wanting to pick him up and comfort him.

Merri surprised all of them. She stood up and walked away a few feet, her back to them, folding her arms tightly across her chest. "I hate my ivory skin!"

Even Danny stopped crying and stared at his sister. Matthew's brows rose in surprise, then drew together as he tried to assess the unexpected outburst. "Why?"

Big sobs shook her small shoulders. "Come here, Merri and sit on my lap."

Slowly, she walked over to her father and climbed up into his lap, heaving gasps of air as if she'd been crying for hours. "Why do you hate your ivory skin?"

"Because I want to play in the sunshine without long sleeves and...and I want to swim in the daytime like Danny did."

Matthew held her tightly. "Danny won't swim until you can, Merri."

"B..but I don't want to be different than my friends. They make fun of me. Th...they say: 'Merri has milky skin,' and then they laugh."

"How long has this been going on, Merri?"

"A long time. Every time Mommy took us with her to her friend's houses who have kids to play with and every time I went to parties."

"Did you tell your mother about this?"

"Yes."

"What did she say?"

"She said that my friends were just jealous 'cause they didn't have pretty skin like I have."

"Do you believe that?"

"Yes. I want to have pretty skin like Mommy, but I wish I...." The tears started up again.

Remorse bore down on Matthew. Why hadn't he been aware of this? He should have noticed something...some little thing that would have given him a clue! "Merri, listen."

"What?" she asked, stopping the tears for a moment.

"You know, I'm thinking that if your mommy were here right now she'd probably say, 'go ahead and swim in the daytime and don't worry about your skin anymore.'"

"She would?"

"I think so." He gave her a reassuring smile.

The tears dried up instantly and she threw her arms around her father's neck, "Oh, thank you, Daddy."

"Yippee!" exclaimed Danny. "We get to go swimming in the day time! We get to go swimming in the daytime!"

~~~~~~~~~~~~

Matthew, having just put the children to bed, walked into the family room where Pipit was reading. She looked up. His face looked a little haggard.

Sensing her presence, he said, "Here's the alarm clock you requested."

She got up and took it from him. "Thank you."

"I can see you had quite a harrowing day today."

"I'm sure it will get better,"she said without conviction.

Matthew smiled. "That's a good positive attitude. I hope you can soon believe it. Now, I want to discuss something with you. Arthur and I feel that it's important for you to see a doctor. I'm going to make an appointment for you with my neurologist."

"But Matthew, I don't have any money, and who knows if I have insurance."

"You can pay me back when you learn who you are."

"No. I'd rather not plan on that."

"Why?"

"Because I don't know whether I'll even be able to pay you back after I learn who I am."

"My neurologist is a very busy doctor, Pipit, so I'm sure he can't get you in for at least two or three weeks. I'm making an appointment for you—you're going and that's that."

Chapter Eleven

The jangling of the alarm clock awakened Pipit with a start. Slamming her hand on the off button, she groaned, wanting to go back to sleep. Matthew had asked her to set it for 6:30! She sat up dreading another day with Merri, certain that not only had she never taken care of children, but certain she was not cut out for it—under any circumstances.

Quickly brushing her teeth and washing her face, she looked at herself in the mirror. Maybe the reason her hair was so short was because she swam a lot, hoping it was this rather than her sense of style. Throwing on a pair of knee length shorts and T-shirt, and slipping on the sandals, she went to the kitchen.

Trying to think what to get for breakfast, hating it all the while, she decided that at least she knew how to scramble eggs...or she felt she did. Pulling out a can of orange juice from the freezer, she made that first, then broke the eggs. Learning from her mistake of over-cooking the burgers last night, she waited to cook the eggs until the toast was made. She'd just about finished the toast when Matthew appeared.

"Pipit, would you mind helping me a minute?"

"Not at all, Matthew." She followed him into his bedroom.

"I usually wear a shirt and tie under a sport coat." His face carried a look of frustration. "But as you know, I can't see the colors I'm putting together. Could you pick out something for me? Mike usually gets to do the *honors*," he added with a grimace.

Her heart wrenched for him. "Yes." She picked slacks, shirt and sport coat and told him what they were.

"Perfect. Thank you, Pipit."

"You're welcome. Don't feel hesitant to ask me to help you in any way, Matthew. Shall I start the eggs?"

"Start in five minutes. I'm going to get the children up so you don't have to."

~~~~~~~~~~~~

"Is it time yet?" wheedled Merri for the umpteenth time.

"No. As I said, we have to wait until it warms up outside. You keep checking it for me."

"I'll help her," Danny said, running outside with his sister.

Matthew had given the children chores for today. Merri had to help with the dishes, and sweep the kitchen floor. Danny had to empty the garbage and wipe off the kitchen table. All this in addition to making their beds and straightening their rooms. They had eagerly pitched in so they could go swimming.

At last it was warm enough outside. Pipit carefully applied SPF 45 all over Merri and SPF 10 on Danny. She decided to start using less block on Merri as her skin became more used to the sun. The child was too pale. Finally, the three trudged off to the swimming pool.

"Show Merri how fast you can swim, Pipit," Danny said.

Pipit stepped in and swam for her as she had for Danny. Returning, she smiled at Merri.

Merri smiled back. "I know how to swim, but I can't swim fast like you. Will you teach me?"

"Yes. But it will take a lot of practice."

Merri was a different child all day—one who acted like she'd been given a reprieve from punishment.

Pipit read to them and played games with them so they wouldn't want to watch so much television.

Only when she began to fix a meal of frozen french fries and fish sticks, did Merri sit on the bar stool and begin her running dialogue: "That isn't the way my mommy does it," or "Mommy didn't do it that way." Here it was only the second day, and she felt if she heard that statement one more time she'd scream.

That night, Pipit fell into bed totally exhausted, and when the alarm went off the next morning, she knew for certain she wasn't cut out for this job. But where else could she go with a false name and no memory? About to put the pillow over her head and doze for a few minutes, she remembered she had to help Matthew pick out clothes.

Standing in the kitchen, she tried to figure out how to make the French toast the children had asked for. What kind of a person was she that she didn't even know how to fry hamburgers? She pulled down a cookbook of Diane's and looked up French toast.

Somehow, she managed to get through breakfast, help Matthew pick out clothes, monitor the children's chores and clean up the kitchen, muttering more than once, "This is no life for me!"

Again, the day warmed up enough to swim. She let the children play in the pool a little longer while she sunbathed, feeling that she sorely needed that leisure.

Bribing the children with an inside game, they finally agreed to get out. While they dressed, she showered.

They had just begun their game, when the doorbell rang. The children ran to the door. "Stop, you two!" Pipit yelled, "I have to be there with you to answer the door." They actually minded her and waited. Fearing that it might be Elinor, she looked out the peep hole and saw a woman in a colorful hat.

Her heart pounding, she opened the door slightly. "Yes?"

"Hello. I'm your neighbor and Diane's friend, Flo Henderson."

Pipit breathed a sigh of relief. The children pulled the door open wide, and squealed. "Aunt Flo!" They threw their arms around her.

Stooping down she hugged them both at the same time. "How are my two budding little artists? You ready for another art lesson from Aunt Flo?"

"Yes, yes!" they both replied enthusiastically.

The woman raised up and smiled at Pipit. "Margo told me about you. I'm so happy you've come to help poor Matthew." She swept into the house and closed the door. "We must go into the family room and get acquainted. I hear your name is Pipit, yes?"

Pipit was only able to nod as she followed the children and the exuberant woman into the other room. Flo seated herself on the couch and patted a place on both sides of her. The children clambered up and sat beside her.

Surely, Pipit thought, *she can't be for real.* Her short, light brown hair looked windblown under the hat. Long false eyelashes framed her brown eyes. The overdone eyeshadow, blush and ruby-red lipstick fit perfectly with the dangling earrings and colorful sarong. All the while she'd been studying her, Flo had been chattering on. What she'd said, Pipit had no idea, but managed to squeeze in a question. "The children take art lessons from you?"

"Oh my yes, the little darlings, and what talent they have. I came over to meet you and invite you over to see their artwork. You see, Diane has been very kind to me. She has arranged art shows for my work and she invites her rich friends. All she had to say was: 'I love her work,' and they would come to the show and buy from me. Wasn't that lovely of her? The least I can do is give the children free art lessons, don't you agree? Where in the world did Matthew ever find you? You are so precious and quaint. You must meet Diane's friends in the neighborhood. Everyone loved Diane." She stood up with a flourish, "Come, Pipit, let's tiptoe over to my place and I'll show you the children's art, then I'll put them to painting while I show you mine."

Pipit, feeling out of breath just listening to the woman, found herself following her and the children out the door and up the road to a modernistic, Spanish-style stucco with a large front courtyard.

Flo opened the black wrought iron gate of the courtyard. "Run along inside, darlings, and put on your painting smocks while I show Pipit the sculptures and statues here in the courtyard."

"Okay, Aunt Flo," Merri said. "Come on, Danny."

"You aren't related, are you?" Pipit asked.

"No, but the children are such loves, I told them they could call me aunt. Come over here and see this sculpture, Pipit. It was created by Mel Broderick who lives down the street."

Pipit couldn't react to the odd metal design, but found she really didn't have to. Before she could even take a breath to speak, Flo was pointing out and explaining that Mel's wife, Bobby sculpted that marvelous statue of the desert fox. Pipit examined the strange looking object from two different angles and couldn't see any resemblance to a fox. While she was doing this, Flo was going on about the other creations.

"Now," continued Flo, "let's go in and see what the children are up to."

"Are there really desert foxes?" Pipit asked, quickly slipping a word in.

"Yes, but Bobby has never seen one, or even a picture. That creation is just from her wonderful imagination. Mel and Bobby were also close friends to Diane. They loved her—like everyone who knew her."

Pipit followed Flo inside and was greeted by a room just as colorful as the clothes she wore. It looked like an art gallery, with a mixture of antiques and modern furniture. A warm, inviting feeling emanated from it—something Pipit needed at the moment.

Flo quickly ushered her through the room, and down the hall into a cluttered colorful studio with a large easel. On a table were small clusters of oil paints, water colors and paint brushes. Empty frames, canvases and unframed pictures were leaning against the wall and cabinets. Encased in one wall was a huge window that reached almost to the ceiling. Underneath it in the corner, Merri and Danny sat at a small table, painting.

"Get all your paintings out of the drawer, children, and show Pipit."

Eagerly, they did what she'd asked and began talking at the same time.

"Wait a minute," Pipit said, "let's take turns. You start first, Danny and then Merri." They looked like ordinary children's drawings and paintings to Pipit. Gratefully, Flo's effusiveness overrode her efforts to remark on them, making it possible for her to simply nod and smile.

After the little art show, Flo said, "Get back to your painting, children, while I show Pipit my art work."

Returning to the large room in the front, Flo showed her the paintings one by one, telling her the names and a brief story about each. Pipit was surprised that she liked so many of them. Most were modernistic in style with intriguing color combinations. Others were desert scenes and other scenery. When Flo wound down, Pipit conveyed her opinion of the paintings. Flo, genuinely pleased, thanked her.

Suddenly, they heard a scream from the other room. Pipit ran back."What is it, Merri?"

"Danny daubed some paint on me!"

"You got some on me first," retorted Danny.

"But I didn't mean to."

"You did, too."

Pipit looked at her watch and realized it was lunch time. "Come on, kids, let's go have lunch, but first thank Flo for her kindness."

They responded quickly, and soon they were having a race down the street to their house. Though the unexpected change in her routine had revived her flagging spirits, she was glad to be back home. *Home?* she thought. *Diane's home!* It will always be Diane's home, and the thought deflated her. Why, she had no idea, other than the fact she herself was homeless.

After lunch, she read to the children and then suggested they do something on their own. "We want you to play with us, Pipit," Danny said."

"Yes! Let's play a game."

"Aren't there any children in the neighborhood for you to play with?"

Merri hung her head, "No. Mommy always had to take us to play with her friend's kids in Scottsdale."

"Do children ever come here to play?"

"Sometimes Mommy's friends come here and bring their kids."

"Danny, do you have any toys?"

"I have some in a box in my closet."

"Do you have some in your room, Merri?"

"Yes."

"All right, I want you both to go to your rooms and play a little while so I can go to my room and rest."

Merri looked at her quizzically. "Are you tired, Pipit?"

"A little. I'm not used to swimming."

"Oh." They both ran out of the room to do as Pipit had requested.

Surprised at their obedience, she went into her room and lay down to think and soon fell asleep. It felt as thought she'd only slept a moment when Merri shook her awake, but her watch told her she'd slept thirty minutes.

"Danny and I are hungry. We want a snack."

Pipit groaned and closed her eyes. Always, they needed something; she never had a moment to herself.

~~~~~~~~~~~~

On the stove, store-bought spaghetti sauce was warming, and in another pan water was heating for the spaghetti. Tearing the lettuce leaves for the salad as Margo had taught her while on their grocery trip, she thought about Matthew. His spirits had improved slightly, but still—he wasn't the Matthew she'd become acquainted with in the cabin. Nevertheless, she was looking forward to his coming home. She needed someone to talk to besides little people, and she certainly couldn't say she'd had a conversation with Flo.

She heard the front door open and shut. "Children, your daddy's home." Glued to the television, they didn't move. Quickly going over, she turned it off. A howl issued from both of them. "Your daddy's home! Go greet him." Her enthusiasm infected them.

"Daddy, Daddy!" they yelled running into him as he walked into the room.

He smiled. "Well now, that's a greeting that revives my tired bones." Crouching on his heel, he hugged them both at once. Standing up, he turned to a sound in the kitchen. "Pipit?"

"I'm here, Matthew. We're *all* happy to have you home."

"That's nice to hear. How did the day go?"

"Tell your daddy about our day, children."

They both began chattering at once. "Whoa there, let's go sit down on the couch and take turns." After he'd heard about their swimming and the visit with 'Aunt Flo,' he turned to the cook. "Flo is quite an experience, isn't she?"

"An experience describes it perfectly, but it was a change I needed."

Matthew's faced sobered as he put himself in Pipit's place. "How would you like to attend a musical sometime soon?"

Pipit's face lit up. "I would love that."

"I'll call Arthur and Mamie and we four will go together."

"What about the children?"

"We have a babysitter in the neighborhood we use. We'll take the children another time."

~~~~~~~~~~~~

After everyone had eaten some of the over-cooked spaghetti covered with bottled sauce and had taken as many bites of the wilted salad as they could handle, they cleaned up the kitchen and settled in the family room.

Pipit knew she was used to better cooking because her own was so abhorrent to her. Matthew was reading to the children and she was poring over a cook book, determined to learn how to cook. Tomorrow, she was going to visit Margo and get a good recipe and really work at making a decent meal.

Closing the book, Pipit felt lonesome for the Matthew she'd known in the cabin. When she heard Matthew come to the end of the story, she said, "Matthew, why don't you sing and play some fun songs for the children?"

"Oh yes, Daddy, sing a funny song." pleaded Merri.

He smiled. "All right," he said, getting up and carefully finding his way to the piano. "The ones you *know*, you have to sing *with me.*"

For the first time since coming here, Pipit felt a semblance of contentment. She loved to hear Matthew sing. His was the voice that had saved her life...the voice that had touched something deep inside. After some time, Matthew stood up and told the children to go get ready for bed.

At last they were alone. "Matthew, would you sing one of those old songs you sang up at the cabin—for *me*?"

His face closed. "I'm sorry, Pipit, I...I can't."

"Why?"

"I just can't," he pronounced abruptly.

Disappointment seeped through her like water through a sieve. She got up and grabbed a magazine and walked quickly to her room, shutting herself away from this family that wasn't hers.

Chapter Twelve

"From what the weather report said, Pipit, the day is going to be too cold to swim."

She was in the closet, picking out something for Matthew to wear when she heard him tell her this unwanted news. Now what was she going to do with the children all day? The news only added to the depression she'd awakened with this morning caused by Matthew's refusal to sing for her the night before.

Exiting the closet, she laid the clothes on the delicate blue comforter on Matthew's neatly made-up bed. She told him what she'd picked out. Instead of thanking her as he'd done everyday previously, he said, "The clothes hamper in my bathroom and the one in the children's bathroom are getting full. Would you please do some wash today?"

"Wash?"

"Yes. You do know how to wash don't you?" he asked with an edge to his voice.

"I really don't know, Matthew," she retorted flippantly.

"I can't believe you don't know how to do that."

"How would I know how to do that, Matthew?" she asked, her voice dripping with sarcasm. "As Arthur said, I was probably a spoiled rich kid."

In no mood to deal with this new attitude, Matthew heaved a sigh. "Will you please try to figure it out and do the wash today? And in a couple of days, the bathrooms need to be cleaned."

"The bathrooms?" Not only hadn't the wash crossed her overtaxed mind as she'd been trying to adjust to her new situation, and deal with the children, but cleaning the bathrooms hadn't either. Feeling embarrassed at her ignorance, she blurted out, "I'm not cut out to take care of children, cook or clean house. I resign." She plunked herself down on the bed.

Matthew heard her sit down. "Diane didn't like us sitting on the bedspread, Pipit."

"What can Diane do about it?"

"What did you say?" he asked a bit ominously.

His tone of voice caught her attention. "I said: what are you going to do about it?"

"You're acting like a spoiled child, Pipit."

"Why not? That's what you and Arthur think I am," she stated, not making a move to get off the bedspread.

"Are you going to go get breakfast?"

"No," she said folding her arms tightly. "I resign."

Surprising her, Matthew sat down on the off-limits bedspread, a smile hovering about his lips. Reaching up, he fingered her hair. "It feels like the bad haircut, as you call it, is growing out."

Tongue-tied for a moment, she replied, "What does that have to do with anything?"

Ignoring the question, he asked, "Do you mind if I feel your face to see what you look like? I'm not sure how blind people do this, but I suddenly have a need to know what my spoiled rotten nanny/maid looks like." Then he smiled the heart-stopping smile she'd so sorely missed.

Her mutiny melted into a gooey puddle inside. She turned towards him. "Be my guest."

Both hands found her face and ever so slowly, and ever so gently his fingers felt her forehead, her brows, her nose, cheeks and jaw line, chin, then her lips, lingering on them a little longer. The breath she'd been holding came out in a rush.

His hands moved down to hers and held them tightly. "Forgive me, Pipit. I've been harsh with you. I...I'm still struggling with my grief. Everything here reminds me of Diane and I can't seem to let go of it."

"Do you think it might help if you gave away all her clothes or boxed them up for Merri to see one day?"

He stiffened and dropped her hands. *I've done it again*, she thought. "I'll go get breakfast, Matthew," she said quickly.

"No, wait." He paused. "Thank you for staying on."

"You're welcome," she muttered as she left the room.

~~~~~~~~~~~~~

The episode with Matthew had upset Pipit's fragile, emotional equilibrium. Trying not to think of his hands on her face, his tenderness, his apology, she went about gathering up the wash. Sorting the clothes, it began to feel familiar, grateful that she might not be totally ignorant in this area.

The children were watching a video in place of swimming. Her thoughts turned to their plight. They needed to have friends to play with. Since she had no memory of how she felt as a child, she wondered how she knew this. Why did Matthew and Diane buy a house way out here in 'artistville' away from people who had children? She reminded herself that this was none of her business. Nevertheless, it was her *concern* since she had to care for the children day in and day out—sighing over the 'day in and day out.' Not since she first woke up in the cabin, had she so desperately wanted her memory to return.

After the wash was all completed, folded and the children had helped put it away, the three of them put on jackets and walked over to Margo's house. Her husband, Phil answered the door. He was only a little taller than Margo with gray strands through his curly black hair. His dark brown eyes smiled before his mouth did. "You are Pipit."

"You're Phil," she replied smiling.

"I sure am. Hi there, kids. Come on in, all of you."

He led them through the foyer into the comfortable looking family room/kitchen. Margo got up from the couch, and greeted them enthusiastically. Pipit noted that Margo's coloring was just the opposite of Phil's. Her short casually curled hair was blonde, and her eyes were blue. They were dressed in knee-length khaki shorts and white T-shirts, and both were well-tanned with a plethora of laugh lines at the corners of their eyes.

Margo smiled at the children. "I do believe I might be able to find some chocolate chip cookies somewhere. Sit down at the table and I'll look for them."

"Yay!" they chorused, clapping their hands.

With the cookies and a glass of milk before them, Margo could turn her full attention to Pipit. "How's the cooking going?"

"What cooking?"

Margo laughed. "You ready for further instruction from the ol' pro here?"

"More than you know. I need to at least make one good meal during my career as cook/maid/nanny or we're all going to starve to death. Especially me."

Pipit came away from the Stillman household with a recipe for one of their favorite casseroles and a few ingredients that the recipe called for. Margo had also instructed her how to cook a vegetable they'd purchased at the grocery store, and how to make a luscious fruit salad with the fruit she had on hand. Determined to make a good meal tonight, she began early while the children sat at the table, drawing pictures and coloring.

When Matthew walked in, he said, "Something smells awfully good in here."

"Daddy, Daddy!" they yelled, running to him and throwing their arms around him.

He swallowed the lump in his throat. It had been a long time since they'd greeted him as they had lately. It started shortly after Pipit arrived.

After the accident, he wasn't able to be the father they were used to, so he could hardly expect them to be enthusiastic about him coming home from work. A thought struck him—even before the accident, they *rarely* greeted him like this. The memory disturbed him. When he was a child, his father coming in after work was the highlight of his day, and he had more than once wondered why his own children didn't feel the same way.

"Come and see the truck I colored, Daddy." Remembering his daddy couldn't see, he said, "I mean, I stayed in the lines."

"And I drew some flowers," Merri said.

~~~~~~~~~~~~

The meal had turned out well. Matthew complimented Pipit and thanked her. The children also liked it. Pipit felt pleased over their reactions, and over accomplishing her goal. She was determined to keep it up. Soon, she would need to go grocery shopping again, but first, she needed more menus and recipes from Margo.

As soon as they had cleaned up the kitchen, Pipit got a book from the bookshelf, and disappeared into her bedroom. The children needed to be alone with their father she told herself. In reality, she knew it was because she was still hurt at Matthew's abrupt refusal to sing a song for her. He hadn't apologized to her for that, and somehow, she knew he wasn't going to.

She needed to find out her identity! Every day she hoped that she'd start to remember, but she hadn't. Several times she had called Arthur to see if anyone had found her car yet. He told her he had checked and as of yet, the snow hadn't melted enough. Feeling the answer would be the same as a couple of days ago, she dialed Arthur's number anyway.

Matthew *felt* Pipit leave the room more than he'd heard her. He didn't think much about it until she didn't return. Why did she leave? He preferred that she stay here with him and the children. Her presence lifted his spirits, as it had at the cabin. He had no idea why Pipit had this effect on him. It was probably as simple as the fact that she was a woman, and he missed female companionship.

Chapter Thirteen

It was the seventh night Pipit had left right after dinner and gone to her room, and the loneliness of each subsequent evening was becoming more unbearable. Though the specific memory was lost to her, loneliness from the past came through loud and clear. As difficult as her life was at the moment, she realized Matthew and the children had eased her heart...and now she couldn't be with them in the evenings when she needed it the most. A gentle knock on the door interrupted her brooding thoughts. "Come in."

Matthew stuck his head in. "Danny and Merri are *both* wanting you to tuck them in."

"I'll be right there, Matthew." Last night, for the first time, Merri had asked for this. She had happily acquiesced, not quite believing she was beginning to win Merri over. It had been ten days since she started taking care of the children and it was Danny who first started clinging to her. It had started a couple of days ago with him wanting to sit by her and lean his head against her arm...so hungry for a mother. Then last night, tucking Merri in had turned out to be another special moment.

~~~~~~~~~~~~

The next afternoon, Pipit realized that the routine—the cooking and caring for the children was coming a little easier. She'd had several more successful meals and a couple not so successful, but on the whole she felt she was improving in her domestic skills. Though pleased over her improvement, she continued to hope that one of these days the memories which lurked at the edge of her consciousness would suddenly come into clear focus—then she could leave this daily drudgery.

She and the children had just come back from a walk and visit with Flo, a promise she'd made because the weather wasn't warm enough to go swimming today. The phone rang and Pipit ran to the nearest one. "Hello?"

"Hello, love. This is Flo. Mel and Bobby Broderick just called and asked to meet you. We'll all be over in about thirty minutes. Is that all right?"

"It is. Thanks, Flo. I would like to meet them." Somehow, Pipit knew that Flo wasn't a person she would ordinarily seek out for a friend and she suspected that she might feel the same about the Brodericks. But she needed friends, as well as the diversion they provided from her hum-drum life. She found that she was actually looking forward to their visit.

"Can we watch cartoons, Pipit?" Merri asked.

"Yeah, can we?" Danny repeated.

"All right, but just for an hour. Mr. and Mrs. Broderick are coming over in a little while. You might want to come into the front room and say hello to them."

"Okay, we will." Merri said, running over to the couch and picking up the control.

Pipit straightened the family room a little and then went into the kitchen to look at the menu for dinner. "Meals, meals," she muttered. "A never ending round of meals. I think I'd like to have a cook." She studied the recipe for the chicken casserole, trying to calculate how much time it would take. First, she'd have to boil the small whole chicken in water as Margo had instructed. The doorbell rang.

They're a little early, she thought as she opened the door. Sucking in a quick breath, Pipit stared at the stunning woman standing on the doorstep. The woman seemed equally shocked at seeing her. The cream silk suit accentuated the woman's short, stylishly turned under dark hair. She stood regally straight, and the hand that gripped the handbag tightly in front of her, displayed a huge, sparkling diamond. Speechless for a moment, Pipit wondered who...Elinor! She'd almost forgotten about her. "Uh, may I help you?" she asked, feeling as though her heart would pound right out of her chest.

"Who are you?" the woman asked sharply.

"Mr. Melloy hired me as housekeeper and nanny. May I ask who you are?"

"I'm the children's grandmother, Elinor Halstrom," she stated, pushing past Pipit and stepping in. "Where are they?"

"I'll go get them, Mrs. Halstrom."

"Never mind, I'll find them."

Pipit nervously followed the obtrusive woman into the family room.

"I see you are letting the television do your work as nanny." Before Pipit could react, Elinor stepped over to Merri and Danny. "Grandmother's here, children." No response.

Pipit quickly went over to the television and turned it off. Immediately, they both responded indignantly.

"Your grandmother Halstrom is here to see you."

Startled, they looked up. "Grandmother!" they both said at once, getting up and hugging her.

"Come and sit beside me," she said, sitting on the couch, "and tell me how you are."

Eagerly, they sat beside her. "You certainly have a dirty face, Danny," she said giving Pipit a disapproving glance.

"We went to see Flo and she gave us a chocolate ice cream cone and I forgot to wash my face."

Without reacting to his happy announcement, Elinor, turned to Merri. "My, but your hair looks terrible. You need it brushed and washed."

"Daddy helps me wash my hair and he always brushes it."

Elinor's icy gray eyes held Pipit's. "You mean you let a blind man wash and comb this child's hair?"

"I don't *let* Mr. Melloy do anything, Mrs. Halstrom," she replied in a low voice, carefully trying to hold back her anger. "These are his children, and he has chosen to take as much care of them himself as he can."

"As he can? How can a blind man take care of children?"

"Daddy isn't a blind man," Merri said, almost in tears. "I mean, he doesn't seem very blind to me."

Elinor took Merri into her arms. "You poor baby. Don't feel badly, Grandmother is here to look after you."

Danny, his eyes big and solemn, sat as still as a mouse beside his grandmother.

Suddenly, Elinor sat Merri back down on the couch and faced Pipit. "Who are you?"

Calmly and coolly, Pipit answered. "As I said, I am Mr. Melloy's housekeeper and..."

"Housekeeper? Hmph, I see no evidence of housekeeping here. What is your name?"

Pipit stood up and walked into the kitchen area. "I think I had better call Mr. Melloy and tell him you are here."

"No! You sit right down, Miss, I don't need Matthew here right now."

Ignoring her, she picked up the phone on the kitchen counter and dialed. "May I speak to Mr. Melloy, please?"

Elinor glared at her.

"Mr. Melloy, this is Pipit."

Matthew understood at once. "Elinor's there. I'll be home as fast as I can, Pipit."

The phone went dead, but Pipit continued talking. "Mrs. Halstrom is here and I'm sure you'd like to see her...All right, we'll be waiting for you, goodbye."

Pipit picked up the chicken and proceeded undoing the plastic bag. "I was just preparing dinner, Mrs. Halstrom. Would you care to stay and eat with us?" she asked, hoping with all her heart she would refuse.

"No thank you, but since you called Matthew, I do have something I want to discuss with him. What is your name, young lady?"

Seeing the children subdued and frightened made Pipit angrier, but she knew she had to answer. "Pipit Bordeau."

"What kind of a name is that?"

"It's French."

"How in the world did Matthew find you?"

"Find me?" she hedged.

"Did you come looking for a job or did he advertise?" she asked, impatience edging her words.

"I think you had better discuss this with Matthew," she said without thinking, then quickly covering her slip, she added, "as you call him, Mrs. Halstrom."

Tight-lipped with anger over Pipit's refusal to answer her question, Elinor turned her attention back to the children. Suddenly, she took Merri's face in her hand. "Merri, what has happened to your skin?"

"N-nothing, Grandmother."

"But your lovely ivory skin is tanning." She looked over at Pipit. "Are you allowing Merri out in the sun without protection?"

"As I said, *I* do not allow the children anything. They are Mr. Melloy's children. I take instruction from him." Hoping to avoid more discord in front of the children, she decided to slip away and forget about dinner. Placing the chicken back into the refrigerator, she pretended to engross herself in wiping up. Soon, she escaped into her bedroom, deciding to stay there until after Matthew had arrived and talked with his mother-in-law.

~~~~~~~~~~~~

It seemed forever before Pipit heard Matthew enter the house. She was grateful that he was here to deal with Elinor instead of her. What she really wanted to do was escape over to Flo's. It was then she realized that Flo and the Brodericks had not come, and decided that Flo knew Elinor's car and decided to visit another time.

About thirty-five minutes later, Pipit heard the front door open and shut. Shortly there was a knock on her door. Putting down the book she'd been trying to read, she opened it to see Matthew. "Hi," she said, "I see you are a little bloodied, but still breathing."

"Barely," Matthew said, grimacing. He shut the door. "I put a video in for the children because I need to talk to you."

She took his hand and led him over to the couch. "Sit down, Matthew."

He sat, still holding her hand, gave it a squeeze, then let go. "Congratulations on handling Elinor. She was quite miffed over the fact that you wouldn't answer her questions the way she wanted."

Pipit sat down beside him. "She's a scary woman. No wonder you needed someone here to help you out. She attacked your ability to wash and comb Merri's hair and my housekeeping. Both, I concede, do need improving."

He smiled. "Of course. She wants Mrs. Danville to come for a while starting sometime next week and take care of the children so you can spend all your time cleaning and cooking."

"Are you letting her come?" she asked apprehensively.

"I am for now. I don't want to rock the boat. Letting Mrs. Danville come for a while buys me time until I regain my eyesight. When I do, a lot of things are going to change."

"She spoke quite harshly in front of the children and they were frightened."

Matthew's jaw overworked itself a moment, then slowly he explained, "Elinor is good to the children, but if she gets backed into a corner, she speaks her mind whether they're present or not. That is one thing that has to change—now."

They sat in thoughtful silence, each trying to deal with the situation as best they could, both feeling helpless with their different challenges.

At last Matthew spoke softly into the silence. "Pipit, why do you leave us after dinner and stay in your room?"

The question took her by surprise. How could she answer it? "Well...uh...it didn't seem to matter whether I was there or not. You and the children are a family. I'm an outsider. You need to be alone with your children. They need to have their father's total attention."

He leaned his arms on his thighs, and bent his head toward the floor. "Pipit, in the short, difficult eleven days you've been here, you have accomplished what I couldn't possibly accomplish by myself. You have calmed the children down, they are emotionally more stable and much happier. They aren't fighting like they used to. You say you feel you've never taken care of children, but you have a way with them. Children can't be fooled. If an adult doesn't care about them or feel kindness toward them, that adult can't fake it. Children can immediately sense those things. You care, whether you know it or not or whether you want to or not."

Pipit felt like crying. She had no idea that she'd done that much for the children. She couldn't see the kind of progress he talked about. But then, she hadn't been around the children before so she couldn't compare. The only progress she could see was in her ability to cook and manage the household chores. Matthew's assessment left her feeling happier than she'd felt since leaving the cabin. But still, there was the hurt over his insensitive refusal to sing for her.

Her silence went on so long, he sat up and faced her, wishing he could see the expression on her face. "What is it, Pipit?"

"I'm so happy that I have made a little difference, but...I still feel I need to leave after dinner."

"I assure you, we don't need to be alone. Please stay with us."

She had to tell him. "I guess *I* need to leave."

"*You* need to?" he asked, surprised. "Can you tell me why?"

"I know it's foolish feeling as I do, but I can't help it."

"Please tell me how you feel, Pipit."

"You were different at the cabin, Matthew. Here, you've put a wall of grief around yourself and I feel lonelier around you than away from you."

He shook his head. "How lonely and hard it must be—trapped here with no memory, no driver's license, day in and day out taking care of someone else's children, cooking, washing and..."

"It's more than that, Matthew."

"More?"

"Yes. Your wonderful singing voice saved my life, and later when you sang for me at the cabin, it kept something alive in me. It also evoked emotions that have memories, memories that I feel need reckoning with. A week ago, you refused quite abruptly when I asked you to sing a song for me."

Matthew's brows knit together, a troubled expression replaced the concerned one. His chest heaved. "I'm sorry I hurt you, Pipit. I'm not quite sure why I refused—why it's hard for me to sing the kind of songs *here* that I sang at the cabin. I've tried to analyze it, but I'm afraid I dislike introspection. I think I've run from it for years. All I can say is it has something to do with Diane."

He reached for her hand and held it tightly with both his. "If you'll stay with us in the evening, I promise I'll work on this problem I have and try to sing for you. Uh...I hate to lay this on you," pausing, he let go of her hand, and ran his own hand though his hair, "you have enough burden to carry, but to tell the truth—I *need* you, Pipit. Your presence lifts my spirits. It did the moment you fell on our doorstep at the cabin." He found her hand again. Lifting it to his lips, he kissed it, then got up and felt his way out of the room.

Chapter Fourteen

Just before leaving for the Scottsdale store Saturday morning, Matthew held out a handful of fifty dollar bills. "Here is your first two weeks salary, Pipit."

Surprised, she took the bills and counted them. "Five hundred dollars! But, Matthew, I owe you for the clothes I bought."

"I deducted that. Well, I must be going, Mike is waiting. See all of you tonight."

Pipit stared after him. She really had no idea if he was underpaying or overpaying her, but suspected it was the latter since he and the children had to live through her muddled attempts at cooking and cleaning.

The children seeing her preoccupation, took advantage and turned on the cartoons.

Hardly aware, she set the money down on the counter and automatically began cleaning up the dishes, thinking about what Matthew had said the night before. For the first time, she woke up this morning before the alarm. Also for the first time since arriving here, she looked forward to the day with a tingle of excitement. Had she ever felt needed before?

Had anyone ever needed her? Whatever the answer, *Matthew needed her,* and it gave her a reason to get up. It took the monotony out of making breakfast this morning.

As she wiped off the counter, she stopped and stared at the money and suddenly, she realized what having it meant. No longer was she stuck in this house unable to go anywhere because she couldn't drive—she could call a taxi! She and the children could go any where they wanted. Where could they go on a Saturday? "Of course! That's where we'll go."

Besides, the man who cleans the pool as well as the yard man were coming today, which meant no swimming or playing outside. Excited, she cleaned rapidly, finishing in what had to be for her, record time.

Turning off the television, Pipit said, "I have a surprise."

"What?" they both said at once, their eyes bright with excitement.

"We're going to do something different today. We're going to go for a ride in a taxi cab."

They both looked puzzled, so she explained what a taxi cab was. "We're going to go down to your daddy's store in a taxi and watch him sell pianos. But—when we walk in, we're going to have to be quiet as mice and not let him know we're there, and then we'll surprise him. Do you think you can do that?" They nodded vigorously, grinning with anticipation. "Then," her voice turned low and secretive, "maybe we can kidnap him and take him to lunch with us."

"Yay!" they exclaimed, jumping up and down.

"You need to go make your beds and pick up your toys while I go shower and get ready."

~~~~~~~~~~~~~

Pipit found a blow dryer in one of Diane's drawers and attempted to style her straight hair. It was longer now and a little easier to manage. Putting on some makeup for the first time since she bought it, she found that she wasn't quite so plain when she took time to enhance her eyes with mascara and eye shadow. Slipping on a slim long skirt of dusky blue and a white knit top, she realized she didn't have any jewelry or perfume. When looking for the hair dryer, she'd seen Diane's beautiful jewelry and had smelled her perfume. Once more, she had come away feeling depressed for reasons she couldn't understand, other than knowing instinctively Diane's taste in clothes, jewelry and perfume were not hers.

Her spirits soon revived after she'd called a taxi from Scottsdale. Since the weather was still cool, she helped the children dress in warmer clothes, combed their hair, and then the three of them waited impatiently for their ride. The children squealed when, at last, they heard a horn.

On their way, Pipit felt as excited as the children while they planned their careful entrance into the store. Merri said she would 'ssh' the clerks who knew her and Danny.

"How often did your mother take you to the store?"

"Sometimes when Mommy went shopping, she stopped in to talk to Daddy."

~~~~~~~~~~~~

In between customers, Matthew's thoughts wandered back to Pipit. He'd sensed a difference in her this morning. Though she hadn't said anything about his request to stay with him and the children in the evenings, he felt something positive from her. Was he asking too much of her in her condition? He'd asked himself this over and over the night before as he lay in bed thinking.

Mike broke into Matthew's thoughts. "Matt, a customer is requesting your services out on the floor. She wants you to play several different pianos for her."

Each time, Matthew churned inside over having to be led around in the store, "All right, Mike, hand me your arm."

~~~~~~~~~~~~

The taxi turned off Scottsdale Rd into Lincoln Village and parked in front of the store. The driver got out and opened the door for the three occupants. Pipit paid him, took hold of the children's hands and walked to the front door. Through the glass, she could see Matthew sitting at a piano playing. She smiled at the children conspiratorially and put her finger to her lips. Trying to be inconspicuous as possible, they entered and wove in and out of the pianos until they came to a piano next to the one Matthew was playing. Pipit sat down on the piano bench and pulled the children down beside her.

Since the bench faced the side view of Matthew, Pipit watched him look up at the customer now and then, smiling the familiar warm smile she'd seen at the cabin. When the song ended, he explained the quality of this particular brand of piano.

"Would you play this piano now?" the customer asked pointing to the one Pipit and the children were sitting at.

Scrambling up, the threesome tiptoed to the next piano bench, the children stifling their giggles with their hands.

Matthew played another song and again extolled the virtues of that brand. The indecisive customer asked so many questions, the children got restless. Finally, and just in time, the customer said she'd have to bring her husband in to hear the tonal quality of the different pianos.

Mike, noticing the customer was about to leave, started over to Matthew to help him back into the office. Merri ran over to him and put her finger to her lips. Pipit and Danny followed her.

"This is Mike. He picks up Daddy every morning," whispered Merri.

"I'm Pipit Bordeau, Mike," she said in a lowered voice. "I take care of Matthew's children."

He smiled. "Nice to meet you. Matthew has told me about you."

"It's nice to meet _you_," she replied softly. "Would you do us a favor, Mike?

"Sure."

"Would you please tell Matthew a customer wants to hear him sing as well as play?"

He was puzzled until Pipit pointed to herself, then he smiled and nodded. Mike reaching Matthew just as the customer left, told him of the request.

"Where is the customer?"

"Sitting on a piano bench a few feet away."

"Is he or she interested in a piano?"

"I don't know. You know how some customers are, Matt," he teased, "some come in to here just to be entertained."

Matthew wasn't in any mood to entertain. "Ask her or him..."

"It's a she."

"Ask her if she's interested in buying a piano."

"Ma'am, are you interested in buying a piano?"

Pipit smiled and nodded.

"She is Matt."

This happened now and then at this store, but today Matthew felt annoyed, certain that the singing wasn't necessary. Nevertheless, he acquiesced and began.

Pipit mouthed a thank you to Mike. As usual, Matthew played and sang a song from a bygone era. She smiled at the children and sighed as she listened. At the end of the song, Pipit clapped and the children joined in.

Matthew turned toward the clapping. All of a sudden two children pounced on him, laughing. "Daddy, Daddy!"

The look of total surprise was worth the price of the taxi. "Merri? Danny?"

"Yes, Daddy, we came down to surprise you."

"How...how did you get here?"

"We came in a taxi," announced Danny.

"Pipit?"

"I'm here, Matthew," she answered as she went over and stood beside him.

He grinned. "What a...welcome surprise. But you spent a bundle getting here, Pipit. Why would you spend your money like that?"

"I figured this was the only way I could get to hear you sing."

Matthew was silent for so long that Merri piped up, "Pipit wanted us to surprise you, Daddy."

"And we're going to kidnap you," Danny said, beaming from ear to ear.

"Kidnap me?"

"Yes," Merri said, "so we can take you to lunch."

"This is quite a conspiracy," he said, chuckling. "Was this Pipit's idea?"

"Yes. Can you go, Daddy?"

"Kidnaping means I have to go," her daddy said, smiling and hugging her.

"It does? Oh goody!"

"Goody!" repeated Danny.

"But I don't think it's quite lunch time, is it, Pipit?"

"Not quite."

"Can you sing and play some more, Daddy?"

"Now I know for sure this is a conspiracy."

"I had nothing to do with that last request," Pipit stated, "did I, Merri?"

"What?" she asked puzzled.

"Did I tell you to ask your daddy to sing and play some more?"

"No, I thought it up myself," she replied

Matthew smiled. "Most of the time I only play here at this store so the customer can hear how a piano sounds. It's at the Phoenix store I sing a song once in a while for someone if they want to hear it."

"Let's go to the Phoenix store then, Daddy."

"I'm going there Monday, Merri, but maybe I can sing some more here. Mike?"

"Yes, Matt."

"Are there any customers in the store?"

"Not a one."

"Okay, Merri, I'll sing for you. Is that all right with you, Danny?"

Danny nodded, grinning.

"I can't hear a nod, Danny."

"Oh, that's right. Yes, sing for Merri and I'll listen."

"Good boy," Matthew said, patting Danny's small knee.

Mike smiled and sat down on another piano bench. In addition to his other duties, Matt had asked him to stick around when he was out on the floor to guide him from piano to piano or back into the office.

Pipit went around to the back end of the grand piano so she could see Matthew's face while he sang, noting the difference in his demeanor here at the store.

Before Mike or Pipit were aware, several customers had walked in and soon they gravitated toward the compelling music. Two more came in and went over to the small group clustered around the man at the piano.

When the song ended, Danny requested *School Days.* Afterward, Merri requested *Thank Heaven For Little Girls.* Matthew's audience couldn't be held back; at the end of the last song, they clapped.

Startled, Matthew asked, "Mike, do we have some customers here?"

"Yes, Matt, I was listening, not watching. Sorry."

"May I help some of you?" Matthew asked, smiling.

~~~~~~~~~~~~

At Cassie's Cafeteria, Mike, Merri and Danny sat at one small table eating and Matthew and Pipit were eating at the one next to it. Matthew had insisted that Mike drive rather than pay for a cab. And Pipit insisted that the meal was her treat.

Mike entertained Merri and Danny by asking them silly questions and the children chattered and laughed, almost forgetting to eat.

"So you feel rich enough to hire a cab?" Matthew asked, smiling.

"Not rich, independent. Thank you for the money. It has temporarily taken away the feeling of being trapped. I needed this today."

His face turned pensive. "If I could see, I'd take you places so you didn't feel so trapped."

"You could hire a taxi," she teased.

He smiled. "You got me there. I could, but it goes against my frugal grain to spend that much on transportation."

"Apparently, I don't have a frugal grain."

"It's your money to do with whatever you wish. This is a big treat for the children."

"It is," she said watching them for a moment. "They like Mike."

"They do. They've known him for a couple of years. I hired him when he was putting himself through college at Tempe. He graduated in music then got an MBA. I'm grooming him to manage the Scottsdale store. The business is growing and I can't do it all, especially now."

"You are a good salesman, Matthew. The children and I listened for quite a while."

"You were there that long?"

"Yes, but I'm glad the lady left when she did. The children were beginning to get restless. Especially Danny."

Matthew smiled as he pictured it. "I don't know how they sat so still and quiet during all that."

"I told them that was what we were going to do—watch Daddy sell pianos."

Matthew laughed, lifting Pipit's spirits a notch higher.

"So here you are," declared an imperious voice above them.

Startled, Matthew's head raised up toward the voice, and Pipit looked up into the face of Elinor Halstrom.

"Grandmother! Grandmother!" Merri and Danny burst out, jumping down from their seats and hugging her.

"Hello, my darlings," Elinor responded, patting them both. "Now go sit down and finish your lunch. I need to talk to your daddy."

They scrambled back into their chairs and resumed their visit with Mike.

"What are you doing here, Elinor?" Matthew asked, struggling not to show his irritation.

"I went into the store to speak with you and one of your sales people told me you were here."

"Can't this wait, Elinor?"

"No. It cannot. I'm in the middle of organizing a charity and I'm extremely busy."

His voice low and controlled, Matthew asked, "What is it you wanted to speak to me about, Elinor?"

"I came to tell you, Matthew, that Mrs Danville will be there to care for the children starting Wednesday of next week. I need her up until then. And—I suppose Miss Bordeau is sleeping in Mrs. Danville's quarters. Would you please find her another place to stay besides under Diane's roof."

Pipit watched Matthew stiffen, his hand clench. "Elinor," he paused to take a deep breath, "Miss Bordeau is from out of state. She will be staying where she is."

Elinor lowered her voice for the sake of the children. "May I remind you, Matthew, that I paid for that addition so Diane could have more help."

"I would be glad to reimburse you for your expense, Elinor."

Elinor's lips tightened. Her eyes giving Matthew a warning he couldn't see, she responded with curtness. "Very well, Matthew, for now Mrs. Danville will drive back and forth. We'll discuss it again later." With that, she turned to the children and gave them each a kiss. "Grandmother will see you again soon."

Her presence lingered like gray smog on the valley floor— diminishing the sunshine. Matthew and Pipit ate silently. When they were almost finished, Matthew spoke. "I'm going to take the afternoon off, Pipit. Mike will drive us home. You won't have to pay for a cab."

"The children will be happy. They need to spend more time with you."

~~~~~~~~~~~~

That evening, Pipit lay in bed thinking of the day. The weather had turned warm by the time Mike had driven them home so she'd suggested they all go swimming. Matthew had hesitated. "I haven't been swimming since the accident; I don't know."

In the end, Matthew took the plunge and the four of them played water games. Afterward, Matthew told Pipit to order pizza and root beer. The children were the happiest she'd ever seen them. They missed their daddy—the daddy who smiled often and whose warm, heartfelt laughter boosted everyone's spirit. Today in the store and in the swimming pool, he'd given them an abundance of both.

To settle them down for bed, Pipit read to the children while Matthew listened. To their delight, he remarked on the story as they went along.

She whispered into the darkness. "What will it be like with Mrs. Danville here?" Resentment churned inside her at the thought of someone else taking care of the children. This so surprised her, she sat upright. It had only been two days ago that she found it a burden taking care of them, cleaning the house and cooking. Even though it was the best alternative, silently, she had daily resisted it—and the lack of personal freedom that came with it. And now she was resenting Mrs. Danville coming to help? She shook her head.

Moonlight streamed into the open window and a chilly desert breeze blew in as she analyzed this change of heart. It wasn't long before she realized it was because Matthew had so candidly admitted he *needed* her presence. In her narrow and empty world, it felt as though she now had a tangible connection to another human being, and it gave her a sense of responsibility for that human being—Matthew, as well as his children. How long this would override her own desires and needs, she had no idea.

Lying back down, she pulled the covers up to her neck and stared at the ceiling, her mind wandering back to the touching moment she'd experienced tonight. Since the children again requested she tuck them in, she had tiptoed toward Danny's room. Finding the door open, she was about to step in when she saw Matthew kneeling with Danny beside his bed. Danny was praying. Walking quietly past, she went on down the hall to the family room to wait until they were through. She'd already said good night to Merri, who, she was sure had also said prayers with her daddy kneeling beside her.

"Did *I* pray?" The question filled the quiet room. She knew about God; she knew about the Bible—but did she pray?

Chapter Fifteen

Matthew awakened Sunday morning more rested than he'd been since the accident. He stretched and smiled as he thought about the day before and the wonderful surprise Pipit had arranged for him by bringing the children to the store, then kidnaping him for lunch.

Even Elinor's intrusive visit hadn't spoiled the day. His total involvement with the children all afternoon and evening had brought him such joy, he realized he needed it every bit as much as they did. And all this because of Pipit.

He lifted the face of his watch and felt the time. It was 6:30. He felt his good spirits slipping away as the early hour once more brought its usual panic over not being able see the dawning light of morning. If he could accept his blindness, he knew the anxiety would eventually lessen. But according to his doctor, there was hope, and he clung to that hope like a wood tick clinging to human flesh and like the tick burrowing its head, he buried his in denial of anything less than sight.

Remembering it was Sunday dampened his spirits further because he was so limited in what he could do. He was used to working hard and staying busy—much to Diane's displeasure. A wave of remorse swept over him. If only he could push time back, he wouldn't work on Saturdays. He would spend more time with Diane and the children. He had neglected her. Trying to dislodge the painful memories, his mind turned to the present problem—Sundays. On Sundays, he felt trapped; he wasn't able to drive himself and the children to church, let alone do anything else.

Getting out of bed, he headed for the shower. Afterward, he grabbed his old jeans and T-shirt from the familiar hook. Why he dressed quickly this morning he had no idea. Habit, he guessed.

Out in the hall, he stopped at both Merri's and Danny's doors and heard their soft breathing. They had been up late so he didn't expect them to awaken at their usual hour. Entering the family room, he wondered if Pipit was awake.

"Good morning, Matthew." The greeting came from the kitchen area.

He could almost *see* the daylight through her cheerful voice. He smiled. "Good morning, Pipit. What are you doing so early in the kitchen?"

"I'm looking for a recipe for waffles. I thought sausage and waffles might make a good Sunday morning breakfast."

"Sounds great. Wish I could help."

"You can. You can make the orange juice," she said placing the frozen juice and pitcher on the counter.

"Maybe I could manage that," he said starting to walk around the bar.

"I feel like Merri," Pipit said. "She stood up to Elinor and said: 'Daddy doesn't seem blind to me.'"

Matthew stopped in mid-movement, momentarily overcome with emotion. Quickly swallowing it, he felt his way around the bar. As he took a step into the working area of the kitchen, he stumbled over Danny's toy truck and pitched forward. Instantly, Pipit grabbed him, holding him until he could right himself. He clung to her shoulders, totally distraught and humiliated.

"It's all right, Matthew. It's nothing to be upset about. I should have noticed the truck there."

He pulled her into his arms and his chest heaved with involuntary sobs. Embarrassment rapidly brought them to a halt. Stiffening, he dropped his arms from around her and found that *her* arms were still tightly wrapped around *him*.

"Matthew," she murmured against his shoulder, "you are going to see again. I feel it." The minute she said it, she wondered how she could feel so sure.

Slowly, he raised his arms and held her as tightly as she held him. "Thank you, Pipit," he whispered, aware of how good it felt to hold a woman again. But—she wasn't Diane. Pipit's body felt firm and strong—Diane's soft and fragile.

Immediately feeling the change come over Matthew, Pipit instinctively knew he was thinking of Diane. With the exception of Mamie's embrace, it was the first physical solace she'd had since she awakened on that snow covered mountain. She felt swallowed up in comfort when his strong arms wrapped around her pulling her in against his muscled chest. He dropped his arms too quickly. She needed more. In spite of it, she giggled.

"What, Pipit?" he asked, surprised by the sudden humor amidst the emotion.

"Now I understand the term, 'bear hug.'"

It took a moment before he could respond. "It's rather unusual, isn't it?"

"What?"

"Getting a hug from a *grizzly* bear. At least that's what I've felt like for months."

~~~~~~~~~~~~

After lunch when they were all helping with the clean up, Pipit said, "I have a great idea. Let's go for a walk. The weather is delightfully warm this afternoon."

Matthew hesitated, still hating to have people see him being guided.

Danny spoke up eagerly. "I'll hold your hand, Daddy, so you won't fall. I'm sorry 'bout not putting my truck away."

Matthew swallowed hard a couple of times. "Thank you, Danny. Let's go on that walk," he responded with a cheerfulness he didn't feel.

Before they stepped outside, Pipit explained, "Kids, you'll have to take turns holding your Dad's hand because I have to hold on to this one."

Matthew smiled as Pipit took hold of his right hand and Danny the other, remembering how she had taken his hand that first day up in the cabin. He remembered how surprised he'd been that her slim fingers had felt so strong, her hand so firm. She was still taking the responsibility of guiding him and he continued to allow it. For some reason, her hand had given him emotional strength up there in the cabin, and it continued to do so now.

The foursome walked down the road since there were no sidewalks between the spread out houses. The warm sunshine felt good on Matthew's face and his spirits rose.

They stopped and said hello to Flo. Next, they stopped at the Brodericks and several other neighbors. Matthew introduced Pipit and visited each family on their porch for a few minutes. Everyone remarked on how happy they were to see Matthew out.

Back on the road again, Pipit said, "Merri and Danny, walk ahead of us a little ways. I want to talk to your daddy."

"Can we race?" Danny asked.

"No," his dad said. "Stay close to us, there are cars driving by. We can have a race in our back yard when we get home."

Matthew turned to Pipit. "What do you want to talk to me about?"

"I have had an ulterior motive for this walk—to find children for Merri and Danny to play with."

"You should have told me. Diane always insisted on knowing the parents of the children before they played with them."

"If we find any children in the neighborhood, I thought that we both could start getting to know their parents today."

"Pipit, Diane was particular about the children's playmates."

She was silent a moment, then she spoke, carefully enunciating each word."In other words, she would only let them play with children of the upper crust."

"Pipit..."

"Why did you and Diane choose to live in a neighborhood where there are no children?"

"I chose it in order to move as far away from Elinor as I could and still get to work. At that time, Merri was a baby and I didn't think about playmates."

"Do you give me permission to see if I can find some children?" she persisted.

"Mrs. Danville won't allow it."

"They're your children, Matthew."

"As I said before, Pipit, for now, I'm going along with what Elinor wants. I need to buy some time, until my sight returns."

"It's a shame, Matthew. Children need to live in a neighborhood where they have friends to..." she stopped and gripped his arm tightly with her free hand. "I've just had a flash of memory!"

He stopped. "You have? Merri and Danny stop. We're turning around and heading home."

"I don't want to," Merri said.

"Can we go looking for lizards?" Danny asked.

"Not today. Another day. Let's go home and have a race and play some games."

He responded with exuberance. "Okay!"

"Okay," echoed Merri.

"I can hardly wait, Pipit," he said, excitement in his voice, "tell me what you've remembered."

"I remembered a neighborhood. It was a neighborhood of small homes with nicely kept yards. A group of children was playing on one of the front lawns. I didn't see myself, but I know I was one of them...and that the front lawn belonged to the house I lived in as a child. Maybe I still do."

"What does it look like?"

"It's a small white stucco house with flowers, bushes and trees. And I know I was happy there—but, that's all." Her face distorted in frustration. "That's all I remember."

"Nevertheless, Pipit. This is a breakthrough, so other memories are sure to come."

Chapter Sixteen

Monday morning after Matthew had left for work, Pipit sent the children in to make their beds and straighten their rooms. She had no way of knowing what other children were like, but even with Merri's bouts of temper tantrums, she and Danny seemed to be unusually obedient. Flo's effusiveness over Diane must not be exaggerated as she had first suspected. She had come to believe that Diane was as wonderful as Flo said she was. "So why am I dreading the arrival of the ominous Mrs. Danville, the woman Diane apparently trusted to help care for her children?" she asked herself, scrubbing the frying pan vigorously, unable to shake the pall that had settled over her.

The relentless wash had piled up and they were getting low on food in the house. Would she ever get used to the never ending cycle of cooking, cleaning, washing and grocery shopping? And day after tomorrow those duties would be hers without the enjoyment of caring for and doing things with the children! In the beginning she had also been reluctant to care for them. She smiled, remembering how it hadn't taken long to become attached to them, making the job seem easier.

Impulsively, she decided to chuck all the household chores and make the most of the next two days with the children, and she knew exactly what they would do today.

~~~~~~~~~~~~~

In the taxi, the children were bouncing with excitement about going to their daddy's Phoenix store. Pipit had told them that they were going to sneak into the store and watch their daddy sell music and instruments, then kidnap him again.

Pipit wasn't quite sure how Matthew would feel about their shenanigans today. He'd been such a good sport last time. She hoped he would be today.

Merri and Danny finally settled down and looked at the books she had them bring so she would be free to go over again the simple memory that had flashed into her mind yesterday afternoon. Her evolving past life was as suspenseful and intriguing as a mystery novel—and like some mysteries, just as frightening—even though that memory carried with it the feeling of a happy, carefree childhood. No matter how she tried, she couldn't recall any more, so several times she went over the sequence of events that led up to the memory.

She'd been relaxed and happy yesterday as she, Matthew and the children walked together, feeling the pleasant warmth of the Arizona sun. But there was more to it than just feeling relaxed. Something had triggered the memory—maybe her desire to look for playmates for Merri and Danny. As she'd learned before, she couldn't force it. She had no choice but to wait for a set of circumstances that could spark another memory. Trying to squelch her rising impatience, she reasoned that it could happen any moment, tomorrow...the next day...anytime.

The cab driver interrupted her thoughts. "We're here, Ma'am. Melloy Music Center."

The children squealed in excitement. "We're here, Pipit!" exclaimed Danny.

Pipit paid the fare, then to the delight of the children, she motioned for them to follow her. Crouching, they pretended to be sleuths, tiptoeing toward the front door of the store and peeking through the glass.

"There he is!" Merri said, "he's playing the clarinet."

Pipit looked at her in surprise. "How do you know that's a clarinet?"

"Mommy brought us here and taught us all about each instrument and then she took us to symphonies and told us what instruments were playing. Didn't she, Danny?"

Danny nodded in wide-eyed agreement.

Pipit thought about this a moment. At the latest, Danny would have been only three and Merri four. What an education Diane had given them—painting lessons, symphonies, trips to the library.

As they stepped inside, a female clerk recognized the children. Merri put her finger to her lips, then smiled.

The clerk, taking the cue, came over to them and whispered. "Hi, Merri. Hi, Danny. Are you trying to surprise your daddy?"

They both nodded, grinning.

"And we're going to kidnap him and take him to lunch," Danny whispered.

"How fun for him," she replied.

"I'm Pipit Bordeau. Matthew hired me to take care of the children."

"Hello. Matthew has told us about you. I'm Shelly," she whispered, leading them to a place near Matthew, and pulling over a couple of chairs.

"Thank you, Shelly." Pipit said. "Do you have books with songs from the forties and fifties?"

"Yes, we do. I'll get them for you."

Mike, who was now helping Matthew get around at both stores, was standing near him. He smiled at the threesome, and Merri laid a finger over her lips, grinning.

It wasn't long before Shelly returned. She handed two music books to Pipit just as the customer Matthew had been playing for decided on her purchase.

"Shelly, would you please take care of this customer?" Mike asked. "I've got another customer here." He smiled at Pipit.

After Shelly and the customer left, Mike took the music books Pipit was handing him, knowing what she wanted. "Matthew I have a lady here that would like to have you sing a couple of songs from these two books?"

"Give me the names of the songs she wants to hear."

Mike gave him a couple of titles.

Pipit gave Merri and Danny a secretive smile and they responded with their own.

The three waited while Mike read some titles. Matthew nodded and began playing *I'll Be Seeing You*. After that one, he played *Blue Berry Hill*, then *Chantilly Lace*. When the last song ended, Danny couldn't contain himself. He ran up to him and Merri followed.

"Surprise Daddy! Surprise!"

Again, Matthew's face registered total surprise. He laughed. "Hey, you two, is this going to be a daily occurrence?"

"We're going to kidnap you again, Daddy." Danny eagerly blurted out.

"Pipit?"

"Yes, Matthew."

"Where is that customer who wants to buy these books?"

"You are speaking to her, that is, if I like the selections of songs in it. I may have to hear five or six more before I decide, however."

Matthew grinned. "Oh, no you don't. I'm on to your tricks."

"Can we go now, Daddy?" Danny asked.

"What time is it, Pipit?"

"It's almost noon."

"It's lunch time. Let's go. Hey, Mike, want to go to lunch again with your fan club?"

"Sure do," he grinned.

~~~~~~~~~~~~

The small booths at the fish and chips place couldn't hold all five, so again, the children and Mike sat together in one, Pipit and Matthew in the other.

"I could get used to eating out like this, Matthew," Pipit said. "In fact, we all may have to, we're getting low on food again. I guess when Mrs. Danville comes, I'll go check with Margo and find out when she's going grocery shopping."

Matthew only half-listening, asked, "Have you had any other flashes of memory since Sunday?"

"No. I'm just going to have to wait, and somehow I feel patience isn't one of my qualities. Have you had any change in your eyesight, Matthew...any change at all?"

"You know, this morning as I was getting ready for work, I noticed a change. I used to believe that the blind saw only darkness. That isn't the case."

"It isn't?" Pipit asked, surprised.

"No. Those who read braille and are considered blind retain light perception, which is the ability to see the contrasts between light and dark. This morning when I awoke, it was still dark outside. By checking my watch, I know when the sun comes up. When it came up, I felt I saw a greater contrast. I have an appointment with the doctor this afternoon. By the way, *your* appointment with doctor is in two weeks. I wish it could be sooner, but that was as soon as he could get you in."

"Tell me about Mrs. Danville, Matthew," she said, changing the subject.

"About twenty-five years ago when Mrs. Danville was thirty-five, Elinor hired her to be her private secretary, and general factotum. Mrs. Danville had married ten years before and her husband was killed in a construction accident. Three years later she applied for the job with Elinor. She and her husband weren't able to have children. Because she took a liking to Diane, Elinor hired her in spite of the fact that she had no education, nor social skills. Elinor educated her and Mrs. Danville has always been grateful to Elinor for hiring and teaching her. Through the years she's become an outstanding and extremely loyal employee to Elinor. I believe she's now about sixty. She loves Merri and Danny, and Diane found her help invaluable." Pipit was silent so long, he asked, "What is it, Pipit?"

"I'll miss taking care of the children."

It was Matthew's turn to be silent. After a while, he said, "If it were up to me, I would choose you over Mrs. Danville, Pipit. I'm sorry it has to be like this. However, any day your memory may return and you'll be gone."

Changing the subject to something more pleasant, she asked, "I want to take the children to the zoo tomorrow, Matthew. Can you get off and go with us?"

"I wish I could, but I have an important staff meeting in both stores. Besides, you are using up your money quickly. I have an idea. I'll arrange for Mike to pick me up a little later, and we'll drop you off at the zoo, pick you up afterward and drive you home."

"That would be helpful, thank you," she said, feeling disappointed.

"Also, I'll pay for the tickets and give you money for lunch. And thank you, Pipit for this great surprise again today." He lowered his voice. "The only thing that could make it better is if I could see, then the four of us could go out together as a family without having to have a chauffeur along."

Did Matthew realize what he'd just said?...'go out together as a family.' She didn't think so. Anyway, it sounded good to her. Matthew and the children were the only family she had right now.

~~~~~~~~~~~~

After the children were in bed, Matthew turned on the television and listened to the early news, then flipped it off.

Pipit, who was curled up on the couch reading, asked, "What did the doctor say today, Matthew?"

"He said the change was a good sign and that the improvement should be more rapid from now on. However, there is a small chance that it will be permanent blindness."

"I don't know how I can feel so strongly about this, Matthew, but I feel that you will be able to see again."

He smiled. "You sound so certain, Pipit. It gives me hope." He paused. "You know, I'm anxious to hear what the doctor has to say about you, but..." He hesitated to finish.

"But what, Matthew?"

"But nothing."

"Please, Matthew, tell me."

"I'm afraid I've come to rely on you more than I should, Pipit. I'm curious as heck about you and I want your memory to return...yet, a part of me wants you to remain here with us. I know it isn't fair of me to feel this way since you need to get on with your life."

"Maybe I don't have a life to get on with. Maybe my life is here with you and the children."

"I wish it could be, but it can't, Pipit. Part of me knows that. You would just end up being like Mrs. Danville...a lonely woman pretending to be part of a family, but in reality having no one to care for her and look after her in her later years."

For some reason, it felt like Matthew had just dealt her a blow to the stomach. In reality, Matthew 'needing' her didn't mean very much. It had only given her something to hang on to for a short time. When Matthew regained his sight, that 'need' would evaporate. Though still trying to catch her breath after the blow of Matthew's words, she realized there was a part of her that was as fearful of Matthew regaining his sight as he was of her regaining her memory.

She stood up and walked toward her room. "Good night, Matthew."

Surprised by her sudden departure, he didn't react until she was at the door. "Good night, Pipit." *Why did she leave like that? Did I hurt her feelings?* he asked himself. *I had to be honest with her, didn't I?*

Without her presence, the room seemed unbearably empty, but it was all mixed up with the emptiness Diane left behind and he couldn't tell which was which. He groaned. "Oh Diane, Diane why did I have to lose you?"

Chapter Seventeen

Wednesday morning after Matthew left for work, Pipit hustled the children to help her clean up in readiness for Mrs. Danville. *Strange*, she thought, *they didn't act excited to have her come, nor did they act like they didn't want her to come.*

The house needed a real cleaning. She probably should have done it yesterday instead of taking the children to the zoo, but they had had such a wonderful time, she didn't feel guilty in the least. Matthew and Mike had picked them up at 3:30 in the afternoon, so she was able to get dinner over early. This enabled her to go over to Margo's to find out when she was going grocery shopping. As it turned out, Margo wanted to go right then. At least, she was prepared in this area for Mrs. Danville's arrival.

Pipit had just finished the breakfast dishes when the doorbell rang. Walking quickly, she opened the door to a tall, prim stick-of-a-woman. Her gray-streaked black hair was pulled tightly back into a french bun, emphasizing her long sharp nose and thin lips. Cold, piercing brown eyes looked Pipit over disapprovingly. The woman wore a black dress, a stark contrast to Pipit's white T-shirt and tan shorts.

"Mrs. Danville?"

"Yes." The one word reply hung in the air like a challenge. Finally, she added, "You must be Miss Bordeau." She made it sound like over-ripe sauerkraut.

"I am. Please come in."

She stepped in. "Where are the children?"

"They're cleaning their rooms. Go in and have a seat and I'll get them."

Pipit went in and told Merri and Danny to come out and speak to Mrs. Danville. "Okay," Merri said. Danny said nothing, just followed his sister. Pipit found this curious.

The two walked over to Mrs. Danville who held out her arms. They went into them. "Let me look at you," she said, after a quick hug. "My, but you have both grown since I've seen you. Sit down beside me and let's talk about what we are going to do today."

"When it's warm, Pipit takes us swimming," Merri announced.

Mrs. Danville straightened her back and glared at Pipit. "You know you are going against Diane's wishes don't you?"

"I only know that it is Mr. Melloy's wish that they swim. You may discuss it with him if you like."

"Well, today children, we're going to resume your painting lessons with Mrs. Henderson. Your grandmother has requested it." Looking up at Pipit, she said. "I assume that is all right with you, Miss Bordeau." It was obvious the statement required no answer.

"As I said before, Mrs. Danville, you may discuss the children's curriculum with Mr. Melloy. As of now I'm just the cook and housekeeper."

Mrs. Danville looked around the room. "Housekeeper? Elinor told me about your so-called housekeeping."

"It is a little casual, isn't it? Kind of like the way I'm dressed," she said, smiling, determined not to get drawn into contentiousness.

"Diane kept the house spotless."

"Did she have a maid?"

"Well, yes, but in between, she kept it spotless. Didn't she children?"

They both nodded solemnly.

"Well...if you'll excuse me, Mrs. Danville, I'll get the wash started. It has piled up so high, none of us has a thing to wear. You see, we've been playing for four days straight, haven't we?" She smiled at the children.

They grinned widely, nodded vigorously.

"Well then, in that case we had better get on with our painting lessons and reading."

Pipit escaped in search of the wash.

~~~~~~~~~~~~

Pipit pulled the casserole from the oven and placed it on a cooling rack. She'd had more time to concentrate on the meal so she was anxious to taste it. Dipping a spoon in and blowing it cool, she put it in her mouth. She grimaced in frustration and disappointment. It didn't taste as good as she thought it would!

The children and Mrs. Danville walked in from painting lessons at Flo's, and immediately, Merri climbed up on a bar stool and announced crossly, "I'm hungry."

Danny climbed up beside her. "Me too. Mrs. Danville wouldn't let us have an ice cream cone over at Flo's!"

"Maybe we had better eat before your dad gets home then. I've set a place for you Mrs. Danville. You are eating with us, aren't you?"

"Of course. It's a long drive back to Elinor's. Now, if I were able to stay in my own quarters, it would be much easier. Diane was much more considerate of me than Matthew."

Pipit glared at Mrs. Danville for talking like that in front of the children.

Turning her attention to them she said, "I'm going to call and find out when your daddy is coming home." She walked quickly out of the room to phone from her bedroom. Plunking herself down on the bed, she fumed. Just then, she heard the front door open and shut. Matthew was home! Hopefully, Mrs. Danville would watch what she said around him. Soon, she heard the happy greetings from Merri and Danny.

She entered the kitchen in time to hear Matthew courteously greet Mrs. Danville. "Good evening, Matthew," Mrs. Danville returned, coolly.

Pipit added her greeting. "Good evening, Mr. Melloy."

His face lit up. "Good evening, Pipit. How was it today not having to look after these two ruffians?"

"I got the wash done for a change and a little cleaning. Dinner is ready. If everyone will be seated, I'll get it on the table."

Danny jumped down from the stool and sat at the table.

Merri followed him. "That's my chair!" Merri said, shoving him.

"It's not either. I get to sit by Daddy tonight."

"You can both sit by me. What is the matter with you tonight, Merri?"

"Nothing," she sulked.

After everyone seated themselves and had taken a portion of the casserole and the vegetable, Danny pointed to the spoonful of casserole on his plate. "I don't like this."

"I like it, you're just a baby, Danny," Merri taunted.

"I'm not either! You're a baby!"

"Stop it. Both of you," Matthew ordered. "What is the matter with you both? I guess the day at the zoo was too tiring. You're both going to bed early tonight."

"It was the sun on Merri's skin, Matthew," Mrs. Danville stated. "You know how the sun wore her mother out. Now about the swimming..."

"The children are swimming when it is warm enough. Pipit will take them."

"But, Matthew..."

"That is the way it will be, Mrs. Danville. I've already covered this with Elinor."

Mrs. Danville ate in silence for some time, then looking at Pipit, she said, "Diane was a wonderful cook, and she was very health conscious. For instance, she would have had another vegetable with this casserole and maybe a fresh salad."

Pipit couldn't believe her ears. Mrs. Danville was determined to keep Diane's memory alive by criticizing others. "How *kind* of you to point that out, Mrs. Danville," she gushed with sarcasm. "Maybe *you* should take over the cooking since you are so full of ideas on what we should eat."

Mrs. Danville bristled. "I only take care of the children. That is the way Diane wanted it."

"That's too bad. Then I guess you'll just have bear with my less-than-nutritious meals, Mrs. Danville."

Matthew broke in quickly to avoid further escalation of the barbed exchanges. He asked the children questions about their day. Finally, the meal ended and Mrs. Danville left for home.

Hurriedly, Pipit cleaned up the kitchen, wondering if she could stand another day of having Mrs. Danville here, let alone a week or—until her memory returned! She could hear Matthew bathing the children and their irritability. As soon as possible, she escaped into her bedroom and sat down on the small couch thinking. How could only one day with Mrs. Danville cause the children to regress so much?

Chapter Eighteen

Pipit had little to say as she helped Matthew with his clothes Thursday morning. What could she say at this point without causing him greater concern? When he left for work, she sat down with the children and hugged each one. "I missed you yesterday. Maybe it will warm up enough to go swimming."

"I hope so," Merri said. "I missed you too, Pipit."

"I did, too," Danny said.

The doorbell rang, but before she could even get up, the door opened. Pipit ran into the foyer and found Mrs. Danville putting her keys away in her purse.

Noting the expression on Pipit's face, Mrs. Danville said, "Diane gave me a key to the house. No need for concern." Walking past Pipit, she went on into the family room.

"Good morning, children. Did you have a good night's sleep?"

Neither one responded. Mrs. Danville laid her purse and jacket down on a chair and went over and sat down on the couch with them. "We're going to be very busy for the next three days. Your grandmother and I have planned some wonderful things for you to do."

"If it warms up, Pipit is going to take us swimming," Merri stated.

"We won't have time for that, Merri. We have too much to do."

"But I want to go swimming."

"I want to, too," added Danny.

"We're going to the library this morning, and then we're driving to your Grandmother's house to have lunch with her. She misses you and wants to see you."

"Oh, okay," Merri said, her face losing its pout. "Can I check out some books and take them to show grandmother?"

"You may. She may even read one or two to you. Now, let's go into your rooms and change into something presentable and we'll be off."

Pipit watched them disappear into the hallway, and tears stung her eyes. "I could have taken them to the library if I only had a driver's license," she mumbled. Stepping over to the window, she stared out, deciding that the last thing she wanted to do was stay in this house alone today!

Turning quickly, she headed for her bedroom talking to herself. "I still have money left. I'll call a taxi and go to downtown Scottsdale and look into the shops." She picked up the phone and called, then went back out to see the children off.

Merri and Danny came running in to hug her goodbye. She hugged each one, fighting back tears. "Have a good time, you two."

"I want you to come with us," Danny said.

"I do too," Merri said eagerly. "I'll ask Mrs. Danville if you can." Before Pipit could stop her, she ran over and asked her.

"Miss Bordeau needs to stay here and clean the house, Merri."

"Mrs. Danville is right. I need to clean the house. I'll see you tonight. Will you bring the children back in time for dinner, Mrs. Danville?"

"No. Their grandmother wants them to stay and see their grandfather so we'll all be eating dinner with them," she said ushering them to the front door. "I'll bring them home in time for bed."

As Mrs. Danville closed the door behind them, Pipit went back into the bedroom and changed into a skirt and knit shirt with a matching short cropped-cardigan. Checking her hair in the mirror, she wondered if she could find a beauty salon and have it styled. Quickly putting on mascara and eye shadow, she grabbed her purse and went into the family room to wait for the taxi.

In the cab, Pipit informed the driver that she was new to the area, and asked him where there was a good place to shop in downtown Scottsdale.

"I can drop you off at Fashion Square Mall or you might want to see old town Scottsdale. It's quite a tourist attraction, and has some interesting shops."

"I think I'd like to go to old town Scottsdale."

Still feeling lonely and a little lost, Pipit focused on the scenery during the thirty-minute drive on Scottsdale Rd. Still bemused by the names of the streets, particularly noting Dynamite Rd. as they stopped at a light. They passed fenced ranches; one of interest to Pipit was an Arabian horse ranch. As they drew closer to town, major shopping appeared on both sides. They stopped at a light on

Frank Lloyd Wright Blvd. South of another uniquely named street, Jack Rabbit Rd., they passed Lincoln Village where Melloy Piano Center was located. She wished she could drop in and say 'hi,' but the last thing she wanted was for Matthew to know she was sluffing her duties today.

For the first time, Pipit really noticed Scottsdale. It was a beautiful, orderly and clean city with stately palms and greenery planted wherever possible. Arriving at Scottsdale Rd. and 5th Ave., the driver pulled off and opened the door for her, suggesting she start by walking down 5th Ave.

Intrigued, she began sauntering down the quaint and narrow street. On both sides connecting shops with old-fashioned western facades drew her curiosity.

The weather had turned warm and delightful. Feeling like a bird out of a cage, she did just as she pleased. She window shopped, wandered in and out of several colorful shops...boutiques, an oriental rug store, an art gallery, and an Indian craft store. Reaching what was apparently the street center, she came upon a distinctive fountain with five rearing horses. Gazing at it a moment, she walked on past it and discovered a shop called Pierre's Custom Perfume. She stepped inside. Pleasant, flower-like scents filled the small room. Behind the counter, rows of small brown labeled bottles filled narrow shelves. A cushioned wicker couch and chair, surrounded by plants on wicker stands, looked inviting. Seating herself, she sighed. Window shopping, she realized, tired her more than swimming.

When the one customer left, the man behind the counter addressed her. "I'm Pierre, may I help you?"

"Maybe," she said standing up and stepping to the counter. "How much is your custom perfume?"

"It depends on what scent of flower or flowers you use and how many. I do not use any artificial chemical scent, only oil from the flowers. The test is free. Would you like to find out what flower scents you like best?"

"Yes, I would, thank you."

"What flowers do you like best?"

Her face clouded. "I don't know." She had no idea what she liked, and she certainly didn't want to tell him about her memory loss. "I like so many, maybe you could help me out."

"Of course. Do you like heavy sweet scents or light delicate scents?"

Remembering that she didn't care for Diane's heavy sweet perfume, she said, "Light delicate scents."

He turned and pulled several bottles down. Opening one, he ran the glass stem lightly across a small strip of blotter paper and handed it to her.

"Nice," she said, "what flower is that?"

"That's sweet alyssum." Opening another bottle, he repeated the same sequence.

"I don't care for that one."

After several bottles, he found another one she liked. "That is the flower called sweet pea. Let me put both together on a blotter."

Pipit watched him, intrigued by the whole process. He handed her the blotter to smell the mixture of scents.

"Mm, I like that."

"All right then, let's give it the skin test. Rub the blotter of the mixed scent on the inside of your wrist and see if you like the scent on your skin."

She did as he said and smelled her wrist. "Mm, it's nice on my skin, also."

"Good," he said smiling. "Shall I make up an ounce for you?"

"How much would an ounce cost?"

"Let me check. I'll be right back." He quickly returned. "You see, there are some rare flowers and some imported flowers, but both these flowers are grown in America so an ounce would only be $160."

She gasped. "I can go to a department store and get perfume much cheaper than that."

Pierre smiled condescendingly. "But they are not perfumes that are customized to your taste and sense of smell. Mine are fragrances from the pure oil of the flower."

Pipit calculated in her mind how much she had left of her funds. She decided that she had enough for the perfume, as well as a hairstyle and still have some left over. "All right," she said, "make up an ounce for me. How long will it take?"

"About thirty minutes. I have the oils in the back."

She paid him and said, "I'll wait for it."

~~~~~~~~~~~

Seated in the first beauty salon she found, the hairdresser fingered through her hair. She had talked him into squeezing her into his busy schedule. "You have a lovely texture to your hair. I believe it's long enough to style it in the more feminine fashion you asked for."

When he was through, she studied herself in the mirror and decided she'd been lucky to find this hairdresser. He made her look almost pretty. She paid him $90 and left to find a place to eat lunch.

Stopping at a small place called The Tea Room, she went in. The hostess seated her and she ordered the luncheon plate of the day. It was a delicious chicken salad, a delicate green molded salad, and colorfully cut carrots, celery and cucumber, accompanied by a plate of three kinds of small sweet muffins. She sighed as she savored the tasty meal, wishing she could make food taste this way.

After lunch, she sauntered in and out of the shops until boredom set in. Glancing at her watch, she saw that it was 3:30 and knew it was time to call a taxi and go on home to prepare dinner for Matthew. The thought of entering the empty house with only the memory of the mysterious Diane hovering around deterred her. Spying a bench in front of one of the shops, she sat down. Then it dawned on her. Had she saved enough taxi money to get home? Opening her purse, she counted her money. Thirty dollars and the taxi cost more! "How stupid of me,"she muttered. "What am I going to do?"

Getting up, she walked on, feeling trapped and powerless. Loneliness settled over her. She felt she had no one on this earth to turn to. She didn't have enough money, she couldn't drive, and worst of all, she couldn't remember! Stopping and taking several deep breaths, she tried to be calm.

Calling Matthew for help is the last thing I want to do, but what else can I do? she asked herself. *No, I just can't do it!* She began to walk aimlessly. Glancing every now and then at her watch, she twice approached a pay phone only to draw back. Twice, she checked her money hoping that somehow it would turn out to be enough.

At last it was 4:30. She had to make a decision. Matthew would be going home any time now. Still she hesitated. The seconds on her watch were ticking away like the count-down on a bomb...5...4...3...2... Convulsively, she grasped the phone and dialed the Scottsdale store.

"Melloy Piano Center," the voice answered.

"Is Mr. Melloy in the store today?"

"He is. Would you like to speak with him?"

"Yes I would, thank you."

"Hello," The timbre of Matthew's voice was just as low and resonate on the phone as it was in person.

"Hello, Matthew, this is Pipit."

"Is everything all right? You sound upset."

"The children are fine. Mrs. Danville took them to the library and then to Elinor's house for lunch and dinner to spend time with both grandparents. Is that all right with you?"

"It has to be. What's the matter, Pipit?"

"I'm stranded," she said, feeling mortified.

"Stranded? Stranded where?"

Reluctantly, she answered. "In old town Scottsdale. I couldn't bear to stay in the house without Merri and Danny so I called a taxi to bring me here to shop. I...I spent so much money, I don't have enough to pay for a taxi home."

There was silence on the phone a moment, then Pipit heard a warm burst of laughter, allowing her also to see the humor in the situation, relieving the tension in her shoulders. "Well," he said, still chuckling, "if you aren't the biggest spendthrift I know. I guess I'll have to raise your wages to support your habit."

She laughed weakly. "Thanks for making me feel better, Matthew."

"Tell me where you are and Mike and I will pick you up in about twenty minutes."

~~~~~~~~~~~~

On the way home in the car with Mike and Matthew, Pipit realized all the frightening emotions had dissipated and she was feeling less alone. To her relief, Matthew and Mike talked about business rather than teasing her about the silly fix into which she'd gotten herself.

When they arrived home and entered the house, Matthew said, "You smell nice, Pipit. Did you buy some perfume?"

"You like it then?" she asked, pleased.

"Very much."

"It should smell good, it cost $160 an ounce," she said as she took his hand and walked into the kitchen to see what to do about dinner.

Matthew whistled. "Maybe you got taken."

"It's custom perfume from the natural oils of the flowers. I chose two flower scents that I liked and he made me the perfume out of those."

Matthew smiled and sat down on one of the bar stools. "I guess it's worth the price then."

"I had my hair styled too. It looks better than when I first arrived at the cabin."

"How much did that cost?"

"Too much. I think old town Scottsdale may be rather expensive."

"I wish I could see your new hairstyle, Pipit."

"I wish you could, Matthew," she said in a wistful voice. "It's really no fun looking nice for myself only—even though it does make me less homely."

Matthew chuckled. "I can't imagine you being homely, Pipit. Arthur doesn't think you are."

"He doesn't?" she asked, heartened.

"Nope. Oh, by the way, speaking of Arthur. He called me at the store the other day and he and Mamie with their son Randy, and his wife, Joan, and their children are coming this Saturday night. Randy and Joan are going to stay with the children while Arthur and Mamie take us out to dinner and to the Broadway musical, *Beauty and the Beast*."

"They are? Now I have something to look forward to while I endure two more days with Mrs. Danville."

"Arthur thought you might feel that way. He knows you've been working hard here and thought you'd appreciate a change...especially since I can't take you anywhere myself without a chauffeur."

~~~~~~~~~~~~

Not long after Pipit had cleaned up the kitchen, Mrs. Danville entered the front door with two tired children. They followed her into the family room. "Matthew," she said, "Here are the children. See to it they go to bed early."

"Hey," he said, opening his arms wide. They both ran into them. "Did you two have a good time?" They both nodded, forgetting to speak out loud for their daddy.

"I'll be going, Matthew," Mrs. Danville said."I'll be back in the morning. Goodnight, children." She turned and briskly walked out.

"Pipit!" Danny said, running over to her and hugging her. Merri followed him with her own hug.

"Thank you for remembering to hug me, too," she said, smiling at each, her heart full. "Why don't you go back and sit by your father and tell him everything you did today."

They ran back and sat by him and Danny began the narrative. Merri reached across and slapped Danny in the face. "I get to tell it first."

Danny began sobbing as if his heart would break. Pipit felt like hers would also. Matthew picked Danny up and held him on his lap. "Merri must be tired or she never would have hit you like that."

"Yes she would! She's been mean to me all day."

"You stay here with Pipit, Danny," he said placing him on the couch. "Merri and I are going to her room."

Pipit quickly went over to the couch and put her arms around Danny. "I'm sorry, Danny." He clung to her until he was through crying. Soon, his father returned and took him by the hand and together they went into his room to prepare for bed.

After Danny's prayer, Matthew lay down beside him thinking about the actions of his children. He'd tried to talk with Merri, but she'd sulked and even hit at him, reverting to her past behavior before Pipit entered their lives. *Why?* he asked himself. If he didn't know better, he'd think it was Mrs. Danville's influence, but, Merri had acted like this almost since Danny's birth—long before Mrs. Danville came to help Diane. And even after she came to help, Diane had cared for the children herself most of the time. Mrs. Danville only came once in a while for a few days when Diane was in the middle of one of her projects.

While waiting for Matthew, Pipit wondered why Merri was turning on Danny. The question hung heavy on her heart. Mrs. Danville seemed to care for the children.

"Somehow, things have to change for this family!" she whispered. But at the moment, the possibility of a change for the better seemed hopeless.

Matthew returned, found a chair and seated himself. Pipit could see by the expression on his face that things hadn't gone too well.

"Pipit?"

"Yes?"

"Would you mind reading to me?"

"I'd be glad to, Matthew. What shall I read?"

He got up and went to the spot in the bookcase where he always kept it and picked up his family Bible.

She quickly got up and took it. They seated themselves and Pipit turned to the New Testament. Just holding the book made her feel more hopeful over Matthew's situation. She began reading. Forty-five minutes later, Matthew said, "Thank you, Pipit, I think we'd both better call it a night."

Chapter Nineteen

Mel Osborne lifted the blade of the snow plow slightly. Since there had been a brief warm front, the snow on the road had melted almost to a slush. He didn't want the blade to scrape the already beleaguered road. When spring came, invariably they would find big chuck holes in the asphalt from the temperature changes.

Up ahead, off the road, something glinted in the sun. He stared hard at it. "Good grief, Tim," he said to his partner sitting beside him. "Do you see what I see?"

"What, Mel?"

Mel pointed to the spot. "See that shiny gray metal in the ditch beside the road."

"Yeah. What do you think it is?"

"I hope it's not what I think it is."

"An automobile?"

"Yeah," he said, driving as close as he could and stopping.

"Wait a minute, Mel, I think I remember some of the guys at the department talking about a man who called and told everyone to watch for a car that went off the road up here. The man said he thought it was probably covered by snow because he couldn't find it himself. Neither one of us were there that day."

"All I remember, Tim, is that a woman kept pestering us to clear the roads up here just as soon as those blizzards died down. Let's get out and see if we can shovel enough to take a look."

They each grabbed a big snow shovel from behind the seat and waded through the still deep, but wet snow. "Whatever it is, it must have been completely covered by those big drifts we got up here."

They shoveled hard and fast. "It *is* a car, Mel!" Neither of the men mentioned the nagging dread they felt at the possibility of finding a body in it. Each was breathing hard and sweating even though it was still cold.

"Get on the other side, Tim, and let's clear the front windows on both sides so we can look inside."

They shoveled and shoved the snow clear of both windows. "There, Mel, I think we can see in now." Their hearts pounding, they both bent down and looked in.

"It's empty, Tim!"

Tim grinned with relief, but it was short-lived. "The front door is ajar. That means whoever was in this car got out and could have frozen to death trying to find somewhere to go."

Mel's face was grim. "That means we have to wait until the thaw. No way could we find a body now under all this snow."

"Wait a minute, Mel, there's something inside. Come on over to this side and see if we can get this door open wider."

The two men shoveled vigorously, and finally were able to pull the door open a little further. Tim, the more slender of the two reached in and pulled out a small purse. His face pale, he said, "It was a woman, Mel."

"Open it, Tim."

Gingerly, Tim opened the purse. Pulling out a wallet, he found a driver's license. They both stared at the blonde-haired young woman. "Her name is Elizabeth Cabot. She's from Palm Springs, California."

Both were silent a moment, then Mel said. "You know, Tim, there's a cabin around the bend. Maybe she found shelter there."

"But, Mel, hardly anyone comes up in this area in the winter."

"I know, but it could have belonged to the man who wanted us to watch for a car that went off the road."

"The chances of that are slim. But we can hope."

"Let's get back to the office and give this information to the boss."

~~~~~~~~~~~~

Julia Cabot, her arms folded tightly across her mid-section, faced her husband, Calvin. "Cal, something is wrong. I know it. In Liz's note, she said she'd call in three weeks and tell us where she is and now it has been twenty-five days."

"Calm down, Julia, you know how independent Liz is, how she's traveled alone. Even when she traveled all over Europe, she only had the companionship of an older woman. And remember that time we didn't hear from her for almost ten days from the time she said she'd call?"

"But that was a miscommunication, Cal. Liz always does what she says she'll do. Besides, she just got engaged! I just don't understand it." Most of this conversation had been repeated daily, but usually with tears of frustration.

"Maybe you're right, Julia." Calvin Cabot didn't want to tell his wife that he'd felt uneasy ever since he'd learned that Liz hadn't left a message for Kirk. She'd accepted his proposal and his ring Friday evening and the next day, Saturday, she left, leaving only a note. Her leaving like that when she seemed so happy left him feeling more than puzzled. "Has Kirk called this morning?"

"Not yet. But I'm sure he will. He calls every day, sometimes twice a day."

This wasn't news to Cal. The whole conversation was simply daily emotion Julia had to get out. Three days ago they had contacted the police in several cities in California and reported her missing. These were places Liz went now and then. The police hadn't taken them too seriously once they had questioned the Cabots and found out that Liz was on the go often, and that she'd only been gone one day past the time she said she would call.

Julia picked up the worn note Liz had left them and read it out loud once more, hoping somehow they would pick up a clue. *"Dear Mom and Dad, I have to get away for a while. Please don't worry about me. I'm fine. If I'm not home before, I'll call you in three weeks. Love, Liz."*

"Don't torture yourself, Julia. I'm sure we'll hear from her any moment now." Calvin didn't believe what he was saying, but somehow he felt better saying it.

"I just wish we knew which city, which state..." The phone rang and Julia grabbed it. "Hello."

"Mom, have you heard from Liz yet?"

Disappointed at hearing her youngest daughter's voice rather than Liz's, she said, "No, Linda, we haven't."

"What are we going to do, Mom?"

"I don't know. I've got to go, dear, I have to talk with your father."

"Okay, Mom. Talk to you later."

"Let's go eat lunch out on the patio, Julia, you didn't eat breakfast this morning."

They left the bedroom and walked down the hall together and as they reached the foyer, their other daughter Claire walked through the front door. "Hi," she said. "Any news?"

"No, Claire. Your dad and I are going out on the patio to eat lunch. Want to join us?"

"Okay."

The three ate in silence for a while, then Claire spoke, "I just don't understand Liz. She was very much in love with Kirk and she was so happy when he proposed."

Calvin sighed. This conversation was worn out also, but he bore it in silence.

"I know," her mother said. "I've gone over and over it in my mind trying to find even one clue as to why she'd leave like this. I've talked to Kirk in depth and he has no idea why she left."

"How is he taking it by now?"

"More worried, just like we all are."

~~~~~~~~~~~~~

Mrs. Danville, arriving slightly later that morning, took off her coat and without a word of greeting got right down to business. She slid in the CD and sat down with the children to listen to the classical piece of music.

Pipit was amazed that Danny sat so still. Shortly, Mrs. Danville, turned the music off and asked, "Now, children, can you tell me what instruments were playing?"

Pipit, who was in the kitchen area trying to look over some recipes couldn't help herself. "Do *you* know, Mrs. Danville?"

Mrs. Danville shot her an angry glance. "Of course. Having lived with the Halstrom family for so long I've become quite educated in the arts. Diane educated the children also. She took them to symphonies as often as was possible."

"How nice," Pipit said, feeling a little annoyed. "And how nice that they can hear their father sing and play."

"It would be nicer if Matthew would take voice lessons like Diane wanted him to. His voice is untrained."

"It doesn't sound untrained to me."

"Have you had music training, Miss Bordeau?"

"I am a connoisseur of fine singing, Mrs. Danville."

"Please, Miss Bordeau, take care of the house cleaning and let me get on with what Diane would want me to do."

"Is it warm enough to go swimming yet, Pipit?" Merri asked in a small plaintive voice.

"I'm sorry, Merri, but it's too cold today. Maybe it will be warm tomorrow."

"Miss Bordeau, I'm taking the children to the library again tomorrow. You see, Diane was an intellectual. She hosted many book reviews and she read every book that was reviewed. She wanted the children to learn to love reading."

Pipit nodded and left the room quickly. She would have to go over the recipes another time. The way Mrs. Danville talked about Diane bothered her terribly, and she wasn't quite sure why. And yet...for some reason, she felt terribly sorry for Mrs. Danville. She had no life of her own; it consisted almost totally of living some-one else's just as Matthew said. Wasn't that what she herself was doing? Living someone else's life? All of a sudden she felt smoth-ered. She couldn't stay in this house another minute. Throwing on a sweater, she headed for the front door to go for a run.

~~~~~~~~~~~~

After a harrowing time putting the children to bed, Pipit and Matthew were trying to relax in the family room. Matthew flipped on the television and tried to find something he could enjoy which didn't require sight.

"Is there something you would like to watch, Pipit?" he asked.

"No. I feel too edgy. Mrs. Danville is making me so nervous I don't know how I'm going to hold out, Matthew."

He flipped off the television. "I'm feeling the same way, Pipit."

They sat in silence for some time. Pipit paged aimlessly through a magazine, oddly wondering if she were an intellectual like Diane. Probably not since all she managed to do was page through maga-zines!

"Pipit?"

"Yes, Matthew."

"You've heard of a marriage of convenience haven't you?"

She was so shocked at the question she couldn't answer immediately. "Wh..what are you getting at, Matthew?"

"I'm feeling so desperate, I...I feel like asking you to marry me."

This statement triggered such emotion, such unsettling thoughts Pipit couldn't say a word.

"Pipit?"

"Yes, Matthew."

"What are you thinking?"

The obvious finally struck home; it was just a rhetorical statement. Matthew only said it because it was impossible. The marriage would be illegal with a fake name. "What *could* I think, Matthew?"

"Oh, I don't know. What I meant was, if your name were real, I might dare ask you to marry me for a short while, and then, of course, we would annul it later so you could...."

"That's so flattering, Matthew," she interrupted with sarcasm.

Surprised at the sarcasm in her voice, he quickly recanted. "Please forget what I said. I didn't mean it the way it sounded, Pipit. I'm sorry."

She laughed.

Surprised, Matthew frowned. "Why the laughter?"

"It just struck me how ludicrous the whole thing is. Poor Matthew, who had such a beautiful wife, is now so desperate, he's willing to marry a homely woman until his sight returns."

The silence turned heavy. At last, Matthew asked, "Where in the world did that come from, Pipit?"

"I have no idea."

Chapter Twenty

Saturday morning as Pipit laid out Matthew's clothes, she thought of the night before. She and Matthew had said goodnight under strained circumstances. They still felt strained. Matthew entered the room dressed in his old jeans.

"I have your clothes laid out, Matthew."

"I'm sorry. I should have told you. I'm not going to work today. I think it has been too hard on you dealing with Mrs. Danville alone. I've called and told her that I'm staying home today and not to come."

Tears sprung to her eyes. Why, she wasn't sure. She blinked them back rapidly and tried to say something, but nothing would come. Sensing something, Matthew felt for her. She backed away. "Pipit?"

"I'll go get breakfast, Matthew." Her voice betrayed her. She tried to walk past, but he managed to grab her hand.

"What is it, Pipit?"

"Please, let me go, Matthew."

"You're crying."

"No I'm not," she said, her voice breaking.

He wrapped her in his arms and she collapsed against him. Tears came rushing out in a torrent. Some time later, she gained control. Matthew, still holding her, with one arm pulled a tissue from his pocket and handed it to her.

"Thanks," she whispered, wiping her eyes and nose. "I don't know what came over me, Matthew."

Still holding her tightly, he said, "You've gone through a very traumatic experience that not only impacted you physically and mentally, but emotionally. You've only cried once that I know of and only a little up at the cabin. From what I've come to know of women, they need to release emotion more than once. I had begun to think you were going to hold it in indefinitely, and I know that wouldn't do you any good."

"Thank you for...for being sensitive...for understanding. It takes away the embarrassment."

He let go of her and held both of her hands in his. "About last night, Pipit...I keep forgetting that you think of yourself as homely. I can't see you so all I see is your character—your soul so to speak—and I find it beautiful. But you had no way of knowing this, and I'm sorry. And—you had no way of knowing that I don't feel I could *ever* marry again...even if it were a marriage of convenience for a short while. It was a thoughtless, off the top of my head remark, spoken out of frustration."

Pipit couldn't respond for a moment. She was touched by his sincere compliment and yet, at the same time, she was confused. Pain clutched at her heart. "Thank you, Matthew," she managed, her voice sounding raspy to her ears. Pulling her hands away gently, she half-whispered, "I...I need to go fix breakfast."

~~~~~~~~~~~~~

Saturday turned warm and they all went swimming after lunch, releasing frustrations that had built up in all them. Merri was on her best behavior so Danny was happy.

Pipit was looking forward to the evening. She'd been anticipating it all week and even more so when this morning Matthew had informed her that Randy and Joan were bringing dinner for themselves and the children so she didn't have to cook. When Pipit told Merri and Danny that their cousins were coming, they were exuberant.

When it came time to get ready for the evening, Pipit found herself humming. After showering, she styled her hair like the hairdresser taught her, then put on makeup. At last, she got to wear the one nice dress she'd purchased with Mamie. The last touch was the special perfume. Though her eyes said otherwise, she felt beautiful. "Maybe my 'beautiful soul,' as Matthew put it, is peeking through." She smiled. "Don't I wish."

She heard the doorbell ring and the squeals of the children. Excited voices issued from the foyer. Everyone was already assembled in the family room when she entered.

Arthur gave a low whistle. "Can this be the wounded little Pipit who fell on our doorstep?"

"It is, Arthur. It's good to see you again."

Mamie got up and went over to Pipit and gave her a warm motherly hug. "You look lovely, my dear. The dress we picked out is very flattering."

"Thank you, Mamie," she said, her face glowing.

Mamie introduced Pipit to Randy and Joan and their two children, Becky and Johnny. Pipit noticed that Randy took after Mamie, short, brown-haired with a big smile and an outgoing personality. His wife, Joan, was just the opposite—a small, dark-haired girl, friendly, but reticent.

"Hey, we're glad to finally meet the amazing Pipit Dad and Mom have talked about," Randy said, grinning.

"I'm happy to meet you and Joan. Thank you for giving Matthew and me this special break."

Danny ran over to Pipit. "These are my cousins! They've come to play with us."

Pipit crouched down and hugged him. "I'm so glad. Have a good time while I'm gone, will you?" He grinned and nodded.

Merri pulled herself away from her cousin Becky, ran over and also hugged Pipit goodbye.

~~~~~~~~~~~~

Seated next to Matthew in the SUV, Pipit couldn't help feeling as though she was out on a date. Wondering if Matthew felt uneasy about the arrangement, she studied him. He seemed relaxed, so she leaned back and enjoyed herself.

Around the table at the steakhouse, while waiting for their orders, Arthur and Mamie were full of questions about the children, Elinor, and Mrs. Danville. After they both answered the questions, Arthur asked, "Pipit, have you had any change in your memory?"

She told them of the one brief flash. "There are times when I think that any moment I'll remember something and then it doesn't come."

"Sounds like it won't be long, Pipit," Arthur replied.

Pipit enjoyed the meal and the visit immensely. She felt safe and very much at home with these three, almost as if they were family. Actually, she told herself, they were all the family she knew. After finishing their dessert of pie, they left for the theater.

Arriving at Gammage Auditorium on the campus of ASU, Arthur found a parking space. Matthew chose to hold on to Arthur's arm rather than have Pipit hold his hand. He was concerned that people who knew both him and the Halstroms would get the wrong impression and that it might get back to Elinor.

When they found their seats, Pipit quickly arranged to sit by Mamie, putting both Mamie and Arthur between her and Matthew. It was obvious to her that Matthew didn't want them to be seen together as a couple. She wished it could be otherwise, because she felt good being close to him.

Matthew felt both relieved and disconcerted at Pipit's maneuvering. It would have been nice to sit by her. As always, her presence would have soothed his battered emotions.

The musical was wonderfully delightful and uplifting to Pipit. She wondered if she were musical. At least, she knew she appreciated music and that it must have been a big part of her life. She glanced over at Matthew often during the performance and found him either smiling or a pleased expression on his face—and realized he needed to do this more often.

~~~~~~~~~~~~~

When they arrived back at Matthew's place, they found that the children were all asleep and Randy and Joan were watching an old movie. Randy looked up as they walked in, and flipped off the television. "Hey, how did it go?"

"Great," Matthew responded. "The food was good and the musical was just what Pipit and I needed."

"It was!" Pipit agreed enthusiastically. "Thank you, both." She turned to Arthur and Mamie. "And thank *you*. I don't think you realize how much I needed this special evening out."

"Oh, we can imagine," grinned Arthur.

The six of them had visited only a few minutes, when Arthur said, "Matthew, can I talk to you in private for a few minutes?"

Surprised, Matthew nodded. "Of course. Let's go into the front room. Hang tight, everyone, we'll be back soon."

When they left, Pipit said, "I understand Matthew worked for your father on the cotton farm, Randy."

"He did. I don't know what we would have done without him at the time he came. Although he was only fifteen when he came to live with us, he...."

"Only fifteen? I thought he was older when he worked for you."

"I guess Matthew didn't tell you. He and his parents lived in Weatherford, Texas. He was only fifteen when he came home one day from school to find his home, and the peach orchards leveled by a tornado."

Pipit gasped. "Oh no. How terrible. Were his parents..."

"They were killed, and the two hundred acres of peach trees were destroyed."

"I've been so caught up with my own problems, I haven't even asked Matthew about his life."

"That's certainly understandable, my dear," remarked Mamie.

Randy continued. "My father and Matthew's father were brothers as you know. They were very close so of course my parents took Matthew in, and immediately he became part of the family." Pipit was surprised to see Randy blink back tears. "To quote the words from the song, *Matthew,* by John Denver: '*He came to ease my daddy's burden and he came to be my friend.*' The words of that song always touch me because it describes my cousin Matthew so perfectly. Matthew didn't inflict his grief upon us, he just helped out and I really thought he came to be my friend. And like the song says, Matthew '*found the family Bible,*' and he read it regularly."

Mamie interjected. "We feel that's why he was able to handle the grief of losing his parents. It had to be, because he was an only child, and he and his parents were very close."

"Yes," Randy continued, "as it says in the song, '*he was raised on love.*'"

Pipit reflected on this new insight into Matthew. After a moment, she said quietly, "Thank you for telling me this, Randy."

~~~~~~~~~~~~

After they were seated, Arthur said, "Matthew, I wanted to talk with you alone because I've heard from Pipit's parents."

Matthew's back stiffened at the news. He felt a flood of emotions. He wasn't sure he could handle this right now. "You have?" he asked, incredulous. "How...how in the world did they..."

"A man from the highway department in Eager called me yesterday. He told me that they had a short warm front come in and it melted the snow just enough that when two men were up there with the snow plow, a small part of the car was showing. They suspected it might be an automobile so began shoveling. They found her purse and, of course, a driver's license." Matthew held his breath. "Her name is Elizabeth Cabot. She's from Palm Springs, California."

Matthew mouthed the name. "Elizabeth. I've always liked that name."

"Yes. Not a homely one as she suspected." He grinned. "The men hightailed it back to Eager, sure that Elizabeth Cabot had gotten out of her car and had frozen to death. Their boss, whom I talked with about looking for the car when the snow melted and with whom I left my phone number, immediately called me. I informed him that Miss Cabot was alive and well. I told him to call her parents and have them call me, that I would tell them everything."

Matthew exhaled a heavy breath and ran a hand through his hair. "I can hardly believe all this, Arthur. It's good news...for Pipit...or Elizabeth. Awkward to call her that. Go on."

"Well, I got a call from them almost immediately. They have been scared to death.

Apparently, she left a note for her family telling them she had to get away for a while and not to worry and that if she didn't return sooner, she'd call them in three weeks. Well, it has been twenty-six days. Four days ago, they reported her missing to the police in a couple of cities where Pipit went sometimes. They didn't dream she'd go up into the snow country."

"Did you inform them of her condition, Arthur?"

"I did. At first they couldn't believe that their daughter wouldn't know them. She has two younger sisters who are both married and also live in Palm Springs. They've all been beside themselves with worry, I guess."

"She's not married then."

"No, but she's engaged."

"Engaged?" Somehow this didn't feel possible to Matthew. Pipit felt like *his* responsibility; he shook his head, trying to rid himself of the thought.

"They'll be here tomorrow afternoon to take her home."

"Tomorrow? So soon?"

"Can you blame, them, Matthew? They wanted to come today, but I told them that we had tickets to see the musical tonight."

"No, I guess I can't blame them. But it's so abrupt, I...I guess I'm like *Professor Higgins* in *My Fair Lady,* though unable to grow *accustomed to her face,* I've grown accustomed to her—presence. The children will be devastated. What am I going to do, Arthur?"

Arthur studied his nephew curiously. "She's good with the children, I can see that. How has she done with the cooking and cleaning?"

Matthew chuckled. "That has been an adventure for her as well as us. But she's been a trooper, Arthur, and stuck with it and is actually learning to cook rather well, and she's managing to keep the laundry up now. It has been hard for her. I don't think she's used to doing it. Does she come from a wealthy family?"

"I have no idea."

"How old is she?"

"I don't know that either. How are we going to handle this? Should we tell her now or let her parents show up and see if seeing them brings her memory back?"

"Wow, what a decision. What do you think, Uncle Arthur?"

"When you don't know what to do, you always call me 'Uncle' Arthur. Just coincidence?"

Matthew grinned. "You know it isn't. As I asked, what do you think?"

"Well, I'm inclined to let her be surprised or shocked at their arrival and see if that doesn't jog her memory."

"I'm inclined that way, also, but I'm concerned about what the shock might do to her. I think it will feel as abrupt to her as it does to me." He frowned in thought for a moment. "I guess it's best to let her be surprised."

"All right," Arthur said, standing up. "Let's get back to the group."

Chapter Twenty-One

From the moment Matthew woke up Sunday morning, confusion settled over him. He felt despondent. Mentally, he went over the questions swirling around in his head. What will the day bring? How will Pipit react to seeing her parents? How will the children handle Pipit leaving—if she does leave. Why in the heck would he question her leaving? Wishful thinking he was sure; he'd come to depend far too much on Pipit's help. The act of bringing her here was mainly to help *her*, but this morning, he felt that the arrangement had been more help to him and the children than to her. How would this afternoon affect all their lives?

Pipit awoke, stretched and lay in bed thinking of the night before. The wonderful evening they'd spent with Matthew's family was one she'd always remember.

"What can we do today to make it nice for the children?" she asked aloud. As always, the thought of fixing three meals today dampened her spirits. "Oh well, 'Pip ol' girl,' as Arthur might say, at least Matthew will be home all day."

~~~~~~~~~~~~

It was a beautiful morning, so Pipit suggested that she and Matthew sit out on the patio and watch the children play since he'd vetoed their request to go swimming. Matthew left the back door open so he could hear the doorbell, even though the Cabots had told Arthur they would arrive sometime in the afternoon. Pipit had asked him why he was preoccupied this morning and all he could come up with was he was thinking about what a nice evening they'd had the night before—which was partially true. Going out to dinner and to a musical with Arthur and Mamie had cheered him up, but the news afterward had numbed him.

"Watch, Daddy," Danny said as he ran and took, what was to him, a big jump.

"Watch me, Daddy," Merri mimicked Danny.

"What are they doing, Pipit?" he asked, his heart sad that for a moment they'd forgotten that he couldn't see them.

"They're running and jumping. Tell them I think they are both fast and good jumpers."

"Pipit says you are potential Olympic contestants."

"Huh?" Merri asked.

Pipit laughed. "I said you were fast runners and good jumpers."

"Oh. Watch us do it again."

"Why don't you have a swing set out here for the children, Matthew?"

"Diane tried to discourage them from playing outside too much because of the summer heat and Merri's fair skin, as well as hers."

The doorbell rang, and Matthew jumped visibly. "What time is it, Pipit?"

"It's 11:30."

Could that be them? he wondered, his heart racing. "I can't imagine who that could be this early, Pipit. Would you please guide me in to the front door?"

"We'll be right back, kids!" she yelled, while taking hold of Matthew's hand. Almost to the foyer, she said, "Maybe one of the neighbors has come to visit us."

As she opened the door, Matthew tightened his grip on her hand. "Mamie and Arthur!" she exclaimed. A radiant smile spread across her face. "What are you doing here *today?*"

Matthew let out a sigh of relief, and Mamie said, "We brought over a pot roast. We thought you would appreciate another vacation from cooking. Randy and Joan are here, also. They're getting the children out of the car, and bringing in the dessert."

"I can't believe our good fortune," Matthew said, grinning.

Both Mamie and Arthur had noted the expression of relief on Matthew's face. "I'll just go put this on the stove," Mamie said, "Vegetables have been cooked with the pot roast and it's all done, so just as soon as all of you are hungry, we'll eat."

"That won't be long," Pipit said, following her into the kitchen, leaving Matthew and Arthur in the foyer, "because all Matthew and the children wanted this morning was cold cereal."

Randy and Joan entered, and Randy clapped a hand on Matthew's shoulder. Lowering his voice he asked, "Hey, how are you doing today?"

"Not too great. I'm feeling uneasy about the whole thing."

"That's why we came," Joan said. "Randy and I are going to take care of Merri and Danny in the family room or outside when they come."

"And to give you moral support, Matt," Randy added.

"I need it! Thanks."

Their children raced ahead to find their cousins, and Joan followed placing her cake on the counter, noting that Becky and Johnny had found Merri and Danny in the backyard. "I'm glad it's warm today so the children can play outside," she said.

"Me too," Mamie said, giving her a knowing glance. "Let's set the table and get ready to eat right at 12:00."

"I'm all for that, Mamie," Pipit said, "it smells so good. How lucky can I get—two days in a row I don't have to eat my own cooking."

"Matthew said you were doing well with your cooking," Mamie replied.

~~~~~~~~~~~~

After dinner, the family all gathered outside to enjoy the warm February afternoon.

Pipit felt more content than she could remember feeling. Extended family made life richer. But—it isn't mine! Pushing this unsettling thought aside, she decided to just enjoy what she could. She found herself delighting in the play and antics of the children, very aware of how carefree and happy Merri and Danny were acting today. She turned to Matthew and saw the same somber expression she'd noticed this morning. She frowned in concern. What could be the matter? He was so upbeat and cheerful last night at the restaurant and during the musical.The doorbell rang and it seemed to Pipit that the whole family froze. *How odd*, she thought. "I'll answer it," she said.

She got up and quickly stepped into the kitchen. It wasn't until she had arrived in the foyer, that she noticed Matthew, Mamie and

Arthur had followed right behind her. She laughed. "I guess we'll answer the door in a group."

Turning the knob, Pipit opened the door. For several seconds, Pipit and the couple on the doorstep stared at each other, then both the man and the woman exclaimed, "Elizabeth!" Their arms outstretched, they stepped in.

Pipit, shocked, backed up. "What?"

The couple froze in their tracks, both overcome with emotion. "We're your parents, Liz," the woman said—her tear-laden eyes begging Pipit to recognize her.

Pipit panicked. "Matthew? Mamie...Arthur? Who are these people?"

Matthew reached for Pipit's hand and held it tightly, and Arthur said, "They are your parents, Pipit."

"How do you know, Arthur? They can't be! I don't *know* them," she said, backing up against the small entry hall table. She knew she sounded irrational—she couldn't seem to help it.

The man spoke gently. "Elizabeth. Elizabeth Cabot. That is your name. I am your father, Calvin Cabot. This is your mother, Julia Cabot."

"Matthew..." she began, her voice shaking with emotion. "how can I know they are really my parents?"

Arthur took over. "Let's all go into the front room and sit down together and I'll tell you the whole story, Pipit."

"Why do you call her Pipit?" the woman asked.

"I'll tell you that also."

Calvin and Julia Cabot sat on one of the sofas. Pipit, holding Matthew's hand like a drowning person would a lifeline, led him to the other one. Mamie and Arthur seated themselves on the two chairs. Julia Cabot's face was pale with anxiety, and Matthew could feel Pipit shaking.

Arthur began the story from the beginning and told the Cabots everything as he had promised them over the phone. Afterward, he turned to Pipit and told her the part of the story she didn't know; the finding of her car, and the call from Eager that followed. "I told the official in Eager to call your parents, and, of course, your parents quickly called me."

Arthur looked over at the Cabots. "I understand that you left Palm Springs immediately and went up to Eager and picked up the purse the two men found." Calvin nodded. "I assume then that you have the wallet with you?"

They nodded, and Julia reached into her purse, pulled it out and handed it to Arthur. "Could I have yours also, Mrs. Cabot?" She nodded, fighting back emotion as she searched for it. Finding it, she handed it to him.

Matthew placed an arm around Pipit's slender shoulders and gave her a squeeze of comfort. He felt her body stiffen as Arthur said, "Here are both wallets."

Pipit took them hesitantly. She opened up the woman's first, dropped it in her lap, then opened up the one that was supposed to be hers and looked at the face on the driver's license. Matthew heard her gasp. "It's me, Matthew." She studied the address, then picked up the other wallet and compared the addresses. Panic set in. Her chest heaved—rapid breaths turned spasmodic. "But...but I don't know them, Matthew." His arm tightened around her shoulders, trying to soothe her, while his own emotions hovered close to the ragged edge. Pipit looked across at the stricken couple and at last managed to say, "I...I'm sorry that I don't recognize you."

"It's all right, darling," Julia Cabot said.

"N-no it isn't all right. I...I know this sounds unreasonable, but I only know Matthew and his children. I only know Mamie and Arthur and their children. They...they are all the family I know."

Cal Cabot spoke gently. "Liz, *we* are your family and you are more likely to regain your memory if you'll come home with us *now* and see your two sisters and all the familiar surroundings. We came to take you home."

Pipit tore herself out of Matthew's grip, stood up, stepped rapidly around the couch and stood behind it in front of her vacated spot, her hands gripping the back. "I...I can't go home with you...I need to stay here and take care of the children, I..." Tears glistened in her eyes. Mamie and Julia simultaneously stood up to go around and comfort her. She backed up, and held her palms outward. "No! No one touch me." Her hands covered her face as she backed up against the wall and sobbed. Matthew's heart swelled with pain for Pipit, for himself and for his children. Tears rolled down both

Julia's and Mamie's cheeks. Calvin blinked back his emotion as did the other two men. They all waited until Pipit's sobs quieted down, finally stopping.

No one moved. They continued to wait for Pipit to speak. At last, she asked, "How can I leave you in the situation you're in, Matthew?"

Matthew turned his face toward her. "You have to leave, Pipit. It's in your best interest."

She inhaled a spasm of breath, letting it out carefully. "But...but I thought I would only leave when my memory returned. How can I leave with people I feel are total strangers to me?"

Slowly and gently Calvin explained. "Elizabeth, you said in the note you left us that you would call in three weeks if you weren't home by then. As your mother has said over and over the past five days, 'Liz always does what she says she'll do, something has to have happened to her.' We gave you one day leeway, but the next four days were hell for us. We notified the police in several cities. Your mother could hardly eat, she has hardly slept and neither have I."

Pipit remained silent, thinking, still standing, her back against the wall.

"Can you really say no to these people, Pipit?" Matthew asked. "I can feel their love for you. Surely you can also."

"I don't know. All I can feel at the moment is anxiety at leaving you in a terrible situation and...and the children. How can I leave them...now?" she asked. Tears flooded her eyes and ran freely down her cheeks.

Matthew, deeply touched, wondered for a moment if he could answer the way he was supposed to for her sake. "I promise you, Pipit, we'll be all right."

Before Pipit could tell Matthew that she didn't believe he really felt that way, Julia spoke up. "Elizabeth, you are engaged. Your fiancé, Kirk, has been beside himself. You owe it to him to at least come home with us and see him."

Her mother might as well have thrown a glass of ice water in her face, for it had the same effect. The shock of it arrested her erratic emotions, dried up the tears. "I'm engaged?" she whispered in disbelief. Suddenly, feeling the need to sit down, she returned to her seat beside Matthew.

"Yes," Julia said, "and he's a wonderful young man."

"I don't feel engaged."

"You don't feel we're your parents either, but we are," Julia retorted, her patience getting thin. Suddenly suspicious, she asked, "Is there something going on between you and Mr. Melloy? I noticed that you held his hand, and that he put his arm around you."

Mamie raised her brows and glanced at Arthur. *These two have had confrontations in the past,* she thought.

Jolted at this, Pipit returned with abruptness. "Of course not! Matthew is still grieving over the death of his wife."

"Mrs. Cabot," Matthew began, "you've done well by your daughter. She's one of the kindest women I've ever known. Soon after she woke up in the cabin, she found out I was blind. That very morning when Arthur called us to breakfast, she could have walked on into the kitchen and let me fend for myself, but from that moment on, she took on the responsibility of taking my hand and leading or guiding me. As for me, I feel great affection for Pipit...or Elizabeth because she's taken good care of my children. She's worked hard; she's cleaned, cooked and washed. I put my arm around her to try to comfort her as she has tried to comfort me more than once. It was a natural thing to do."

"She's cooked for you....cleaned?" Calvin asked, amazement in his voice.

"She has and she's calmed my children in a way no one else has been able to."

"Kirk who?" Pipit blurted out.

"Kirk Morgan. Does that sound familiar?" Julia asked hopefully.

"No. How old am I?"

"You are thirty," Julia answered.

"I knew I was older. Have I ever been married?"

"No," her father answered.

"Do you want to meet the children I've been taking care of?" she asked, hastily returning to the subject that was dear and familiar.

"Well...yes, dear," her mother said with reluctance, "but are you coming home with us?"

Pipit, fighting back another surge of emotion, turned mute. Everyone held their breath, waiting. In the background, happy squeals of the children in the backyard floated in upon the heavy silence. "Matthew, how can I leave?"

"You have to, Pipit, because I'm firing you."

She laughed, the laughter turning into quiet sobs. Soon they subsided. "Does anyone have a tissue?"

Julia reached into her purse, retrieved one and took it over to her, then sat back down. "Thank you, Mrs. uh..." Pipit stuttered. "What do I call you? I can't call you Mrs. Cabot, and I can't call you mother."

Arthur broke in. "Do your mother the kindness to call her Mother, Pip ol' girl, you can do it, I know you can." He grinned at her.

Pipit couldn't help but smile. "Thanks, Arthur." Turning to Julia, she asked, "Did I call you Mother or Mom?"

"Mother."

Another silence followed. With great difficulty, she replied, "I...I'll go with you. I need to pack, but...I don't have a suitcase."

"I'll lend you one, Pipit," Matthew said quietly, "that way you have to return it and we can see you again."

Pipit swallowed hard and blinked furiously. Never had she been so emotional...or had she? Maybe she'd been an emotional basket case in the past. "Thank you, but I don't want to use one of Diane's. May I use one of yours?"

Matthew paused a moment, for it was one of Diane's he had intended to lend her. It would fit a woman better. "I'll lend you one of mine." He stood up to leave the room, and automatically, Pipit went over and took his hand to lead him.

"No, Pipit. Stay here with your parents. I can find my way," he said feeling regret, for that would have been the last opportunity he'd have to hold her hand.

Arthur filled in the awkward gaps of conversation while they waited.

Pipit felt Matthew had been gone longer than he should have, and was about to go find out if she could help, when he returned.

She took the suitcase from him noticing the odd expression on his face. "What is it, Matthew?" she asked. "Is something wrong?"

Feeling flustered a moment, he replied. "Oh no...no. It's all right."

"Tell me, Matthew."

In almost a whisper, he said, "You'll find out, Pipit. I promise you."

She gazed at him perplexed, then turned away abruptly. "Mamie, would you come with me to pack?"

"I certainly will, dear." She followed Pipit out.

Matthew also left to wait in the family room.

Arthur remained with the Cabots to visit and answer any questions they might still have.

Chapter Twenty-Two

Pipit set the suitcase in the foyer, and went into the front room to announce, "I'm packed, but I have to say goodbye to the children." Avoiding addressing her parents, she finished with, "Please come into the family room so they can meet you."

Julia and Calvin eagerly stood up and smiled at their daughter. It was Calvin who replied, "We'd like to meet those children."

Matthew had waited in the family room while Mamie went out to bring Merri and Danny inside, leaving Randy, Joan and their children outside to avoid confusion. When she came back in with the children, she found Pipit and her parents waiting.

"Merri and Danny," Pipit said, "come here." They went over to her. "I want you to meet my mother and father, Mr. and Mrs. Cabot."

"Oh," Merri said wide-eyed.

"How do you do, young lady," Calvin said, reaching for her hand.

Danny looked up at Pipit. "I didn't know you had a mama and a daddy."

Everyone laughed, easing the tension which had filled the room. When Julia and Calvin finished greeting the children, Pipit said, "Both of you come and sit down on the couch with me. I want to tell you something." They scrambled up onto the couch, one on each side of her. Putting an arm around each, she squeezed them. With the sudden realization that she had become more that just fond of these two children, her heart did a painful flip-flop. She closed her eyes a moment, trying to gather strength. "Merri and Danny, I...love you."

Matthew's heart felt clamped in a tight vise.

Merri smiled. "I love you, too, Pipit."

"I do too," Danny said.

"What I have to tell you is this—my mother and father came here today to...to take me home with them."

"Why?" Merri asked.

"Because I've been gone a long time and they've been lonesome."

Merri's expression changed to one of eagerness. "Can we go stay with Becky and Johnny until Pipit gets back, Daddy?"

The vise tightened. Here it comes, Matthew thought. "Merri and Danny, Pipit isn't coming back. She's going to go live with her parents."

"But I thought she was going to live with *us*," she replied, her voice quivering.

Tears welled up in Danny's eyes. "I don't want her to go."

Pipit pulled them both close. "I don't want to go, but I have to, but I promise I'll come back and see you—soon."

Tears sprang to Merri's eyes and rolled down her cheeks. "No! I don't want you to go, Pipit."

"Me either," Danny cried.

If I ever needed self-control, it's now, Pipit told herself as she silently gulped back the knot lodging in her throat. She glanced at Julia and Calvin Cabot and saw compassion in his eyes and tears in hers. Her heart softened. Turning her gaze to Matthew, she saw him struggling to keep a neutral expression on his face. Recalling his somberness this morning, she realized Matthew knew about her parents coming. He knew last night! That's why Arthur wanted to speak to him alone.

"Merri and Danny, come here to me," their father said.

"No!" screamed Merri, clinging to Pipit. "I don't want Pipit to go."

He spoke softer. "I don't either, Merri. Please, both of you come here."

Reluctantly, they both went over and stood before their father. Taking hold of each of their arms, he said, "Pipit borrowed my suitcase. She has to return it, so she'll be be back to see us."

"But I want her around my house," wailed Merri.

"I do too," Danny said in a tremulous voice.

Merri broke out of her father's grasp and ran back to Pipit, whose battle to hold back her emotion failed; tears came as fast as she blinked. Merri climbed up on the couch and hugged her, refusing to let go. "I'm not going to let her go, Daddy," she sobbed.

By this time, Danny had broken loose and had run to Pipit, also clinging to her. Pipit hugged them tightly, her tearful eyes begging for someone to help.

Mamie came to the rescue. "Matthew, will you let the children go home with Randy and Joan so they can play with Becky and Johnny for a few days?"

Matthew spoke loudly so as to be heard above the children's crying. "Merri and Danny, do you want to go stay with Becky and Johnny for a few days?"

Their crying died down. "Will Pipit be here when we come back?"

Arthur stepped in. He walked over to the children and took hold of both their arms and gently pulled them away from Pipit. "Let's go outside and play with Becky and Johnny and then we'll have a treat."

Reluctantly, they allowed their uncle Arthur to lead them outside, and Pipit broke down. Mamie sat beside her and hugged her. "Children are resilient, Pipit. They'll be all right."

"But will I?"

Matthew rose and spoke through tight vocal chords. "I think you had better take your daughter and leave, Mr. and Mrs. Cabot."

Arthur came back just in time to join all of them at the front door. Calvin picked up the suitcase and turned to address Arthur and Matthew. "How can we ever thank you for saving our daughter's life?"

"Yes, thank you," Julia said. "If you hadn't been there....if you hadn't taken such good care of her...she might have..." She couldn't go on.

"And thank *you*, Mr. Melloy," Calvin went on, "for giving our daughter a place to stay until we could find her."

"I assure you, Mr. Cabot, she was far more help to me than I was to her."

Pipit rolled her eyes in skepticism. Turning, she threw her arms around Mamie. "Thank you for coming here today to help us...for everything."

Mamie gave her a warm smile, "We'll be looking forward to your visit, Pipit."

Next, Pipit gazed at Arthur, his warm eyes, his grinning face. "You're going to be all right, Pip ol' girl," he said, "you're quite a woman."

Throwing her arms around his neck, she kissed him on the cheek and gave him an affectionate smile. "How does one thank someone who has saved one's life?" Feeling another surge of tears behind her eyes, she whirled around, her back to everyone, remaining this way until she had successfully stemmed the flow.

At last, steeling herself to say goodbye to the most important person, Matthew, she managed to look at him. His face was an emotionless mask. "I guess it's time to say goodbye to you, Matthew." She reached for his hand and shook it. "Thank you for my life—and for trusting your children with me so I could have a place to stay."

He let go of her hand and held out his arms. His voice sounding slightly ragged, he asked, "How about a 'grizzly bear' hug goodbye?"

She stiffened. "We'd better let it go with a handshake, Matthew, I've cried enough to last a year. I hope everything works out well for you and the children." With that, she wheeled around abruptly, stepped to the door and went out.

As the sound of the car receded in the distance, it felt to Matthew as though a light had gone out. "Goodbye, Pipit," he whispered. "Come back to us." It sounded like a prayer.

Chapter Twenty-Three

The ride in the back seat of the Lincoln Town car was smooth and comfortable. Pipit leaned back and attempted to relax, trying not to think about Matthew and the children, trying not to think of the unknown world into which these two strange people, who claimed to be her parents, were taking her.

Questions crowded her mind, questions about them, herself, her sisters, and most unsettling of all—her fiancé. She still didn't feel engaged. Wouldn't she *feel* engaged if she were? But as the woman in the front seat, her mother, pointed out, she hadn't felt that they were her parents, yet they were. What kind of a man was her fiancé? Did he look like Matthew? She smiled at that last question. How could she be that lucky? Was she ready to ask about him? Was she ready to *hear* everything? Could she handle that knowledge while in her emotional state? No, she answered herself. She remained silent.

Because Calvin and Julia had found their daughter safe, and were taking her home, the silence was bearable.

Calvin sensed they needed to give Liz some space, and he hoped Julia felt the same way. He hadn't had a chance to talk to her about it. Did they really know Elizabeth? She'd never exhibited any interest in children, so the affection she had shown to the Melloy children and their attachment to her amazed him and he was sure it had Julia.

Julia's mind flitted from one random thought to another. She wondered how Kirk would take Liz's loss of memory. He'd put up with a lot from her when he was trying to win her love. Liz had refused to have anything to do with him at first. Surely his love could survive *this* trial. This was a match she had wanted for a long time. Kirk was a charming and outstanding young man from a well-to-do and prominent family, and she had promoted the relationship in every way possible. Julia shook her head ever so slightly; she didn't understand her oldest daughter, Elizabeth. Linda and Claire were so much like herself in their goals, and their outlook on the life they'd established in Palm Springs. Liz wasn't beautiful like her sisters, and she had done everything she could to get Liz to dress nicely, to wear makeup to enhance her eyes, her nicest feature, but she had refused. Though Liz had told her several times why, Julia knew she would never understand.

The first thing she and Cal had to do she was take Liz to a doctor, a specialist...probably a neurologist. She felt impatient. She wanted to ask Liz if she remembered *anything*, no matter how small! But something told her to wait until she became more accustomed to them, when she wasn't feeling so emotional. It seemed that somewhere she'd read that some head injuries actually change a person, making them temperamental, emotional. This thought unsettled her. She wanted Liz and Kirk to marry. Linda and Claire had married well, and she desperately wanted the same for her oldest.

Gradually, Pipit relaxed enough to realize how exhausted she was. Leaning her head back, she closed her eyes and dozed. It wasn't until they pulled into the parking lot of a nice steak house on the western edge of Phoenix that she awakened.

"Are you hungry, Elizabeth?" Her father asked. No answer. "Elizabeth?"

"I'm sorry. I just can't seem to answer to Elizabeth. You couldn't call me Pipit, could you?" The look of consternation on both their faces gave her the answer. "Never mind." She glanced at her watch and saw that it was a little after 5:00. "I don't feel hungry, but I should be able to eat something."

After the hostess seated them and they had ordered, Pipit smiled at her parents for the first time. "Thank you for giving me a lovely name. I was sure it would be as homely as I am."

"Homely?" her father asked, frowning. "You know, we've gone through this with you before."

"You have?"

"Yes. And nothing we could say ever changed your mind."

"I'm not surprised when I look in the mirror," she said, a small smile on her face.

She studied her mother for the first time. She was stunningly beautiful. Her hair, short and blonde, was perfectly styled for her oval face; her blue eyes were large with long, dark lashes. Her makeup was impeccable and the blue linen sheath, with its short matching jacket fit well on her trim figure. "Why didn't I get your looks, Mrs. ...uh Mother?" she asked, the familiarity awkward on her tongue.

Julia gazed at her daughter, pained. "We've had this conversation before, also."

"Oh." She turned her gaze to her father. He, too, was blonde, but his face was longer, his nose long and narrow, his chin strong. "I got your looks, I see. Not that you are homely like I am," she quickly assured him. "You are very nice looking, but..."

"No need to explain, Liz." He smiled. "I know. My looks go well on a man, but not on you, as you've said before. I disagree with you. I find your looks interesting and distinctive."

"That's a nice way to put it. Does my smile light up my face as yours does?" she asked, smiling.

"It does. Everyone tells you that."

"Who do my sisters take after?"

"Your mother."

"Oh-oh, I can see the problem already. I was probably insecure. Feeling mousy beside them, I probably slunk into a corner and bit my nails."

Her father laughed long and hard. Her mother only smiled. It was her father who responded, "Just the opposite. You exhibited more confidence than any young woman should have."

The waiter placed a large, scored, deep-fried onion on the table with a sauce in the middle for dipping. All of a sudden, Pipit's mouth watered. She pulled off a piece, dipped it in the sauce. "Mm, delicious. One thing I'm not going to miss is my own cooking!"

Calvin and Julia both laughed.

~~~~~~~~~~~~

Back on the road by 6:30, Pipit felt more relaxed. The dinner had been excellent and though the conversation was a little sparse, it had been pleasant because she had not asked any more questions about herself and her life with them. She'd find out soon enough. Instead, she had answered their questions about her waking upon the mountain, finding the cabin and her time there with Matthew and Arthur.

In the car, conversation was non-existent. During the silence, she couldn't keep her mind off Matthew and the children. This brought her so much anxiety, she decided to do her best not to think about them. It was then that she made the firm decision not to go back and see them until she had regained her memory. What would be the use? She would never feel whole until she remembered everything.

Leaning her head back, she slipped into a deep sleep. Several hours later, her father's voice awakened her. It was dark out. Sitting up straight, she found that her neck and shoulders were stiff. "Did you say something, uh...Dad? Is that what I called you?"

He smiled at her through the mirror. "Yes. I said we're entering the beautiful city of Palm Springs, 'the place of sun-filled days and starry nights.'"

"Sounds nice," she said in a small voice.

Fifteen minutes later, her father looked through the rearview mirror. "We're almost home, Liz. How do you feel?"

"Nervous."

"No need to feel nervous. Your sisters will be waiting for you at the house. They've been beside themselves with worry over you. We've called them and told them about your memory loss, so they're prepared."

"Have you informed uh...Kirk, my...uh fiancé?"

"Before we left to go get you, we called him and told him we had found you and that you'd had an accident, but you were all right physically. We didn't tell him about your memory loss, and we were indefinite about when we were going to go get you.

"Your mother and I decided that you had better get settled and reacquainted with your sisters, and your home before we called him because he'll want to come right over when we do. When you feel ready, we'll discuss with you how and when to tell him of your condition."

"Thank you, Dad. Uh...Do most people call me Liz rather than Elizabeth?"

"Yes," he replied.

Even though it was dark, Pipit could see the homes getting larger, the landscaping more elaborate. Soon, her father turned and stopped on an apron of brick paving in front of a wrought-iron gate, flanked by thick, square brick posts. These were connected to a low, cream colored stucco wall which surrounded the area inside. The gate opened and closed after them. The brick road, lit from the ground on each side, and edged by flowers and tall palms, wound through beautiful grounds to a magnificent cream stucco rambler with a large front portico. Instead of following a fork that led around to the back, her father stopped under the portico.

The porch was brightly lit. A potted tree stood on each side of the high double door inset with stained glass windows. Potted plants and flowers surrounded two white wrought-iron benches on either side of the large porch.

Pipit was speechless. Her parents turned around to her, their expressions anxious, hopeful. "Does this look familiar to you, Liz?" her mother asked.

She shook her head. "I'm sorry, it doesn't. This is a beautiful home. Arthur asked me if I was a spoiled rich kid. Maybe I am."

Her father laughed and said, "Well, we've given you a lot and you've had many opportunities. You'll have to judge for yourself as to whether it has spoiled you."

Just as they stepped out of the car, the front door burst open and two young women came running out to Pipit, tears of relief and happiness glistening in their eyes. Arms open wide to hug her, both drew back when they saw no sign of recognition from their sister. Confused and disturbed, they didn't know what to do.

"Liz," her mother said, "this is Claire, your sister, who is just one year younger than you, and this is Linda who is two years younger."

Pipit, a little overcome by their beauty, and the affection in their eyes, managed to say hello.

There was a brief pause before Claire cried, "Oh, Liz," throwing her arms around her, "we're so grateful we found you." Pipit, touched by her sincere affection returned her hug.

Next, Linda threw her arms around her. "We've been so scared!" she exclaimed, pulling back and studying her sister. "Your hair has grown out. It looks cute."

Surprised by the compliment, Pipit stuttered, "Th...thank you."

"You really don't remember anything? Us?" Linda asked, incredulous.

Pipit shook her head slowly. "I'm sorry."

"That's all right, Liz," Linda replied sympathetically, "I'm sure it will come back. Come on in and we'll show you to your room."

Calvin got his daughter's suitcase out of the trunk as well as his and his wife's overnight cases and led them all inside. Julia watched Liz carefully as did the other three. They were disappointed that her face revealed no sign of recognition, rather, an expression of awe.

"This is a gorgeous house. You must be *very* rich, Mr. and....I mean Dad and Mother." She frowned. "But this doesn't feel right. I had one small flash of memory. It was when I was asking Matthew why he didn't live in a neighborhood where there were other children for Merri and Danny to play with."

"And what was that, Liz?" her mother asked. They all held their breath.

"It was a memory of a neighborhood with a lot of old trees and small houses, not even middle class, I would say, but nicely kept up. A group of children were on the front lawn. I didn't see myself, but I knew that I was among the children and that it was my front lawn. The house was a small white stucco."

Julia and Calvin looked at each other and he asked, "Was there anything distinctive about the front porch?"

Pipit thought about it. "Yes. The entrance to the porch was a small stuccoed archway."

Thrilled that her daughter remembered something, Julia explained."That was our home in Los Angeles where we lived until you were fourteen, almost fifteen. You loved that neighborhood and didn't want to leave it, and all your friends." Julia glanced at her husband and daughters.

Pipit both saw it and felt the undercurrents. "Please, don't hide anything from me. I need to know what kind of a person I was...am."

"Well," her mother continued, "you resisted moving into this home and living what you termed, 'the uppity life style' here in Palm Springs."

"That was years ago. Didn't I ever adjust?"

"It's very involved, Liz," her father said. "Let's get you settled and take one step at a time."

"All right," Pipit said, her curiosity beginning to override the anxiety she felt over the strangeness of this life. Though knowing it once had been hers, it felt as though it belonged to someone else.

"Let's take your suitcase to your bedroom, Liz," her father said, taking the lead through the foyer to the wide intersecting hall which ran the length of the house. Turning left, he led her down that hall to another, branching off to the right. At the end of this hall was her bedroom. Pipit looked around, examining every detail. Her family watched her closely, hoping to see some kind of expression on her face that would indicate she saw something familiar.

Pipit noticed the carpet first. It was the color of rich vanilla. A large bay-side window at one end of the room housed a small library under the wide sill—two long shelves packed with books. Family pictures, a lovely plant in a basket, tall wooden candle sticks and a clear vase filled with fresh flowers decorated the sill. *I must like to read,* she thought.

A small wheat-colored sofa sat at an angle on the right of the window. Across from it was a small overstuffed chair with an ottoman. Behind that was a L-shaped desk of light wood with a computer and printer.

The queen bed on the opposite wall was a four poster of the same light wood as the desk. The bedspread and pillows were a mixture of lemon-yellow, apple-green and golden wheat. Lovely watercolor paintings hung on the walls.

"This is a lovely room," she murmured.

"You redecorated it several years ago," explained Claire.

"I like my taste," she said, disappearing into the dressing room, opening and closing drawers. Her family stood at the door of the dressing room watching. Next, she stepped in the large U-shaped, walk-in closet, shocked at the number of clothes filling the space. "Did I wear all these?" Once again she saw the glances between her mother and her sisters.

"At one time or another, you wore a number of them," her mother answered.

Pipit spoke quietly as if speaking to herself. "It will be interesting to compare the few clothes I have in Matthew's one suitcase with these to see if I have the same taste as my old self. However, these clothes here look much more expensive." Pivoting on her heel, she walked out of the closet and back the bedroom.

She gazed at the four anxious faces. "I know you want to ask me questions as much as I want to ask you, but would you mind—could I be alone now? Since it's past 10:30 all of you must be as tired as I am."

The look of disappointment on the faces of her sisters was brief. They both smiled and nodded, and Claire responded. "We'll come back over tomorrow afternoon, or is that too soon?"

"I don't know," Pipit answered frankly. "I do need to get reacquainted with you, but..." her voice trailed off.

Linda replied a little too brightly, "Take your time, Liz, we'll come over only when you're ready to have us."

"I'm sorry that I don't know what I want or don't want. My emotions are up and down and all over the place."

Her father shepherded the group toward the door. "We'll see you tomorrow morning, Liz. Have a good night's sleep." He pulled the door shut behind them.

Pipit stared at the door, numb and lonely. She turned and slowly walked to the window, gazing out at the moonlit grounds of the immense backyard.

Arthur was right, she thought. *I must have been spoiled.* The glances she saw, the undercurrents she felt made her wonder if she wanted to learn about herself.

Turning from the window, she stepped over to the small sofa and sat down heavily. Her gaze traveled around the room again, realizing that her small room at Matthew's felt more familiar than this one. Her unwilling mind naturally slid from her room at Matthew's to Matthew himself, wondering how he was, how Merri and Danny were. Tears silently rolled down her cheeks. Would Matthew regain his sight in time to keep Elinor from taking the children from him? Edginess propelled her up off the sofa, moving in jerky steps about the room.

A sudden realization that now she knew who she was, she could drive! She had a driver's license! If she wanted to, she could leave here, go back and continue helping Matthew until he regained his sight. It certainly would be easier this time; she wouldn't feel so helpless, so dependent. She could drive Matthew and the children anywhere they wanted to go. And she could get away herself now and then instead of calling a taxi!

The elation over the freedom that was now hers, left almost as quickly as it came as she remembered the decision she'd made while on the way here. She could be more help to Matthew if she were whole. Acting on the thought, she decided to do everything she could to return to normal. *By learning everything about myself,* she thought, *my past life and what kind of a person I was, surely something will trigger my memory, as well as give my injury time to heal completely.*

More at peace, she recognized how exhausted she was. Opening up Matthew's suitcase, she pulled out her nightgown. Undressing quickly, she slipped it on, pulled down the inset blinds, and without even brushing her teeth, crawled into the large comfortable bed.

Chapter Twenty-Four

Pipit's internal time clock, unwillingly developed while taking care of Matthew and the children, awakened her at 6:00 AM. She awoke with a feeling she hadn't had in her short memory—excitement. Disoriented only a moment, she looked about the strange room. The first thing she remembered was her decision just before falling asleep. For some reason, it felt like she was embarking on an adventure—a far cry from the fear and apprehension of coming home with two people who felt like strangers. She was going to get acquainted with Elizabeth Cabot, and hoped with all her heart that she liked her. If not... Her thoughts would not allow her to go further in that direction.

Stepping quickly out of bed, she went into the dressing room, trying to discover the elusive Elizabeth. Picking up a bottle of perfume, she smelled it. She liked it, though not quite as much as her custom perfume. Checking out the skin care and makeup, she was happy to find she was well supplied. There was every shade of eye shadow she'd ever want, every color of lipstick, and brown mascara for her lashes. Next, she looked into drawers that contained jewelry, surprised that there wasn't more of it. What there was, she liked. So far, she and Elizabeth had the same taste. She smiled at herself thinking of Elizabeth as a different person. The large closet drew her next. Turning on the light, she began examining the clothes. She liked them also, but to her surprise, a great number of them still had the sales tags on them. The price of each was a little staggering considering her small salary at Matthew's. Why hadn't she worn these wonderful, glamorous clothes? She looked through the clothes which seemed to have been worn, and they, too, were stylish. Near the front of one side of the closet were what looked like some well-worn items—all casual clothes—shorts, knee length shorts, jeans, khaki pants, T-shirts, casual pull-over sheaths, cotton blouses etc. Pipit frowned. Something was wrong here. But what?

Leaving the closet, she brought her suitcase into the dressing room and found places for the clothes and makeup she'd purchased with Mamie in Chandler. Finding a shelf for the empty suitcase in the closet, she undressed and got into the shower.

Afterward, she found a drawer full of underclothes, then sat down and blow dried and styled her hair, deciding that she needed to go to a salon again. She took her time picking out the proper skin care and makeup. How nice it felt to have time to pamper herself; something she certainly hadn't been able to do at Matthew's. Putting on a slight amount of base, she powdered her face with a soft brush, then applied a hint of blush...just enough to look natural. Blue eye shadow went on next and then mascara. Why hadn't she been more aware of how long her lashes were? She'd noticed before that mascara enhanced her eyes, but hadn't noticed the length of her lashes.

Eagerly she entered the closet and tried to decide what to wear. What a treasure trove of clothes! She picked out a cotton pant set which still had the tags on them. The top was a pale blue, short-sleeved, boxy cut cardigan, under which was a lace edged knit tee. The matching pants with cargo pockets went on first.

Next, she slipped on a pair of white sandals and went to look at herself in the mirror. Frowning at the tags, she rummaged through the drawers, found scissors and cut them off. "What jewelry should I wear?" she asked her reflection. She decided on a pair of small silver earrings and a silver bracelet. Saving the custom perfume for a special occasion, she dabbed herself with what was already there. Studying herself, she wondered who she was dressing for. "Pipit, that's who," she stated with a satisfied smile.

Feeling a flutter in her chest, she realized that she was ready to go exploring the house and grounds. Wondering what time breakfast was, she glanced at her watch. It was 7:30. Stopping to make the bed first, she opened the door and peeked out into the hall. She couldn't see or hear anyone. Taking a deep breath to calm herself, she walked out of her bedroom, retracing her path of the previous night. Reaching the entry to the foyer, she looked left. The view through the spacious open living room, overlooked the patio and the wide landscaped backyard.

Stepping into the foyer, she noticed for the first time the beautiful oil painting hanging above a lovely table. Across from the painting, open double doors revealed a large library with wall to wall books, a desk and rich leather furniture. Her attention returned to the living room. *Surely*, she thought, *this home had been designed for entertaining; it was much too large for the small Cabot family.*

A glass door between two large, ceiling to floor windows, led out onto the patio. In the right corner of the room, stood a tall, graceful kentia palm. In the left corner a large tree-like ornamental fig towered toward the ceiling. Pipit couldn't imagine her fifteen year old self not liking this lifestyle with its beauty and culture.

A mahogany grand piano stood near one window. Off-center, a grouping of five chairs surrounded a large square glass-topped coffee table held by finely carved lindonwood legs. On top of the table, among other tasteful decor, an ornate sage vase held a desert plant which sprouted four lovely orangish, vertical-shaped flowers. The chairs were different styles and fabrics. The right side of the room held another grouping of sofas and chairs, and on the left a round lindonwood table with four padded club chairs. *The hues and shades of color were pale gold, light tan, reddish beige, all subdued and elegant*, Pipit thought.

Her empty stomach led her out of the living room and down the main hall in the opposite direction from the bedroom wing. She passed a large and lavishly decorated dining room on the right. Finding the kitchen on the left, she noted that it also faced outward to the patio. It was a large professional type kitchen with expansive windows. A sturdy woman, bending over to retrieve something in the refrigerator, stood up with a green pepper and a tomato in her hand. Startled, the woman stared at her. "M...Miss Liz?"

"Yes?"

"It's really you?"

"It is. And who are you?"

"Who am I?" the woman asked, suddenly concerned.

"I'm sorry. Didn't my parents tell you that I had an accident and sustained a head injury?"

"They said you'd been in an accident, but that you were all right."

"I woke up with no past memory. I didn't even know my name."

"My gracious!" the woman declared. "You poor dear. My name is Mabel. I'm the chief cook around here. My daughter, Millie helps me part time."

"I'm sorry I don't recognize you, Mabel. I'm starving so I came in here wondering when breakfast was. It seems no one is up."

"I'm surprised you are. You're usually a late sleeper because you stay up so late."

"I do...did? Hmm. That changed while I was away." She watched Mabel start breakfast. "I'm certainly glad we have a cook. My cooking is terrible."

"*Your* cooking?" Mabel asked, stopping in mid-movement.

Pipit told her briefly of her stay with Matthew.

Mabel laughed. "Will wonders never cease...*you* cooking!"

"I guess it is a wonder. But I'd really like to learn how to cook well. Will you teach me?"

Mabel stared at her shaking her head. "That knock on the head has certainly changed you for the better, Miss Liz."

"Didn't I want to learn to cook?"

"Not in the slightest and mentioned it more than once to me. Even in Europe, you always ate out. Never did a thing for yourself as far as cooking was concerned."

Pipit slid onto a bar stool and watched Mabel cutting up the pepper and tomato. "Was I lazy, Mabel? Please be frank, I want to know what I was like."

"Lazy? I wouldn't say that, but..." she stopped.

"But what?"

"You were strong-willed and stubborn."

For some reason, that assessment didn't surprise her. "What are you making, Mabel?"

"An omelette. Your parents usually eat breakfast at 8:00."

"What can I do to help?"

"Help?"

"Oh...I guess I wasn't much help."

Mabel shook her head. "You...uh can cut this ciabatta bread and we'll crisp it in the oven."

"I'm sorry, I don't remember where the knives are."

Mabel pointed to a drawer. "You never knew where they were or for that matter where anything was in the kitchen. You were totally uninterested."

After cutting a few slices of bread, Pipit watched Mabel prepare the three individual omelettes, and place them in a warmer. Getting the orange juice out, Mabel said, "Since the weather is supposed to be warmer this morning, your mother requested that the meal be served out on the patio."

"That sounds wonderful."

"You always liked that. You were an outside girl. Would you like to carry this tray of glasses, utensils and napkins out and place them on the table?"

"That's easy enough," she said, picking it up and heading toward the screen door. Pushing it open with her shoulder, she stepped outside and gasped in awe at the beauty of the plants, flowers, and the lovely furniture that filled the huge patio. Beyond the patio, across the expanse of terra cotta brick inset with flower beds, she viewed a long, gently curved pool. It was surrounded by plants, flowers, windmill palms, comfortable lounge chairs, umbrella tables and chairs. "How could I not have just loved all this?"

"What?" came a voice behind a large potted plant.

Pipit set the tray on the table and turning to the voice found that it belonged to an elderly man holding a watering can in his hand. He stared at her. "Miss Liz?"

"Yes."

Happiness sparkled in his deep-set eyes as he smiled affectionately at her. "I knew your folks went to fetch you, but I didn't know that they'd be able to bring you back so soon. We're all mighty relieved that you're all right. I almost didn't recognize you, you look so nice."

"Well, I don't recognize *you*," she replied, studying his thin wrinkled face and his unruly white hair.

"You're joshin' me."

"No, I'm not." Explaining her circumstance as briefly as possible, she sighed, knowing that she'd have to go over this same path with everyone.

His warm gray eyes reflected shock, then compassion. "I knew your parents had received a call telling them where you were, but they didn't tell me that you had lost your memory. That explains why you didn't call. I'll tell you this much, Miss Liz, we're just glad to have you home safe and sound in any condition."

"Thank you. I'm sorry, but...who are you?"

"I'm one of the gardeners. My name is Horace. I take care of all this," he said with a sweeping gesture that took in the whole expanse of the backyard. "Except of course, for mowing," he amended, "I'm gettin' too old for that. Where have you been all this time, Miss Liz?"

"I've been staying with a family where I did the cooking, housecleaning and taking care of children," she answered, smiling sweetly, knowing it would shock him as it had her parents.

Horace's chin dropped slightly, then a grin spread across his face. "Well, I'll be a cotton eatin' bollworm! Serves ya right; hope it did you some good."

"You didn't like me, I take it."

"Just the opposite. I'm very fond of you. I suppose you liked me as well. You asked my advice often enough."

"Did I take it?"

"Rarely."

"Why?"

"I guess because you were always hell-bent on goin' nowhere."

"Liz!" a voice behind her exclaimed.

Pipit pivoted around. It was Julia—her mother. So concerned over Horace's last remark she could hardly return her mother's smile, nevertheless, she said, "Good morning, Mother." Her father appeared. "Good morning, Dad."

"Good morning," they chorused, both smiling.

"You look lovely, my dear," her mother said, pleased. "You've never worn that outfit."

"I know. I had to cut off the price tags," she said, taking the glasses and utensils off the tray and placing them on the table. "Excuse me, I'll take this tray back into the kitchen and see what I can do to help Mabel."

Calvin and Julia stared at her retreating back and then at each other. Horace quickly busied himself with the flowers, smiling.

It wasn't long before Pipit returned and sat down at the table with her parents.

"Mabel wouldn't let me help." She pulled a face. "I think she thinks I'll be in the way."

Presently, Mabel came out with a tray and placed the food before each of them. "Good morning, Mr. and Mrs. Cabot."

"Good morning to you, Mabel," Calvin said. "Thank you for the breakfast."

She smiled. "It's what I'm getting paid for," she said, walking off.

A gentle warm breeze floated through the patio. It was pleasant and relaxing, but Calvin's and Julia's attempt to carry on a conversation with Liz during breakfast wasn't too successful. She was quiet and withdrawn.

Pipit gazed out at the view beyond the patio. "How many acres, Dad?"

"Two and a half."

"Will you both excuse me?" she murmured, "I would like to look around the grounds."

When she had meandered far enough away, Julia stated with anxiety. "I'm going right in and call Dr. Reuben, the neurologist Dr. Strong recommended."

"Good," her husband replied, pushing his chair back and standing up. "I think I had better get to work, Julia," He bent down and kissed her. "I'll see you later this afternoon."

~~~~~~~~~~~~~

Pipit followed the winding terra cotta path, at times flanked by beds of desert plants and flowers, interspersed with tall lacy-leafed jacaranda trees. It was all so beautiful, she could hardly take it in. Why didn't this feel even a little familiar? The path curved around a group of citrus trees and led to a white latticed arbor nestled in a group of feathery-leafed, sweet acacia trees. Smiling, she stepped inside and found two seats, one across from the other. Sitting down, she found that it hid her from anyone who might be out on the path or grounds. "What a charming little hideaway," she murmured, wondering if she'd come here very often. It was some time before she asked the question that had hung uneasily in her mind. *Why was I 'hell-bent' on going nowhere?*

"Liz!" The husky whisper came from just outside the arbor. She jumped up, startled.

A man stood at the entrance gazing at her, his brown eyes brooding, hurt. "Why didn't you call and tell me you were back?"

She stared back at the strikingly good-looking man with a golden tan and sun- bleached blonde hair. Incredulous and nervous, thoughts darted through her mind—this couldn't be Kirk! Surely, her mother wouldn't send him out here when she'd requested some time to get acquainted with her sisters first.

The man glared at her. "Why are you staring at me like that?" he demanded as he lifted his foot to step inside.

"Stop!"

He withdrew his foot. "What the hell?"

"Who are you?" she asked.

"Who am I?! What do you mean by that, Liz?"

Her voice rose. "Who are you, I asked?"

"I'm your fiancé, remember?" he replied with sarcasm.

"Did Mother send you out here?"

"No."

"How did you know I was home and how did you know I would be out here?"

"I happened to be driving by last night when you got home. I returned home and waited and waited for your call. I finally gave up and came over. I've been half out of my mind with worry, Liz, and all I get now is an interrogation?"

"I asked you how you knew I was out here?"

His eyes narrowed. "I can't believe all these questions. I'm the one who should be asking the questions and getting some answers. Mabel answered the door and told me you were in the backyard. I didn't even go in, I just came around."

Though relieved her mother had kept her word, she felt a keen disappointment that, of all people, she didn't recognize the man to whom she was supposed to be engaged! Noticing that his brown eyes were dark and angry, she took a step backward as he stepped inside. "Don't touch me," she whispered menacingly, surprising herself.

"Don't touch you?" he asked incredulously.

172 Alene Roberts

"I don't *know* you. I had a head injury which took away my memory. I didn't even know my own name. I didn't recognize my own parents or sisters. And I don't recognize you."

Shocked into silence, he frowned and shook his head, trying to absorb the unbelievable and disturbing news. "Wh...what? You...you don't remember *anything*?"

"No."

"Surely this isn't permanent?"

"I don't know. I certainly hope not."

"Why didn't your mother tell me?"

"She was intending to tell you when she called to let you know I was home, but she and my father felt I needed to get reacquainted with my own sisters, and become more accustomed to this place...my home before I see *you*."

Kirk was speechless for some moments. "This is all rather unbelievable." His face hardened. "But where have you been?"

"It's a long story. Do you mind if I don't go into it right now?"

"I do mind. Where's your engagement ring?"

Pipit looked down at the bare finger of her left hand. Why hadn't she thought of that? "I don't know."

"Don't tell me you lost it! It was almost a carat."

She gazed at him aware that he hadn't asked her how she was. He seemed more upset over losing the ring than over the fact that she'd been hurt. "I'm feeling much better, thank you."

A chagrined expression flitted briefly across his face. "I'm sorry, Liz. I've been so worried, I'm not thinking straight. I do want to know how you're feeling. I want to know everything. Can we sit down here so you can tell me?"

"No. Please give me some time and space, Kirk."

"I would think you've had plenty of time. It has been a month since you ran off!"

"Is that all?" It seemed much longer to her as she struggled to care for Merri and Danny.

"Is that *all*!?"

"Please leave, Kirk. You have no idea what I've been through."

"How can I know what you've gone through?" he asked, his voice more gentle. "You won't tell me."

It finally sank in. "I ran off?" she asked. "What do you mean?"

"We just got engaged and the next night we were supposed to meet at the country club in the gazebo. You didn't show up. You just left, leaving a note for your parents, but not one for me."

"Oh. I didn't know. No wonder you're angry and hurt. I have no idea why I did that. All I can say is—I'm sorry, but you'll have to give me a little more time. I'll call you when I'm able to see you again and tell you everything."

He let out a heavy breath. "All right, Liz. I'll give you what you ask, but I hope it won't be long before you call."

"I hope so, too," she said quietly.

Kirk stepped out of the arbor, then turned to face her. "Are you all right physically?"

"I believe so."

"Good. You look very nice this morning."

"Thank you," she said, pleased.

"Your eyes...they're beautiful. You look different somehow." With that he turned and quickly walked away before she could respond.

Chapter Twenty-Five

Pipit remained in the arbor for some time, trying to analyze Kirk Morgan, and her reaction to him. She had leaned forward and watched his long smooth strides move him quickly out of sight around the bend, very aware of his nice build—particularly his broad shoulders.

What do I feel? she asked herself. Surprise, and concern. Surprise at her first reaction—the involuntary distrust of the man she was supposed to be engaged to, which soon turned to concern over why she'd run away. Why run from such an attractive man, and one who sincerely seemed to be hurt by it? Who did she think she was—*Snow White* the fairest in the land? She doubted that she'd had many suitors, if any, besides Kirk Morgan. This thought galvanized her to go find her mother and ask some pertinent questions. She hadn't known where to start until now. Apparently, it would fall into place logically when she felt a need to know something.

Nearing the house, she noticed her mother staring out the window of a room which also faced the patio. When Julia saw her daughter, she opened one of the french doors and motioned her in.

Pipit entered and glanced around, noting that this room must be the family room since it was furnished a little more casually than the front room, but still a little too elegant for the likes of Merri and Danny. Would her mother allow children to play in here?

"Liz," her mother began without preamble, "I saw Kirk walking out of the yard about twenty minutes ago. Did you see him? I want you to know I didn't call him, nor did I know he was here."

"I know. He found me on his own."

Before Pipit could formulate her first question, her mother asked, "Tell me about it. How did he react? How did you? Did you tell him about your condition?"

Pipit walked over to one of the grayish-green couches in front of the entertainment center, kicked off her sandals and curled up. Her mother sat down on the other one, and waited while her daughter examined the room.

Pipit first noticed the rug underneath this grouping of furniture. Its background was white, outlined by a couple of border lines of light tan—the color of the carpet underneath, with a pattern of sparsely scattered, gray-green leaves and peach colored flowers. An attractive bowl of peach silk flowers on the glass-topped coffee table carried the accent of color. Two upholstered armchairs flanked the couches.

Off further was a bar, in front of which was a small round table surrounded by four chairs. Another set of couch and chairs stood at the opposite end of the room; all this for entertaining she supposed.

Focusing on her mother, she noted her anxious and questioning expression, so she began relating everything that had transpired between herself and Kirk.

What Liz told her answered all of Julia's questions. She sighed. "I'm certainly glad that's over, Liz. You must allow him to see you soon. You need to get reacquainted. I'm sure it will help you remember because you were in love with him and you were so happy when you finally decided to accept his proposal."

"If I was so happy, why did I run off and not even leave him a note?"

"That's what your father and I have asked ourselves over and over. The only possible answer I can come up with is, somehow, the note did not get to him. Maybe it was inadvertently thrown away, or lost. Maybe you just needed to get away for a while and think about the big step you had just taken. After all, you had three near engagements or rather three other proposals, and you were the one who broke off all three relationships. You told me the night you were engaged that you wanted this one relationship to last."

"Three other proposals?" Pipit asked, shocked. "I felt almost certain that Kirk was my first and only suitor."

Julia laughed. "You couldn't be more wrong, Liz. You've had many young men after you."

"But...but how could that be? I'm the 'ugly duckling' of the family."

The expression of pain that came across her mother's face seemed tired—as if it had traveled there many times. "If you feel that way, it's because you chose to look like an ugly duckling, Liz—insisting on wearing only the plainest, most casual clothes, choosing to cut your hair far too short for the shape of your face, choosing not to wear makeup. You seemed bent on trying to look as unattractive as possible. I'm amazed Kirk even gave you a second glance."

"Why?" Pipit shook her head as if to reject what she'd heard. "Why did I do all those things?" She stood up and moved about restlessly, feeling distress for her mother, as well as for herself.

"I wish I knew. Your father doesn't know, your sisters don't know."

"Why *did* Kirk give me a second glance?"

"It's a mystery that any of the young men came after you."

The remark struck a deep and painful place in Pipit, and knew it did for the woman in front of her. "I can see how frustrated you've been. I'm sorry."

Julia crumbled under the unexpected sympathy. Pipit sat down and put her arm around her mother. "I'm sorry for causing you so much pain."

Her mother pulled a tissue from her skirt pocket and wiped her eyes. "Thank you, Liz. Now, maybe you can understand why I'm nervous about you and Kirk and why I want you to get reacquainted soon."

"I'll call him just as soon as I visit with my sisters. I feel I need to get to know them first."

"Thank you." She smiled a bit wanly. "With your memory gone, you are much more understanding and kind, Liz."

Pipit contemplated this with some disquiet. "I hesitate to ask my next question."

"Go on, Liz, ask it."

"I was going to say, since I had no dearth of boyfriends, what was it that attracted them to me? It certainly wasn't my looks. Was it my personality?"

Julia looked down at her lap, her brow contorting. She was silent.

Pipit held her breath, then exhaled sharply. Standing up, she said, "You know what, Mother?"

Julia raised her head and looked up at her daughter. "What?"

"I don't think I like Liz Cabot. I think I'll remain Pipit." She walked out and ran to her room locking the door. Throwing herself onto the bed, she cried. "What kind of a person was I?" The rest of the questions she had about Kirk Morgan would have to wait.

~~~~~~~~~~~~~

A tapping sound was coming from somewhere. Pipit opened her eyes. She'd fallen asleep.

"Liz?" The voice came from the door.

Pipit got up and went over and opened it.

"Are you all right, Liz?" her mother asked.

How could I be? she wanted to say, when as Liz Cabot I was rebellious, homely and apparently lacking in personality. Instead she said, "Yes."

"Your father and I are having lunch out on the patio. Would you like to join us?"

"I'll be right there after I freshen up."

A few minutes later, she found her father and mother on the patio engrossed in the newspaper. "Hi, Dad."

Calvin put his paper down and smiled. "Good afternoon, Liz."

In spite of her mother's stark and painful revelations, Pipit realized she was hungry. "This food looks wonderful," she said, seating herself at the table. "How nice that I don't have to fix it."

They ate in silence for a while, then her mother said, "I've made an appointment for 10:00 AM tomorrow morning with Dr. Reuben. He's a neurologist, Liz."

"Thank you."

"I hear you saw Kirk this morning, Liz," her father said.

"Yes," she replied swallowing a mouthful.

"And?"

"And I have some more questions."

"Shoot."

"How did I meet Kirk?"

Her father frowned, thinking. "I'm not sure."

Her mother spoke up. "We've known the family for years, Liz, so it was natural that you and Kirk were thrown together at country club galas, golf tournaments and parties."

"How old is he?"

"Thirty-six," replied her mother.

"Has he ever married?"

"No. He's been the most sought after, eligible bachelor in our social circles."

"Did I seek after him?"

Her father laughed. "Nope."

"Good. Apparently he was a little picky to remain single so long. So...if he was so picky, why did he choose me? I'm told I tried to look unattractive and apparently my personality was the same."

"Your personality?" her father questioned, surprised. "Why, Liz, that isn't so."

Ignoring his protestations, Liz turned to her mother. "Is there a good hairstylist I could go to, Mother?"

Julia's face lit up. "Of course, dear. Francois has been wanting to do something with your hair besides cut it. He's effusive over the texture of it. Would you like me to make an appointment for you?"

"I would, thank you." She questioned herself. *Do I want to look nice for Kirk? For myself? Or...Matthew? Now where did that come from? Matthew couldn't see it even if he were here!*

Chapter Twenty-Six

Three-thirty the next afternoon, Pipit waited restlessly for her sisters to arrive. She had asked her mother if she might visit with them alone.

Staring out the window of the family room, Pipit's thoughts returned to Matthew and the children. How far away and unreal her time with them seemed at the moment. What a different world she lived in now.

Her mother had taken her to see Dr. Reuben, a neurologist, early that morning. After a physical and mental examination, his opinion, reinforced by the one memory she had, was that her full memory would probably surface in the near future. It was only a matter of time.

"Hello, Liz," Claire said as she and Linda entered the room.

"Oh, hello to both of you," Pipit said, whirling around. "Thank you for coming."

"Thank you for letting us," Linda said.

When the three had seated themselves, Linda asked, "How are you feeling, Liz?"

"I'm feeling a little more at home, thank you."

"Mother told us what Dr. Reuben said," Claire added. "We're anxious to have our sister back."

Pipit studied these two beautiful girls—her sisters. They could almost be twins except Linda was very blonde and Claire was strawberry blonde. Both had large blue eyes and perfect features like their mother. This afternoon, though both wore casual dresses, they looked stylish and perfectly groomed.

Launching directly into it, Pipit began, "I need to ask you some questions and I don't want you to whitewash the answers. I gather that I tried to look even more unattractive than I am and that I didn't often make an attempt to dress nicely. Since that seemed to be the case I was certain that Kirk Morgan was the first man who ever paid any attention to me." Her sisters looked at each other and smiled. "But Mother informed me that wasn't so, that I've had three other proposals. Needless to say that surprised me. I then asked her if I was so unattractive, what was it that drew men to me...my personality? Mother looked down, an unhappy expression on her face and wouldn't answer...so if I was homely with no personality, what drew men to me...Dad's money?"

Both Claire and Linda were smiling. It was Claire who spoke first. "Mother has been so concerned about you she can't see past her nose. I'm afraid, in her presence, you only displayed sarcasm and rudeness to the men who came around. We saw how you were when she wasn't around, and we've tried to tell her, but until she sees it herself, she won't believe it. However, you were tolerably decent to Kirk in her presence."

"It sounds like I was unkind to Mother."

"You and Mother are like oil and water, Liz," Linda explained, "You are much different than she is. In fact, you are different from Claire and me."

"How?"

"We all liked it here in Palm Springs and fit in with the lifestyle very easily when we moved here, but you refused to. You said it was superficial and snobbish."

"Isn't it?"

"No," Claire answered. "The neighborhood we lived in, in Los Angeles, began to change. Neighbors we'd known for years began moving out and the new people moving in were not the same caliber, and it had become quite dangerous living there. Dad had a lot of businesses and a lot of real estate, one of which was a large date grove here in the Palm Springs area, and since he and mother both liked warm weather, they decided to move here. By that time, Dad had become quite wealthy and Mother, who has always wanted to be part of the social scene, insisted on living in this neighborhood."

"Oh, Liz, you'll love it here," Linda said, glad for the opportunity to try and influence her sister since she was now a little like a newcomer to Palm Springs. "It's always so exciting; something is going on all the time. Broadway musicals, country club parties, golf tournaments where many movie stars come. In fact this month, February, is when the golf tournaments takes place. And, Liz, you were once an avid golfer and liked to go to the tournaments."

"You were also a champion swimmer and won medals in high school. You were so good at tennis, you could have become professional," Claire added.

"Could have? Didn't I keep on with all those things?"

Claire smiled. "No. You got bored, you said. You graduated and got your masters from California State University at San Bernardino in Art History. You worked in an art gallery here for a while, then you went to Europe. We've all gone to Europe several times, but you stayed there, and became the manager of a large art gallery in Paris."

"So that's why I can speak French. How long was I there?"

"Five years. You've been home about a year."

It sounded to Pipit as if they were talking about a stranger—someone accomplished, not her. Pulling her thoughts back to these two lovely young women who were her sisters, she said, "I understand you both are married. Tell about your husbands."

"This is so strange having to tell you all this, Liz," Linda said. "I married before Claire. I married Bruce Beckstrom four years ago. His family is a wealthy family here in Palm Springs. He works in his father's brokerage business."

Claire responded next. "My husband's name is Kelley Thorton. I've been married three years. My husband also works with his father. They've been in real estate here for ages."

"I see you both married well."

Claire and Linda looked at each other, then back at her. Claire remarked, "Though you liked Bruce and Kelley, you used to say that very thing, but in a sarcastic tone."

"I wasn't a very nice person was I?"

"We thought you were wonderful, Liz," Linda contradicted. "You were a wonderful older sister to us."

"That's hard to believe."

Claire smiled at the remark. "Nevertheless, it's true. We were very close. You were very protective of us and kept us out of trouble. We were so naive, but you never were, for some reason."

"Oh, Liz," Linda began, "we're so anxious to ask questions ourselves."

"Of course you are. You want to know everything that's happened to me." They nodded vigorously. Pipit began at the beginning when she woke up on that wintry night. They were wide-eyed and intrigued when she told them of the music and the voice that had guided her to safety. Claire and Linda were enthralled. They laughed when she told them of her misadventures in cooking, and Merri's running dialogue during her first pathetic efforts. Pipit left nothing out, telling them of her panic, of her emotional ups and downs. They laughed; they cried. When she was through, Linda and Claire were silent for a few moments.

"What's going to happen to Matthew?" Linda asked.

"I don't know. I try not to dwell on it since I can do nothing to help him right now. Even reviewing it has made me feel anxious. I don't know whether calling the children will help them or disturb them."

"Do you miss Matthew?" Claire asked pointedly.

"I'm still riding an emotional roller coaster trying to adjust to being Liz Cabot...so, no."

"This is quite a drama, Liz," Claire said. "We'll be on the edge of our seats waiting for the second act...then when the curtain drops on the third."

"It is quite a drama isn't it?" smiled Pipit. "Now, since I told you about 'my' children, what about yours?"

"Ours?" they asked almost simultaneously.

"You've been married for a few years. Don't I have any nieces or nephews yet?"

They smiled and shook their heads.

"Why?"

"You knew once," Linda said. "We're still young. We want to golf, travel with our husbands, play a while before we have to settle down with children."

Their sister frowned at them. "That sounds a little selfish."

Indignantly, Claire blurted out, "Selfish? You could barely tolerate children, Liz, and never once did you ever mention you wanted them."

"I'm sorry if I offended you, but when I was trying to care for Merri and Danny, I *knew* that I had been a selfish person because it was so hard for me to care for others. I resented not having time for myself."

"Hey, what's going on in here?" a deep voice said. The girls turned around to see Bruce, Linda's husband.

"Hi, darling. Come and say hello to Liz."

"Liz," he said, pulling her up from the chair and giving her a hug. "It's mighty good to see you here safe and sound. You had us worried."

"Thank you. Bruce, isn't it?"

"Yes. Sorry about your accident. Hope your memory returns soon."

"Thank you, Bruce. Me too." Pipit liked him immediately. He was average height, clean cut, with thinning blonde hair and a wide, warm smile.

Just then, Julia entered and announced that dinner was ready in the dining room.

Pipit was pleased that her sisters and their husbands were invited to dinner. As they entered the dining room, Kelley walked in, slipped his arm around Claire and gave her a kiss on the cheek.

"I'm glad you could make it so early, Kelley," his wife said.

Everyone greeted him except Pipit who mentally appraised him. A big man, slightly overweight, dark-haired and nice looking. Stepping over to her, he took both her hands in his. "Liz! It's great to have you home at last."

"Thank you.'

"Did you have a good visit with your sisters?"

"I did. They tried to tell me what kind of a person I was."

"I'll add my two cents. You were a great sister-in-law."

"Thank you, that helps. You see, I'm getting mixed reviews," she said looking pointedly at her mother.

Everyone laughed—except Julia.

Chapter Twenty-Seven

Wednesday afternoon, Pipit stared at herself in the mirror. Her mother had taken her to see Francois, the hairstylist, that morning. He gave her a body perm and re-styled her hair. Pipit had watched the transformation in amazement. Parting it on the left side, he brought her hair over the right half of her forehead, then behind her ears with slight curls showing against her neckline just below her earlobe. He styled an attractive swirl of hair over her left temple. The style had widened her face and made it look less long. She was more than pleased.

After returning home, she had given Kirk a call—mainly to please her mother. She had accepted his invitation to take her for a drive around Palm Springs and then to dinner. He was due any minute. It all felt like a wonderful dream—this lifestyle, after what she had been through living at Matthew's. She had chosen to wear a periwinkle pant suit with gold jewelry—another outfit that hadn't been worn. A sliver of excitement slid through her when her mother knocked on her door to announce Kirk's arrival.

Julia glowed with happiness as she watched Kirk's expression when he saw Liz.

She followed them out onto the porch and waved goodbye as they drove off in Kirk's silver Mercedes.

Kirk turned to her and smiled. "You smell delicious. Is that new perfume?"

"Yes. It's a custom perfume I had made for me in Scottsdale one day when I was able to escape the children for a while."

"The children? What children?"

"It's a long story, Kirk."

"Don't you think I deserve to hear the story—everything that happened to you after you left?"

Something deep down was churning inside her. Rubbing her brow, she hoped it would help bring the broiling emotions to the surface where she could examine them, remember their origin.

"Well...don't I deserve it?" he demanded.

She turned slowly and examined his angry face, then his handsome profile as he turned to watch the road. "I don't know. I don't know you."

His foot pressed the gas pedal, his jaw rippling in anger, he turned a corner sharply.

"I see you have a temper," she remarked quietly.

His foot let up the gas pedal, and he let out an explosive breath. "I'm sorry. I've been so upset about you leaving, and now that you've returned, I find that I still don't have you."

"I can only imagine what you have gone through and what you are going through now."

Leaving the Rancho Mirage area, Kirk drove through town center on Fred Waring Dr., passing the city hall. They drove the palm-lined road silently for some time while Pipit studied the buildings, the businesses. It looked familiar and yet it didn't. Turning left on Jefferson St., Kirk eventually drove southwest on 42nd Ave. until they arrived at a place called Palm Desert Resort. Finding a parking place, he pulled in and smiled at Liz. "This was one of your favorite places to walk around. We used to come here and end up in a special place and talk. Does is look familiar at all?" he asked hopefully.

"Palm Springs, in general, looks a little familiar—yet it doesn't. This place is no different." Kirk looked disappointed. "You and I are going to have to be patient. I don't think we can force this."

"You're right. Let's go for a walk."

"Let's," she agreed. He got out and went around for her. Together, they walked along the sidewalk that eventually led them through trees and flowers. "This is beautiful, Kirk."

It wasn't long before a small alcove made up of trees and flowers appeared, and in the middle was a white bench. "This is where you and I have had some long talks." He gestured. "Shall we?"

She nodded and they seated themselves. Kirk studied her and as he did so, he fingered her hair. "Your hair looks nice. You've fixed it differently. I like it."

She smiled. "Thank you, Kirk."

Without warning, Kirk pulled her to him and kissed her. She fought it, trying to pull away, but his kiss only became more ardent. Suddenly, an electric jolt went clear through her, and her arms seemed to have a will of their own, winding themselves about his neck. Passion fogged her thinking as she returned his kiss. When finally they pulled apart, Kirk's face was one of exultance. "You haven't forgotten how you *felt* about me."

Breathlessly, Pipit muttered. "I don't recall the love I felt for you, but I experienced the physical attraction—and it scares me."

Rankled, Kirk's voice rose. "Not again!"

"You mean I've said that before?"

He stood up and paced back and forth in front of her. "Before you left for Europe, I tried to date you more than once, but you refused me, telling me that when I touched you, you felt too much physical attraction for me and that it scared you. I couldn't understand it then and I don't understand it now."

"Can I change the subject, Kirk?"

Still chafing, he nodded. Running a hand through his hair in frustration, he sat down.

"I'm sure you could have your pick of all the beauties around, Kirk. Why did you choose me? Surely, you can't deny that I'm rather plain."

"Plain?" A sardonic smile crossed his face. "Well, you don't have the looks your sisters have, but you managed to intrigue all the guys around."

"How? I can't imagine that. My mother thinks I had the personality of a prickly pear cactus."

He laughed. "Liz, you had the most caustic tongue of any one I know. And you used it when we guys needed it...and sometimes when I didn't think we needed it. But you were fun and stimulating because you were knowledgeable about a lot of things, and..." His voiced trailed off.

"And what?"

"Oh nothing," he quickly replied, irritated that he'd almost told her.

"We're not going any further in getting reacquainted if you don't tell me the 'and.'"

He unsuccessfully tried to think of something else to tell her. Exhaling an impatient breath, he said, "All right, Liz. And—you were *unavailable*—in more ways than one."

It took a few moments to sink in. When it did, the smile that crinkled her eyes came from deep inside her. "Thank you, Kirk. Now, will you give me a few more details?"

Her smile always affected him. "You were so protective of your sisters, you were the *bane* of the male population of Palm Springs." He noted her surprise and smiled. "You three Cabot girls were known as 'the virgin sisters.'"

At this, Pipit's jaw dropped, and for a moment she was speechless. "You mean, I wouldn't let them..uh..." She couldn't finish the sentence.

Kirk helped her out. "It wasn't just that you wouldn't let them, but you were so close, the three of you, you kept reminding them of the things your parents taught you before they moved to Palm Springs."

"Before?"

"You told me that your father had instigated Bible reading every morning before you moved to Palm Springs, but that, to quote your sarcastic statement, 'it had been put aside because of the lifestyle of the rich and famous they had adopted.'"

When Pipit had internalized this startling information, she smiled at him gratefully. "Thank you for telling me, Kirk. I think I might finally begin to like Elizabeth Cabot."

It was Kirk's turn to be surprised, as well as puzzled. "You talk as if you weren't her."

"As far as I know now, I'm Pipit, not Elizabeth."

"Pipit?"

"I think it's time to explain what happened to me after I left." She told him everything, but as briefly as she could, not nearly as detailed as she had told her family. She watched Kirk's expression as she did so. At times, his face reflected concern and sympathy and other times his face hardened as it was at this moment.

"Is this uh...Matthew interested in you?" he asked tersely.

"I'm sorry, I did leave something out. His wife, Diane, was the most beautiful and near perfect woman I've ever heard about. Matthew can't forget her; he won't let her go. It has been over nine months since she died and he hasn't rid the closets and drawers of her things. No woman could compete with the memory of Diane."

Some relief crossed his face, but not all. "But how do *you* feel about *him*?"

"How do I feel about him?" she asked, her brows twisting. "Why...I feel compassion toward him and his children. I'm concerned that he may lose his children to his mother-in-law. She'll take him to court and try to get custody of them if his sight doesn't return."

"Oh." He stared straight ahead, rubbing his chin in thought for a moment, then facing her he said, "I can see that you're concerned over the problem he has, but for some reason I sense that isn't all you feel."

"Why, Kirk, you're jealous of him," she replied, amazed.

"Are you telling me that I have no reason to be, that you don't care for him in some way?"

Pipit abruptly stood up and walked a few feet away, her back to him, suddenly feeling irritated and impatient with his incessant questions. Without turning, she said, "When two people are thrown together like we were, Kirk, you naturally learn to care for each other. I learned to care for his uncle Arthur, but," she turned around and faced him, "you are forcing me to focus on my feelings for Matthew in a way I never have, and it's uncomfortable."

Kirk's eyes narrowed suspiciously. "Why?"

She sat down beside him, and glared at him. "I don't know. It's probably because I feel about him like...uh I would a brother."

"I hope that's it, Liz, but your anger makes me wonder."

"I'm not angry!"

He laughed. "Oh?"

It took only a split second to realize it was true. She smiled sheepishly. "You're right. My emotions have been up and down and all over the place, Kirk. It has driven me crazy. The neurologist told us this happens with a head injury."

For the first time, Kirk's face reflected total relief. "Of course. I've heard that." He reached for her and pulled her close. "That makes me feel better."

"I'm glad," she said, pulling away. "But please, Kirk, let's not be physical. I need some time."

He dropped his hands and stood up. "Damn! Do we have to go through all this again, Liz?"

"Again?"

He got up and paced restlessly. "You pulled this on me before. When I finally convinced you to go out with me, it was a little like trying to melt the ice queen."

Pipit laughed. "I would hope so."

He stopped in front of her and gazed down at her smiling face. A smile flickered across his own. "It isn't amusing, Liz."

"I don't remember this, Kirk, but it's obvious that all the women would be spell-bound by you, that you could wind any woman around your little finger. I suspect it was time one of us pulled you up short."

He laughed and sat down. "You're more like the Liz you don't know than you realize." He took her hand and said, "Okay, I'll do my best to behave for a while. How about we go for another drive before we go to the restaurant?"

~~~~~~~~~~~~~

The drive had been pleasant since both Pipit and Kirk were more relaxed following their talk. Eventually, they wound up at Del Rio's, Palm Desert, because Kirk, like Pipit was dressed more casually with only an open-collared shirt under his sport coat.

After the hostess seated them, Kirk said, "You liked this place. You particularly liked to dine on the patio in the summer under the stars. Does it look familiar?"

"It's strange that I remembered the movie star/singer as we drove down Frank Sinatra Dr., but not this place. The doctor explained to us that amnesia is puzzling to physicians, and it certainly is to me."

"And to me," he said. "I guess I had better tell you a little about this place. They tell us that everything served here is authentic, fresh and healthful, including fresh handmade tortillas daily."

"Sounds wonderful. When I was Liz," she said with a grin, "I probably took all this for granted, but Pipit certainly doesn't. After trying to cook and having to *eat* my own cooking, dining at a nice place like this is a treat beyond compare."

"I can't imagine you cooking, Liz," he said in disbelief.

"Believe it or not, I now want to learn how. Mabel said she'd teach me."

The waiter appeared and asked if they would like something to drink. Kirk ordered a Tequila, white Blanco. When the waiter turned to Pipit, she asked Kirk, "Did I drink?"

Kirk hesitated and for a moment was tempted to say yes, but knew he couldn't get away with it. "No."

"I wouldn't care for anything," she said to the waiter.

When the waiter left, she asked, "I didn't drink? Why?"

"In the first place, you didn't like the tired, sleepy effect alcohol had on you and secondly, you told me you didn't even want to drink when you became a serious athlete. But more than that, you had a close friend whose parents were alcoholics and you saw how they neglected her, how she suffered...then became an alcoholic herself."

Her face turned serious. "Was I worried about your drinking?"

"At first, but then, I too have had several friends like yours. I made a pact with myself to only drink sparingly—one at a meal and maybe one at a party."

"How serious an athlete was I?" she asked, wanting to change the subject.

"Serious enough to try to beat me," he teased.

"Did I beat you?"

"As a matter of fact you were so determined and so competitive, you beat me a couple of times both in tennis, and golf."

"You must be good, then," she teased.

"Actually, I've played in a couple of tournaments with some movie stars, but it's more of a hobby to me than a serious sport. How about a game of golf tomorrow afternoon?"

"I think I'd like that, if I remember how to play."

"I'll pick you up at 2:00. Is that all right?"

"Do you work?"

"I do, but I'm my own boss. My father and I have real estate holdings, mortgage companies and a few other things."

"Two is fine."

Speaking of my father, he and my mother are anxious to see you. I'll take you over to the house after the golf game."

The waiter brought Kirk his drink and took their orders.

"Do they like me?"

"Very much. They wondered if I would ever get married."

"Did I like them?"

"I'm not sure. You were quite reserved around them."

"Hey Kirk, good to see you," a man said passing by.

"Good to see you, Sam."

From then on, it seemed to Pipit that everyone who knew Kirk arrived at the restaurant and stopped to talk to him. Some knew her and spoke to her, and she tried to act as though she knew them in return. In addition, Kirk pointed out people of consequence, as well as a couple of movie stars who were at other tables.

"Do you know the whole town, Kirk?"

"We've lived here all my life...so I know a great many."

The food was placed before them. It tasted so good to Pipit that she ate until she had to undo the top button of her pants.

"I have tickets for the 13th annual Frank Sinatra Celebrity Invitational Golf Tournament on the 16th at the Desert Willow Golf Resort. Will you go with me?"

"That sounds impressive. I'd like that, thank you."

They had visited a few minutes after dessert, when Pipit said, "I feel a little tired, Kirk. I think I had better get home."

"You were never tired, Liz, are you all right?"

"I think it's the after-effects of the head injury as well as the emotional teeter-totter I'm constantly on that makes me tired. But I'm feeling better day by day."

About twenty minutes later, Kirk walked Pipit to the door. She shivered from the night chill. He took her hand and kissed it. "That will have to do for now. See you tomorrow at 2:00, Liz."

"Good night, Kirk and thank you for the drive and dinner." He nodded, smiled and turned toward his car.

As Pipit opened and shut the door, her mother appeared. "Have you been waiting for me?"

"As a matter of fact I have. I've been anxious to hear how your afternoon and evening with Kirk went."

"It was quite enlightening, but it has left me emotionally and physically exhausted. May I tell you about it tomorrow morning?"

Julia was disappointed and also concerned. "Are you all right, Liz?"

"I'm fine. It's just emotionally taxing trying to remember and not being able to."

"You go on in to bed, dear, and we'll talk tomorrow morning at breakfast."

"Thank you, Mother. Good night."

Chapter Twenty-Eight

By 8:00 the next morning, Pipit was just about to go to breakfast when she heard a knock at her door. Opening it she saw a strange face—a woman dressed in a light green uniform. "Hello, Miss Cabot. I'm here to change your sheets, and clean. Also, if you have any wash I'll take it down to be done. And your mother told me to tell you that breakfast would be served in the dining room."

"Uh...do I know you?"

"Yes, you do. I'm Leona. Your mother told me about your accident and your condition. I'm sorry, Miss Cabot. I hope you'll be all right soon."

"Thank you, Leona. How often do you clean and gather up the wash?"

"It varies, but usually every three or four days."

Pipit smiled. "What a life. I could get used to this." She walked past her down the hall toward the dining room leaving Leona staring after her, puzzled.

"Good morning," she said as she entered the dining room.

Their faces lit up. "Good morning, Liz," her father said.

"Leona gave you the message I see," her mother said. "Any time you wish to sleep in, Liz, let me know ahead of time and I won't let her disturb you."

"Sounds good after the kind of work I had to do while staying with Matthew. And imagine having someone do my laundry," she said helping herself to a bowl of fruit and a poached egg.

Pipit looked up in time to see the wide-eyed glance that passed between her parents. " Did I take all this for granted?"

"More than that, Liz," her mother said, "you've resisted it while at the same time allowing yourself to become...uh..."

"Spoiled by it," her father finished.

"Now, Cal, that isn't what I was going to say, exactly."

"Of course not, Julia, that would mean we *all* are a little spoiled being waited on continually."

"I *know* I was spoiled by it," Pipit said. "I didn't know a thing about cooking, and I'd almost forgotten how to clean—and I resented having to do it."

"But you did it anyway," her father said, smiling.

"I did, but not well. And it still bothers me to think about it—but not enough to not enjoy being waited on," she replied, pulling a face.

Julia could wait no longer. "When will you be seeing Kirk again?"

"This afternoon for a game of golf...if I remember how to play."

Her mother smiled, pleased. "Would you like to tell us about your time with Kirk yesterday afternoon and evening?"

Pipit ate a couple of bites and stared into space. "It's strange, but having amnesia is like being able to start out with a clean slate, so to speak. All the rebelliousness and antagonism I apparently felt in the past are gone from my memory. I've heard both favorable and unfavorable remarks about Elizabeth. As I find out bits and pieces of information about myself, it seems strange, but I can stand back objectively and view Liz and Pipit at the same time as if I were neither one. And just as importantly, I'm able to view my relationship with you both, my sisters, and Kirk—objectively—and see both sides, incomplete though that may be. And hopefully, when I regain my memory I'll be a better person."

This unexpected disclosure left her parents speechless for a moment, then her father said, "That's quite profound insight, Liz."

She gave her father a small grateful smile, then recounted briefly her time with Kirk the day before, leaving out the personal things. Her mother's face reflected disappointment. "Later, I'll tell you the details you want to hear, Mother."

"Thank you, Liz," her mother said, touched at her sensitivity. "How about inviting Kirk to dinner tomorrow night?"

"Sounds fine. I think I'll watch Mabel prepare that meal and try to learn something."

"Why?" her mother asked.

"Because I felt so inept at Matthew's house. If I'm ever in a situation where I have to do for myself or others, I want to know how."

~~~~~~~~~~~~

Kirk and Liz were finishing up their golf game. "You almost beat me, Liz," he said grinning. "You certainly didn't forget how to play golf."

"I didn't, and I enjoyed the outing and being on this beautiful course. Thank you."

"Are you ready to go 'meet' my parents?" he asked, chuckling. "It seems strange asking that since you already know them."

"I...guess I am."

"They also want you to stay for dinner."

"All right. My mother asked me to invite you for dinner tomorrow night. Can you come?"

"You bet! I want to spend as much time with you as possible."

The golf course was not too far from the Rancho Mirage area and soon Kirk was driving into it. He said, "As you see, we live in the same area."

Taking Clancy Lane, he drove two blocks and turned into a driveway, stopping before a black wrought iron gate. It opened slowly, and after he'd driven the winding terra cotta brick road for about 200 feet, a magnificent estate appeared—a two-story, Mediterranean-styled house with spectacular grounds surrounding it. It was white stucco with a cream and peach tile roof and a wide cherry wood front entry. The windows were long vertical panes divided by wide slats of cherry wood. Ornate wrought iron balustrades surrounded the small balconies of the upstairs windows.

Within the circle formed by the driveway, directly across from the entry of the home, a three-tiered fountain bubbled water into a curved, octagonal tiled pond surrounded by pink, yellow and white flowers. Directly in front of the house were planters filled with flowers and tall palms.

"This is one of the most beautiful homes I've ever seen in my short life as Pipit."

Pleased, Kirk replied. "I'll build you one like it if you want."

Suddenly overwhelmed by it all, Pipit turned silent. When he could see she wasn't going to respond, he got out and went around for her. At the front door, Kirk pushed the bell. "Mother likes to be forewarned when I arrive with company."

A butler answered the door. "Good evening, Mr. Morgan," he stated formally, "your mother is waiting for you in the sun room."

"Thank you, Gerard."

Pipit noted that the inside of the home was as opulent as she expected. Entering the plant-filled sun room, they found Mrs. Morgan reading. "Oh, there you are, Kirk." Standing up, she gazed at Pipit and spoke cooly, "It's nice to have you back, Liz. I hear you had an accident."

The woman before her stood straight-shouldered—elegant in a soft silk dress with a single strand of choker pearls. If there were any strands of gray in her hair, they were well hidden. Her blonde hair was combed back into a stylish bouffant.

"Yes, I did have an accident, Mrs. Morgan."

Nan Morgan's voice turned to ice. "When you disappeared so suddenly, I'm sure the note you must have left Kirk was misplaced somehow."

"Mother...please," admonished Kirk.

"I'm sorry, I don't remember anything, Mrs. Morgan. I may have left him a note, I don't know."

"I hope you did, my dear, I certainly hope you did." She smiled, but her green eyes held no warmth. "Please have a seat, both of you. Your father will be here, momentarily, Kirk."

Before they could even sit down, Dick Morgan walked in. "Well you're here already." He walked over to Pipit and took both her hands in his. "My dear girl, we're certainly relieved that you're all right."

"Thank you, Mr. Morgan," she said, noticing that he was as striking, in his way, as his wife. His thick hair was silver white and though there were some wrinkles in his tanned face, he was still handsome, his smile charming.

"Sit down, all of you," Nan Morgan said, "Dinner will be ready shortly."

"I know I knew this once, but how many children do you and Mr. Morgan have, Mrs. Morgan?"

Though prepared for Liz's memory loss, this was Nan's first evidence of it and it surprised her. She paused before replying.

"I have two daughters younger than Kirk. They are both married and living in other states. Kirk is our only son."

"Liz may not remember *us*, but she remembers how to play golf, " Kirk said, grinning. "She almost beat me this afternoon."

"I hope you remember how you *feel* about our son," Dick Morgan stated, his eyes turning hard. "We want to get this marriage on the road."

"I'm afraid it will take some time, Dad," Kirk said.

"Neither one of you are getting any younger," his father snapped.

"I think I had better leave and let you three discuss this," Pipit said, standing up.

"No, Liz," Kirk said. "I want you to stay. Dad, you and I and Mother will go over it tonight, later." He turned to Liz. "You see, since our talk, I haven't had time to discuss the situation with my parents."

"All right, son," his father said. "I'm sorry, Liz, but as you might guess, we've been concerned about Kirk getting around to giving us some heirs."

Pipit heard no apology in his voice, so she said nothing.

"Excuse me, Mrs. Morgan," a young woman dressed in a maid's uniform spoke from the door. "Dinner is ready."

"Thank you, Joanne. Shall we?" she asked, standing and smiling with practiced graciousness.

Kirk took hold of Liz's arm and followed his parents to the dining room. Pipit decided to not cause a problem by leaving, but wondered if she had ever felt comfortable in this house.

Chapter Twenty-Nine

After breakfast, Pipit, dressed in jeans and a sweatshirt, resumed her trek around the acreage behind the house. It was a little chilly, but sunny as usual. Her mind went back to the dinner the night before with the Morgans. She had suspected that her own mother was something of a snob, but compared to Nan Morgan, she was a model of humility. And it was obvious that Dick Morgan was used to getting his way, no matter who he stepped on—and that included his own son. Something was eating at Kirk during the meal. He had tried to carry on a civil conversation with his parents, but he ended up talking mostly with her, irritating his mother.

As she rounded a bend, she came upon the old gardener kneeling on the ground pulling up weeds from a flower bed. "Hello, Horace."

He turned and grinned. "Hello to you, Miss Liz. How are you?"

"I'm learning a lot about myself and my family...so I guess I'm fine. How are you?"

"Middlin' well, I'd say."

"Could I ask you a question, Horace?"

"Pull up a seat here on the lawn and ask away."

She sat on the lawn crossed-legged. Horace joined her, resting his wrists upon his knees, his soiled, bony hands hanging loose.

"You said I used to come and ask you for advice."

"You did, but your mother didn't always like the advice I gave you."

"This time, I'd like to ask you what you think of Kirk Morgan."

A smile spread across his weathered face, producing furrows of lines. "You've already asked me that."

"I did?" she asked, constantly surprised at how Elizabeth kept surfacing and becoming one with the person she thought of as herself—Pipit. "What did you say?"

"I would rather not say, Miss Liz. You need to discover what *you* thought of Mr. Kirk Morgan."

"You must not have liked him."

"That's not true. I liked him well enough. He was nice to me, and he seemed to care about you."

"I wish I knew how I felt about him. I have enjoyed being with him the short time I've known him in this rerun of my life. But it seems that if I really loved him, I would remember that or feel it."

"You did love him, Miss Liz. You never would have become engaged to him if you hadn't. You were a no-nonsense girl who faced things straight on."

"That reminds me, something has happened to my ring. I don't know whether I lost it up in the mountains or if I took it off and put it somewhere. Excuse me, Horace, I think I'll run up and look for it."

Breathlessly, she entered the dressing room and started rummaging through her jewelry. It wasn't there. She looked under everything in every drawer. Still no ring.

Quickly going back into the bedroom, she went over to the desk and searched through every drawer. She was about to give up when she decided to look inside a stationery box, hoping to find a note that she might have written to Kirk. Lifting the box from the drawer, something rattled. Removing the lid and the small stack of paper, she saw a ring. Picking it up, she studied it. It was a large solitaire set in an unusual setting. She felt nothing. It was as if she'd never seen it or worn it. Hesitantly, she slipped it onto her left finger. It fit.

Resuming her search for a note to Kirk, she raised each empty sheet of stationery, page by page, certain she was wasting her time. Why would she slip it under blank pages? But that was exactly what she had done; she came to one she'd started! "Dear Kirk, I..." then nothing. Underneath that page she'd started another one. "Dear Kirk, When..." then stopping as before.

On both pages, the paper bubbled in several places. Looking closer, she realized they were water marks. Were those tears? A feeling of sadness for Elizabeth Cabot crept over her. What could have happened to make her take off the ring, not even finish a note to Kirk, and run away? Tears rolled down her cheeks and she didn't know why. She made a couple of decisions. She decided not to show Kirk the unfinished notes, and to return the ring to him until she regained her memory. Taking it off and putting it back into the box, she was seized with a sudden feeling of loss—of what might have been.

Remembering that Kirk was coming for dinner, she headed for the kitchen to find out what Mabel was fixing. She wanted to watch Mabel's deft fingers, her methods, and her wonderful ability to use herbs and spices to season foods, hoping that some of it would rub off on her. She was struck by a thought. Why? She had given her parents a reason, but what was it really that drew her back to the kitchen?

~~~~~~~~~~~

It was 5:55 PM, almost time for Kirk to arrive, when Pipit entered the dining room and found her mother fussing over the floral centerpiece. "How pretty, Mother."

"Oh, hello, Liz," her mother said straightening up to look at her. "You look very nice in that crimson silk. One thing this memory loss has done for you, Liz—you've had the desire to look your best."

Puzzled, Pipit asked, "Even when I was beginning to fall for Kirk, didn't I try to look nicer?"

"A little, but there was still something that kept you from 'conforming,' as you put it."

"I must have been a real trial to you, Mother. I'm sorry."

Tears glistened in Julia's eyes as she reached for her daughter and gave her an affectionate hug. "Thank you, Liz. That soothes my heart more than you know." Releasing her, Julia quickly returned to the business of dinner. "Now, since you don't remember, we serve cocktails in the front room before dinner. I'm joining your father there now."

Hearing the bell, Pipit walked quickly to the door and opened it to a pensive looking Kirk. "Well, that's some rainy-day expression you're wearing, Mr. Morgan." She gave him a bright smile. "Come on into the sunshine."

He smiled. "Thanks, Liz. I feel better already. But I'm still upset over the way my parents treated you last night."

"Well, Kirk, I can hardly blame them. I ran out on their son. It's understandable that they would feel hurt and be a little resentful toward me."

He nodded slightly. "I had a talk with them last night," he added glumly, "but they are a little insistent about us setting a date for the wedding."

She changed the subject. "I found the ring, Kirk."

His face lit up. "Where?"

"Let's talk about it after dinner. Mother is serving cocktails in the front room."

"Good. I need one."

When they stepped across the foyer and into the living room, Julia and Calvin were already there. They greeted Kirk warmly.

~~~~~~~~~~~~~

After the delicious meal Mabel had prepared and Millie served, Pipit suggested that she and Kirk visit in the family room. It was a chilly February evening and not conducive to a walk. Calvin and Julia left the two to themselves.

Pipit seated herself on a chair and motioned Kirk to one of the couches.

"Please, Liz, sit here beside me."

She hesitated a moment, then got up and sat beside him. "That's much better," he said, his eyes admiring her. "I like you in that color."

She smiled. "Thank you." Reaching into a pocket, Pipit pulled out the ring she had found and handed it to Kirk. "It's a lovely ring, Kirk."

An expression of relief passed over his face. "I'm glad you like it. Will you wear it?"

"I can't. I'll have to fall in love with you all over again or wait until the memory of our relationship comes back to me. I will accept it then and we can go on as planned—unless there turns out to be a reason I can't. I don't want to have to return it to you and hurt you again."

"It won't matter, Liz, I'll be hurt regardless. My parents will be much happier if you wear it now."

"Don't they understand that I don't remember my feelings for you?"

"Yes, they understand, but they are very determined people."

"Do you want me to wear it, Kirk, knowing it wouldn't mean anything, that it wouldn't mean a commitment on my part?"

"I...uh, no, I guess not." He put the ring in his pocket, and slipped his arm around her shoulders. Grateful that she didn't resist, he gave her a squeeze and she laid her head upon his shoulder. They stayed that way for some time, silent, contemplative.

"Liz, how about dinner tomorrow night?"

"Sounds nice. How shall I dress?"

"It's upscale, so dress accordingly. I'll pick you up at 7:00"

After Kirk left, her feeling was one of relief that the ring was now back in Kirk's possession, and that he had accepted her reason for returning it. However, her relief was tempered by concern. Knowing how Kirk's parents felt, she wondered how they would handle this.

Chapter Thirty

Pipit was excited. Early that morning, Claire had called and said that a restaurant, where they had often lunched together, was having a fashion show during lunch, and asked if she would like to come. She had accepted eagerly. *Life here in Palm Springs was as busy and exciting as Linda had said*, she thought, slipping on another one of her nice dresses. Also, she had discovered a row of hats all along a top shelf of the closet. Finding one that went with the dress, she tried it on. It was a fine woven straw with a wide turned up brim. "Well, if I don't look like a model of fashion, myself," she said smiling at her reflection, noting as she had many times before, that when she smiled, she looked less plain. Preening in front of the mirror, she wondered again why Liz had refused to dress up, and at the moment she felt a little impatient with her 'alter ego.'

She found her mother in the foyer waiting for a friend to pick her up for lunch, an engagement she'd made over a week ago. "I'm sorry you can't go with us, Mother."

"Why, Liz, you look positively glamorous!"

"I do?" she asked, awe written all over her face. "But...I don't know if hats are in style."

Her mother smiled. "You always wore what you wanted to before, so why not now?"

Hearing the honk of a horn out in front, Pipit said goodbye to her mother, went out and opened the back door of Claire's waiting Lincoln Navigator SUV.

"Wow!" Linda exclaimed as Pipit climbed in. "Is this really our sister?"

"I think she's an imposter," Claire replied, smiling.

"You're right and her name is Pipit," came the response from the back seat.

"You look fabulous, Liz," Claire remarked, driving out and onto the street.

"That's what mother said. But I don't know if hats are in style."

They both laughed. "You really are Pipit, not Liz. Liz was always the kind who set her own style and even started trends herself. You were quite an individualist. However, hats are in if you want to wear them."

"Good."

"How are you and Kirk getting along, Liz?" Claire asked.

"When I explained the situation, he agreed to take it slow and actually start all over."

"That's amazing from what I know of Kirk," Linda said.

"What do you both think of Kirk?"

"We don't know him real well, Liz," answered Claire. "We're younger than you and he's about six years older than you are, so that's quite a gap. However, we did know his reputation—that he went through women like my husband goes through a bag of potato chips. He had very little patience with women. He dumped them if they did anything he didn't like, and there was always another one waiting in the wings. We were impressed with the way he pursued you, though, and stuck with it until you gave in and dated him. He seemed to really care for you, so naturally, that would make us like him."

~~~~~~~~~~~~

The three, seated around the small table at the restaurant, had just been served. Pipit took a couple of bites of the food she'd ordered. "Now if I could make food taste like this, I'd be happy," she exclaimed. "Do either of you cook?"

"No. We're both lucky—we married wealthy men."

"Somehow, I think it's good for a wife to cook for her husband once in a while and especially if she has children."

"Why?" they asked at the same time.

"Oh...I don't know. What if you had financial reversals and you couldn't afford a cook?"

Just then the fashion show began. Soft music played in the background as the hostess announced each model, pointing out in detail the fashion statement of the clothes. The models strolled through and around the patrons, stopping and turning, parading the upcoming new spring fashions from several prominent stores in Palm Springs.

Pipit, remembering her trips to downtown Phoenix and Scottsdale, watched, wide-eyed over the elegant, high class, stylish clothes. It seemed that the base, courser fads of fashion which were popular today among the general population, were not the fads of wealthy society. "My compliments to high society," she whispered to Claire. "Elizabeth would agree, also, I'm sure."

Claire laughed. "Maybe you know her better than I do, then."

~~~~~~~~~~~~

In spite of the fact that she had stuffed herself at the luncheon, Pipit was starving and looking forward to going out to dinner with Kirk tonight. She applied the last of her makeup, then went into the closet and pulled out her choice of evening wear, an elegant mint-green suit with mint-green embroidery down the center. Dabbing on her favorite perfume, she grabbed the small ivory purse that matched her heels, and walked quickly out of the bedroom into the foyer, hoping Kirk would arrive soon. Sure enough, the doorbell chimed. Before she could put her hand on the knob, her parents appeared to see them off. She opened the door and invited Kirk in.

"Good evening, Mr. and Mrs. Cabot," he greeted smiling.

Calvin nodded. "Good evening, Kirk."

Julia smiled at him warmly. "You two have a good time, tonight."

"Thank you," he said, guiding Liz out the front door and closing it behind them. "You look good enough to eat, Liz," he said, opening the car door for her.

"That's an interesting compliment, Kirk. My limited memory tells me I haven't seen you in a suit and tie. You look handsome."

"Thanks," he grinned. "I thought tonight would never get here," he said as he placed himself behind the wheel, and turned toward her. His fingers caressed her neck a moment, then he turned the key and drove out. "I'm taking you to another one of your favorite places, Liz, the Sirocco restaurant at the Renaissance Esmeralda Resort. Sound familiar?"

She shook her head. "I'm sorry, no."

His disappointment was apparent.

"Kirk, it has only been seven days since I arrived. Let's try to be patient. I want to remember as badly as you want me to, maybe more so."

Kirk didn't respond, so they rode in silence. Before long, he turned on East Palm Canyon Dr. and drove until they reached Indian Wells Lane. Turning into the resort, he parked the car and silently led her into the Sirocco. He spoke to the head waiter. "I have reservations for two. Kirk Morgan." Immediately, they were warmly welcomed and led to a table by a large window.

Pipit gazed out at the breathtaking view of waterfalls, fairways and mountain vistas. She looked around. The Sirocco was elegant, but had a warm, inviting ambiance. Off somewhere, a classical guitar was playing. Smiling at Kirk, she murmured, "How romantic."

"I hope so," he said, his eyes piercing hers.

"May I take your order for wine, sir?" the waiter asked.

"The lady will have nothing, but I will have Cabernet Sauvignon."

"I'll bring it right away, sir."

"This restaurant serves wines from an award-winning list of vintage, domestic and imported bottles."

"Maybe I ought to try a small glass. You make it sound good."

"No way, Liz. I don't want you falling asleep during the meal."

"It's just that I don't know that I do that. I kind of wanted to try it and see."

"I talked you into drinking a glass of wine one time after we'd been dating awhile. You were adamant about how it would affect you, but I didn't believe you. So...you showed me. Pretty soon, your face was in your plate, so to speak."

She laughed. "I don't want to miss one moment of this evening, so I guess tonight isn't the time to try it."

The waiter placed the wine before Kirk. "May I take your order now, Mr. Morgan?"

"Do you mind if I order for you, Liz? I know what you especially like here."

"Please do."

"We'd like two appetizers of Champagne Baked Hearts of Artichokes with Herb Butter."

"And the entree, sir?"

"The young lady here would like the Grilled Ahi Tuna with Fried Polenta, roasted Peppers and Saffron Leek Sauce. I would like Mushroom Crusted Rack of Lamb with Celery Root, Mashed Potatoes and Mustard Jus."

When the waiter left, Kirk said, "The two chefs here claim they use the freshest and finest regional ingredients, many of which they say are organically grown. Fish and seafood are flown in daily from both coasts."

"I'm thoroughly impressed, Kirk. I'm certain I'd be impressed with the price, too."

He shot her a surprised look, and smiled. "You have *never* mentioned price to me, before."

"If you remember, I worked for Matthew Melloy and he paid me. I worked hard for that five hundred dollars."

Kirk's face closed. "Has this Matthew contacted you since you've been home?"

"No, and I don't expect him to."

"Have you contacted him?"

"No. I've thought of calling the children, but I decided that it would do more harm than good at this point. However, I did promise them that I would go back and see them sometime."

He frowned. "Why?"

"Because they were very upset when I left, and so was I."

"You'll get over it and so will they."

"Kirk, I learned to love those motherless children, and they became attached to me."

"How could that be?" he asked, then added a little desperately, "You weren't with them all that long,"

"I know, but we were all living under emotionally fraught circumstances during that time. Maybe that made it possible, I don't know."

Kirk looked away, his face troubled, his hand closed into a fist. Pipit studied him, and pain pricked her heart. Somewhere deep inside, she cared for this man. Reaching over, she took his fist in both her hands and gently caressed it. "Kirk, I can only live in the present here because I don't remember the past. Let's enjoy the present together and hope the future brings us both happiness. We have to have hope."

His hand relaxed and took hold of one of hers. "Liz...Liz, I love you."

Those three words buoyed her heart. "It hurt me to see your pain a moment ago, Kirk, and for the first time, I know that in some hidden place I care for *you*."

He picked up her hand and brought it to his lips. "Thank you."

The waiter appeared, placing the delectable looking appetizers before them. "It looks wonderful, Kirk." Her smile was affectionate.

Letting out a hopeful breath, he returned her smile.

They ate in silence. The beautiful classical guitar music surrounded them, lending a glow of warmth to the communication and understanding that had just passed between them.

Chapter Thirty-One

Sunday turned out to be a satisfying day for Pipit and her family. Linda and Bruce, Claire and Kelley, and Kirk all came to dinner and afterward they retired to the patio and visited most of the afternoon. The weather was warm and sunny—the kind that draws golfers from everywhere to Palm Springs.

Later, when the family had dispersed, Pipit suggested that she and Kirk take a walk around the grounds. "I would like to know our history, Kirk—when we first met and when we got acquainted and when we began seriously dating."

"That's a subject I don't mind talking about," he replied, smiling. "Let me think where to start. Well, when you and your family moved to Palm Springs into the Rancho Mirage Area, your parents seemed to fall into the same social circles as my parents. You were a gangly fifteen-year-old and I was a twenty-year-old student at Harvard, home for vacation. I didn't pay much attention to you. You were just a kid.

"I got my MBA at Harvard and came home to work with my father. One day during a swimming party, there you were—a twenty-year-old all grown up. We were thrown together often on the weekends when you were home from Cal State. I tried to take you out when you were twenty, when you were twenty-one, and again after you had graduated and working at an art gallery here in Palm Springs. You turned me down every time...the first and only girl who ever turned me down, and I don't mind saying, I was burned over it.

"You left for Europe when you were twenty-five and only came home for holidays, and for both your sisters' weddings. When you came back to stay, about four years later, I tried again. Believe me, that's not my nature so far as women are concerned. But it paid off. You finally accepted a date. We dated for six months and got engaged. You know the rest, Liz."

"Were you ever engaged before, Kirk?"

"No. I could never get that far in any relationship until you."

"My family tells me that I was almost engaged three times, or rather had three other proposals."

"I know, and it bugged the hell out of me."

"Did you know those men?"

"I only knew one of them, but I understand the other two were from Palm Springs also."

"I've been told I broke it off with all three. Did I tell you why?"

"No. I really didn't want to talk to you about anyone else in your life. Don't any of your family know?"

"No. I guess I kept it to myself."

"Sounds like you," he said, reaching for her hand and leading her into the arbor where he slipped his arms around her. "I don't like talking about your past loves. How about the man in the here and now who loves you?"

Pipit squirmed. "Please, Kirk, I asked you..." His lips were on hers before she could finish. She couldn't help responding to his kiss, but this time, she was able to hold her emotions in check. When they pulled apart, she said, "Let's go inside, Kirk."

He smiled in triumph. "All right. Let's go plan what we're going to do next week."

~~~~~~~~~~~~

The following week was a whirl of activity. Monday night, Kirk came over with a dozen red roses for Valentines Day. Tuesday, he and Pipit went swimming in the Cabot's pool. Wednesday, the 16th, they attended the Frank Sinatra Celebrity Golf Tournament which brought the biggest names in show business to Coachella Valley for the benefit of the nonprofit Barbara Sinatra Children's Center at Eisenhower Medical Center. Pipit, again, mentioned how amazed she was that she had recognized so many of the stars when she couldn't even remember herself. Kirk and his family knew some of the stars, and introduced her. Her parents also attended as did Claire and Linda and their husbands.

Kirk told her a few of the important names who had golfed in Palm Springs: Gerald Ford, Eisenhower, George Bush, Ronald Reagon, Bob Hope and Bing Crosby.

Friday, the 18ᵗʰ, Pipit, her mother and sisters attended the Barbara Sinatra Children's Center benefit fashion show and luncheon. The narrator of the fashion show explained to the patrons that the clothes were furnished by Saks Fifth Avenue, debuting their spring collection. She informed them that they were designed by the House of Travilla, begun by the legendary designer Bill Travilla, reminding them that he created costumes and wardrobes for more than 250 screen legends in more than 200 of the most popular films and television series of all time. She explained to the ladies that Mr. Travilla's gift for enhancing a woman's femininity with his designs brought him respect and admiration from such superstars as Betty Grable, Jane Wyman, Ginger Rogers and Joan Crawford.

Pipit was entranced. She was also impressed that many wealthy people combined their social activities with fundraisers, contributing to worthy causes. *Did Elizabeth appreciate this*? she wondered.

Saturday night, Kirk took Pipit to Verdi's *Aida* at the magnificent McCallum Theater. Everyone who was anyone was there, Kirk told her. During the intermission people who knew her and her parents came up and greeted her. Awkwardly, she tried to reciprocate, but found it emotionally draining.

Sunday evening, Julia announced to her daughter that she was giving a party the following Saturday celebrating her safe return.

"Only if you will tell your...our friends about my amnesia. It's too exhausting trying to be polite and act as if I know them."

"Your father and I already added a note of explanation to the invitations we sent out last week."

Pipit sighed. "I'm about partied out, Mother, but that sounds nice."

"Did *anything* last week seem familiar?" Julia asked anxiously.

"No, but don't worry, Mother. Surely it can't go on much longer," she stated wearily.

~~~~~~~~~~~~

The following week turned out to be just as full. Monday, Kirk took Pipit golfing. Tuesday, her mother and sisters took her to lunch and then over to the art gallery where she had worked, hoping it would jog her memory. Wednesday, Kirk took her to the La Quinta Classic Horse Show. Thursday, her father took her out to see his date grove and then to dinner, just the two of them, for a father-daughter chat. Friday, Pipit begged off from all activities and spent the day resting, thinking and working with Mabel in the kitchen preparing for the party Saturday night. Strangely, she enjoyed this last activity as much as anything she had done the past week.

Chapter Thirty-Two

Julia was determined to make the party a major event. Preparations for it began several days before and continued early Saturday morning. The house was a beehive of activity. Maids were busy cleaning and freshening the house. Deliveries were arriving from the florist—bouquets of fresh flowers for the center-piece on the buffet table and other significant places.

Though a caterer provided the basic buffet foods, including unusual fruits, imported cheeses, shrimp and crab cocktails, Mabel, her daughter Millie, Pipit and Julia joined in preparing the French beignets. These were small custard filled, delicately sweet cake buns—Julia's specialty. By 6:00 PM everything was prepared and ready for the guests.

Just before the guests began to arrive at 8:30, Julia turned on the stereo system, and put in a collection of CD's appropriate for conversation. Fifty couples were invited. Julia had her usual butler employed for such occasions.

The guests were greeted by Julia and Calvin with their daughter, Liz, by their side. Julia then graciously directed them into the bar in the family room if they wanted cocktails, into the front room, family room or patio to visit with the other guests as they chose and to the dining room buffet when they desired to eat.

Outside, the weather was pleasant. The french doors of the family room were wide open as was the door of the living room. Guests rotated from the living room by way of the patio to the family room and bar, finding their way back to the dining room.

Kirk and his parents were among the first to arrive. Kirk took Pipit's hands in his, smiled and kissed her forehead. "I'll see you when you finish greeting all the guests."

Nan and Dick Morgan oozed with the appropriate courtesy as they greeted Pipit and her parents. After the effort of returning their greeting, Pipit was particularly happy for the next arrivals: her two sisters and their husbands.

All of the guests greeted Liz warmly, and offered hope for her speedy recovery. The last of the guests arrived. When Pipit turned to go into the dining room to get a plate of food, Kirk was by her side.

"At last, you're alone," he said, grinning.

She returned his smile. "Hi, I'm in need of some nourishment after greeting all those well-wishers. Want to join me?"

"You bet. The table of food looks wonderful, as always."

They escaped with their plates to an alcove of the patio and visited. After a short while, Julia, a small frown of irritation on her face, found them,

Quickly erasing the displeasure, she spoke to her daughter. "Liz, if you and Kirk are through eating, would you please mingle among the guests? After all, this evening is in your honor."

Pipit sighed. "We'll be right there, Mother."

She and Kirk mingled with the guests for awhile, but as it happens often with group visiting, they soon got separated. The music was pleasant and relaxing, and Pipit found herself able to enjoy the task a little more than she'd expected. She was unaware, at first, that the music had changed, but soon the haunting melody penetrated her consciousness. Startled, she realized it was *Matthew* by John Denver.

Moving to a quiet corner, she listened. The words in particular—*he came to ease my daddy's burden, he came to be my friend*—touched her heart. Poignant emotion overcame her. Squeezing through the guests, she rapidly walked to the peaceful solitude of the library. Closing the doors behind her, she was inundated by bewildering and conflicting emotions about the Matthew she had left behind in Arizona. *Why was this happening?* she asked herself. She had put all consideration of Matthew and his predicament out of her mind. There was nothing she could do to help while in this amnesiac condition...so why?

She remembered what Matthew's cousin, Randy, had told her, that the words in the song, *Matthew*, mirrored Matthew Melloy's own life—his selfless service to Randy and his uncle Arthur. It also reflected his courage, at the young age of fifteen, to endure his grief and loneliness alone, not inflicting it upon the family who took him in. No. Not alone. He brought his family's Bible, found almost untouched in the rubble left behind by the tornado's terrible destruction.

Unwelcome tears blurred her vision and she blinked furiously. "I can't do this! I have to be out there with the guests." No matter how she argued with herself, she was unable to stop the flood of emotion and tears.

The library doors opened abruptly. Distressed, Pipit quickly turned her back on the intruder.

Closing the doors quickly behind her, Julia asked, "What in the world are you doing in here, Liz? Kirk has been looking all over for you."

"P..please go get Dad, will you?...and don't tell Kirk where I am. Just tell him, I'll be with him soon."

Frowning at Liz's back, Julia turned and walked out. Soon, she and Calvin returned, locking the doors behind them. When Calvin saw his daughter's tear-stained face, his concern heightened. "What is it, Liz?"

"Where is our family Bible, Dad?"

"What?!" he asked, shocked at the question. "This hardly seems the appropriate time for that, Elizabeth."

"It certainly isn't!" Julia's patience was at an end. "What has that got to do with being a good hostess?"

Pipit knew she was acting irrational, but the words came out anyway. "I'm worried about Matthew." Tears rolled down her cheeks. "He found his family's Bible...where is *our* family Bible?"

Julia and Calvin looked at each other. "Maybe we should call Dr. Reuben," Julia said to her husband.

"No!" cried Pipit. "I don't need a doctor. I just need to have my question answered."

Calvin went over to a bookshelf, pulled down a Bible and slapped it down on the desk. "There! Now, may we go tend to our guests?" he asked sharply.

Tears still sliding down her cheeks, she said quietly, "Not yet. I need you to answer another question. Why did we stop reading it when we moved here?"

"How do you know about this?" her father asked, shocked. "Has your memory returned?"

"No. Kirk told me."

"Kirk?" her mother asked, incredulous. "Why would...how would Kirk know anything..."

"Apparently I told him about it when we were dating."

Her parents were silent. At last, her father muttered, "I...I don't know why we quit. The move here was a big step in our lives...we had so much to adjust to..." His voice trailed off.

"I see you don't really know." The tears suddenly dried up. Spying a box of tissues on the desk, she pulled one out and blew her nose. "I'm sorry. I know I've been overly emotional and have sounded quite illogical. What triggered all this was a song you had on the stereo. I'm fine now. Don't worry," she added a little too buoyantly.

She walked quickly to the door, unlocked it and walked out without glancing back at her stunned parents. Running to her bedroom, she quickly repaired her mascara, then rejoined the party.

Winding around the visiting guests, she spied Kirk who was watching for her. "Hi,"she said as she walked up to him. "I'm sorry. I needed to get away from the crowd a moment. Just another emotional jag caused by this darn situation of mine."

He scrutinized her. "Have you been crying?"

"Does it show?"

"A little."

"Let's get out of here, Kirk. Let's go for a walk until my eyes look better."

"Fine with me. I'd love to have you to myself."

They walked quickly until they were out of sight, then Kirk asked, "Why were you crying, Liz?"

"I don't know," she answered honestly.

"Surely something must have happened?"

Pipit felt guilty not telling him about it, but she truly didn't understand it herself, and she knew if she tried, it would just make him jealous...and for no reason. "The music, the crowds maybe...I don't understand it."

"I wondered if your parents were pushing it to have this party so soon."

"I think they were. Even though everyone here tonight knows my condition, it's still a strain because they know me, and I don't know them. Such an odd set of circumstances."

"How about we plan next week, Liz?" he suggested, wanting to take her mind off the situation.

She rubbed her tight shoulder. "I...uh think I need to have the next three days to myself to relax and let down, Kirk. Maybe the fast pace we've kept has slowed my recovery."

He was silent for so long, Pipit looked over at him. "What is it, Kirk?"

"I hate not seeing you for three days because Wednesday morning I have to go out of town on business. I won't be back until noon Saturday."

Her brow crinkled, and a small frustrated sigh escaped. "I'm sorry. I don't like the idea either of not seeing *you* for a whole week, Kirk, but I'm feeling a little overwhelmed at the moment."

Hiding his disappointment, he put his arm around her. "Then a week of rest will be good for you. When I get home Saturday, my father and I have an important business lunch at 1:00 at Twin Lakes Country Club. We should be through about 3:00, maybe 3:30. Would it be possible for you to meet me at the...." he stopped.

"What is it, Kirk?"

"I don't know whether to ask you to meet me at the gazebo as I did before. Maybe that gazebo is bad luck for us."

"I'll meet you there. I can get to the country club, but you'll have to tell me where the gazebo is."

He told her how find it from the parking lot of the club.

"I'm sure I can find it. Now, I think we'd better get back before Mother sends the bloodhounds out after us."

~~~~~~~~~~~~

After she and her parents had said goodnight to Kirk and the last of the guests, Pipit felt as empty and drained as the cocktail glass, inconsiderately left on the exquisite antique foyer table beside her. She was relieved that her mother had hired extra help to clean up. All she had to do was go to bed. Before going to her bedroom, however, she went into the library, picked up the family Bible and took it with her.

When she had washed her face and put on a nightgown, she picked up the book and got into bed, wondering why she brought it. Opening it up, she answered herself. "If fifteen-year-old Matthew Melloy found help reading this after his parents were killed, maybe I can find some help, too."

Chapter Thirty-Three

Sunday afternoon, Pipit's sisters and brothers-in-law came over to visit and to compliment their parents on a very successful party.

"Thank you," Julia said, pleased. "I believe everyone enjoyed themselves."

"How could they help but," Linda said, "the food was delicious, as always when you entertain, Mother."

"It was, Julia," Calvin added.

Pipit felt forced to say something. "Thank you, Mother and Dad, it was easier than I thought it would be. Now, when I see any of those people, they'll at least understand when I look a little blank and act a little stupid." She smiled.

"Why isn't Kirk here?" Claire asked.

"I told him that I needed to have a few days to myself. We've been going at such a fast pace, I feel a little strung out."

"I hope you and Kirk are planning on attending the big Debutante Ball this Friday at the country club," Linda said.

"Kirk is going out of town Wednesday and won't be back until Saturday noon."

"Oh no!" Linda exclaimed. "It's the biggest, most elaborate event of the year! Well...you can come with us, anyway, Liz."

"Thanks, but no thanks."

"You refused to attend what was supposed to be your *own* debutante ball, also, Liz," Claire added smiling.

"I did?" She looked over at her mother, knowing how much that must have upset her. "I'm sorry, Mother."

"That apology is a little late, Liz," her mother said, still chafing over her daughter's behavior in the library the night before.

After a couple of hours more of visiting, Claire and Kelley excused themselves and went home. To Pipit's relief, Linda and Bruce left soon after. She was still struggling over the strange episode from the night before, and it was difficult to visit.

Now alone with her parents, she said, "Dad, I need to talk to you about my car. It's probably still buried under the snow in the

Arizona mountains. I'll be needing it. I don't want everyone having to taxi me around indefinitely. Do you think it will be usable?"

"I'm afraid not, Liz. You left the door ajar, and when they pulled it out, I found out that the drifting snow had completely ruined the upholstery. It could have resulted in other problems too, so I just got rid of it. I've already bought you another car. It's a Buick Skylark. I've had it in one of our garages waiting until you were ready to be a little independent."

Happy and relieved, she got up and kissed her father. "How thoughtful of you, Dad. Thank you!"

"You're welcome, Liz."

"Did you also pay for the other car?"

"No. You did."

"Do I have any money of my own?"

"I'm sure you have some. Not much, however. You spent everything you made in Paris, plus the money I furnished you so you could travel around Europe with Elise."

"Who's Elise?"

"A friend of yours, a widow of fifty. She's a friend of the owner of the art gallery you managed."

"Oh. Well, I guess I'll go rummage around in my desk and see if I can find my check book."

"I believe it's in the small purse that the men found in your car, Liz," her mother said. "I placed it on a shelf in your closet the other day."

~~~~~~~~~~~~~

Monday morning, Pipit awakened feeling more relaxed knowing that nothing was pending, that no one was expecting anything of her. She decided not to eat breakfast with her parents and, instead, just rummage in the kitchen for something later. She luxuriated in the jacuzzi, then took her time dressing. Casual and relaxed was going to be her motto for the next three days. In spite of all this, however, she still felt unnerved over her reaction to the song, *Matthew.* "I have to forget it," she told herself sternly, but still her thoughts drifted to Merri and Danny, wondering how they were, hoping that Elinor wouldn't cause problems.

As soon as she felt her parents had finished their breakfast, she left the room and went into the kitchen to visit Mabel, hoping it would take her mind off what she couldn't control—Matthew's situation.

~~~~~~~~~~~~

All day Monday and Tuesday proved to be what she needed. She swam, walked, read and helped Mabel in the kitchen. Thoughts of Matthew and the children began to fade and feel far away—unreal. By Wednesday afternoon, she felt restless. Surprisingly, by Wednesday evening, the restlessness turned into loneliness for Kirk! Was she remembering her feelings for Kirk or was she falling for him all over again? *But how could that be?* she argued with herself. *I hardly know him.* In spite of this logic, the next two days dragged on endlessly. Friday evening, she found that her excitement at seeing Kirk on Saturday had accelerated to a such a point, she felt like a bubbling tea pot.

She awakened Saturday morning with butterflies in her stomach.

At breakfast, her father studied her. "You are certainly effervescent this morning, Liz. What's up?"

"It's strange, Dad, but I find that I've missed Kirk. I'm excited to see him again."

Julia beamed. "I'm happy to hear that, Liz."

Calvin studied her, puzzled. "Are you remembering or are you starting to care for him all over again?"

"I've asked myself this...and I don't know. During this amnesia, I have felt a lot of emotion I couldn't define, so emotions apparently aren't forgotten...at least in my case. They just have to be sorted out and placed where they belong. The mystery is—where do they belong and when will the pieces begin to fit together?"

Julia's face showed weariness from concern. "We'll be relieved when that mystery is solved, Liz, especially for your sake."

"The interesting thing, Mother and Dad, is I feel that I may be awakening to my love for you. It's feeling more comfortable and familiar here with you." The expression on both her parents faces made her want to cry. "At least I've made that much progress."

Julia blinked backed tears. "Thank you for telling us that, Liz."
Her father nodded in agreement. "We're anxious to have our daughter back whole, even though," he smiled, "we do like the 'Pipit' side of you."

~~~~~~~~~~~~

In her excitement, Pipit decided she'd leave early. She was driving herself to the country club, and in case she took a wrong turn, she'd have plenty of time to correct it. Besides—it was possible that Kirk would be there at 3:00 instead of 3:30, and she wanted to be there waiting for him.

She had picked out a dress to wear, certain that Kirk would be wearing a suit since he was attending a business meeting. Studying herself in the mirror, she decided that the sparkle of happiness in her eyes made her more attractive; she hoped Kirk noticed. And she hoped her excitement would make it apparent to Kirk how much she had missed him.

Kissing her mother goodbye, she said, "Wish me well, Mother. This feels like the first time I've driven."

"You were always an excellent driver, Liz." Julia scrutinized her oldest. "You know, you look absolutely glowing."

Pleased that her mother noticed, she smiled. "I'm glad it shows."

Sliding behind the wheel of a car felt natural, she realized, as she turned the ignition of the new Skylark. The feeling of independence exhilarated her. She felt confident, as well, since she had a map, and had been told by her father how to get to the country club.

Taking several different streets out of Rancho Mirage, she followed her father's directions. Eventually, Twin Lakes Country Club appeared on the right. Turning into it, she felt a flutter of excitement. She glanced at her watch and saw that it was only 2:45. Parking the car as close as she could, she got out and found the path that Kirk had told her about. Stopping a moment, she took a couple of deep breaths to calm her racing heart. Sauntering slowly, she enjoyed the beautiful grounds, the flowers and the tall graceful palms whose fronds gently swayed in the warm gentle breeze of this first Saturday in March. There was a feeling of spring in the air, or was it in her heart?

As the path rose upward toward a cluster of trees, her excitement increased. But suddenly, something inside her changed. Like a door slowly opening, she knew she had seen this path before! Her heart pounded. Her chest heaved with breaths that almost came too fast. Entering the stand of trees, she stopped only a moment to catch her breath. Moving on, the path curved around a large fan palm, then dipped sharply, and there it was on the right—the *gazebo*. She froze—a heaviness descended upon her. A deluge of memories came tumbling into her mind so fast she could hardly take them in. She turned to run, but stopped by the fan palm, struck with the realization that she had stopped here before—had, in fact, *hidden behind* the trunk of this very tree! It was then that she remembered—with blinding clarity—why she had run away almost two months before.

Leaning against the tree for support—the occurrence—so clear in her mind, seemed to be happening all over again. Reliving it—the pain felt unbearable. She slumped to the ground. She remained huddled behind the tree, shaking. A glimpse of the time told her it was almost 3:00. She had to leave before Kirk came! But the pain inside her chest rose up into her throat, choking her. Bowing her head, she rested her chin upon clenched hands, unable to move.

At last, the shaking abated. She stood up and walked unsteadily down the path toward the car, her mind still whirling with returned memories, now overlaid with memories of her life as Pipit. *I have to get home and sort it all out*, she thought. "But this time," she murmured, "I'm not going to run away. I'm going to face it. My alter-ego 'Pipit' has done that much for me, at least."

Opening the car door, she sat down heavily, feeling as though a knife had been thrust into a still tender wound. However, the pain was much greater this second time—the dimension of her understanding of Kirk, and her feeling for him had broadened—her perspective deepened—as though she were viewing three dimensional scenes on a wide movie screen, but from different angles at the same time, melding the different aspects of her grief into one big boiling pot.

In spite of this, while driving home her mind amazingly seemed to rise above the maelstrom of emotion and calmly deliberate on how to break the news to her family. Learning from her 'Pipit side' that all the painful things she'd kept to herself through the years, in order to save her family distress, had only caused them confusion and pain. She had to be open and frank now, and not allow them to suffer anymore because of her.

When she entered the house, every muscle quivered in apprehension at the prospect of breaking the news to her family. She made her legs move toward her room. Before she could reach it, however, she ran into her mother.

Julia's surprise at seeing her daughter back so soon, turned to concern. "Liz, you're pale. What is it? I thought you were meeting Kirk."

"I...I was supposed to, but—my memory has come back."

Liz said it in such a flat voice, it didn't register at first. "It has?" Julie finally asked. Liz nodded. Julia, tears filling her eyes, opened her arms and gathered her daughter to her bosom. "Oh, Liz! I'm so happy to have you back."

She clung to her mother. "I need to tell you how it happened, and why I ran away, but I...I think I need to be alone for a while first."

Julia released her daughter, studying her face. "All right, Liz." Her heart full of apprehension, she watched Liz move down the hall to her room.

Immediately, Julia went into her own bedroom and dialed Calvin. His comforting voice answered. "Cal, something is terribly wrong. Liz went to meet Kirk only an hour ago and she's already back, looking pale and shaken. She told me her memory had returned, but the way she said it frightened me."

What should have been an occasion for celebration was overshadowed by concern. "I'll be right there, Julia. I think you had also better call Claire and Linda and have them come over."

Not long after she'd hung up from calling her daughters and telling them that there was news about Liz and to come over as quickly as they could, the phone rang. Julia picked it up and said, "Hello."

"Hello, Mrs. Cabot. This is Kirk. I'm worried. Liz was supposed to meet me at Twin Lakes Country club at 3:30. I'm still waiting and it's 3:55. Is she there by any chance?"

Julia was more than puzzled. Whatever caused Liz to look so pale and distraught, it wasn't because she had seen Kirk! Not certain what she should tell him, Julia replied. "Kirk, Liz's memory came back to her and apparently she needed to return home."

"Her memory? It did? Oh...that's great news!" Julia could hear the relief and excitement in his voice. "May I speak with her?"

"She indicated she needed to tell her family first, Kirk," she explained, not certain if that were the case, but she knew *they* needed to hear about it first. "I'm sure she'll be anxious to talk with you afterward."

"All right, Mrs. Cabot. Tell her to call me as soon as she can."

"I certainly will, Kirk."

~~~~~~~~~~~~

By 4:45, the Cabot family, with the exception of Liz, was assembled in the family room discussing their happiness over the return of Liz's memory, as well as their anxiety over her frightening reaction.

Calvin stood up and moved to the door decisively. "I'm going to go ask Liz if she can come out now and tell us about it."

Liz heard the knock, and knew it was time to go talk with her mother. She opened the door. "Dad! I didn't expect to see *you*."

"Your mother called me and your sisters. She told us that your memory has returned." Liz nodded, but Calvin saw no joy in her eyes. "She felt that something was terribly wrong. Is that right, Liz?"

"Yes, Dad. I'm ready to tell all of you about it."

Together, they walked to the family room. Liz gave her sisters a small grateful smile. "Thank you for coming."

"You really have your memory back, Liz?" Linda asked almost in disbelief.

"Yes."

"We're happy for you, for us," Claire said, "but *you* don't seem happy about it. Why? Tell us, Liz. You're scaring us."

Liz sat down in one of the chairs and faced her family, dreading to tell them the terrible news. "I'm very relieved to have my memory back—but with it came a painful experience."

"Are you going to tell us about it?" Claire asked pointedly.

"Yes." She began slowly, hesitantly. "I was supposed to meet Kirk at the Twin Lakes Country Club in the gazebo. I left early so I could be there waiting for him. Well...when I was walking up the path toward it, something inside me started to change. The path looked familiar, but at the same time....a feeling of..." She searched for a word that would describe it. "When I turned a bend and saw the gazebo, a feeling of...of oppression came over me. I stopped. It was then that my memory came back...all at once...so overwhelmingly that I could hardly take it in. I turned around to run. But instead, I stopped by a fan palm, recalling that I had hidden behind it when...when something occurred two months ago. It was at that moment—I remembered why I had run away." She paused, not wanting to go on.

Her family waited, fearful and anxious. "Go on, Liz. We're here for you," her father said.

She took several deep breaths trying to ward off the crushing emotions. "When I remembered, it was as if it were...as if it were happening all over again."

Walking quickly up the path, Liz's excitement escalated. She was to meet Kirk in the gazebo at 7:00. It was only 6:30, but she wanted to be waiting for him when he arrived. He'd been tied up with business all day and he'd asked her to meet him. She looked down at her engagement ring, remembering his proposal the night before and his happiness when she accepted.

Just before turning the bend in the path, she heard familiar voices. Slowing down, the gazebo came into view, and to her surprise, Kirk's father had just stepped up into it and grabbed his son's hand. Kirk had arrived early, too!

Stepping quickly behind the tree so as not to be seen, she decided to wait until his father left. She wasn't in any mood to see Dick Morgan. Their voices floated up clearly to her ears.

"Congratulations son! Your mother told me about your engagement just as I got off the plane today. She said you were meeting Liz here, and since I had planned a business golf game here at the club,

I thought I'd come over and give you a pat on the back for a job well done. You've earned that partnership."

"Thank you, Dad. It was hard work, but I did it..she finally fell for me."

Dick Morgan chuckled. "If she only knew we planned this out together. When I urged you to marry the girl, I really didn't think you'd succeed since she'd turned you down so many times years before."

Kirk smiled. "Back then, she had no idea the reason I kept asking her out was because some friends of mine bet me that I couldn't seduce her. I took the bet. I was sure they'd won, but the laugh is on them. The ultimate seduction is—marriage."

Dick Morgan's laugh was ugly, guttural. "You're right, Kirk! When did you set the date?"

"We haven't yet."

"Make it soon, son. When I asked you, our financial problems were sticky, and now our cash flow is worse. I don't know if Cal Cabot will go for a merger of some of our assets or not, but we've got to get the show on the road and try, or there won't be a business for you to be a partner in. The stock market hasn't been good to me this year, so set the date for your marriage as soon as you possibly can. It will take time to work on Cabot. I've got to go now and meet my golf appointment. See you at home."

Liz, shocked and disbelieving at what she'd just heard, wondered for a moment if she had imagined it. But the moment passed, and her trembling legs led her back down the path to her car, almost as if they had a will of their own. She was numb. As she drove, the shock, the grief, the numbness passed, and she was left only with a cold rage. She knew what she had to do.

Her mother and father were at a dinner party so she could pack and leave before they got home. She had to get away...far away. Facing Kirk right now, would be too painful. Bitterly, she laughed. It had happened again. Kirk was marrying her for her money—just as the other three had tried to do! "I've been such a fool! Of course they all wanted to marry me for my money, who would want to marry the 'ugly duckling' of the Cabot family?"

"Now you know everything," Liz said quietly.

During most of the account, Julia had covered her face in horror. Calvin's face had turned hard and angry. Claire and Linda had stared in open-mouthed shock.

Now—they all sat there stunned, speechless.

Liz stared at the floor, feeling completely drained—caved in. After a few moments, she broke the silence. "When I overheard this that day two months ago, I didn't want any of you to be as upset as you are now. I thought that if I could get away for a while and get my emotions under control, none of you need know why I decided to break it off with Kirk. So I left a note, and decided to go some place different—a ski resort. In the snow storm, I took a wrong turn. You know the rest."

Her mother shook her head in distress. "Oh, Liz, if only you would have confided in us, we..."

"I apologize to all of you for not confiding. That's why I'm doing it now. Thank you for being here to support me this afternoon." Her voice broke, but she quickly steeled herself.

"But Liz," Claire said, "I'm confused. You indicated the other three men wanted to marry you for your money. I don't believe that."

"I don't either," Linda stated.

Calvin drew his brows together in troubled thought, but Julia added her opinion. "I agree with your sisters, Liz. I could tell—anyone could tell that each of those young men cared for you. They couldn't have faked *that*."

"They were only attracted to me because they couldn't get what they wanted from me as they could from the other girls they took out."

Another round of shock registered on her mother's face, as well as the other three.

It took some moments for her mother to get a grip on herself. Finally, she spoke, purposely ignoring Liz's last distressing revelation. "Liz, those boys came from well-to-do families. How could they be wanting to marry you for your money?"

Calvin gently contradicted her. "Julia, their parents weren't all that well-to-do. They were people who desperately wanted to be part of the social set. They mortgaged their souls, so to speak, in order to do so." Julia's brows rose in astonishment.

Liz went on, anxious to get it all over with. "Even though I wasn't seriously interested in Rob, Charles or Kevin, I discovered, one way or another, they each wanted to marry me mainly because of your wealth, Dad. That was hard for me to learn. After that, as you know, I left for Paris."

"No wonder it took Kirk so long to convince you to go out with him when you returned home from Paris," Linda said. "And how devastating it was for you to finally fall in love with him, and...and then find out that he too..." She didn't dare go on.

"Speaking of Kirk, Liz," Julia said through angry tight lips, "he called, worried over why you didn't show up at the gazebo. I told him your memory had come back and that you may have wanted to tell us about it first. He seemed thrilled about it and told me to tell you to call him as soon as you could."

This news brought more disturbing and conflicting emotions to Liz. She stood up. "May I be excused now? I need to go to my room and sort it all out. If Kirk calls, Mother, tell him that I'd like him to come over tomorrow evening." Her mother nodded, grim-faced.

Before Liz could reach the door, her father stopped her and encircled her in his arms. "Liz, I can't tell you how grieved we are to hear about Kirk."

His words brought tears dangerously close and her rigid body relaxed a little. Her voice came out in a hoarse whisper. "Thank you, Dad." She turned back to the little group—feeling their grief and empathy. "Thank you...for listening...for being here for me. I love you all."

~~~~~~~~~~~~

Liz stood by her bedroom window watching Horace working at a flower bed, remembering the many enjoyable conversations she'd had with him. She gazed for some time at the beautifully land-scaped grounds. The peacefulness that emanated from the beauty her eyes beheld, contrasted markedly with the upheaval going on inside her.

Turning from the window, she sat down on the small couch, her hands clenching and unclenching, unable to let down, let go. Every muscle, every nerve felt intractable, her heart felt iron-hard—heavy. Yet, there was the ache, deep and tangible over having been twice rejected by the same man! Not in reality, of course, but experiencing it, forgetting it, then the sudden vivid remembrance had the same excruciating effect.

As the afternoon wore on into evening, the shock of all she'd experienced began to wear off. Suddenly, bitterness and anger propelled her off the couch. "How dare Kirk pursue me for the reasons he did!" she muttered, moving back and forth. "How dare he take his father's challenge! How dare he express love for me! How could he betray me like that?!"

Several hours later, exhausted, and half-sick to her stomach, she changed from her dress, washed her face and slipped on silk pajamas and house slippers. Opening the bedroom door, she padded down the hall toward the kitchen. She pulled out a carton of milk from the refrigerator, poured herself a glass and sat down at the table sipping it. Feeling tense, almost to the breaking point, she wondered if she would ever sleep again.

Back in the bedroom, she turned off the lights and slid between the fine woven sheets and lay there rigid for some time. Finally, turning on her side, she curled up and willed herself to relax, her mind to turn off.

At 2:00 AM, after tossing and turning, a remarkable understanding finally found its way into her overworked mind. She hadn't *grieved enough*; she hadn't had time! When she'd learned the shocking truth of Kirk's deceit two months ago, she had rushed out of town. Twenty-four hours later, she found herself wandering in the mountains without any memory of the incident, her grief suspended, repressed. She wasn't suffering *twice* over it as her emotions had led her to feel—she hadn't had time to suffer over it even once!

Gradually, her muscles relaxed, allowing her heart to give into the grief, the tears to flow mercifully.

Chapter Thirty-Four

The bright sunlight streaming through the windows surprised Liz. It seemed but a moment ago that the moonlight cast its soft glow over the room. Looking at the time, she was shocked that it was late—ten o'clock! She was grateful that she'd finally fallen into a heavy, forgetful sleep. She lay there staring at the ceiling, thinking of what was ahead of her, dreading the day.

An enveloping sadness crept around her heart and stayed. Gone was the anger toward Kirk. She realized she still loved him, or at least, still had feelings for him.

Her growling stomach drove her out of bed. Stepping into house slippers and slipping on a matching silk robe, she shuffled out of the bedroom and headed for the kitchen. Though food didn't sound good, she knew she had to put something into her stomach or be sick.

The smell of coffee lingered in the kitchen, but Mabel wasn't there. Opening up the refrigerator, she pulled out a jug of milk, and found a box of cold cereal. She was spooning in the last bite when both her parents walked in.

"We saw your bedroom door ajar, Liz," her mother said, "so we came looking for you."

Surprised to see her father home at this hour, she looked at him questioningly. They sat down at the table with her. Liz felt a pang of concern as she gazed at their faces. Her mother's face was drawn, her lids swollen as if she'd been crying. Her father's eyes looked heavy.

"Neither one of you got much sleep last night either, did you?"

Ignoring the question her father asked, "How are you, Liz?"

"I may be doing better than you. I'm sorry to put you through this."

"No more of that, Liz," her father said, his voice tired and exasperated. "We're family, remember? So how are you?"

"I'm better than I was last night, Dad, thanks. But I'm dreading the visit with Kirk. Has he called?"

"He called last night," her mother said. "I answered the phone and I don't think I hid my feelings toward him very well. He's concerned and wants to come over this afternoon. I told him I would ask you, and call him back. He wanted to know why you couldn't call him instead of me. I told him you weren't feeling very well."

"Thank you, Mother. I didn't want to even speak to him until we were face to face. Will you please call him for me, and tell him this afternoon is fine. I want to get it over with."

~~~~~~~~~~~~~

Liz, dressed casually in jeans and a blue T-shirt, stood before the arbor waiting for Kirk. It was almost 2:00 and he was due any minute. She had instructed her mother to send him out here because it was more private than the house. The warmth of the afternoon was mellow, spring-like. The flowers of the acacia trees were beginning to bloom, producing their masses of yellow balls, filling the air with a sweet fragrance. A black and yellow oriole, perched on one of the limbs, warbled softly, interrupting with harsh metallic trills. *Spring is a time for happiness*, she thought. If only...

"Liz?" His voice was barely audible, and unsure.

Slowly, she turned around and faced him. "Hello, Kirk." She stepped inside the arbor.

He followed and sat where she indicated, across from her, his face troubled. "Your mother said that your memory has returned. But something is wrong. What is it?"

Liz's throat hurt. In a voice hoarse and hesitant, she replied, "I remembered why I ran away."

Her expression alarmed him. "I'm almost afraid to ask—but why did you?"

She'd gone over this in her mind several times, and now she couldn't think where to start. With the fingers of both hands, she rubbed her forehead a moment, the lump in her throat more painful. She wanted to cry...but not for herself, for Kirk; he looked so vulnerable, so fearful. "I...I left early yesterday to meet you in hopes you could arrive earlier. I wanted to be there waiting for you. I missed you while you were gone." An expression of hope crossed his face, making it more difficult for her. "As I walked up the path toward the gazebo, something started happening to me. The path was familiar. When I came to the fan palm where the path curved, and dipped down to the gazebo, all the memories came rushing back so fast I wanted to run to my car, but all I could do was lean against the tree. It was then that I remembered why I ran away."

Kirk leaned forward, his breathing heavy with anxiety. "Go on, Liz," he whispered.

"Remember when I was supposed to meet you at the gazebo over two months ago?" He nodded. "I was so happy about our engagement the night before that I wanted to get there early, just as I did yesterday—and I did." She could see that it hadn't sunk in. He only looked puzzled, waiting for her to go on. "I arrived early— almost the same time you did, and moments before your father walked up to congratulate you."

Kirk frowned. "You couldn't have, I didn't see you."

"Just before I started down the path, I heard your father's voice. I stopped and waited behind the tree until he left because I wasn't in the mood to see him. Your voices floated up to my ears as clearly as if I were right there."

Still, Kirk frowned, puzzled...then slowly the frown disappeared, and the blood drained from his face. "You...you heard our...conversation?"

Liz nodded.

His mouth opened to speak, but instead he bent his head and stared at the ground. One hand reached up and rubbed his mouth. The moments, fraught with emotion, dragged by unbearably for Liz. Placing both elbows on his thighs, he gripped his hands together and continued to stare at the ground. Liz waited.

After some time, he sat back and gazed at her, agony in his face. "No wonder you ran away," he managed to say. "But, Liz, it wasn't what it seemed...that is, I didn't mean what I said. I only said those things to my father because that's the way he thinks...the seduction part, that is. He's had mistress after mistress." He waited for Liz's reaction, but she gave him none.

He continued, but the words came out slowly, hesitantly, hoping to tell her in a way she could forgive him. "But...that isn't all. I...I need to go back to when I tried to date you years ago. Yes, my friends bet me that I couldn't...that I couldn't seduce you. Yes, I took their bet, but..." He leaned forward, his voice rose, "it was because I was so damned intrigued by you, Liz. That's the real reason I tried to date you. I swear to you...Liz, that's the truth.

"It's true that my dad challenged me to marry you, but it didn't take much because I was still intrigued by you. However, the joke's on me, because I really fell in love with you, Liz." He studied her, looking for a sign that she believed him.

"You deceived me, Kirk. You were marrying me for my money...for Dad's money."

"No, Liz." The words were wrung from him in a paroxysm of agony. "I was marrying you because I loved you, and because you're strong. I need your strength behind me...I" His voice broke; his eyes watered. Liz waited silently until he gained control. "Believe me, Liz, I only said those things to my father to get his approval...I...I never have had his approval. I thought that maybe this one time he'd..." A single tear moved down his cheek. He couldn't go on, embarrassed at confessing his weakness.

Liz blinked back her own tears, for she knew it was true that he'd never had his father's approval. Touched by his vulnerability, she desperately wanted to fill his need. "I believe you, Kirk. And...I believe you love me."

Profound relief crossed his face. "You do? Then...you forgive me for..." He couldn't repeat it.

"I forgive you, Kirk."

"Thank you, Liz, thank you!" He rose, took a step and held his arms open toward her. "Then...you'll...marry me?"

"No."

Looking as though she had slapped him, he stumbled backwards and sat down heavily. When he'd gained some composure, he leaned toward her, his eyes pleading. "Liz...I need you! I can be the man Dad always wanted me to be with you by my side."

Liz got up and sat beside him, taking one of his hands in hers. "Kirk, you can't be the man your dad always wanted you to be because your father will never be satisfied. He'll always be critical and unapproving—no matter what you do, no matter how you try. Besides, do you really want to be that kind of a man?"

Kirk pulled his hand away and put his arm around her shoulders, and held her tightly for several moments before he could speak. "You're right, Liz. I...I haven't wanted to admit it because I...want money, and my dad has it. I...maybe I want the power it brings."

"You are smart and capable, Kirk. You don't need your father. Why don't you move away from here and be your own man?"

Kirk stood, pulling Liz to her feet with him. He slid his arms around her and held her close. "I can do that if you'll marry me, Liz. I'll give up any hope of money from my father if you will." He leaned back and gazed anxiously into her face.

Pulling her arms free, she took his face into her hands, stood on tiptoe and kissed him tenderly on the lips, then spoke gently, "I love you, Kirk...but I can't marry you."

In desperation, he took her in his arms and kissed her insistently. Liz realized that she no longer felt the physical attraction she once had. All she felt was sadness that she no longer loved him enough to marry him. Something had died there at the gazebo two months ago. And she knew it was permanent.

Stricken, Kirk let go of her, feeling the change in her. "I don't know what I'll do without you, Liz."

She took his hand, her eyes averted, thinking. Marrying Kirk would destroy them both. His weakness, his need for approval would be transferred to her. He would never gain the strength he needed to be his own man.

Finally, she looked up into his sorrow-struck face and spoke tenderly, "You will find someone else, Kirk, I know you will. But not here in Palm Springs in your father's shadow." She paused. "I feel we both need time to think, and make some decisions about our lives. I think it's best you go now." She stepped out of the arbor. He reluctantly followed her and accepted the hand she held out to him. Hand in hand they walked slowly toward the house and around to his car.

Julia had watched them through the window as they walked together, holding hands, and she was frightened. She didn't want her to marry Kirk! Her night of soul searching had brought about some painful introspection. If she hadn't insisted on living here and wearing their wealth on their backs, so to speak, would Liz have been hurt like she had? She was still gazing out of the window when a voice spoke.

"Mother?"

Julia turned from the window. "Where's Kirk?" she asked apprehensively.

"He's gone home."

"I saw you walking hand in hand. Did you make up?"

"During our conversation, I realized that Kirk really does love me, and I told him that I loved him." Her mother gasped. "Let's sit down, Mother, and I'll tell you everything that happened between us."

Chapter Thirty-Five

Julia, Linda and Claire, planned a full week of activity for one purpose only—to take Liz's mind off Kirk. All week they attended art shows, a fashion show, a musical, golfing and lunches at nice restaurants. Calvin joined them for dinner two different evenings. Though sadness, and anxiety over Kirk hung on, all the activity did have its desired effect; Liz found herself enjoying her family in a way she never had. They laughed together, enjoyed memories together and felt closer than they had for a long time. It wasn't until Friday afternoon, after having lunch with her mother and sisters at their favorite French restaurant, Gigi's, that Liz begged off going with them to a charity ball that evening. "If I have to flash a glowing smile at one more of the intelligentsia of Palm Springs, I think I'll throw up."

Julia and her daughters glanced at each other. It was Claire who voiced the thought. "Well, we have the 'real' Liz back at last," then the three burst out laughing.

Liz just rolled her eyes at them. "Why don't we get in the SUV and go exploring the desert, and get sand in our shoes hiking?"

Linda and Claire stuck up their noses at the suggestion. "You know we don't like hiking in the desert...or anywhere else." Linda said.

"Except the golf course," added Claire, smiling.

"How about you, Mother," Liz asked, a twinkle in her eyes, "are you game?"

Julia smiled. "You know the answer to that, Liz."

"All right then, I guess I'll just have to call Kirk and..."

"No!" they chorused. "We'll go with you."

Liz laughed. "Gotcha! Never mind. I think I'll just take a swim and watch an old movie. If you want to join me instead of going to the ball and getting bored stiff, feel free."

~~~~~~~~~~~~

The weekend dragged by for Liz. She could hardly keep from picking up the phone and calling Kirk to see how he was doing. When Sunday evening rolled around, Kirk came over. Standing on one foot then the other at the doorstep, he smiled hesitantly. "Will you go for a ride with me, Liz? I would like to tell you something."

So glad to see him, she replied with eagerness. "Yes, Kirk. Come in while I tell my parents I'm leaving."

"I would rather wait outside, Liz—for obvious reasons."

When Calvin and Julia learned where Liz was going, they protested.

"Don't worry, it will be all right, I promise you."

Liz and Kirk were silent while he drove to that part of Rancho Mirage where the homes gradually ascended the lower mountain slopes.

Liz didn't have to ask where he was taking her. She knew. He drove up the familiar area, winding past all the homes to the highest point of the road. Parking in the only vacant lot left, which belonged to his father, he got out, opened the door for Liz and together they hiked to their usual spot on this brown, rock-studded slope.

They sat down on their favorite rock and looked out over the valley. This was the place where they always went when they wanted to be totally alone, and when they didn't have time to get into Kirk's jeep and go to Palm Canyon—the canyon belonging to the Cahuilla Indian tribe.

Liz's heart was heavy, realizing they would never hike together again. Kirk loved nature and hiking as much as she did. Gazing dreamily over the valley, she thought of the happy times they had spent walking through Palm Canyon, which boasted of having 3000 palms growing in the region. The lushness of the canyon attracted a multitude of wildlife, especially birds. Last December, she and Kirk had watched hoards of cedar waxwings, Lawrence's goldfinches, and western bluebirds descend upon the canyon.

She blinked back tears and tried to be light. "It feels good to be here, Kirk. I would rather associate with the lizards and the rattlesnakes than go to one more social activity or go to one more public place where we might run into the 'creme de la creme.'"

Kirk smiled. "I see the rebel of the Cabot family is back in full swing."

She returned his smile with a small sad one. "How are you, Kirk?" she asked, studying his face.

"I've been better. I've missed you, Liz."

"I've missed *you*, Kirk."

He gazed at her intently. "Any glimmer of a chance you've changed your mind?" he asked, his eyes pleading for an affirmative answer.

"I wish there was, Kirk, because I still care for you—but no."

He looked away, his face grim with defeat. Picking up a rock, he threw it with a violent jerk of his arm. "I didn't think so." After a time, still looking straight ahead, he said, "What I wanted to tell you is—I've applied for several jobs in California. I told my father this morning that I was no longer going to be working for him, that he needed to find someone to replace me."

Liz let out a sigh of relief. "Thank you for telling me." A tear escaped and slid down her cheek. "I feel that things are going to go better for you from now on, Kirk. Remember, I'll be pulling for you."

Kirk turned to look at her and saw the tear. He pulled her close. "Thank you for caring about me. I guess...deep down in my gut, I never really felt I would be lucky enough to keep you. You're too good for me, Liz."

"No, Kirk..." So choked up, she couldn't go on. They sat together for some time, hanging on to the closeness they felt, knowing that it soon had to end.

"Could I have one good kiss goodbye?" he whispered.

She nodded. He kissed her long and desperately, and she returned it, dispirited over their final parting.

Chapter Thirty-Six

O nce more Liz forgot to pull the blinds the night before, so Monday morning bright rays of sunshine awakened her. Glancing around the lovely room gloriously bathed in light, she wished her feelings reflected the cheerfulness it invited. Instead, she felt lost and lonely. Her blissful state as 'Pipit,' was gone. She had to face reality—who she was, and what she'd done with the almost thirty-one years of her life.

Paris had been an escape, and she loved the culture she found there. The many visits to the Louvre, and the trips around Europe had enriched her life remarkably—but at the moment, it felt as though her life had been one self-indulgence after another.

"What am I going to do now?" she murmured. The prospect of working in another art museum dismayed her. But she needed to go to work; she couldn't go on living off her father at her age!

Several times she'd thought of teaching art history on the college level. This had sounded interesting to her, and at the moment it still did. Struck by this thought, she realized she might be able to get a teaching position at the California State University branch right here in the Palm Springs Area called Coachella Valley Campus.

She hadn't thought of it before because she'd wanted to get away from Palm Springs. Now, it sounded good to live at home and teach. With a masters and her experience working in a Paris art gallery for five years, it was unlikely she would need to get her doctorate to teach at CVC.

This thought so lifted her spirits, she quickly stepped out of bed, threw on a swimming suit and ran out for an invigorating swim. It required only a few laps to make her realize how out of condition she was. Breathlessly, she pulled herself up out of the pool, slipped on the cover-up and walked to the patio where her parents were having breakfast.

"Good morning, Liz. Have a good swim?" her father asked, smiling.

"I did. It felt good and it released some tension." She sat down and told her parents she'd decided to apply for a teaching position at CVC. Their reactions were gratifying.

She got up and kissed them both. "I hope I'll soon be independent so you won't have to support me at all anymore. I think I'll go down to the campus this morning and get an application."

~~~~~~~~~~~~~~

The trip down to the university had given her life some purpose. She set the application on her desk, and went into the closet to change into something casual. As she did so, she was hit by a feeling of guilt; a promise broken.

She had promised Merri and Danny that she would visit them soon, and she realized that to a child 'soon' is an entirely different concept than it is to an adult. Now that her memory had returned, she could go back as a whole person. *I've got to go now*! she thought. The sudden sense of urgency surprised her.

Leaving the dressing area, she sat down on the chair and thought about it, wondering how Matthew was, wondering if his sight had returned...if not, what was the situation with Elinor? She didn't relish thinking about this; she was still trying to get her equilibrium after the emotional 'yo-yo' she'd been on over Kirk. Feeling a little unnerved, she got up, stepped to the window and stared out. "I need a few more days to get myself grounded before I go see the children...and yes, Matthew. I need at least three more days." She made the decision to leave for Arizona early Friday morning.

~~~~~~~~~~~~~~

Liz broke the news of her pending trip at dinner. By the look of concern on her mother's face, and the frown on her father's, she knew they were not pleased.

"I promised Merri and Danny that I would come and visit. When you make a promise to children, it should be kept. You both taught me that by your own examples."

Neither Calvin nor Julia could think of a good counter argument, but Julia made a stab at it anyway. "Liz, from what you told us, Mr. Melloy is embroiled in a custody problem with his mother-in-law. Don't you think it would be best to visit when that is all resolved? After all, you've been through a lot. You need to heal."

"I understand what you're saying, Mother, but I would like to get the visit over with so it won't interfere with my application and follow-up at CVC. Also, I feel at loose ends right now, so maybe it will take my mind off my own problem. More importantly though, I owe Matthew and his uncle Arthur my life. If I can help out by cheering up the children for a short while, I would like to do that...and I would like to leave knowing it's all right with you."

Her parents were silent a moment, then her father said, "If you feel this is something you have to do, then, of course, we're behind you, Liz. Just be careful; your soft heart has led you into difficulty more than once."

Liz smiled. "I can't imagine what difficulty I could possibly get into by visiting the children, but" she added, feeling her spirits lift, "I promise I'll be careful, Dad."

~~~~~~~~~~~~~

The next three days were busy with preparations for the trip, packing, shopping for gifts for the children and a trip to the salon. By Thursday night, she knew she'd gotten carried away with her packing, but then, the 'Pipit' in her was still appreciative of the lovely wardrobe and she couldn't make up her mind what to take, so she packed more than was necessary.

When placing a toothbrush into her cosmetic bag, she remembered why she hadn't had her teeth straightened. It was her own decision. The slight overlap of one front tooth over the other, gave her teeth character, she'd felt. She still did.

Also in the cabin, she remembered wondering why she'd had her hair cut so short and unattractively, why she hadn't worn so many of her beautiful clothes. She knew now, but she wasn't proud of the answers. They seemed very immature to her. *If the world was going to think of her as an 'ugly duckling,' why try to be anything else, besides—wasn't short hair easier to manage when swimming a couple of times a day? Why try to dress to impress people, when she was bored stiff with the social amenities expected of her?*

Of course she'd been bored with it all, but out of respect for her parents, she needn't have worn her non-conformity like a protective suit of armor!

Chapter Thirty-Seven

Early Friday morning, Calvin took several trips to the car carrying Liz's suitcases, including the empty one that belonged to Matthew. "Why did you pack so much, Liz?" He frowned as he placed the last of them in the trunk. "Are you planning to stay for a long time?"

"No." She smiled at the concern on his face. "I certainly don't want to end up as the housekeeper and nanny again. It's not my style. I really don't know why I'm taking so much, except I finally appreciate my wardrobe and have enjoyed dressing more attractively."

"I'm certainly glad to hear that, Liz," her mother said, walking into the garage in time to hear the conversation.

"I've put some money into your checking account, Liz," her father said.

"Thank you, Dad," she said, feeling a little chagrined. "You know, I should be independent of your financial support at my age. That's why I'm making preparations to go back to work."

"As you know, Liz, you have a large trust fund. Remember, when you turned thirty, you came into that money. You are free to use it whenever you choose. However, as long as you are under my roof, I'll continue to support you."

"I know, Dad, and I appreciate that—and the fact that you have confidence I can handle my inheritance. If I were you, I don't think I would have that confidence in me. I don't have much to show for my almost thirty-one years of age. I'm not married, and I don't have a career to speak of."

"But you are the most level-headed daughter we have," he remarked, smiling.

She smiled and hugged him. "Thank you. Somehow, you always manage to make me feel better about myself."

Hugging her mother, she said, "I'll call you when I get there, or when I find Matthew. He'll either be in the Phoenix store or the Scottsdale store. I need to talk with him before I rush out to see the children. *The Wicked Witch Of The West*, Mrs. Danville, may be upset if I show up unannounced."

"All right, Liz," her mother replied, "but I do wish you weren't going."

Without addressing her mother's statement, she hurriedly got into the car, smiled and waved goodbye, backed out and headed toward the street.

The drive through Thousand Palms and Indio was pleasant. The desert after that was a tedious drive. She reached Blythe in two hours, stopping to get a cold drink and then drove across the Colorado River and on through Quartzsite, a small place surrounded by gray rocky desert.

This grayness would be reflecting her own life today if it weren't for the fact that she now had some direction, and was on a mission of mercy. "Mercy for whom?" she asked aloud. On the road this morning, she felt excitement at the thought of seeing Merri and Danny...and, she had to admit, excitement at the thought of seeing Matthew...so this trip was for herself, also—a closure, so to speak. This time, she would say goodbye without any further promises.

Arriving at the outskirts of Phoenix, she pulled into the parking lot of a business, picked up her cellular and called Melloy Music to see if Matthew was there.

"Melloy Music," the voice said.

"Is Mr. Melloy working there today?"

"He is. Would you like to speak with him?"

"No thank you. Do you know when he'll be leaving for lunch?"

"As a matter of fact, he mentioned that he'd take the late lunch at 1:00 or 1:30."

"Thank you." Liz hung up, relieved that when she arrived at the store at 12:00 noon or shortly after, he'd still be there and she wouldn't have to wait.

She couldn't help but think how much Phoenix reminded her of Palm Springs. At last, she drove into the parking lot of Melloy Music. Turning off the key, her heart pounded with excitement as she got out of the car and walked toward the store.

Peeking through the window of the door, as she and the children had done, she saw Matthew at one of the pianos playing a piece for someone. *Maybe he has his sight back*! she thought, her hopes rising. She opened the door, walked over and stood behind him, listening and watching him. Her heart sank, for he wasn't reading music; he was playing by ear and the customer was holding the music.

When he was through, the customer said, "That's the one I was looking for. Thank you, Mr. Melloy."

He turned and smiled at her. "You're certainly welcome."

The customer left and Matthew remained sitting, waiting for Mike. Soon, Mike headed their way. When he saw her, his face lit up and she put a finger to her lips, motioning him to go back. He smiled and nodded.

Liz seated herself in the chair the customer had vacated, and studied Matthew's face. She was shocked. His face looked drawn; under his eyes, dark circles accentuated the desperation she saw in his face. Suddenly stiffening, he masked the emotion, aware that someone was near.

"Uh...may I help you?" he asked.

She didn't reply, remembering that he had been able to sense her presence before, wondering if he still could.

His brows drew together in thought and bending his head slightly, he asked hesitantly, "Pipit?"

"I'm here, Matthew."

For a moment he didn't speak. She saw that his lower lip and chin trembled slightly, then he whispered hoarsely, "I knew it!"

"Elizabeth is here also," she said quietly.

"You have your memory back!" He held out both hands to her.

Scooting the chair closer, she leaned over and placed her hands in his. "I do, Matthew. It's wonderful to see you again."

He squeezed her hands so hard, it almost hurt. "I'm happy for you."

"Thank you, Matthew, but I see your sight hasn't returned."

His smile disappeared. "No."

"I have a car and money in my wallet. How about going to lunch with me so we can talk."

Matthew laughed. "I can imagine how great it must feel to be able to drive and go where you want to."

"Almost as great as it would be for you, Matthew. Can you go to lunch?"

"Well, since you're able to drive, I can. That leaves Mike here to help."

Liz motioned Mike over. "It's nice to see you, Mike," she said, smiling.

He grinned. "It's great to see you, Pipit."

"Mike, meet Elizabeth Cabot. Her memory has returned."

"Hey, I'm glad to hear that, uh...Elizabeth."

"Thank you. I've invited Matthew to lunch. Do you mind?"

"Not at all. I'll go to lunch later."

"Thanks, Mike," Matthew said standing up. He smiled when Liz took his hand, led him out of the store and to her car.

She opened the door for him. "My father bought me a new Buick Skylark."

"Nice." He seated himself. When she went around and got in on the other side, he added, "I guess your car is still up on the mountain. It won't be long before they can get it out. I hope it will be usable."

"They've already gotten it out, and it wasn't; that why the new one. Where would you like to go eat, Matthew?" she asked before starting the car.

"You decide. I'm not very hungry, Pipit...uh, Elizabeth. It's going to be difficult calling you anything, but Pipit."

"My family calls me Liz. You can call me that, or Elizabeth. If you slip, Pipit still sounds right to me. We'll have to explain to the children and let them choose what they want to call me."

"You want to see the children?" he asked, concerned.

"Of course. I promised them. That's why I've come."

If only your memory had returned sooner, it might not have happened! he thought.

His mind darted back to the day Pipit left. Even with his family all there, he'd felt a deep loss. At first, he attributed it to an overdependence on her help with the children. But as the days wore on, he sorely missed the peace he had felt in her presence. It wasn't long before Merri slipped back to the way she was before Pipit arrived, and Mrs. Danville and Elinor conveniently used this for their own purposes, blaming it on his blindness.

He responded finally. "After Merri and Danny returned home from spending a couple of days with their cousins, they cried for you for several days, and have continued to ask about you, but..." his face reflected agony, "Pipit, it may be too late."

Liz scooted the seat back and turned to face Matthew. "What's wrong, Matthew?"

"The children are at Elinor's. The Child Protection Services, through the pressure of Elinor and her high-powered attorneys, came out and told me I had to give Elinor temporary custody until the court hearing Monday morning."

"No!" exclaimed Liz. "The court hearing?"

"Yes. Elinor is taking me to court for custody of the children. My sight has not improved at all and the doctors can do nothing for me."

"Why? What did they say?"

"The doctors are now calling it psychogenic visual loss, which means they don't think there is anything physiologically wrong with me anymore. In other words, they think it's post-traumatic stress."

"Did they give you more tests?"

"Yes, and after conferring with several other doctors, they're telling me that my injuries were not such that would cause blindness for this long."

"Do you believe it's post-traumatic stress, Matthew?"

"After thinking about it for a few days, I decided that they're probably right."

"Then, it's possible your sight will return! What is *their* prognosis of that possibility?"

"They're as puzzled as I am. They said it could be permanent or—if and when my sight returns, it will probably be spontaneous improvement. They have found that has been the pattern."

"You mean one minute you couldn't see and the next, you could?"

"That's what I understand."

"What can I do to help, Matthew?"

"Well, once again, as you did when you fell on our doorstep, you've cheered me up." He smiled at her. "Thank you. But other than that," he added dispiritedly, "there's nothing you can do."

"Would Elinor let me see the children?"

"No. She's been upset that they've cried for you."

Liz shook her head refusing to accept it."This can't be happening, Matthew. There has to be something we can do about it." She felt overcome with frustration. *Matthew can't lose his children!* she screamed inside her head. Merri and Danny need to be with their father! Then she asked an obvious question, "What about your uncle Arthur and aunt Mamie. Couldn't they take them?"

"No, they can't. Elinor is a closer relative, and in addition to that, she has the money and power."

"You know, I'm not hungry either, Matthew. Let's eat later. Do you have to go to work this afternoon?"

"No. What would you like to do?"

"I would like to go to your house where we can talk. We have to figure out some way to stop Elinor."

"All right," he said, grateful for her company, "but I'm afraid we won't come up with anything. Mamie, Arthur and my lawyer have been trying for about three weeks to help me think of some way to keep Elinor from taking the children."

Her mouth set in a grim line, Liz moved the seat up and started the car, drove out of the parking lot and headed for Cave Creek. Matthew pulled out his cellular and called work telling Mike he wouldn't be back this afternoon. After that, both were silent for some time, then Liz asked Matthew how the rest of his family were. Matthew asked about hers.

When they arrived at the house and had seated themselves in the family room, Liz looked around the room. Loneliness for the children crept over her. Feeling frustrated and helpless, she asked, "Does your attorney think you have a chance?"

"He's concerned because Elinor seems to be holding most of the cards."

Restlessly, Liz got up and moved about the room, thinking.

Matthew could hear her walking around, and was touched that she cared enough to be this upset. He heard her mutter, "We have to think of something!"

After about ten minutes, Matthew begged her to sit down. She did as he asked. Sitting in the chair next to the couch where

Matthew was seated, she scrutinized his face. As usual, he was concealing his feelings.

Her mind flitted from one thing to another, searching frantically for something that maybe Matthew and his lawyer hadn't thought of—then felt foolish. How did she think she could come up with something when they hadn't been able to?

Once, in the cabin, she'd asked herself if she had ever prayed. She had. However, after she'd graduated from college she became too busy, as Horace put it: "hell-bent on going nowhere." Her prayers flew up to heaven only in times of unhappiness. And here once more, in heartache, she contemplated praying for help, feeling guilty because she had neglected her prayers in between. Making a vow to Him and to herself that this would change, she once more sent up a fervent, emotion-filled prayer, begging Him for help. She knew *she* didn't deserve it, but since Matthew and the children did, her faith felt stronger.

Feeling restless himself, Matthew sensed that he needed to give Pipit—Liz, he reminded himself—time to go over in her mind any possible options, as he had done for weeks. He knew the outcome. She had to accept the hopelessness of it for now, as he himself was still trying to do.

Unexpectedly, Liz's thoughts turned to the evening she'd taken her family Bible upstairs after the party. She had opened it when she got into bed that night and read out of it trying to calm herself after the irrationality she'd displayed in the library. The verse that had stood out then, came to mind: "...*Inasmuch as ye have done it unto one of the least of these my brethren, ye have done it unto me.*"

Puzzled over this, she knew there was nothing she could do for Merri and Danny. It was hopeless...*unless*...the idea that came startled her. No! She couldn't do it. Matthew would never do it! But the idea would not go away. She panicked. How could this be an answer to her prayers? But—somehow, she knew it was.

Her hearted pounding, she prayed for courage. Taking in several deep breaths to calm herself, she said, "Matthew, I've thought of a solution."

Surprised, Matthew knew that whatever it was, it couldn't be a solution, nevertheless, he was touched. "Oh? What?"

She said it bluntly, for there was no other way. "We could get married."

Shocked, Matthew was unable to respond.

"You mentioned it once, Matthew, remember? I know you weren't serious, you were only speaking out of desperation. I know you said that you could never marry again, even it was a marriage of convenience for a short while. But do you have any other solution? Do you have any other choice?"

"Liz," his voice came out in an incredulous whisper, "I thought you were engaged."

"I was. I'm not now."

"Why?"

"I would rather not talk about it."

"You...you didn't call it off because of...me, did you?"

Liz's laugh came out harsh. "Now that's good, Matthew. Why would I do that? Why would any woman want to involve herself with you? You're in love with a ghost. You keep her clothes, her perfume and jewelry just as she left it. No woman could ever compete with the memory of Diane."

Matthew flinched. "Liz Cabot has a biting tongue, I see."

"Biting or not—it's a fact."

When Matthew had regained his composure, he said, "I can't have you sacrifice yourself like that, Liz."

"I haven't done much with my life, Matthew, in fact I've led a life of self- indulgence. It certainly won't hurt me to do this." She cringed, remembering what she'd said to her father just before leaving for Phoenix: 'I certainly don't want to end up as the housekeeper and nanny again.' And that was exactly what was going to happen if Matthew accepted the only chance he had to keep his children!

"What if my sight never comes back? I can't have you stay on indefinitely. You have to live your own life."

"I still don't understand why I feel this way, but I feel you'll regain your sight, Matthew. But if it turns out that you don't, surely by then we will have been able to find a reliable woman who would be willing to live in and care for the children. At least, we will have beaten Elinor."

Desperate, Matthew knew he had no choice but to *consider* Liz's offer. However, he could already see several problems. Addressing the first, he said, "I'm concerned at how attached the children will become. It will be harder when you leave the second time."

"Oh. I haven't had time to think of that; we have so little time to do something. Let me think, how could we handle that up front?" She answered her own question. "We'll just have to be open with the children. We'll have to tell them that I've come for a visit, but that I'll have to leave in a while."

"I don't know why I even considered it for a moment. It's impossible, Pipit...Liz. There is no way we could possibly get married before Monday morning."

"We would have to fly to Las Vegas and get married," she said quickly. Though she heard herself say it, she could hardly believe she had. She'd always thought it terribly uncouth and totally unromantic to marry that way. But then, in reality, they wouldn't really be getting 'married.' Not in the real sense, she told herself. She covered her face, her heart full of anxiety.

"I can't believe you just suggested that? Why are doing this for us, Liz? Why are you willing to?" he asked, still incredulous.

"Because...I love Merri and Danny and they wouldn't be happy with anyone but you. They belong with you. Secondly, you and Arthur saved my life."

"Anyone would have done the same."

"Not in the same way," she replied softly. "Well...are you going to accept my proposal?" she asked forcing a light-hearted tone. "Actually—I wouldn't be caught dead proposing to a man, Matthew. This truly is a once-in-a-lifetime opportunity."

He laughed. "You are an amazing woman, Liz. I accept, but only because I have no other choice."

"Thanks for the compliment."

"You're welcome," he chuckled. "We need to get your suitcases in, so we both can pack a light overnight bag to take to Vegas. I need to call my lawyer and tell him we'll need to meet with him Saturday afternoon when we get back." Warming to the idea, he added, "First, we need to make plane reservations for tonight, then call a hotel for a reservation. I hope it's not too late to get either one."

It was only then that Liz remembered she hadn't called her parents to inform them she'd arrived. What in the world could she tell them? There was no possible way she could make them understand what she was about to do. Deciding to call only to inform them that she'd arrived safely, and that she'd call in a few days with information of where she would be staying, her thoughts moved on.

Remembering her mother's misgivings about her coming here, her heart felt weighed down. She and her father had been so happy that she had some direction—a worthwhile goal. Surely, she could explain that she would be able to go on with her plans in the not too distant future. After all, they knew her well enough to know that a *career* of housekeeper/nanny was the last thing she would choose. After the court hearing, she would explain everything to her parents. She tried to reassure herself that in some small measure they would be able to understand. Wouldn't they?

Chapter Thirty-Eight

Matthew waited for Elizabeth to pack a small suitcase. He'd suggested that they be dressed up in case the marriage could be performed immediately upon their arrival. She'd already helped him pack, pick out his suit, shirt and tie. His spirits had risen considerably, feeling hope for the first time since Elinor announced she was taking him to court.

Still, he felt guilty. Allowing Elizabeth to make this sacrifice for him and his children was too much to ask of her; she had never married. How terrible for her to be married, for the first time, in the 'marriage mill' of Las Vegas! But he didn't feel guilty enough; his children came first. Hopefully, she wouldn't think of this as a 'real' marriage, just a ritual they were going through in order to be successful in court Monday.

Liz closed her small bag, and tried to calm her erratic heart before leaving the room, glad that she had called a taxi. She was feeling too nervous to drive! She should be questioning the appalling step she was taking, but she wasn't. In spite of her conviction that this was what she needed to do, she still felt terribly anxious. Deciding it was perfectly normal under the circumstances, she picked up her bag and went into the family room to wait with Matthew for the taxi.

Liz felt they had been lucky so far; things seemed to have fallen into place. When she called Southwest Airlines, they had only two seats left together. Then, while trying to pack, she'd called the only casino hotel in Vegas she could remember, the Rio. It was so busy, she had to hold a long time before she could get to a live person, and when she did, they only had one suite left with two queen beds. She reserved it for Matthew, hoping the hotel would have a cancellation for her by the time they checked in.

She sat down on the couch. "Matthew, We're in luck again. I was able to get a room reservation at the Rio for one of us. I'm concerned, though, about getting another one if the Rio doesn't have a cancellation when we arrive. I wonder if we can get a room somewhere else on a weekend."

Matthew frowned in thought. "I know it will make you uncomfortable, Liz, but it's probably best we stay in a room together in case Elinor sends her snoops out to check up on us." He grinned. "Look at the bright side—this is the second time my sightlessness will have proven to be very convenient."

She was just about to ask when the other time was when they heard the honk of the taxi.

~~~~~~~~~~~~~

It wasn't long before the plane dipped down at McCarran International Airport. Since they had carried their suitcases on board, they were able to head directly to the curbside to pick up a taxi.

Walking with the crowds of people through the large airport, past rows and rows of noisy slot machines, they reached elevators which took them to the first floor. The curbside was crowded with people also wanting a taxi. The wait seemed interminable until they got one. As they climbed in, the odor of stale and recent tobacco assailed their nostrils. Liz, feeling tense, folded her arms tightly across her mid-section.

Feeling like the novice he was, Matthew self-consciously asked the cab driver how a couple went about getting married in this town. The driver, who apparently had been asked this question hundreds of times, nonchalantly told them that they had to go to the Clark County Court House to get a marriage license first, informing them that they would need the exact change of thirty-five dollars.

"You could go ahead and get married by a Justice of the Peace at the Marriage Commissioner's office, which is only a block from the courthouse, or you could go to a wedding chapel. Both cost thirty-five dollars. But it's mighty busy on weekends. Couples have to stand in line at either place."

"How late does the courthouse stay open?"

"Twenty-four hours on weekends."

Surprised by the answer, Matthew contemplated it a moment then asked with more confidence, "Is there a jewelry store that could furnish us quickly with plain wedding bands?"

"Yes sir. Shall I drive you there?"

"Please. We'd like you to wait for us and then take us to the courthouse." He turned to Liz. "Amazing. Never heard of a courthouse staying open twenty-four hours. Marriage is big business in this city."

They were silent during the drive, both not wanting to let the other one know how they were feeling. The driver stopped in front of the jewelry store. When they entered, a clerk asked, "May I help you?"

"We would like wedding bands please," Matthew said.

"Silver or gold? Plain or with diamonds?"

He turned to Liz. "Gold or silver?"

"I like gold."

"Two plain gold, please."

The clerk soon placed a velvet-lined tray of gold bands on the counter. "We need rings that fit right now," Liz said.

The man seemed unfazed by this request, measuring their fingers and fitting Liz first, then Matthew.

Matthew pulled out his credit card. Liz helped him find the place to sign on the bill. The clerk, oblivious to Matthew's lack of sight, frowned when Matthew didn't take the sack held toward him. Liz took it, and together they walked out of the store to the waiting cab. Before they gave further instructions to the driver, Matthew had Liz check his wallet for exact change, and she checked hers.

On the way to the courthouse Matthew, uneasy over how Liz was feeling, gathered his courage and asked her.

"A little numb—and a little sad for couples who do it this way. How are you feeling, Matthew?"

"More grateful to you than I can express."

The cab pulled up in front of the Clark County Courthouse. Matthew handed Liz his wallet and she paid the driver, who then got out and opened the door for them. Each gripping their own suitcases, Liz took Matthew's sweaty hand with her cold one, and stared at the building in front of them.

"Would you like to know what the building looks like, Matthew?"

In spite of his apprehension, his basic interest in everything spoke. "Yes, I would."

"It's flat-roofed and is an odd color for a courthouse—aqua, cream and gray. There are steps up from the sidewalk to a landing with a short thick wall. All along the wall, people are sitting and standing. There are two entrances. At the left entrance, people are sitting on the steps, and some are just walking around."

"Maybe they're jurors, Liz."

"I hope you're right—that they aren't all waiting for marriage licenses."

In trepidation, they walked up the steps and entered the main entrance on the right. To anyone who might be watching, they looked like just another nervous couple in love, wanting to get married.

"Straight ahead, guards are stationed at metal detectors," Liz explained to Matthew. "To the right is a rope, guiding couples to a small sign on the wall that says Marriage Licenses. A line of about sixteen people are waiting behind it. The floor is a mottled dirty brown and there are no seats anywhere." Both their spirits sagged.

Liz studied the other couples. All were dressed casually, jeans, shorts, tank tops. Several couples looked downright scruffy—a little like they needed a bath. "I think we're over-dressed, Matthew," she whispered.

He broke into laugher. Startled heads turned in their direction as Liz joined in the laughter. Afterward, Liz felt more relaxed, so she initiated a conversation with the couple in front of them. Hearing their delightful accents, she and Matthew soon learned they were from London, and had come all the way from England just so they could be married in Las Vegas.

When they reached the counter they were given forms to fill out. All they had to do was hand the form in, show their driver's licenses and pay thirty-five dollars, after which they left the courthouse, marriage license in hand.

Crossing the street, as instructed by a helpful man in the courthouse lobby, they walked a little over a block to a building that had a sign saying: CIVIL MARRIAGE COMMISSIONER on it. Entering it, Liz said, "This all seems so unreal, Matthew."

This place was even more depressing than the courthouse to Liz. She felt claustrophobic. The lobby area was small and the ceiling low. The floor, brown painted brick, contrasted drearily with gray cement walls, which looked like a rake had been dragged along them when the cement was still wet. It was crowded. The only seating was on the right—faded orange padded seats with a stationary bolster of the same faded color. The less faded orange walls behind were of the same fabric as the seats.

"Tell me what it looks like in here, Liz."

"You don't want to know."

"No fair. I get to suffer with you."

She smiled and described it.

There was standing room only, but as Liz looked around, she realized not everyone was waiting to get married. Some were relatives of the couples. A group who resembled each other were speaking together in what sounded like German. The woman, who looked and acted like the happy bride, was dressed in a short, tight, floral dress with a flower in her long, blonde hair.

As the crowd shifted, Liz glimpsed a sign on the brown wooden door just beyond the elevators. It said: Civil Marriage Commissioner. She asked a woman why no one was going in and was told that whoever was supposed to be in there was out for dinner and wouldn't be back until six-thirty. She asked Matthew if he'd heard this. He nodded, and ran his hand through his hair in frustration and weariness.

Soon, the front door opened and a blonde woman, who looked to be in her fifties, entered. She was doubled over holding on to a walker. Everyone moved back as she worked her way toward the brown door and entered. The couple at the head of the line followed her, along with others who were family or friends.

Twenty minutes later, they came out, the couple not looking any happier than when they went in.

Another group went in, leaving two empty seats on the bench. Liz led Matthew to them and they gratefully sat down, holding their small suitcases as close and out of the way as possible. Even while seated, Matthew kept hold of Liz's hand, for which she was grateful. In this alien environment, it was the only thing that felt familiar and safe.

The next group to go in was the German couple and their family. When they exited, all were smiling and speaking at once. The bride was beaming.

The couple who was supposed to go next were arguing. The prospective groom was apparently getting cold feet, so he suggested that Liz and Matthew go next. Thanking him, they got up, and went through the brown door. Looking over the high counter immediately in front of them, Liz saw the blonde woman, who smiled and instructed them to sign in, give her their marriage license, and thirty-five dollars. Matthew pulled out his wallet and handed it to Liz, who paid the woman.

Concerned, Liz could see no one around, but the woman. "Where is the Justice of the Peace?"

"You're looking at her," the woman said, smiling. "My name is Pat Murphy."

"Oh," Liz replied, surprised.

"Do you have a witness?"

"No," Matthew answered. "We assumed you provided that."

"We usually do, but we're short-handed today." She picked up the phone and dialed. "Joe, we need a witness. Could you come in?....Thanks."

"Joe is our security guard," she explained. "When it's after five, we can use him if we're desperate." She pointed to a room with a large glass window. "Please go on into the ceremony room and be seated."

Matthew liked the sound of the woman's voice. He relaxed a little and smiled. "Thank you."

Liz led Matthew past the counter, past the window to the entrance. Inside, she led him to two blue, padded chairs, their backs to the window.

She looked around the small pleasant room. To the right hung a large gold-framed mirror above a walnut stained credenza, upon which stood an arrangement of light apricot, silk flowers. On the opposite wall, near the door, stood a white pedestal urn with an artificial plant. Several pictures of trees beside streams hung on the walls. A small walnut desk and chair, placed diagonally across the corner, faced the chairs.

"Matthew," Liz whispered. "This is so much nicer than I expected."

"Describe it to me."

She did, then she noticed for the first time the items on the desk. They brought tears to her eyes, for they were the tender, sweet touches of a woman. "Matthew, on the left of the desk, there's a tall clear vase filled with beautiful fresh flowers. In the middle, near the front edge is a small pink pillow, covered with crocheted lace for the rings." With a catch in her voice, she added, "and as you would expect, there's a box of tissues. It's on the right corner of the desk."

Matthew could hear the tears in Liz's voice and felt them at the back of his own eyes.

Deputy Marriage Commissioner, Pat Murphy, entered with her walker, followed by a cheerful-faced, rotund man in a uniform.

"Please excuse the walker," Pat said. "I've just had back surgery." She seated herself behind the desk. "May I introduce you to Joe, our security guard." She glanced at the paper in her hand. "Joe, this is Miss Elizabeth Cabot and Mr. Matthew Melloy."

He smiled broadly. "Glad to meet you both," he said, then moved to his usual place.

"We're glad to meet you, Joe," Matthew said. "Thank you for helping us out."

Deputy Murphy smiled warmly at the couple before her, knowing the man was blind. "Elizabeth and Matthew, I've seen thousands of couples come into this room, and once in a great while I see a couple who is special. You are one of those. I see in both your countenances that you are unselfish, giving people. As you know, I'm sure, these qualities are imperative for a successful marriage. You are a beautiful couple."

Both touched at her kindness, murmured their thanks. Liz wondered if this gracious woman was the one who had added the special touches to this room, making it an oasis amidst chaos and occasional irreverence.

"If you both will now please stand, we'll begin. You may place the ring or rings on the small pillow."

Liz opened the small purse hanging from her shoulder, pulled them out and placed them, then pulled a tissue from the box.

Pat Murphy, in spite of her back, pushed herself to a standing position. "In the marriage ceremony we now have the couples answer 'I will' instead of 'I do.'

"Now, we'll proceed. Marriage is an honorable estate. It is not to be entered into lightly or unadvisedly, but discreetly and soberly. Into this relationship these two persons come now to be joined. I therefore charge both of you that if you know any reason why you should not be joined in marriage, you make it known at this time." Deputy Murphy paused.

"Matthew Milner Melloy, will you take Elizabeth Cabot to be your wedded wife, to live together in the bonds of marriage? Will you love her, comfort her, honor and keep her, so long as you both shall live?"

"I will."

"Elizabeth, will you take Matthew to be your wedded husband to live together in the bonds of marriage? Will you love him, comfort him, honor and keep him, so long as you both shall live?"

"I will."

"Matthew please repeat after me: I, Matthew, take thee, Elizabeth to be my wedded wife,"

"I, Matthew, take thee, Elizabeth, to be my wedded wife,"

"...to have and to hold from this day forward,"

"to have and to hold from this day forward,"

"...for better or worse, for richer or poorer,"

"for better or worse, for richer or poorer,"

"...in sickness and in health, to love and to cherish."

"in sickness and in health, to love and to cherish."

"Elizabeth, repeat after me. I, Elizabeth, take thee, Matthew, to be my wedded husband,"

"I, Elizabeth, take thee, Matthew, to be my wedded husband,"

"...to have and to hold from this day forward,"

"to have and to hold from this day forward,"

"...for better or worse, for richer or poorer,"

"for better or worse, for richer or poorer,"

"...in sickness and in health, to love and to cherish."

"in sickness and in health, to love and to cherish."

"Now the ring ceremony."

Liz stepped over and picked up the rings and handed hers to Matthew.

"Matthew," Pat said, "please repeat. With this ring I thee wed,"

"With this ring I thee wed,"

"...and with all my love I thee endow."

"and with all my love I thee endow."

Matthew placed the ring on Liz's left hand.

"Elizabeth, please repeat: I accept this ring in token of our constant faith and abiding love."

"I accept this ring in token of our constant faith and abiding love."

"...With this ring I thee wed,"

"With this ring I thee wed,"

"...and with all my love I thee endow."

"and with all my love I thee endow."

Elizabeth placed the ring on Matthew's finger.

"Matthew, please repeat: I accept this ring in token of our constant faith and abiding love."

"I accept this ring in token of our constant faith and abiding love."

"Inasmuch as you have thus consented together in marriage, by virtue of the authority vested in me by the laws of the State of Nevada, I now pronounce you husband and wife." She smiled. "You may kiss the bride."

Liz had forgotten about this part. "You don't have to, Matthew," she whispered.

Ignoring her, he took her face in his hands and held it gently a moment, then bent down and tenderly kissed her lips. He hadn't intended to, but he couldn't seem to help himself—his arms went around her and with his lips still on hers, he gave her a long, heart-stirring kiss. Reluctantly, he pulled his head up, shocked at the emotions the kiss had elicited. He held her close for a moment, realizing how much he had missed a woman.

"I'm sorry, Liz," he whispered into her ear, releasing her.

Struggling with her own emotions brought on by his kiss, she couldn't respond.

"Congratulations, Mr. and Mrs. Melloy," Pat Murphy said, handing Liz the non-certified marriage certificate, explaining where they could send for the certified certificate. "May you have a long and happy life together."

"Thank you," Matthew replied in a subdued voice.

"Yes, thank you," Liz added, wishing she could tell this lovely woman that she had made this difficult time easier, more memorable.

They exited quickly. Now a married couple, they walked hand in hand toward the outside door past the new and burgeoning line of those still waiting. They walked along the sidewalk watching for a cab.

"What time is it?" Matthew asked.

Liz looked at her watch. "It's almost 9:00, and I'm feeling shaky. We haven't eaten since breakfast."

"I'm sorry, we should have..."

"No, it's all right."

"We'll eat at a restaurant in the hotel before we check in."

"That sounds good," she muttered, feeling so tired she wondered if she could even eat.

In the cab, Matthew instructed the driver to take them to the Rio, then put his arm around her. "You're wonderful, Liz."

She only sighed, laid her head on his shoulder and closed her eyes.

Fifteen minutes later, the cab came to a stop. Matthew spoke softly. "I think we're here, Liz."

"Already? I must have dozed."

The driver had squeezed the cab into a tight spot in front of the Rio. The area was packed with cars coming and going, and a crowd of people stood in front.

After Liz paid the driver, she noticed the huge flashing marquee of the Rio announcing its entertainment. She stared up at the twenty story convex building with royal blue, purple and orange tinted windows, remembering that her family had stayed at this same hotel before her sisters were married. She was sure it had been smaller then.

Picking up their suitcases, Liz handed one to Matthew, then gripping his hand, Liz maneuvered through the crowd and entered the building.

Low ceilings with lights of white, orange and blue flickered over hundreds of slot machines. To the left of the entrance, a long line was waiting at the check-in counter. Suddenly, gloom settled over Liz like a heavy wet blanket.

"I have no idea where to find the restaurant, Matthew, but I'll ask someone." Leading him further in, she stopped a skimpily-dressed cocktail waitress and got instructions to a restaurant called the Fiore. There, the host showed them to a square, linen covered table. Wearily, they seated themselves, grateful that what they'd come to Vegas for was now behind them.

Liz looked over the menu and both decided on fish. Matthew asked the waiter if it could be brought quickly.

"We're past the late dinner hour, and not as crowded, so it shouldn't be long."

They were both too tired to make conversation, but Liz felt she needed to be eyes for Matthew. "We're sitting in front of a window, Matthew. Outside, across the walk is a large fountain. Here in the Fiore, there is a peaceful, high-class ambiance. The lighting fixtures are hanging low, giving an intimate atmosphere. The chairs we're sitting on, are padded with green leather with dark-stained wooden arms. The carpet is nice—large green bordered squares with orange and green florals inside. Across the room, chefs are working in plain view of the patrons."

"Thank you, Liz. I feel as though I've seen everything today. I can't tell you what that means to me."

"I think I can understand," she answered.

When the food arrived, Liz explained what was on his plate and where his glass and salad were placed. They ate in silence for a long time. The nourishment began to revive them physically and emotionally.

It was then that Matthew voiced the concern he'd had since the moment Liz first suggested getting married in Vegas. "Liz, I was desperate enough to take the chance that the judge wouldn't question the way we got married, but I'm still concerned."

"I have it all planned out, Matthew." His puzzled expression didn't elicit more explanation from her. She said simply, "Trust me, it will be all right."

Something in her voice made him relax. "I don't know what you could possibly have planned out, Liz, but I guess I'll find out tomorrow when we meet with the lawyer. I'm anxious to get home and get it all over with."

"You mean you aren't even going to take me on a honeymoon?" she asked in half-hearted jest. Immediately, she could tell by Matthew's expression that this was a touchy subject. "Sorry. I guess that's something I shouldn't joke about."

Matthew was having a difficult time. What Liz didn't realize, not ever having been married, is that celibacy for a widower was difficult. Now that they were legally married, there was nothing else he would rather do than have a honeymoon! He smiled wryly at her. "My little angel of mercy, I suspect you are quite innocent."

Puzzled at his remark, and a little embarrassed, she turned her attention to finishing the last few bites in front of her.

~~~~~~~~~~~~~

By the time they left the restaurant, the check-in line had diminished. Only one couple was in front of them. Soon they had the key to the room and were riding the elevator to the sixth floor. Liz found their suite, as the Rio called it. Inside, Liz took Matthew's suitcase and placed it near the first bed, showing him where it was, then took him on a tour of the room and bathroom. "It's a nice room, Matthew. Green carpets and nice floral bedspreads. On the other side of the room is a couch, two chairs, and a coffee table."

Liz found a place for her suitcase. They both remained standing, silent, stiff and uneasy. Finally Liz spoke. "It...it feels so awkward to have to sleep in the same room, Matthew."

"And I feel like a child having to be cared for," he stated bitterly.

Gazing at Matthew's pained face, Liz felt foolish. "I'm sorry, Matthew. Thank you for putting my awkwardness into perspective."

Later, Matthew lay in bed in the dark having chosen to wait and shower in his own familiar surroundings tomorrow night. He could hear Liz showering. His mind unwillingly went back to the marriage ceremony. Making the promises verbally, but not from his heart was one of the most difficult things he had ever done in his life, and he wondered how Liz had managed so stoically.

The warm water of the shower relaxed Liz's tense back and neck. All the emotions that she'd rigidly held in during the wedding ceremony came flooding back. She felt like she had made a mockery of something sacred. Her chest heaved in silent sobs, the tears mingling with the droplets of water.

Chapter Thirty-Nine

Saturday morning after eating breakfast together, Liz and Matthew picked up the suitcases they'd brought down with them and went out to hail a taxi.

On the plane, Matthew fingered the ring on his left hand. He had worn his wedding band for about six months after the accident before taking it off, and this new one felt strange.

Liz noticed. "Me too, Matthew. I don't wear rings so this is going to take getting used to." *It also felt odd*, Liz thought, *sitting together on the plane—now husband and wife.* It sounded strange as she repeated it in her mind.

~~~~~~~~~~~~

Saturday afternoon, Robert Beale, Matthew's attorney sat across the table from Matthew and Elizabeth shaking his head, amazed and concerned. "How could you think this quickie marriage of yours is going to stop Elinor, Matthew? It will look to her just what it is and she'll use it against you."

"Mr. Beale," Liz said, "It will work if you'll ask me certain questions. And if Elinor's attorney asks what I think he'll ask."

"Oh? And what are those, uh...Mrs. Melloy?"

"I would like to discuss them with you in private."

"In private?" Matthew asked taken aback. "You don't want me privy to the conversation, Liz?"

"Please trust me, Matthew. This is in your best interest."

"I don't like the sound of that."

"It isn't something that's important for you to know *before* the hearing, Matthew. If you'll agree to wait and hear it in the context of the courtroom, it will save you unnecessary distress."

Frowning a moment, he reluctantly gave in. "Okay. Lead me out into the waiting room."

~~~~~~~~~~~~

It wasn't until 7:00 PM that the two of them turned into Matthew's driveway. After meeting with the attorney, they had gone out to dinner.

Upon entering the house, they silently went their different directions—Matthew to his bedroom and Liz to hers. It felt to Liz that the marriage hadn't even taken place—that it was almost as it was before she left. Except for one thing. She felt more in control.

After unpacking, she undressed, slipped on silk pajamas and washed her face. Since Matthew couldn't see how she was dressed, she went out into the family room to read. She found him sitting on the couch listening to something on TV.

"Hi," she said, curling up in a chair.

He smiled and flipped off the television. "Hi, yourself. Are you all unpacked?"

"Yes. I thought I was over-packing, but as it turns out, I guess I wasn't. Who knows how long I'll be here."

"What are your plans when you leave, Liz?"

"I have my Masters in Art History. I managed an art gallery in Paris for five years, but I'm tired of that so I've decided I'd like to teach on the college level. I've filled out an application for a teaching position at a branch of California State University in Palm Springs."

"When will you know if you're accepted?"

"I don't know."

Matthew hoped the college wouldn't have an opening for a while. Selfish or not, he desperately needed her here right now.

An awkward silence settled over them. Even though legally they were husband and wife, staying in the house alone together without the children there didn't feel right to either of them.

Just as Liz was wondering how she and Matthew were going to get through Sunday, he said, "We need to drive down to Chandler and tell Mamie and Arthur what we've done. They're attending the court hearing with us."

Relief surged through her. "Of course. We have to do that."

Another silence followed. To ease the tension, Matthew decided that the least he could do for Liz was to play and sing for her as she had once requested. He wasn't proud of the fact that he'd turned her down before. He knew she liked the old love songs from the forties and fifties since she had purchased a couple of song books from those decades and had him play them at the store.

He got up, moved to the piano and began playing and singing.

Liz was surprised since he'd refused to play for her here before.

His voice brought back the memory of that frightening night on the mountain. For the first time since the return of her memory, she recalled how his voice and songs had elicited a deep yearning tinged with sadness. She remembered the frustration she felt at the time, not knowing or understanding these emotions. Contemplating it now, the answers were clear. Though having no memory of the hurts she'd suffered before Kirk, nor memory of the crushing blow she'd experienced at the gazebo, these experiences were obviously the cause. The last thing she remembered, before the accident, was a feeling of hopelessness—wondering if she would ever have the opportunity to love and be loved.

She could listen to Matthew's beautiful, soothing voice all day, but reality would no longer allow herself to be affected by his voice as she had been before, nor by the love songs.

After a while, Matthew got up from the piano and seated himself on the couch.

"Thank you, Matthew. I've never heard a male voice that I've liked as well as yours."

"Thank you, Liz—but I suspect the love songs are what you're really talking about."

"Love songs? I learned some time ago that most of the love songs are written by men to make money, not because they feel them. One well-known composer said he resented writing love songs, but he had to because they sold well. Most popular male singers of today belt out love songs, not from the heart, but for the same reason—money. And you, Matthew, sang for me today only because I had requested it when I was here before...not because you wanted to."

Matthew's face turned thoughtful. "Where's my Pipit? She wasn't so cynical."

"Pipit?" Matthew couldn't see Liz's sardonic smile, but heard it in her voice. "*Princess* Pipit lived a fairytale life, once upon a time, in a cabin with a king, and a prince—his handsome nephew. They took loving care of her and doted on her every need, then she was rudely returned to real life."

A half-smile appeared on Matthew's face. "Returned to reality when she went to take care of the nephew's children, or when she went home with her parents?"

"The drudgery *Princess* Pipit experienced, the cooking, cleaning and caring for the prince's children, made her feel like *Cinderella*. Gone was the doting attention she'd received from the prince. But it was when she left the prince and his two children, that her eyes were opened to real life."

"That's quite a tale, Liz. What happened at home?"

"All you need know is I've grown from my experiences and because of them, I'm closer to my family than I have been for a long time."

"I'm glad to hear that, but I'm getting mixed messages, Liz."

"Let's concentrate on the here and now, Matthew. I want to be here to help you win your children back." She got up and went over to the couch, leaned over and kissed him on the cheek. "We *are* going to get the children back," she stated with determination.

He reached up and pulled her down beside him, feeling the silk beneath his hands. *Diane always wore silk.* Finding her face, with his left hand, he kissed her lips.

The emotions it stirred up in Liz were unsettling. She pulled away. "Why did you do that, Matthew?"

He didn't know how to answer so blurted out, "I feel great affection for you, Liz and much gratitude."

"But *who* were you kissing? Me or Diane?"

Matthew stiffened and withdrew his arm from around her, his jaw rippling. "That wasn't fair, Liz."

"Maybe not, but is it true that in your mind you were kissing Diane?"

"I'm not going to honor that with an answer."

"You already have. Goodnight, Matthew. See you in the morning."

~~~~~~~~~~~~

Matthew awakened to the sightless world he still refused to accept, his heart heavy over the way he and Elizabeth had parted the night before. Mostly heavy over the selfishness he'd displayed by kissing her—trying to satisfy his own needs.

He had lain awake last night thinking about the kiss he gave Elizabeth after the marriage ceremony. He knew he definitely was not thinking of Diane at that particular moment, but here in Diane's house, Diane *was* in his mind when he kissed Liz. It wasn't fair to Liz, and he certainly found out she was too intuitive to be fooled.

He entered the family room in casual clothes and was greeted with a cheery good morning from Liz. His spirits lifted. "You are certainly cheerful after my...uh slip last night. I'm sorry, Liz. It won't happen again."

"It's all forgotten," she lied. Both kisses, like a hot branding iron, had burned themselves into her heart, and she was still too vulnerable and tender over the break up with Kirk to have that happen!

"Something smells good, Liz."

"The cupboards are bare, but I found four eggs, a tomato, a green pepper and a little cheese so I'm making us each an omelette."

"Great. I'm suddenly starved." He wanted to add...*because you've relieved my feelings of guilt.*

~~~~~~~~~~~~

Sunday afternoon, Matthew and Liz stepped up onto Arthur's and Mamie's doorstep. Liz rang the doorbell. It was Mamie who answered. She stared at them in disbelief.

"Pipit! Arthur come here!"

Matthew and Liz had just stepped in and closed the door behind them when Arthur entered the living room. "Pip ol' girl!" he exclaimed. Reaching her, he gave her an affectionate hug.

Mamie hugged her next, then looked into her face. "My, but you look lovely, my dear."

"I...I do?" she asked, surprised.

"You do at that, Pip," echoed Arthur.

"Yes," added Matthew. "I find her quite beautiful myself."

"All right, you three, I just may believe you if you don't quit—besides, Matthew and I have something to tell you."

"Come on in and sit down and tell us," Mamie responded eagerly.

Liz led Matthew to the couch. Mamie and Arthur seated themselves across from them.

Matthew took the lead, telling them of Liz's offer of a temporary marriage to thwart Elinor's efforts to take the children away. "I took her up on it. As of now, we are Mr. and Mrs. Matthew Melloy."

Mamie and Arthur were shocked speechless for a moment, then Arthur responded. "Elinor will see through this immediately."

"That's what Matthew's lawyer said, but I talked with him and suggested several things that made him feel it might work. It's worth a try."

Mamie gave Liz a grateful smile. "It surely is, my dear girl."

"If it works and you beat Elinor at her own game, what about this marriage of yours?" Arthur asked bluntly.

"We'll annul the marriage," Matthew replied.

Arthur shook his head. "This is quite a sacrifice you're making, Pipit."

Before Liz could respond, Mamie added, "And magnanimous beyond words! You and Pipit will stay for dinner won't you, Matthew?"

"You bet. My cupboards are like *Old Mother Hubbard's*. And by the way, you can call Pipit, Liz, now," he said as their eyes widened. "She has her memory back."

Chapter Forty

Monday morning, Matthew directed Liz to exit on Mesa Drive and turn right on Javelina. Driving to the north parking lot, Liz found a space. They got out and walked apprehensively toward the Superior Court of Maricopa County—a four story flat-roofed building made of sandstone adobe brick.

They entered an outer door, then an inner door where they were immediately confronted by two men manning a metal detector. Passing through successfully, Liz led Matthew to the elevators. Their nervousness once more manifested itself in her cold hand and Matthew's sweaty one. They got out on the second floor and found a sign announcing Judge Weiner's Division. Stopping at the open entrance of the courtroom, Liz's eyes first riveted on the judge's high, brown walnut bench with the Seal of Arizona behind it.

Before entering, Liz whispered to Matthew. "I see Elinor and two men."

"Describe them," he asked.

"One is tall and distinguished looking. The other one is slight with a large hook nose."

"The tall one is Wayne Halstrom, Elinor's husband. The other one is Hank Hawkins. His nickname is 'Hawk' Hawkins because of his nose and because of his ruthlessness in the courtroom."

"Mr. Hawkins seems to be trying to placate Elinor. She looks upset."

"What is Wayne doing?"

"He's standing aside."

Matthew smile was grim. "Just as I suspected. I think he may be an unwilling participant in Elinor's battle. Let's go in."

Matthew and Liz seated themselves on the front row across the aisle from the Halstroms. When Elinor Halstrom saw them, she did a double-take—staring at Liz as if she couldn't believe her eyes. Beale strolled in and sat behind the table with Matthew and Liz. Elinor turned away and whispered something to her attorney.

"I may have some good news," Beale whispered to his clients. "Judge Weiner, who I've suspected was in sympathy with the

Halstroms, had a minor heart attack last night and is in the hospital. Judge Greer will be replacing him."

Hawkins came over to them. "Excuse me, Mr. Beale, may I speak to you in private?"

Beale, a tall, dark-haired, big-boned man stood up and looked down at the small man. "You may say what you have to say in front of my client, Mr. Hawkins."

Hawkins paused, then delivered his message. "My client, Elinor Halstrom, wants to postpone the hearing for a few days."

"My client," countered Beale, "wants to get the hearing over with today."

Covering up his consternation over the unexpected change in judges, he blustered, "All right, Mr. Beale, but you may be sorry."

"We'll take our chances, counselor," he said.

The court reporter came in and seated herself in front of the judge's bench a little to the left.

Just then, Flo Henderson dressed in a bright, paisley dress and bright, dangling earrings, breezed into the courtroom, followed by the Brodericks. "Darling, how are you?" she said rushing over to Elinor. Then, just as quickly, she went over to Matthew. "How are you, dear boy?" She stared at Liz in astonishment. "Pipit, is that you? Why, I never would have recognized you, you look lovely with that new hairstyle."

"Thank you, Flo. It's a surprise to see *you* here."

"I've been called as a witness by Elinor's attorney."

Before Liz could react, Hawkins was taking Flo's arm and impatiently ushering her to Elinor's side of the courtroom. The Brodericks knew enough to stay there in the first place.

Liz smiled at Beale. "I don't think Mr. Hawkins knows what he's in for with Flo as a witness."

"I concur with Liz," whispered Matthew. "She could just as easily do us as much good as she could Elinor."

"Great," Beale said.

Mamie and Arthur slipped in and sat in the first row of seats behind Matthew and Liz. Arthur gave Matthew's shoulder a supportive clap and squeeze. "We're praying for you, Matthew."

"Thanks. Glad you got here."

The bailiff closed the courtroom doors, walked up to the front of the room and remained standing. As Judge Greer entered, the bailiff instructed, "All rise, Honorable Judge Greer presiding. Court is now in session. Please be seated."

The judge seated himself. "This is the time set for the case Halstrom versus Melloy, domestic relations 2001-1001. Are the parties ready to proceed?" Receiving affirmatives from the respective counsels, he went on. "Will the parties please introduce themselves for the record."

When that was done, Beale stood up again. "Your Honor, my client has just married Miss Elizabeth Cabot, so he and his wife, Elizabeth, are perfectly able to care for the children. I move this hearing be dismissed."

The name Elizabeth Cabot brought shock to those in the courtroom, their heads swiveling, trying to find her. The greatest disturbance came from Elinor.

Fending off the agitated questions from Elinor, Hawkins shot to his feet. "I object your honor. This evidence was deliberately withheld from us on discovery."

The judge turned to Beale. "Well, Mr. Beale?"

"Your honor, I learned of this development too late to enter for discovery."

The courtroom erupted with everyone on Elinor's side trying to talk at once.

The judge tapped his gavel. "Quiet!" he ordered. "Mr. Hawkins, do you want to confer with your client concerning these new circumstances?"

"Yes, your Honor, but first my client wants to know where this alleged Elizabeth Cabot is that Mr. Melloy was supposed to have married."

"Will you answer Mr. Hawkins' question, Mr. Beale?"

"Certainly." He motioned for Elizabeth to stand up. "This is Elizabeth Cabot Melloy."

Shocked murmurings circulated between Flo and the Brodericks. Elinor loudly expressed shock and outrage.

The judge banged his gavel. "Mr. Hawkins will you keep your client quiet. I'll have no more of this."

Hawkins told Elinor something that not only quieted her, but brought a smug and confident smile to her face. Shortly, Hawkins stated, "Your Honor, we're ready to continue."

"All right. You may call your first witness."

"I would like to call Mrs. Elinor Halstrom to the stand."

After she was sworn in, the bailiff told her to be seated. "Now, Mrs. Halstrom, Mr. Beale has informed us that your son-in-law has just married the young woman who is sitting beside him. Do you still feel it is not in the best interest of your grandchildren to remain with your son-in-law?"

"I do!"

Why, Mrs. Halstrom?"

"Because that young woman is an imposter!"

"Why do you say that, Mrs. Halstrom?"

"I went to visit my grandchildren on the day of January 28th, and found that young woman caring for them. When I asked who she was, she said her name was Pipit Bordeau."

"Why do you think she posed as a different person?"

"Objection! Speculation, your Honor."

"Sustained."

"How do you feel about her giving you a false name?"

"It worries me a great deal. My husband and I do not want a person who is deceitful to care for our grandchildren."

"Thank you, Mrs. Halstrom. That will be all."

The judge addressed Matthew's attorney. "Would you like to question the witness?"

"No questions, your Honor."

Judge Greer turned to Elinor. "You may step down, Mrs. Halstrom. Call your next witness, Mr. Hawkins."

"I call Mrs. Flo Henderson to the stand."

A still confused Flo Henderson went up. Standing before the seat she took the oath and sat down.

"Mrs. Henderson, as a neighbor of Mr. Melloy, did you get acquainted with the young woman who came to care for the Melloy children?"

"I did."

"What did she say her name was?"

She frowned and gazed questioningly at the woman she thought she knew. "She said her name was Pipit Bordeau."

"Were you shocked to hear that the woman who called herself Pipit Bordeau was deceiving you?"

"Objection! Your Honor, that implies intent."

"Sustained. Please, reword that, Mr. Hawkins."

"Were you shocked, Mrs. Henderson, when you learned that the woman who came to care for the Melloy children was not Pipit Bordeau, but in reality Elizabeth Cabot?"

"Oh, my yes! She is such a love, I wouldn't dream..."

"Mrs. Henderson, just answer the question. Don't elaborate. What kind of a father has Mr. Melloy been to his children since the car accident?"

"He was a wonderful father before the accident, but..."

"Mrs. Henderson, answer *only* the questions I ask."

"The poor dear man lost his eyesight as well as his wife so..."

"Please do not comment! Just answer the question."

"I'm trying to, love, but it's complicated. Like any man who has lost his wife and the mother of his children, he..."

Hawkins' voice turned low and menacing. "Mrs. Henderson, answer only the question."

Flo's lips tightened. "He could hardly be the father he was."

"So how long did this unfortunate situation keep him from being the father he was?"

"Well...for a couple of months after the accident, and then the dear man seemed to rally for few a months, but grief pulled him down again."

"What happened then?"

"His uncle Arthur and aunt Mamie took things in hand. They came and got the children and took them to Chandler. His aunt Mamie kept the children and his uncle Arthur took Matthew up to a winter cabin for a rest."

"How do you know this?"

"I called Mamie to see how they were and she told me."

"How was he when he returned home?"

"I don't know. I didn't see him, but I did see uh...or rather I met uh...the young woman they brought back with them to care for the children."

"Thank you, Mrs. Henderson. That will be all."

Judge Greer nodded toward Beale. "Would you like to question the witness, Mr. Beale?"

"I would, your Honor," he replied stepping over to the witness stand. "Mrs. Henderson, did Mr. Melloy go back to work after the funeral of his wife?"

"He did. It was amazing. The loss of his eyesight didn't seem to deter him at all."

"Who cared for the children?"

"Mrs. Danville."

"Who is Mrs. Danville?"

"She is an employee of Mrs. Halstrom."

"Did she take good care of the children?"

"Oh, my yes. She took care of them just like Diane, their mother, would have wanted."

"Did the children like Mrs. Danville?"

Flo Henderson hesitated. "I...don't know."

"Why do you say that, Mrs. Henderson?"

"Because they didn't smile often around her."

"I object!" bellowed Hawkins. " Hearsay, your Honor. Mrs. Henderson wasn't always around while Mrs. Danville cared for the children."

"Sustained."

"I understand you gave the children art lessons three times a week, Mrs. Henderson."

"I did, the little loves."

"How did they act during those times?"

"They started out painting nicely, but they always ended up fighting."

"Be more specific."

"Merri acted hostile to Danny, poor boy. Soon, he started hitting back."

"Were these actions conspicuous *before* the accident?"

"They were." Realizing what she'd said, her hand flew to her mouth, looking nervously at Elinor. "I mean..."

"I understand you and Diane Melloy were good friends. Is that right?"

Flo, obviously relieved at the change in direction answered quickly. "Oh my yes. She was a wonderful friend."

"How did you become friends?"

"Objection. Your Honor, this has no relevance to the issue."

"Your Honor," countered Beale, "this has great relevance if you'll allow me to continue."

"Overruled. You may answer the question, Mrs. Henderson."

"When Diane and her husband moved into the neighborhood, I went over and welcomed them. Diane, always so interested in others, found out I was an artist and asked to see my work. Well, she was so enthusiastic about my paintings, she sponsored several art shows for me—the dear."

"So you feel beholden to her mother to testify in her behalf?"

"Objection!"

"Overruled."

"Of course I feel beholden to her mother. She also sponsored art shows for me."

"Thank you, Mrs. Henderson. That will be all for now." Turning to the judge he said, "I reserve the right to question this witness later if I deem it necessary."

"You're excused, Mrs. Henderson," Judge Greer said. "Mr. Hawkins, do you have another witness?"

"I do, you Honor. I call Mrs. Broderick."

After she was sworn in and seated, Hawkins smiled confidently. "Mrs. Broderick, would you tell the judge about your visit to the Melloy household on January 4th of this year?"

"Yes. It was three-thirty in the afternoon. My husband and I took a meal over to Matthew and the children."

"Who answered the door, Mrs. Broderick?"

"His little five-year-old daughter, Merri."

"What happened next?"

"Merri was glad to see us, and was excited to see that we had brought something for them. We followed her in, and I placed the food on the kitchen counter. The kitchen is connected to the family room, you see."

"Where did you find Mr. Melloy?"

"He was sitting on the couch staring straight ahead."

"What happened next, Mrs. Broderick?"

"We spoke to Matthew and told him we had brought dinner in. He thanked us, but he didn't even smile. This was not at all like Matthew. Danny, his four-year-old son, came running into the room. Merri told her brother excitedly that we had brought dinner. He ran to his daddy and jumped up on his lap and said, 'Daddy the Brodericks brought us dinner.''

"How did Mr. Melloy react to him?"

"He didn't. He just sat there. We tried to talk to him, but he could barely answer, in fact, he could barely answer his children."

Liz listened, shocked at the depths to which Matthew had sunk. She wondered if the death of Diane, and becoming blind were the total cause of his actions, or was it something in addition to that? Something that intensified the tragedy and plummeted him to the depths? Mrs. Broderick's answer to Hawkin's next question broke into her thoughts.

"We left and went over to Flo's, I mean, Mrs. Henderson's and asked her if she knew the Halstrom's phone number. She did, but she told us the Halstroms were on a cruise. She told us not to worry, that she would call Matthew's uncle Arthur and aunt Mamie. We went back over to Matthew's, stayed with the children and saw to it that they ate dinner. When Matthew's uncle and aunt arrived, we left."

"Thank you, Mrs. Broderick. That will be all."

"Would you like to question the witness, Mr. Beale?"

"No, your Honor."

"You are excused, Mrs. Broderick. You may proceed, Mr. Hawkins."

"I would like to call Mr. Arthur Melloy to the stand."

After the usual procedure, Hawkins began, "Mr. Melloy, when you took your nephew, Matthew Melloy, and his two children to Chandler, how long did they stay with you?"

"Three days, then I took Matthew up to our mountain cabin. The children remained with my wife, Mamie."

"Why didn't you take your nephew to a psychiatrist, Mr. Melloy?"

"Because Matthew didn't need a psychiatrist."

"Oh? And how could you possibly know that?"

"Matthew has lived with us since he was fifteen years old. I know him pretty well."

"Why did you take him to your mountain cabin? To practice your own brand of psychiatry?"

"I took him to the cabin to get him away for a few days—away from everyone and every place that reminded him of the loss of his wife, Diane."

"After eight months, it seems that Mr. Melloy should begin to get hold of himself, doesn't it?"

"He held it together all that time...until that day Mrs. Broderick went over—and frankly, I find that quite amazing."

"And on that day when he could no longer hold it together, he had sole care of the children, and apparently, you and your wife were frightened because after three days you separated him from his children."

"Objection! Speculation."

"Sustained."

"All right, tell the judge why you really took your nephew up the your cabin."

"I believe I have already answered that, Mr. Hawkins."

"Placate me, Mr. Melloy, answer it again."

"Objection!"

"Overruled."

"I think Matthew deserved to have a small break—which he had previously denied himself."

"Thank you, Mr. Melloy. That will be all."

"Mr. Beale?"

"Yes, your honor."

In two strides, he stood before Arthur. "Did the cabin retreat help Matthew, Mr. Melloy?"

"Almost immediately. He was soon acting more like himself."

"In what way?"

"Well, not only have I been an uncle/father to Matthew, but we've always had a special rapport. Matthew was soon laughing at my corny humor and he was cracking his own, and I knew he was ready to go back to his children. We had planned on staying four days or less, but we got snowed in."

"Thank you, Mr. Melloy. That will be all."

The judge dismissed Arthur, then turned to Hawkins. "Do you have another witness, Mr. Hawkins?"

"Your honor, we would like to know if Mr. Beale intends to call the new Mrs. Melloy to the stand?"

"Mr. Beale, will you state your intentions?"

"Yes, your Honor, I do intend to call Mrs. Melloy."

"In that case," said Hawkins, "the plaintiff rests."

"Mr. Beale," said Judge Greer, "you may call your first witness."

"Thank you, your Honor. I would like to call Mike Banning to the stand. He's waiting outside the courtroom."

"Bailiff, please call in Mr. Banning," Judge Greer directed.

A couple of minutes later, Beale stood before him. "Mr. Banning, you help manage one of Mr. Melloy's music stores. Is that right?"

"Right. I've been training for quite some time, and now I'm a full-fledged manager."

"Before you entered the courtroom, Mr. Banning, we were told that a Mrs. Broderick visited Mr. Melloy at his home on January 4th of this year. Two days before that, was Mr. Melloy at work?"

"Yes sir."

"In what condition did you find him?"

"I found him his usual self, cheerful, able to manage his affairs, very obliging and helpful to the customers. If you were to ask any of the other employees, they would tell you the same thing."

"One day before Mrs. Broderick's visit, what was he like?"

"Exactly the same."

"How about the day in question?"

"I don't remember Mr. Melloy being different on any day."

"Have you at any time seen him withdrawn and depressed?"

"I saw great sadness and grief in him, but I have never seen him withdrawn and depressed, and I've see him and his children often since I also chauffeur him to his home every night and pick him up the next morning."

"Thank you, Mr. Banning. That will be all."

"Would you like to question the witness, Mr. Hawkins?" Judge Greer asked.

"No, your Honor."

"You may step down, Mr. Banning. Mr. Beale?"

"I would like to call Elizabeth Cabot Melloy to the stand."

"I object!" exclaimed Hawkins. "This woman is a fraud. She called herself Pipit Bordeau when Mrs. Halstrom first met her."

"Your Honor," Beale said, "there is a logical explanation to Mr. Hawkin's objection."

"There had better be, Mr. Beale. Overruled, Mr. Hawkins."

Liz stared unflinchingly into the hostile eyes of Elinor Halstrom, then her gaze traveled to Matthew's concerned and serious one.

Beale looked confidently at Liz. "Will you tell us how you became acquainted with Matthew Melloy, and why you called yourself Pipit Bordeau?"

"I will." She started at the beginning, her eyes glancing now and then at Elinor to gauge her reactions. It was visibly a shock when Liz told of her amnesia. Beale's questions and her answers brought the story to the time she returned to Arizona with her memory intact.

As he and Elizabeth Melloy had previously planned, Beale ended the questions. "That will be all for now, Mrs. Melloy. I would like to reserve the right to question this witness later, your Honor."

"Would you like to question the witness, Mr. Hawkins?"

"Yes, your Honor," Hawkins said, jumping to his feet. Though unprepared for Elizabeth Cabot Melloy's disclosure, and momentarily disarmed, there was a glimmer of victory in his eyes. Sidling up to Liz, he cracked a smile. "So, you and Matthew Melloy got married this weekend. Is that right?"

Liz put on a glowing smile. "That's right, Mr. Hawk."

The smile left his face. "Hawkins."

"Oh excuse me, Mr. Hawkins."

"Where were you married, Mrs. Melloy?"

"We flew to Las Vegas to get married."

With a look of skepticism on his face, and a patronizing tone to his voice, he asked, "Did you really think you and Matthew Melloy could make us believe that this quickie marriage is not just what it appears.?"

"How does it appear, Mr. Hawkins?"

"I ask the questions, Mrs. Melloy."

"I'm sorry," she stated contritely, "but I don't know what you mean by 'what it appears.'"

"It appears that Mr. Melloy paid you a large sum of money to bribe you into..."

"Objection! Conjecture."

"Sustained."

"Have you ever been married before Mrs. Melloy?"

"No."

"No? And you didn't mind getting married in such a crass way...no wedding gown, no wedding reception?"

Her silence wasn't intended, but the tears had begun far down in her chest. She looked down and unconsciously wrung her hands while wondering if a touch of sincere emotion would possibly help since her distress was obviously apparent. All she hoped was that she could control it. She swallowed several times.

"Mrs. Melloy?"

"I...I did mind. I have always wanted a church wedding...a white wedding dress, but..." Her voice trailed off.

"But what Mrs. Melloy?" he asked, his small eyes boring into her.

"But Mrs. Halstrom made it impossible."

"Mrs. Halstrom?" he asked, momentarily taken by surprise. "Why would you blame such a thing on this poor, worried grandmother?"

"Because, when I surprised Matthew by arriving at his Phoenix store Saturday, he told me that Mrs. Halstrom was taking him to court this morning to try to take the children away from him. It was a little late to plan a church wedding."

"It seems to me, Mrs. Melloy that if two people are planning marriage, they would have talked about it previous to last Saturday." From information Elinor had given him after she obtained it from an unsuspecting Matthew himself, he asked the next question. "Also, they would have kept in communication with each other. Did you communicate with each other after you left?"

"No."

"Then this so-called marriage was planned spontaneously on Saturday, right?"

"Matthew mentioned marriage to me a couple of days before I left."

"Is that right. It was planned then?" he asked skeptically.

"Of course not. How could I get married under the false name of Pipit Bordeau?"

"But you talked about marriage and still you didn't communicate?" Hawkins appeared smugly confident.

"My parents told me that I was engaged, but of course I had no memory of it. Why would Matthew communicate with me when he thought I was engaged?"

This surprise was unwelcome to Hawkins, but he quickly recovered. "Why didn't *you* communicate with him?"

"Because it felt hopeless. My past memory was gone."

Hawkins took an uneasy breath. "When did you regain your memory?"

"Nine days ago."

"Did you call Matthew Melloy nine days ago?"

"No."

His confidence renewed, Hawkins asked, "And why not—if you were so eager to marry him?"

"I had to work out some personal problems caused by the breakup of my engagement."

"That sounds very convenient, Mrs. Melloy. You broke off your engagement so you could run off to Las Vegas and get married?"

"Objection! He's badgering the witness."

"Sustained."

"Why did you break off your engagement, Mrs. Melloy?"

"My engagement was broken off before I left home the first time—before my car accident. But since I didn't remember that, when my memory returned, I had to go through it all again, so to speak, and emotionally adjust all over again before I could return to Matthew."

"A lovely story, Mrs. Melloy—one right out of the movies. Maybe you don't realize, but Mr. Melloy married one of the most desirable and beautiful women in Arizona, Diane Halstrom. Do you really expect us to believe that he wanted to marry *you?* So, as I asked before, how is Mr. Melloy going to compensate you for helping him keep the children he can no longer care for?"

Liz winced inside. Matthew's jaw rippling in anger, his hands clenched, he leaned over to Beale and whispered vehemently, "Object!"

"Hang on, Matthew," Beale whispered back. "I didn't know that was coming, but don't worry, we have it planned. Liz has it under control."

Liz spoke deliberately, condescendingly. "Mr. Hawkins, My father's name is Calvin Cabot. He is a very wealthy man. I have a large trust fund to use however I choose, so—I hardly think I need compensation."

Though taken aback by this revelation, Hawkins didn't flinch. His steel-trap mind quickly led him to another conclusion. "I....see. Considering how beautiful Mr. Melloy's deceased wife was, maybe *you* saw an opportunity for a marriage you couldn't possibly otherwise have had. Did you compensate *him*?"

Before his words could sink to the deepest, most tender spot of her soul, and before Beale could utter a word of objection, Matthew shot to his feet. "That was uncalled for!"

"Objection!" Beale yelled immediately after.

The judge hammered his gavel. "You, Mr. Melloy, are out of order. And you, Mr. Hawkins, are out of line. The objection is sustained."

Hawkins was concerned that his present tactics might backfire—but it was the only chance he had. To this point, Elizabeth Melloy had clearly out-maneuvered him. He assumed an aggressive tone.

"Mrs. Melloy, are you aware how few marriages consummated in such haste, survive? Even for a year?"

Elizabeth's voice was low and strained. "No." This was the one area in which they were vulnerable, and they hoped that Hawkins would not use it.

"Well," stated Hawkins, "it's less than 25%. That means there is a 75% chance the children will again be without a mother—then the damage done to them might be irreparable."

Beale jumped to his feet, his face flushed in anger. "Objection, your Honor. Mr. Hawkins is not cross examining a witness, he's arguing his case. There is no way *anyone* can know absolutely that any marriage will last, but these two are obviously very much in love."

Elizabeth's heart had sunk within her when she heard Hawkins argument. Could she really be hurting Danny and Merri more than they had been already?

"I'll sustain the objection," Judge Greer said. "Mr. Hawkins, you may proceed."

"That will be all, Mrs. Melloy," Hawkins stated with confidence. He sat down.

"Re-direct, your Honor?"

"You may, Mr. Beale."

"Thank you. Mrs. Melloy, if by chance, the judge awards custody of Mr. Melloy's children to Mr. and Mrs. Halstrom, what will you do?"

"Matthew and I will fight it. We'll appeal. Matthew has funds to fight it. I have funds. If they're depleted, there are many wealthy friends of mine in Palm Springs who can match the wealth of the Halstroms, and who would consider this a worthy cause."

Matthew was in awe over Liz's maneuvering, and this last statement blew him away.

"How do you feel about Matthew's children, Merri and Danny?"

"I love them."

"You were with them such a short time. How could this be possible?"

"I wondered that myself when someone else posed the same question. As I thought about it, I realized that the children, suffering from the loss of their mother, and I, suffering over the loss of my memory, were brought closer in a shorter than normal period of time while we struggled together."

"Thank you, Mrs. Melloy. That will be all."

"Your Honor, I would like to recall to the stand Mrs. Flo Henderson."

The surprise on the faces of Hawkins and Elinor surpassed that of Flo Henderson.

Beale faced the witness, he felt, who could unwittingly hammer a final nail into the Halstrom's custody case. "Mrs. Henderson, you mentioned how badly the children were acting, Merri in particular, since the accident."

"Yes, the poor little dears."

"I want you to think carefully before answering my next question. You indicated on previous examination that the children's inappropriate behavior had begun *before* the accident. Is that correct?"

Beale could tell immediately that she felt a conflict of loyalties.

"Mrs. Henderson, you swore to tell the truth."

"Why of course, Mr. Beale. I wouldn't consider anything less, but it's complicated, you see."

"Complicated because you feel loyalty to both the Halstroms and Matthew Melloy?"

"Oh yes, Mr. Beale. That's exactly how I feel. You see I think Diane was a wonderful person. Everyone loved her. She was a wonderful mother...but..." she glanced uneasily in Elinor's direction, "Merri didn't act much differently before the accident. I never could understand why she was always so unkind to her little brother."

"Thank you for answering so honestly. Now, think carefully again, Mrs. Henderson. When the young woman you knew as Pipit Bordeau came to care for the children, did any change take place in their behavior?"

"Objection! He's leading the witness."

"Overruled."

Beale exhaled a quiet breath of relief and waited for Mrs. Henderson's answer.

"The first day I visited Pipit and the children and invited them over to my place, Merri was still acting difficult. It wasn't long, however, until I began to see a great change come over her. The hostility toward Danny seemed to stop altogether...as far as I could see. I remember feeling quite amazed at Pipit's way with children."

"Did you see any improvement in Merri when she stayed for a period of time with the Halstroms?"

"No. In fact..." her voice trailed off under Elinor's intimidating glare.

"Please go on, Mrs. Henderson."

"I...I believe, if anything, both children were worse."

"Thank you very much, Mrs. Henderson. That will be all. Your Honor, this is my last witness."

"You may step down, Mrs. Henderson," Judge Greer said. He was thoughtful for a moment before he announced, "There is one more thing that has to take place here. I understand, Mrs. Halstrom, your employee, Mrs. Danville is watching the children in another room. Is that correct?"

A tight-lipped Elinor Halstrom answered curtly. "That's correct."

"Bailiff, will you please bring the children into the courtroom?"

Liz reached over and took Matthew's hand and held it tightly. It was trembling slightly.

"Thank you," he whispered.

Liz, anxious to see the children, swivelled her head toward the doors. Presently the bailiff opened them and Mrs. Danville nervously stepped in, her back rigid and straight, she gripped the children's hands tightly. They both looked confused and frightened, their steps hesitant. Her face grim, Mrs. Danville jerked them forward.

"Mrs. Danville, please approach the bench," Judge Greer stated. When the three halted before the judge, he stood up, leaned over slightly and smiled. "Hello, Merri and Danny. My name is Judge Greer. I understand you have been staying with your grandmother and grandfather. Do you like staying with them?" They both nodded solemnly. "Would you like to live with them?"

"I want to live with my daddy," Merri spoke quietly, her chin quivering.

"I want to, too," Danny added timidly.

Would you like to see your daddy now?"

"Yes!" they chorused.

"He's right over there." Judge Greer pointed the direction.

Their heads whirled around, and they pulled away from Mrs. Danville's grip and ran toward him. Halfway there, Merri stopped and stared at Pipit who was smiling at them.

"Pipit? Pipit!" She raced to her and threw her arms around her. "You've come back!"

Liz hugged her tightly. A lump that felt as large as a golf ball lodged in her throat. "Yes. I've come back just as I said I would."

Danny just stood staring at her, his eyes wide in disbelief. Liz reached out with one arm. He ran to her and she pulled him close.

Matthew sat still, listening to the interaction, hearing every movement of the three beside him, his face no longer an emotionless mask. His lower lip quivering, he swallowed hard.

Judge Greer's voice rose. "Mr. and Mrs. Halstrom, do you see what I just saw?"

Elinor Halstrom glared at the judge. "That woman is an imposter! She can't possibly take my Diane's place."

Wayne Halstrom put his hand over his wife's. "Elinor, can't you see that she's good for the children? Let it go."

Elinor jerked her hand away. "Wayne! How can you say that?!"

The judge slammed the gavel down. "I'm ready to make a ruling. I grant custody of Meredith and Daniel Melloy to their father, Matthew Milner Melloy."

"No!" Elinor cried.

"Mrs. Halstrom, I see that you are a woman who is used to getting your way. I suggest you go home and try to develop some understanding and a little charity toward your son-in-law and your grandchildren. Mr. Hawkins will you escort your client out, please."

'Hawk' Hawkins had lost the higher fee promised if he won the case, but his dislike for Elinor Halstrom overrode his greed. A perverse smile twitched at his lips as he gripped her upper arm. "Come, Mrs. Halstrom."

She stood up. "Let go of me! You're fired." Her chin held high, she stepped to the aisle. Ignoring her son-in-law and grandchildren, she clipped out of the courtroom. Wayne Halstrom followed; a strong, successful financier, yet unable to influence his wife. He was so embarrassed by her actions he could neither smile nor nod at his grandchildren as he, too, left the courtroom. Mrs. Danville marched close behind.

Though overjoyed at the verdict, Matthew, Liz and the others found their joy tempered by the tragic rift Elinor had created.

Judge Greer spoke into the silence. "Mr. and Mrs. Melloy, I congratulate you on your marriage, though hurried and not in the manner you would have liked, your children will thank you one day." He smiled. "I wish you well." His gavel rose and fell. "Case dismissed." He rose.

The bailiff stood up. "This matter is adjourned. All rise."

The judge exited.

Walking to the doors, the bailiff opened them. "We need to clear the courtroom for the next case."

They all silently filed out. In the hall, Liz, hanging onto the children's hands, walked them quickly around a corner, and pulled them aside where they couldn't hear the neighbors congratulating Matthew on his winning the custody battle as well as his marriage. She and Matthew had to discuss what they were going to tell them. Mamie and Arthur followed and suggested to the children they go with them to find a treat in a vending machine.

Liz waited a few minutes before going back to Matthew. She wasn't in any mood to hear congratulations on their marriage.

Flo had been the first to speak to Matthew, ending her conversation with, "As fond of Elinor as I am, dear boy, I'm so happy you got custody of the children."

"Thank you, Flo," he smiled. "Thank you for being so forthright about everything. You helped me win my children."

The Brodericks stepped over to Matthew and apologized for having to tell what they did, and also expressed their happiness over the judge's ruling, and his marriage.

Mike was congratulating Matthew on his marriage when Liz walked up to them. "I'm happy for you both."

"Thank you, Mike."

"I guess you'll be taking off for a few days won't you Matthew?" he asked, grinning.

For a moment, Matthew didn't know what Mike meant. Liz spoke up quickly. "Not for a while, Mike. Our honeymoon will have to wait. The children have been through too much, we can't leave them right now."

"Oh. Hope it won't be too long before you both can take off. You deserve a break after all this."

"Thanks, Mike." Matthew said. "And thanks for testifying on my behalf. I think I'll be going to work tomorrow."

"Okay. I'll pick you up."

As Mike walked off, Mamie and Arthur, with the children munching on candy, returned. "Matthew and Liz," Mamie said, "I think we all need to drive to Chandler and eat lunch at our house. If I'm feeling too emotional to eat out in public, I'm sure you both are much more so."

Liz could have cried, she was so grateful for Mamie's suggestion.

Chapter Forty-One

The children had wanted to sit by both Liz and their father during the drive to Chandler, but since that was impossible, Matthew sat in the back seat with one on each side while Liz drove. Merri and Danny, happy to be with their father again, chattered incessantly—oblivious to the turmoil going on inside Liz and Matthew.

As she drove, Liz had only half-listened to the threesome in the back; she was grappling with disparate emotions as her mind went over the whole court hearing, particularly her part in it...and the final ruling. She fluctuated from happiness and relief that they'd won, to despondency over hers and Matthew's deception. The fact that she had told nothing but the truth on the stand didn't help. During most of the drive, all she could focus on was Judge Greer's kindness afterward—his congratulations and his confidence in their future. It didn't matter, she still felt she had lied to the judge.

When they arrived in Chandler, Arthur transferred the children to his car, suggesting that he and Mamie take them over to Randy's to play with their cousins. He knew Liz and Matthew needed some time alone.

Entering his uncle's house, Matthew settled himself on the couch, assuming Liz would sit down with him. But she didn't. He sat there stiffly, waiting, listening intently, trying to figure out where she was. His heart was so full of gratitude to her, he wanted to hold her hand and thank her the best he could. He'd been blown away by her performance on the stand.

"Liz?"

No answer. "Liz, where are you?"

Barely audible, she replied, "I'm over here by the front window."

He got up and felt his way to the window and found her arm. "What is it, Liz?"

"Nothing."

"The tone of your voice is giving you away, Liz."

"I...was thinking about how kind Judge Greer was."

"And you probably felt as guilty as I did...do. It's against your nature to be deceptive, and it's also against mine." He heaved a sigh. "I'm sorry you're having to go through this, Liz. Saying thank you for making it possible for me to retain custody of my children seems terribly inadequate. I'll be in your debt for the rest of my life."

Pulling her into his arms, Matthew held her tightly. "You did a magnificent job up there on the stand. Though Flo helped, it was really you, Liz, who won the custody battle for me...you with your sincerity, your credibility, and your cleverness." He couldn't go on; he felt a little choked up as he had in the courtroom when she spoke of wanting a church wedding and a white dress. With all his heart, he hoped she wouldn't consider this temporary marriage as her *first* marriage.

They stayed in each other's arms for some time, each trying to gather strength from the other. It was Liz who pulled away.

"I want you to know, Matthew, that if I had to do it all over again, I would do exactly what I did. But you and I didn't have time to go over all the ramifications of how it would affect Merri and Danny. They heard the judge congratulate us on our marriage. Though they don't seem to have understood it, friends and neighbors, I'm afraid, will help them along by calling me their stepmother. If they start thinking of me that way, it will be harder on them when I leave the second time."

"That thought has passed through my mind more than once, Liz, but I've consoled myself with the fact that they would be much worse off being raised by their grandmother."

Liz allowed herself to relax somewhat, knowing Matthew was right.

~~~~~~~~~~~~

Shortly after arriving home, Matthew took two tired children by the hand and led them to their bedrooms. It had been a traumatic day for them and they had played hard with their cousins.

Liz went to her room, and walked around restlessly trying to get up courage to call her parents. She had promised to call when she knew where she'd be staying, which should have been last Saturday night, and here it was Monday evening. She knew that their concern over the delay would be nothing compared to the way they were going to feel over her marrying Matthew. The time had come; she couldn't put it off any longer. She dialed her home.

"Hello." It was her father.

Good, she thought, *they're both home*. "Hi, Dad."

"Liz! We've been wondering why you haven't called. Surely, it didn't take you that long to know where you'd be staying."

"Is mother there?"

"Yes, she is."

"Would you get her on the phone, too, please? I have something to tell you."

His moment of silence told her he felt apprehensive. "All right, Liz, I'll put her on."

Her mother's anxious voice came over the line. "What is it, Liz?"

"Hello, Mother. I'm fine, but I beg you both to try and understand what I'm going to tell you. It will be difficult for you, but please try."

"Oh, Liz, you're frightening me."

"We're listening," her father said.

"When I arrived at Matthew's store Saturday, I went in to see him. He was very happy about my memory coming back, but I'm sorry to report, his sight hasn't yet. I invited him to lunch. When we were in the car, he told me that because his sight hadn't returned, his mother-in-law had convinced Child Protection Services to take Merri and Danny from him, and that she was taking him to court the following Monday morning to try and get custody of the children.

"Mother and Dad, I know Elinor Halstrom, and I know what kind of life they would have with her. They love and need their father; he loves and needs them. I owe my life to Matthew, and I love Merri and Danny so..." She stopped and said a quick prayer.

Julia huffed out an impatient breath of air. "You don't mean you are going to stay there and be a cook and nanny, Liz?!"

"Well...not exactly. I suggested to Matthew that we get married."

"Liz no!" Julia protested.

"It's only temporary, Mother."

"How could you get married that fast?" her father asked, a ragged edge to his voice.

"I suggested we fly to Las Vegas."

"Tell me you didn't, Liz," her mother pleaded.

"We did, but it's a marriage in name only. When Matthew's sight returns, we'll have it annulled."

Her father's voice turned hard. "And what if he doesn't regain his sight?"

"He will, Dad, I feel it. I've always felt it."

"Your 'feeling' may be just wishful thinking, Liz," he replied skeptically. "I hope you're right—for his sake...but especially for yours. You say the court hearing was scheduled for this morning?"

"Yes."

"I suppose they saw through this quickie marriage?"

"They saw through it, Dad, but we circumvented it. We won. The judge granted Matthew custody of his children. I'll tell you about it in detail when you come and visit us."

"Visit you?" Julia asked. "I couldn't bear to watch you in a loveless marriage, Liz, taking care of other people's children when you should be where you can meet men and get on with your own life and have children of your own."

"I could use your moral support. I could use my sisters' moral support, but I understand if none of you can give it."

Liz heard a quiet sob. As she tried to reassure her parents, her voice broke. "I'm sorry I've caused you grief once more. One of my main goals is to ease your hearts concerning me. It will happen one day. I promise."

~~~~~~~~~~~~

After showering and dressing for bed, Liz went into the family room hoping Matthew was still up, feeling the need of his companionship after the disheartening call to her parents. She found him listening to a news channel. "Hi," she said, curling up on the couch.

"Hi," he said, pushing the off button on the remote.

"How were the children when you put them to bed?"

"They were so tired they hardly put up a fuss, but they did ask me several times if you were going to stay and how long."

The tears had been close to the surface after the court hearing, closer still when speaking with her parents, now, hearing that the children already were asking how long she was going to stay, she could no longer hold them in. Her efforts to keep her sobs silent were in vain. Matthew heard them.

Matthew, thoroughly distressed, realized how much more emotional Liz was than Diane. As fragile as Diane seemed, she hardly ever cried, tears rarely surfaced in her beautiful gray eyes—for which he had been grateful. His tenderhearted mother cried easily he remembered. And he recalled how it anguished him. He had stoically let Liz cry before, but tonight, he wished he could pretend he hadn't heard her crying, say goodnight and escape to his room! But he owed Liz so much. "Don't try to suppress the sound of your tears, Liz. Go ahead and cry...let it all out."

Liz felt that her tears could go on for hours tonight, so as soon as she could, she stopped, pulled out a tissue she'd pocketed while talking with her parents, and wiped her eyes. "Thank you, Matthew."

"Have you called your parents, yet?"

"Yes."

"They were upset over our marriage weren't they?"

"Yes, but then we didn't expect anything else, did we?"

"No, I guess not," he replied, his heart heavy over having to use Liz, upset her parents, and in the end hurt his children when the time came for Liz to leave. He was not going to tell Liz that he had decided that if in three months his sight had not returned, he was going to insist on her leaving anyway.

Though reluctant to leave Matthew's comforting presence, Liz said, "I think we both need to turn in. It has been a long and difficult day."

Matthew stood up. "Yes. We need to. See you tomorrow morning—my little snow angel."

Chapter Forty-Two

The alarm awakened Liz abruptly, reminding her that she was back to the old grind she had so disliked. However, it felt easier, now, with her memory, a car and a driver's license! And she was anxious to spend the day with Merri and Danny.

Quickly dressing, she washed her face, brushed her teeth and went out into the kitchen to investigate the food situation. Finding milk and cold cereal the only thing available, she mentally took note that menus and grocery shopping had to be number one on the 'to do' list today, wishing Matthew could afford a cook. How she had taken her wealthy lifestyle for granted these many years!

She looked around the kitchen and family room, aware for the first time since she had returned, that the house needed cleaning, also. "I need a maid."

"What did you say?" Matthew asked.

Startled, Liz turned to see Matthew standing behind her grinning.

"Apparently you heard what I said. I hate being caught talking to myself."

"Would you like me to hire a maid?"

Liz thought about it, but before she could reply, the children came running into the room. They threw their arms around her. "Pipit! Pipit! You stayed," Merri exclaimed, Danny repeating it right after.

"I did," she smiled, crouching down and hugging them both.

"Do we get to go swimming?" Danny asked.

"Hey, you two," Matthew said, "Pipit isn't here to just play with you, she has lots to do. You both need to help her. You need to do your chores."

"We will if..." Merri began.

"I will, Daddy," Danny said.

Merri slapped Danny. "You interrupted me! I was talking."

Danny let out an ear-piercing howl. Liz took his hand and pulled him away from Merri, trying to calm him.

Matthew took Merri's hand. "We need to go into your bedroom and talk."

"No!" She refused to walk.

"Merri, do as I say."

"I don't have to!" she yelled, pulling her hand away. "Grandmother said I didn't have to obey you."

Liz was appalled. "Merri, obey your father."

"No!" She dodged her father's reaching hand.

Liz went over and took Merri's hand and placed it firmly into her father's. Matthew, his face grim, marched her into the bedroom, and Liz had a talk with Danny, informing him that his grandmother was wrong, that he and Merri had to obey their father and her, as well. Danny, his eyes wide over Liz's tone of voice, nodded wordlessly.

"Now, go get dressed, Danny and make your bed."

"I didn't have to make my bed at Grandmother's house."

"This isn't your grandmother's house, is it?"

"No."

"So go do as your father said. Making your bed is part of your chores."

"Oh, okay," he said, walking toward the hall.

Liz fumed as she got out the bowls and spoons for their cold cereal. "Hiring a maid is out!"

"It is?" asked Matthew.

"Matthew! Don't sneak up on me."

He laughed. "I enjoy hearing you talk to yourself. Why is hiring a maid out?"

"After that little display of Merri's, and Danny telling me he didn't have to make his bed at his grandmother's, I've decided that all three of us are going to learn how to work."

Matthew chuckled. "You're an amazing woman for a 'spoiled rich kid."

"Thanks. You're mis-matched, Matthew."

"Huh?"

"That tie doesn't go with your shirt and pants."

"Oh. I didn't want to bother you."

"Bother? Aren't *wives* supposed to be helpmates?" As she said it, it sounded foreign. "Or something," she added, taking his hand and leading him toward his bedroom.

~~~~~~~~~~~~~~

March was the beginning of spring in the desert, and Liz had learned to love the desert. She'd had to in order to survive the summer heat of the more formidable desert of Palm Springs. Unlike many of the residents, her parents only escaped the summer heat for about two to three weeks, and then went on about life as usual, except for more cooling off in the pool.

Though the elevation of Cave Creek was almost twice as high as Phoenix and a little cooler, she was sure that some of the desert flowers would be out now.

She hummed as she put away the last of the groceries, deciding to take the children for a walk and introduce them to the desert wild flowers, certain that this was one area in which Diane hadn't educated them. At least, there was one other thing besides swimming she was better at than Diane.

Her singing stopped as she thought back over the day. The children had begrudgingly done their chores, and in the midst of them had several altercations with each other. In the grocery store, they also begged and whined for everything that struck their fancy. When she hadn't succumbed, they both threw tantrums, making her want to slink down behind the grocery cart. She decided, reluctantly, that they had to be punished. When she had informed them upon arriving home, that because of their actions in the grocery store, there would be no swimming today, they both howled.

The deterioration in their behavior made Liz shudder. She had a new appreciation of the way her parents had raised her and her sisters before they moved to Palm Springs. They had to earn money by doing extra around the house, and babysitting. Her parents were firm in their expectations, giving them clear and solid boundaries.

Things changed when they moved to Palm Springs. It was a big adjustment for all of them, including her parents. She remembered her father seem preoccupied and unhappy for a while. Her mother was also preoccupied, but for a different reason. She wanted to fit in with those around her in the wealthy neighborhood, so she began entertaining in a way she never had. In this distracted state, her parents had allowed maids to make her and her sisters' beds, and do the cleaning they had had to do in their smaller home in Los Angeles. Her mother hired a full-time cook. And of course, her daughters had to have the material things the other children had so they, too, could 'fit in.'

What bothered Liz the most, she recalled, was that they quit reading the Bible as a family. The lack of a spiritual presence left her feeling rudderless and insecure among her parents' wealthy friends.

Yes, she and her sisters had become 'spoiled rich kids' as Arthur had put it. She could see it in them as well as herself.

Glancing over at the children, she saw that they were still content drawing and coloring at the table, so she escaped to her bedroom. Her good mood had evaporated, and she felt totally inadequate as a *mother*—for that was what she had to be for a while. She sat on the bed and let the tears roll freely down her cheeks. "I can't...I just can't do this."

"What can't you do, Pipit?" asked a tremulous voice from the doorway.

"Yeah, what, Pipit?" asked Danny.

Unnerved that they had followed her, she looked up. Their sweet faces were so sympathetic it proved her undoing. She covered her face and cried softly. Small arms wrapped around her on both sides.

"Don't cry, Pipit," came the tearful voice of Danny.

"We're sorry, Pipit," wailed Merri.

All three had a good cry together, after which they looked at each other and started laughing.

"Well, if we aren't a silly threesome. How about we three sillies go for a walk and see if we can find some wild flowers for Daddy?"

"And a lizard, too?" asked Danny.

"Yes, if we can catch it. Do you have something to put it in?"

"I have a little wooden box with a lid," replied Danny, his eyes full of excitement.

"Good. Let's go."

Danny clutched the little wooden box tightly as they went out the front door. Since the front yard desert landscaping blended in with the wild desert, they immediately began looking for lizards. It was delightfully warm and the air smelled fresh and spring-like. The children burst into chatter.

"Be careful, Pipit," warned Danny, "there are lots a prickly cactus around here."

"Look, Pipit, there are some pink flowers!" Merri exclaimed.

"Yes, look!" Danny repeated, excited.

"Oh, aren't they pretty. They're evening primroses just barely starting to bloom. Let's pick them for your daddy just before we go back in the house."

"Okay," they said, their attention quickly shifting to other things.

Able to look outside herself now that she was whole, Liz studied the desert here in Cave Creek. North of them was a large hill covered with dark rocks. She had heard Flo call it "Black Mountain." The land close to it was also rocky, but she noted the desert around Matthew's neighborhood was flatter, less rocky with yellow sandy soil.

"Look, kids, here's one of my very favorite desert trees, a palo verde tree. There is something special about it. Can you guess what it is?"

They stared at the small spindly tree unable to guess.

"All right, let's look at a different tree and I think you can guess." Stepping over to one, she said, "This is a juniper tree." Their curious faces studied it, then looked over at the palo verde.

"I know!" shouted Merri.

"I know!"

Merri shoved Danny. "I said it first!"

Liz took Merri firmly by the arm. "You act like that one more time and we're going back to the house, and I'll take Danny by himself when your daddy comes home."

Merri pouted.

"Was that kind, Merri?"

She stared defiantly at Liz, who waited for her answer.

Danny could see their lizard hunting was about to come to a halt. "It's okay, Pipit."

"It's not okay, Danny." Liz continued looking questioningly at Merri, who only stared back sulkily. Liz took hold of both their hands. "All right, back to the house we go."

"Please, Pipit, Merri is sorry aren't you, Merri?"

"I don't want to go back!" Merri yelled, refusing to walk.

Liz let go of Danny's hand and picked Merri up, who instantly began kicking and screaming. "I want to know what's special 'bout the palo verde tree! I want to know what's special 'bout the palo verde tree!"

Unfazed, Liz stated, between screams, "Come, Danny." Danny followed, tears of disappointment filling his eyes.

Inside, Liz put Merri down, who promptly turned back to the door and opened it to go out. Liz picked her up again. The screams and kicking becoming more vehement, Liz walked quickly to the couch and sat down, holding her tightly, rocking her gently back and forth. *What do I do?* she asked herself. *I don't know how to handle things like this! Matthew I need you! What has caused these kinds of actions?*

Danny sat forlornly on the footstool, still clutching his little wooden box.

It wasn't long before Liz felt Merri's body relax and become quiet; only her spasmodic breathing remained. Liz's first impulse had been to spank her, but she quickly squelched it since the child had gone through so much in her short life.

Liz noticed that Danny was still sitting quietly, and knew by his expression that he was still hoping they could go on their outing. "I'm sorry, Danny."

"I'm sorry, too, Danny," Merri said through a small heaving breath.

Danny's soft heart overcame his disappointment. He crawled up onto the couch and put his arms around Merri and Liz. "That's okay, Merri."

Liz felt like a yo-yo on a string. This morning when the children had hugged her, and apologized, her hopes had soared, only to be dashed while on their short walk. Now they were up...*but for how long*, she wondered. She sighed and murmured, "I like group hugs, don't you?"

The children giggled as the three of them entwined their arms around each other and hugged vigorously.

"Hey, what's going on here?" came a low resonant voice from the doorway.

"We're group hugging, Daddy," Merri said through the giggles.

"Group hugging, what's that?"

"You don't know what that is, Daddy?"

"What is it? Show me."

Merri remembered he couldn't see. "Come over to the couch, Daddy and you can group hug with us."

Reaching the couch, Matthew sat down and immediately the two children jumped up onto his lap, pulling Pipit over with them. "Now let's all hug," Merri instructed.

Matthew's arms went around the children reaching for Pipit who in turn wrapped her arms about him and the children. "Hey, I like this!" he exclaimed. The children laughed and hugged harder.

When they disentangled, Matthew spoke enthusiastically. "This is the best greeting yet."

"Oh-oh," Liz muttered, looking at her watch. "It's dinner time and I haven't even started it." *Will I ever be able to keep a schedule?* she wondered.

"That's all right, we're not hungry yet, are we kids? We three need to catch up. Tell me what you did today."

They eagerly began telling their version of the trip to the grocery store and their short walk into the desert, relating the happy details, as only children can do, forgetting the other.

~~~~~~~~~~~~

Matthew put the children to bed at an early hour. They had gotten up far too early this morning because of their excitement at the prospect of seeing Pipit.

Having finished cleaning up, Liz sat down and picked up a magazine just as Matthew came back in. She glanced up, but said nothing.

Matthew felt her presence, but didn't know where she was. "Liz?"

"I'm in the chair that isn't a rocker."

Puzzled, Matthew smiled and felt his way to the couch. "That's right, it isn't a rocker."

"That's my complaint. It isn't a rocker."

"What is this all about, Liz?"

"You need to buy a rocker."

"The children aren't babies anymore."

"Yes, they are."

He thought about this a moment. "You're right, they are, but what brought this on?"

Liz filled him in on everything, ending with a question. "Why does Merri act the way she does?"

"I'm not quite sure. Probably because strangers from Child Protection Services came and took them away to their grand-mother."

"She's worse because of this, I'm sure, but she was this way when I first came. Why, Matthew?"

That was something he'd asked himself over and over. "I really don't know."

"You don't even have a good guess...a maybe?"

"No."

This answer disturbed Liz. "Apparently you told Mr. Beale that Merri acted this way when her mother was alive because he brought that fact out in the hearing, so you certainly must have given it *some* thought."

"I have, but as I said, I don't know."

"I can't believe a father could be so clueless."

This rankled Matthew. "I would rather not discuss it, Liz."

Liz fumed. She remained silent until her anger was under control. As calmly as she could, she asked, "What are you hiding, Matthew?"

She saw the shock on his face. "Hiding? There is nothing to hide."

"You must be hiding something from *yourself*, then, Matthew, because there *are* some answers somewhere."

His brows furrowed, revealing his troubled state. "Liz, you did it before—you can calm the children."

"I can't do it alone, Matthew!" she exclaimed, getting up and pacing back and forth. "I need your help."

"I'm trying to help."

"I need to have some understanding. I need some 'whys' answered. We need to do more than put *Band Aids* on the children's hurts."

"You're over-reacting, Liz."

"And you, Matthew, are under-reacting. Good night."

Matthew remained in the family room for some time trying to quell the annoyance he felt toward Elizabeth, and trying to justify it. In the end, he couldn't.

He remember the annoyance that had broiled up inside him several months before the accident when his aunt Mamie had told him one day in private that Merri was a confused and insecure child and that Danny was not far behind. His reaction was one of disapproval, feeling that if he discussed Merri with his aunt, it would be a form of disloyalty to Diane. When he related his aunt's remarks to Diane, she was furious as he'd known she would be, and had disagreed bitterly.

Nevertheless, for some reason Mamie's assessment had struck a nerve with him—it involved some guilt over neglecting Diane. What this had to do with Merri's behavior then and now, he had no idea. But he couldn't dwell on it further, for pain consumed him. Merri's problem was all mixed up with grief over Diane's death.

~~~~~~~~~~~~

Liz's frustration hammered inside her as she showered and dressed for bed. *What right did I have to tell Matthew he was hiding something?* she argued. One thing she knew for certain, she deserved answers so she could be more effective with the children!

She thought she knew Matthew. But she learned tonight that he was more resistant and complex than she'd realized.

Inadequacy and defeat were the two words that described her present state of mind.

After she'd turned off the lights, she lay in bed for a long time thinking, wondering if she could hold out until Matthew's sight returned. Her greatest desire at the moment was to pack up and leave and let Matthew deal with his unhappy children himself— then maybe he'd make a greater effort to find out *why* they were unhappy!

Chapter Forty-Three

Liz was distant with Matthew the next morning. He felt her silent reproach. She only spoke when she had to. Could he blame her? She was trying to deal with children who weren't her own. Nevertheless, he left for work blaming her for his miserable night and for his unrest this morning.

After Matthew had gone, and some cleaning had been done by her and the children, Liz took them by the hand, and walked over to Margo's, momentarily ignoring their pleas to go swimming or go for a walk. She had to have some answers!

Apparently the neighborhood grapevine hadn't reached Margo for when she answered the door, she stood there gaping in surprise. "Pipit? Where in the world did you come from? Come on in."

"It's good to see you, Margo," she said, pulling the sulking children inside.

"Hey kids, why the long faces?"

"Pipit won't let us go swimming," Merri retorted.

"And she promised to take me hunting for lizards when Daddy came home last night, and she didn't."

"Oh, Danny, I forgot to explain," Liz said. "By the time dinner was over, it was getting too dark to find a lizard."

"Oh."

"But we will go hunting for one I promise. I don't know when, but soon."

"Come children, I have a video I think you'll like to watch," Margo said, taking their hands.

When the children were safely involved in the movie, Margo said, "Come on over here to the table and let's talk. When did you get back? Why are you back? You left so suddenly, I didn't get to say goodbye. Has your memory returned? Matthew told me that your name is Elizabeth Cabot."

"Yes to both. You can call me Liz if you'd like or Pipit. The children still call me Pipit. Margo...did you know that Elinor had the children taken away from Matthew and took him to court for custody of them?"

Margo's chin dropped. "No. Phil and I have been to Hawaii. We just got back."

"Well, I guess I had better tell you everything." As briefly as she could, she began with their marriage in Las Vegas and ended with the court hearing.

Margo was silent for a few moments. "All this happened the minute my back was turned?" She studied Liz intently. "Do you love Matthew?"

"I only married Matthew to save his children. It's a temporary marriage which will be annulled as soon as his sight returns. We're living in separate quarters." Margo didn't look convinced. "I owe Matthew my life, Margo."

"Hey...it's hard to believe that anyone could be *that* selfless."

"I haven't done anything with my life, Margo," she found herself trying to explain. "I love Merri and Danny. I couldn't bear to have them taken from their father." Not wanting any questions, nor another opinion from Margo, she quickly went on. "I came over because I need to ask you something."

"Ask away."

"The behavior of Merri is concerning me. Were you around her enough to see how she acted with Danny before Diane was killed?"

"Yes. She's a troubled little girl."

Suddenly, a shred of fear went through Liz. "Margo, what if something has happened to her? Physically, I mean."

"You mean like sexual abuse?"

"Yes."

"I haven't told you, but Phil and I married later in life, and before I was married, I was a psychologist. My emphasis was child sexual abuse. I have watched both Matthew's children, particularly Merri. I don't believe she's been abused in that way. She doesn't have the right signals or symptoms. Though I'm not certain, I think you can rest your fears about that. Besides, I saw a change come over her after you had been here only a week."

"Thank you, Margo." Liz said with relief. "Do you have any idea why she acts this way?"

"I've tried to figure it out myself. Diane was a loving mother. But she couldn't hug the children a lot at first because she was never hugged. Her mother was the same. Matthew worked with her, and finally she was able to show more physical affection to the children. She told me one day that she didn't want to be the kind of mother to her children that her mother had been to her. Frankly it was rather amazing to me that she could learn to be a warm loving mother with the role model she had. From the few remarks Diane made, I gathered that her father was more loving, but his whole life was his work, so I assume that he neglected Diane as well."

Liz shook her head. "I've gained some valuable information by talking with you, Margo, but frankly, the information just leaves me more puzzled."

~~~~~~~~~~~~

The afternoon was spent in the library. The children happily looked through children's books while Liz looked for books with lessons on treating one another kindly. She also chose several fun books. After filling out the requisite forms, she checked out the books.

On the way home, Liz stopped for pizza and root beer, much to the children's delight. She had decided to feed them early so that when Matthew walked in, he could stay with Merri while she took Danny lizard hunting.

She and the children had just finished their pizza when the front door opened. "Your daddy's home! Go run and greet him." Instantly, they were up and running, almost knocking him off balance as they wrapped their arms around him.

"Wow! That's an enthusiastic greeting," he grinned.

"We saved you some pizza and root beer," informed Merri.

"Great. I love pizza and root beer."

"Pipit is going to take me lizard hunting right now, Daddy!"

"She is?"

"But she won't take me," pouted Merri.

Taking off his coat and laying it over a chair, he walked toward the kitchen sink to wash his hands. "Liz?" he asked tentatively.

"I'm warming your pizza, Matthew."

"Thank you," he said, turning on the water, realizing that she was still distant with him. The day had mellowed out his own feelings so he was ready for things to be as they were.

"Sit down at the bar or the table, Matthew, your pizza is ready."

"I'll sit at the table."

They collided slightly as they both headed for the table. He gripped her arm. "Sorry, Liz."

She couldn't move for he held her fast, but what was more disturbing to Liz was the touch of his hand seemed to sear her flesh, sending a jolt of excitement through her. Breathlessly she replied, "That's all right, Matthew. Please, I need to put the food on the table."

Still he wouldn't let go. He whispered. "Please don't be distant with me, Liz."

"I need to put this down, Matthew," she insisted, ignoring his request. He released his hand and she put the pizza on the table, and poured him a glass of root beer, her heart still pounding.

"Come on, Danny, let's go."

Gripping his little wooden box, he took Liz's hand.

A scream issued from Merri as she grabbed hold of Liz. "I want to go! I want to go!"

"Merri, you remember why you can't go, don't you?"

Merri refused to answer.

Taking her by the hand, she took her over to her father. "Matthew, please take care of Merri."

He scooted his chair back. Liz picked Merri up and placed her on his lap, took Danny by the hand and rapidly walked him out the front door. She stood a moment on the porch, still feeling the effect of Matthew's touch. *No!* she screamed mentally, *this can't happen to me! Not now. Not under these circumstances!* "Let's sit here on the step a moment, Danny," she managed to say. As they sat, she turned to him. "I need a hug," she said shakily. "A really big hug."

They sat down on the one step of the porch, and Danny hugged her fiercely. "I'm sorry, Pipit, and I know Merri's sorry."

"I know, Danny, I know," she said, hugging him tightly, trying to put out of her mind what had happened in the kitchen. She had been able to repress the feelings she had when Matthew kissed her at the end of the marriage ceremony and once again when they arrived home; she could do it again!

She let go of Danny and stood up. "Come on, we've got to find that lizard."

Sneaking around, they stepped around cactus, squatted to look under low branches of burro brush, peeked around the dense growth of an evergreen salt bush, and still saw no signs of the elusive lizard. Leading Danny toward some rocks, Liz stopped him. "Let's just watch a moment and see if one slithers over the rocks."

After a couple of moments, Danny's excitement got the best of him. "Let's find some other rocks, there's not one here."

"Okay!"

An hour and a half passed and still they hadn't spotted a lizard. "We're not going to find one, Pipit," Danny said, his face full of disappointment.

"This is when we have to develop patience, Danny. Let's look for a while longer."

Thirty minutes later, Danny spied one sunning itself in the golden sand. "Look!" he whispered, "There's one!"

Liz put her finger to her lips and stealthily stepped over, and before the lizard knew what was happening to him, she grabbed it. Danny had the box open, his green eyes, wide with wonder, watching as Liz took the lid from him, placed the lizard in the box and slammed the lid on.

"Wow! You're fast, Pipit."

"I used to live in the desert too, Danny, and one of my favorite things to do was catch lizards."

"It was?" he asked, his little freckled face oozing with admiration for her.

Liz laughed. "It was—but I found that lizards weren't very good pets so I always had to let them go back to their home in the desert."

His face fell. "Can't I keep this lizard?"

"Where would you keep him?"

"In this box, and I can feed him."

"What do you think will happen when you open the lid of the box to feed him?"

"He'll crawl out?"

"So fast, you'll hardly see him, but let's go show him to your daddy and Merri."

"Okay!"

Just before they entered, Liz said, "Go get them and tell them to come outside so we can show them. We don't want the lizard to escape in the house; we'd never find him."

"Okay." Danny burst through the door. "Daddy! Merri! We caught one. We caught a lizard! Come and look."

Matthew and Merri met him as he entered the family room. "Come on outside and I'll show you. Pipit says I have to show you outside 'cause he'll get out."

"You really caught one?" Merri asked.

"Pipit did. She's as fast as...as a race car!"

"Amazing," his dad said.

When Pipit saw the three coming out, she said, "Merri, take your dad's hand and guide him over here." She did as Pipit said.

When they reached Pipit, Danny looked at his sister and dad. "Are you ready?"

"We're ready," Matthew said, "but you'll have to *tell* me about it."

"Oh." Danny's face fell. "I forgot. You can't see him."

Matthew's heart hurt for him...for himself. "That's all right, Danny, I will almost be able to see it if you tell me about it."

"Okay...here goes." He opened the lid just a little bit. "Can you see him, Merri?"

She peeked in. "Yes! I can see him."

Danny opened it wider, and immediately the lizard darted out, ran over his arm and down his leg to freedom. Danny and Merri laughed. "He ran over my arm and down my leg, Daddy!"

"I'm sorry he got away."

"Pipit said they don't make good pets. I wish they did though," he said wistfully.

"I wish they did, too," his dad said, picking him up and hugging him.

~~~~~~~~~~~~

In spite of the discipline Liz had to administer, Merri had requested she tuck her in. Feeling grateful for this, Liz spent some time visiting with her. After awhile Merri made an announcement. "I have nightmares sometimes."

"I did, too, when I was a little girl. Do you wake up and feel scared like I did?"

"Yes. I call Daddy and he comes and hugs me a while then I feel better."

"I'm glad your daddy loves you enough to get up in the night and make you feel better." She leaned over and kissed Merri on the forehead. "Goodnight, Merri."

"Goodnight Pipit. Can we go looking for lizards tomorrow?"

"I have something else fun planned if you and Danny are kind to each other."

"Oh goody!"

Liz entered the family room and found Matthew just sitting without the television on. "I'm going to go shower and go to bed now, Matthew."

"Liz, please come and sit down for a moment before you do."

"All right, Matthew."

"I want to thank you for taking Danny out tonight and catching him a lizard."

"You're welcome. I used to love catching lizards when I was young. That's one thing I can do that Diane couldn't." She meant it as a joke on herself, but it apparently didn't go over that way with Matthew. "Don't take that wrong, Matthew. From what I've heard Diane was almost perfect. All I was trying to say is that I'm glad I can at least do something that Diane couldn't do even if it's only catching lizards."

He laughed. "I'm glad you're a good lizard catcher for Danny's sake. I also wanted to tell you that Merri and I had a good talk while you and Danny were out. She confessed her wrongdoings and promised me she would try to do better."

"Good. I have to know what I'm up against so please answer this one question. Was Diane a good disciplinarian?"

"Not at first, but she learned and she became much more consistent as time went on."

"You and Diane have done a good job with the children. They are very kind-hearted and basically obedient children. That's why I'm puzzled at Merri's erratic hostility toward Danny. I'm going to get ready for bed now, Matthew. Goodnight."

~~~~~~~~~~~~

When Liz turned out the light, she opened her bedroom door. If Merri had a nightmare, she wanted to get up with her. Matthew looked very tired when she left him tonight. Exhausted herself, it wasn't long before she fell into a deep sleep.

It felt as though she had just fallen asleep when she heard a noise. She looked at the clock. It said 2:00 AM. She lay there listening, wondering if it was Merri. It wasn't. It was Matthew! He seemed to be crying out. She jumped up and walked quickly down the hall and through the moonlit family room toward Matthew's bedroom. Reaching his open door, she stood there listening.

"No! No! It's going to hit us! No! Diane...Diane..."

Liz quickly went over to Matthew and touched him. He grabbed her hand. "Diane, you're here, you're all right!"

"Matthew," Liz said softly, gently shaking him. "It's me, Liz. Wake up, you're having a nightmare."

He sat up, dazed. "What?"

"You were having a nightmare, Matthew. I thought at first it might be Merri."

"Liz?"

"Yes, it's Liz. I'm sorry it isn't Diane. Go back to sleep, Matthew." She exited quickly, feeling awkward in his bedroom in the middle of the night. Reaching her bedroom, she debated about keeping the door open. She decided to, and tumbled back to bed only to stare sleeplessly at the ceiling.

A profound yearning welled up in her heart. It was so acute, she almost felt suffocated by it. Oh, how she would like to be loved as Matthew loved Diane.

Chapter Forty-Four

The warm afternoon sun shone down on them as Pipit led the children around to the side of the house.

"What is it we're going to do, Pipit?" Merri asked, her large gray eyes eager.

"Yes, what?" Danny repeated.

"We're going to build a sandbox."

They stared at her a moment, then Danny let out a war whoop. "Now I can use my dump truck!"

"Can we build castles?" Merri asked. "My friend has a sandbox and she builds castles."

"We can build whatever we want to build, but we have a lot of work to do. We have to pick out all the little rocks from the sand, all the weeds, and then find big rocks to put all around it."

"We can do that, can't we, Danny?"

"Yes!"

After they had worked for almost an hour, Danny wiped his sweaty little face, making a smudge across his forehead and cheek. "I'm thirsty, Pipit."

"Me too," Merri said.

"How about we finish it tomorrow? Let's go in and get a drink of water, then go into town and get an ice cream cone."

"Yay!!" they yelled.

"Can we bring one home for Daddy?" Merri asked.

"If we hurry before it melts."

~~~~~~~~~~~~

When Matthew came home that night, Merri and Danny ran to him both talking at once, trying to tell him about their sandbox and the ice cream cone that was waiting for him. Merri shoved Danny so hard, he fell to the floor. His feelings were so hurt, he could hardly cry.

"What did you do, Merri?" her father asked.

"Nothing," she retorted.

"I asked you what you did. I heard Danny fall and I can hear him crying."

"He's always talking when I want to talk."

Matthew's face turned weary. "Come with me, Merri."

"No!" She ran away from him.

"Do as your father says, Merri," Liz said, walking over and taking her firmly by the hand and leading her to Matthew who then promptly took her to the bedroom.

Shortly, Matthew came back in, his coat removed. "Merri is staying in her room for a while, Liz. After we put them to bed tonight, we'll have a talk."

~~~~~~~~~~~~

Matthew bathed and put the children to bed as early as he could. When he was through, he came out and sat down wearily. "What are we going to do with Merri, Liz?"

"Why don't you take off work for the next two days, and with Sunday, that will make it three days you can spend with the children. I think your presence will make any change come about faster. You think I can calm the children, but this time, I don't think I can do it alone."

He thought about the suggestion for a while. He lamented. "There just doesn't seem to be enough things I can do with the children without sight."

"I'll be your eyes, Matthew."

He smiled. "And my comforter, apparently. I think you were in my room last night, waking me from my usual nightmare. Thank you."

"You're welcome, any time," she said lightly.

"I've had them continually since the accident. Have you ever heard me before?"

"No. I've always kept my door closed. Last night I opened my door so I could hear Merri if she had a nightmare. She told me she had them sometimes and that you get up and make her feel better. You looked so tired last night, I decided to do that for you if I could hear her before you woke up."

He closed his eyes and rubbed his forehead. "I don't deserve you, Liz. You are the most unselfish, serving person, outside of my own mother, that I've ever known." The moment he said it, he realized what he'd said—*ever known*. Why didn't he include Diane?

Liz, also keenly aware that he hadn't included Diane, was certain it was just an oversight. A little uncomfortable over the praise, since most her life had not been unselfish and serving, she quickly thanked him and changed the subject. "I have another thought about how you might help Merri."

"Good. What?"

"Randy told me about the tornado destroying your peach orchards and killing your parents."

This took Matthew by surprise. "He did?"

"Yes. And he said everything was destroyed, but that you found the family Bible totally intact. He attributes your ability to deal with your grief to your daily Bible reading."

Matthew's mouth was ajar. "When did he tell you this?"

"The night before my parents came. Arthur had taken you into the front room...probably to tell you about the discovery of my identity."

"Go on."

"Do you think if you began that regular routine again, you might find some answers about Merri?"

"As you know—I can't read."

"I'll read it to you."

He was silent for so long, Liz wondered if her suggestion had bothered him for some reason.

Far from it, for it gave Matthew an additional idea. "What you read to me I can retell to both Merri and Danny the next night just before they go to bed. Thank you for reminding me, Liz. It should help. Anyway it's certainly worth a try."

"We used to read the Bible every night when we lived in Los Angeles. I was almost fifteen when we moved to Palm Springs. With all the adjustments of living among the wealthy, my parents didn't get around to starting up again. I missed it terribly. I feel I could have adjusted to the move better if we had kept up that special routine."

"Interesting. Thank you for sharing that. I've wondered how you could be the wonderful person you are with parents who, on the surface, seemed a little like Diane's."

Surprised by this comparison, she couldn't speak for a moment. Her first impulse was to vociferously deny that there was any similarity between her parents and Diane's. Instead, she asked the obvious question. "How did Diane turn out so well with parents like she had?"

Matthew's smile turned tender. "After I had been dating her for some time I met her parents, and soon I asked that very question of myself. I watched her preoccupied and busy father. I watched her socially gregarious mother who professed great interest in everyone she met...that is, those who were on her social level, and realized her interest was only superficial. Diane picked up this interest in others, but hers was sincere. I asked myself how could this happen."

"Eventually, I learned that my beautiful, but frail-looking Diane belied her appearance. When just a child, she knew her mother didn't love her in a normal way. She was cold and unaffectionate and only did things for Diane for the sake of appearance and to show off her beauty. Elinor basked in all Diane's activities and lived vicariously through her. But Diane was a fighter. Emotionally she pulled away from her mother, told herself she didn't care, and found solace in the affection her father gave her, when he had time, and in friends and acquaintances, and in doing things for others— with charities when she was older." When Liz didn't respond right away, he apologized. "I'm sorry for running on like this, it's just that I need to talk about her now and then."

Liz closed her eyes grappling with the conflicting emotions she'd felt during his portrayal of Diane. She wanted to hear more about Diane from him...yet she didn't. The latter disturbed her. *Why not*?! she asked silently. Irritated at herself, she said, "I've heard that people need to talk about loved ones they've lost. You may talk about her with me anytime you feel the need, Matthew."

The tone of Liz's voice was sincere, but he felt something behind the words; not knowing what, he decided to take her offer at face value. "Thank you. That's nice to know."

"Did you continue your Bible reading when you married, Matthew?"

"No. Like your parents, with the adjustments in marriage, I let it slide. I felt concerned about it once in a great while because my mother use to say: 'There are people who are good, but the Bible could make them better.' When we began having trouble with Merri I thought of another statement my mother used to say when I would resist taking the time to join in our Bible reading sessions: 'Daily scripture reading as a family will produce happy, obedient children, and unite the family like nothing else can.' I remember once when I shot back at her. 'But there are no *children*, in our family. I'm an only child!' I never said that again because tears filled my mother's eyes. You see, she wanted a big family and was always broken-hearted that I didn't have siblings."

"It's nice that you had cousins anyway. Would you like to start the reading tonight?"

"Yes, if that's okay with you," he said, hoping that not only would the Bible reading help Merri and Danny, but would also help get him and Liz back the way they were. He still felt Liz holding back, though it was something he sensed more than what she said, or how she acted.

Chapter Forty-Five

Desperation over Merri's actions drove Matthew to take Liz's suggestion and stay home from work the next two days. He dreaded it. Anything was an ordeal when he couldn't really take part in everything as he had before, but the children's excitement almost made it reward enough.

"Come on, Daddy," Merri said, eagerly taking his hand. "Pipit said you could help us finish our sandbox."

Oh great, he thought. *As if I can be any help*! He forced a smile. "Hey, let's get going."

When the four of them stepped off the front porch, Liz didn't offer her hand as usual. Matthew stopped, certain that Merri couldn't guide him sufficiently over the unknown terrain. "Liz?"

"Yes, Matthew."

"I would feel a little more secure if you held my hand, too, and tell me where I'm stepping."

"I'll walk beside you and Merri. I'll help if necessary."

A half-smile appeared on his face. "Are you trying to wean me, Liz?"

Not wanting a repeat of her experience two days ago in the kitchen, she said, "No. I'm training Merri."

"Great," he muttered under his breath to her. "A five-year old guide is just what I need."

Stepping around the house, they arrived at their unfinished project. "Matthew, you and Merri sit down here and pick out the small stones and sticks from the sand while Danny and I go get some nice big rocks to put around the sandbox."

The children chattered happily, laughed at their Daddy's funny remarks and two hours later they were finished. "Can I go get my dump truck now?"

"Sure, Danny," his father said. "What would you like to do in the sandbox, Merri?"

"Can we build a castle, Daddy?"

"You bet. Liz, go get a pan of water so we can wet this so-called-sand."

Since the 'sand' was just sandy soil, an hour later, a rather muddy castle was built and Liz and Danny made roads and hills leading to it. Aware of what a good sport Matthew was, Liz found herself gazing at his face when he smiled or laughed, or on his attractive hands as he worked the sand. Disconcerted, Liz wondered if she was looking at Matthew a little differently because they were married. Was it a natural psychological reaction? Quickly, she pushed it out of her mind. "Who would like to take dip in the pool before lunch?" she asked.

~~~~~~~~~~~~~

After more swimming in the afternoon, and an early dinner, they all gathered in the family room where Liz read to them the books she'd checked out at the library on being kind to each other. Matthew then asked the children questions about what they'd heard. Both Liz and Matthew had been very aware of how good Merri had been all day, but were still holding their breath. Merri, a good reader already, read a book to her daddy and Danny.

"It's my turn to read one of my books," Danny said.

Merri yelled at him. "No! I'm not through."

"I see that it's time to go to bed," her father stated, "you must be very tired or you wouldn't speak to Danny that way."

"I don't want to go to bed!"

Matthew picked her up and carried her in. "Come on, Danny, you come too."

~~~~~~~~~~~~~

Liz restlessly put a wash in, and folded another. When she returned to the family room, Matthew was leaning on the bar, his face in deep thought.

"Hi. How did your Bible story go over?"

"Very well. I think it's going to help. May we read some more tonight?"

"Yes." She walked over, picked up the Bible and Matthew seated himself. She paged through the New Testament for another one of her favorite stories about Jesus, one that might help the children. She picked out John, chapter 13 and began reading. Finally, she came to the verses which had affected her profoundly as a teenager.

A new commandment I give unto you, That ye love one another; as I have loved you, that ye also love one another.

By this shall all men know that ye are my disciples, if ye have love one to another.

At the end of the chapter, she closed the book and they sat in silence for a short while each engrossed in their own thoughts. For some reason, what she'd read made Liz think of Matthew's life as a young boy so she asked a question that had been on her mind.

"Do you still have the peach orchards or what is left of them, Matthew?"

"No. I sold them when the price of land was high. That's how I got the money to set up both my stores. I actually own the land and building in Phoenix. It took a lot of cash to do this and fill the stores with merchandise."

"Randy said that the song, *Matthew,* fits your life at home. Is that true?"

"It does, as a matter of fact. I was very close to my father as well as my mother. They were wonderful parents."

"Randy said that he truly thought you had come to, as the song says, 'help his dad and to be his friend.' "

Matthew smiled. "He's told me that. I'm grateful I could help. I remember worrying that I would be a burden to them. Thinking about it now, I would not have wanted to be in their shoes—taking in a teenager who had just been orphaned."

"Would you play and sing that song for me?"

"Of course, I'd be glad to, Liz."

She listened to the beautiful melody and touching words. Once more, she felt like crying...crying for the young boy who lost his parents. Matthew's voice itself made her want to cry.

When Matthew finished, he just sat there, finding, as usual, that the song brought back memories of his parents, and his life with them. He wished with all his heart that his children could know them. Perhaps their love could help Merri.

~~~~~~~~~~~~

The next two days were delightful for the children, but difficult for Liz. She realized that her new reaction to Matthew was not going to go away! She decided it was easier to have him at work all day.

Saturday, she had prepared a picnic and had driven all of them to a nice grassy park in Phoenix where there were swings, slides and all kinds of things to climb on. She had to hold Matthew's hand while wandering from place to place in order to watch the children and so she could tell him what they were doing. Just holding his hand had begun to have the same effect on her as when he'd taken hold of her arm in the kitchen. Trying to steel herself against it—was useless.

Part of Sunday was spent singing together and playing quiet indoor and outdoor games. That evening after Matthew had put the children to bed, he came out in good spirits. "This has been a good three days, Liz. Merri had a couple of setbacks, but they don't seem as vehement as they were. Thanks for suggesting I take three days off."

"You're welcome, Matthew." It was obvious to her that she was certainly not having the same effect on Matthew as he was on her. How was she going to last until Matthew could see? If only she could pack her suitcases and leave tomorrow morning!

Chapter Forty-Six

For the next two weeks, Liz kept herself and the children as busy as she could, trying not to think, not to feel. She left Diane's house as frequently as she could, taking the children to the zoo, to a movie, to the library and so forth. When they were out, the children had begged to surprise their daddy and kidnap him again for lunch, but she'd made excuses.

When Matthew was home, Liz found things to do—cleaning, washing, ironing, cleaning out the refrigerator, sweeping the porch, cleaning the pool—anything to keep from interacting with him. The only time she allowed herself to be alone with Matthew was when she was reading to him. Immediately afterward, she made excuses: she had to get the clothes out of the dryer, she had to make something for dinner the next night, she had to go grocery shopping.

One evening, at the end of the third week, Liz told Matthew that she needed to go talk with Flo. She wanted to request that Flo not mention to the children that she was their stepmother, and ask her to also tell the Brodericks.

"Good idea, Liz."

Liz's departure left Matthew frowning in troubled thought. He wondered why he was feeling increasingly lonely over the past week or so. He always missed Diane, but this was a new feeling. Maybe it was because Liz had turned into a workaholic. She was never there with him and the children anymore, it seemed. She was always doing something. He said he would hire help for her, but she didn't want it. Neither would she stay with him in the evenings except to read the Bible. It felt as though she were pulling away from him, and it made him acutely uncomfortable. Maybe she needed to leave and didn't want to tell him.

~~~~~~~~~~~~~

It felt good to Liz to be by herself, away from the tension that had built up inside her, and the man who caused it. She visited with

Flo, who promised she would be careful until the children were more adjusted.

Leaving Flo's place as soon as she could, Liz went on a brisk walk. Tomorrow was the first day of April and the evening was warm, and fragrant with blossoming mesquite. It made her think of home, and all of a sudden she felt homesick.

Her walk turned into a run, trying to ease her unhappiness and homesickness, stopping only to catch her breath for a while, then starting up again.

It was dark by the time she finally faced herself...her feelings. Stopping suddenly, her chest heaved as she gasped for breath, the heaving turning into sobs. She was *in love* with Matthew! Why hadn't she worried about this happening when she made the decision to marry him? "Why?! Why?" she asked the dark silent desert. Only the harsh snapping 'chack' of a mockingbird answered, as if it were mocking her folly. Did she think she was impervious to Matthew's charms just because he would forever grieve over his wife? More sobs choked her until through blurry eyes, she saw car lights winding their way toward her. The surprise helped her gain control as she quickly turned in the opposite direction.

Slowly, she walked back toward Matthew's house. At last, she could face the truth. She had loved Matthew from the beginning— when she first awakened in the cabin, when she followed the sound of his singing, when she was greeted by his wide heartwarming smile. He had wrapped himself around her heart with his ability to see the humor in her brash and impudent remarks, as well as the kindness he portrayed in persuading her to face what she was feeling, encouraging her to voice it while he listened intently.

Who could help but love Matthew? But she had loved him, or so she thought, only as a friend! So, when had it turned into more— the kind of love she felt now? She loved a man who had no room in his heart, no love for anyone other than the memory of his dead wife! Even if he could bring himself to love again, how could he find anyone as perfect as Diane? Anyone as *beautiful* as Diane? *She* certainly couldn't fill Diane's shoes. And no way would she want to! A man would have to love her for herself, plain as she was. Why oh why couldn't she have loved Kirk enough to marry him—the one man who loved her?

At last she arrived back at Matthew's. Entering, she saw the family room empty with only a lamp light on. Quickly getting a drink of cold water, she started for her bedroom.

"Liz?"

She stopped in mid-stride. "Darn!" she whispered, then aloud, "Yes, Matthew."

"I'm glad you're home. I was getting a little worried."

"My favorite time of the year in the desert is spring. I guess I got carried away smelling the fragrance of blossoms, and walked further than I intended. Sorry."

"That's all right. I'm glad you enjoyed yourself. Could I speak with you for a moment?"

"Of course. Do you want me to read to you tonight?"

"No. It's getting late. I just want to talk with you."

Liz sat down on the couch and Matthew, not knowing where she was, also seated himself on the couch. Liz quickly got up intending to move to the chair, when Matthew stopped her. "Don't move, Liz. I'm sorry, I didn't know where you were, but could you stay here closer while we talk?"

"All right." She sat as far away as she could get.

"Liz, I feel that something is wrong. Don't tell me there isn't, just tell me what it is."

Her heart flip-flopped with anxiety. What could she tell him?

"Your silence tells me I'm right. Please, Liz."

"I...I guess I'm feeling a little homesick is all, Matthew."

"Do you want to visit your family for a few days?"

"They aren't very happy with me right now, Matthew. I don't want to face them until I go home to stay."

"Do you want to go home to stay...now?"

Now that she had faced her true feelings about him, she studied Matthew's remarkably appealing face, so uniquely handsome. Her heart begged him to take her in his arms and tell her what she longed to hear. Never in her wildest dreams did she ever imagine she'd be in this unhappy and impossible situation!

"Liz?"

"Uh...what did you say?"

He repeated it.

She wanted to shout, yes because I *love* you and I can't bear living under the same roof with you day in and day out, suffering because you don't love me!

"Liz, your mind is off somewhere, or...you're afraid to tell me that you *do* want to go home now—to stay."

"Yes...I want to go home to stay...and no, I don't." Brightly as she could, she explained. "I hadn't planned on a career of nanny/housekeeper so naturally, I would like to bask in the luxury of people waiting on *me* for a change. But—it's too soon for me to leave, Matthew, you could still lose your children if Elinor got wind of my leaving."

Matthew heaved a sigh of relief. "Thank you, Liz. I don't know what I'd do without you right now." He reached for her hand, but she quickly got up and walked away. Matthew frowned. "You used to let me show a *little* affection, Liz."

She'd rather die than admit the real reason she couldn't let him; her mind raced trying to think of a reason he'd be satisfied with. He was so intuitive about the tone of her voice, she had to put on an act like she never had before. With a joking lilt to her voice, she said, "Being *married*, even in name only, is a little tricky, Matthew. I find I have a tendency to look at you a little differently." She made herself chuckle. "I'm just trying to resist your charms. You don't want the complication of me falling madly in love with you, do you?"

Surprised by this explanation, he just shook his head, a quizzical expression on his face, then a smile. "I...I can hardly believe that would happen, Liz...especially in my condition."

"Don't underestimate your charms, Matthew Melloy." She smiled wistfully at his handsome face, then with the same light-hearted tone, she said, "Well, I'm exhausted. It was hard work planning things for all of us this weekend. I think I'll be relieved when you go back to work."

"Thanks a lot."

"You're welcome. Good night."

"Good night, Liz."

Matthew remained up for a while, thinking over what Liz had said, a feeling of disappointment now mingling with his loneliness.

His affectionate nature had been somewhat satisfied now and then as Liz would let him hug her or just touch her; she was the dearest friend he'd ever had. He was sure she was teasing him, but under the circumstances, he had to honor her wishes. At least, she was going to stay a while, much to his relief, but an anxious feeling came over him. Was he relying on Liz *too* much in every way?

Chapter Forty-Seven

For Liz, Sunday, the first of April, turned out to be a bright, warm day, filled with the promises that always came with spring—renewal of hopes and dreams for the future. It hadn't started out that way, for when she had awakened her first thought was her newly discovered love for Matthew, and an overwhelming sense of hopelessness that accompanied it. Yet as the day wore on, the combination of enjoying Matthew and the children, along with the relief of communicating with Matthew the night before, limited as it was, allowed the sensation of spring to win over her spirits.

It was 2:00 in the afternoon. Liz and Matthew were relaxing on the porch watching the children race and play games. Liz gave running account of their antics, which at times were so comical, the two of them laughed. The beautiful day and the savory aroma of a cooking roast drifting out through the screen door, brought Matthew a feeling that all was well.

The doorbell rang, disturbing their peace. Always nervous that Elinor might show up any time unannounced, he glowered. "Who could that be?"

Liz, not wanting company either, replied as cheerfully as she could. "Let's go see." Taking his hand, they walked into the house to the door and opened it. Neither could have been more shocked, for there on the porch, all smiling and holding a large decorated cake, were her mother, father and sisters.

Happy Birthday, Liz!" they all said at once.

The surprise left her speechless, then she half-cried, half-laughed. "Thank you! You can't know what this means to me."

"Come in!" Matthew said with enthusiasm. "Liz didn't tell me it was her birthday."

They stepped in and took turns hugging Liz, transferring the cake from one to the other. She had thought of her birthday briefly, then put it out of her mind. The support from her family right at this time was something Liz desperately needed.

"Come into the kitchen and put the cake down," she said.

"Cake?" Matthew questioned.

"I'm sorry, Matthew. They brought a beautifully decorated birthday cake. The children will be so excited."

As they entered the kitchen/family room, Linda and Claire glanced around, smelled the cooking roast and looked at each other in amazement.

"Something certainly smells good in here, Liz," her father commented.

"I have a big roast in the oven. Now I get to inflict my cooking on someone else besides Matthew and the children."

"But dear," Julia said, "we were going to take all of you to dinner tonight for your birthday."

"You were? How long can you stay?"

Her father answered. "We thought we'd stay for a couple of days. We've reserved rooms at a hotel in Scottsdale."

"Wonderful! You can take us out to dinner tomorrow night for my birthday. Let me make dinner for you tonight."

"That's all right with me, Liz," her father said, "I like the smell of what you're cooking."

"Liz, you haven't introduced Matthew to us," Claire said.

"Oh, I'm sorry. Your arrival so surprised me, I'm not thinking. Matthew, this is Claire, my younger sister." Claire took Matthew's hand and shook it.

"I'm happy to meet you, Claire," he said.

"I'm Linda," a voice said, taking Matthew's hand next. "I'm Liz's youngest sister."

Matthew smiled warmly. "Having all of you come today is a happy occasion for us."

Julia and Calvin spoke to Matthew last, their polite, but cool greeting created tension throughout the room. Claire soon relieved it. "I see the children. May we go out and meet them?"

"Oh, yes!" Liz exclaimed. "You'll love them."

Matthew's heart swelled to hear Liz's excitement at having her family meet his children.

Out on the porch, Liz called the children over. "Merri and Danny, I have a surprise for you." They stopped running in circles, and stared at the group of strangers, their eyes alight with curiosity. Running over to Liz, they shyly clung to her. "You met my mother and father, remember?" They nodded.

Julia and Calvin, still reserved, greeted the children with courtesy.

"These are my sisters, Linda and Claire."

Both her sisters drew the children out, making them feel comfortable. "Come and see the birthday cake we brought Liz," Linda said.

Merri's eyes widened. "A birthday cake? It's Pipit's birthday today?

"It is," Claire replied. "And we came to celebrate it with all of you."

"She didn't tell us it was her birthday," Danny said.

"Now you know. Come in and see it," Linda said, taking his hand while Claire took Merri's. The rest followed them in.

Liz, touched that her sisters were showing such warmth to the children, hoped her parents would follow their example and unbend, for all their sakes.

"Wow!" Danny exclaimed. "It's big!"

Merri examined it. "And it's so pretty. We have some candles," she said, running to a drawer, taking them out and handing them to Linda.

"Oh, good. Let's see, how many should we put on?"

"How old are you, Pipit?" Merri asked.

"I'm thirty-one."

"Wow! That'll be a lot a candles," Danny said.

Claire looked at Liz. "Should we put thirty-one candles on?"

"If there are enough in the box, go for it."

"Oh goody! Can me and Danny help?"

"You sure can," Linda said.

Julia and Calvin were standing apart watching the whole episode. They noticed Liz edge over to Matthew and whisper something that brought a smile to his face. Their hearts were still grieving over the situation Liz had put herself in. All they could do was hope it would soon end.

When the candles had all been put on, Claire suggested to the children that they wait until after dinner to light them. "But, you know what," she said, "we brought you something. It's in the car. Wait right here and I'll go get it." When she came back, she handed them a sack. "If you already have one, we can exchange it."

They eagerly opened the sack and both tried to retrieve it. Merri, elbowed Danny away. "I started first." Danny looked over at Liz, his lips quivering.

"Danny, Merri did start first. Let Merri get it and then you can hold it."

"Okay."

Merri pulled out a ball. "It's a soccer ball, kids," Liz explained. "You don't have one. It's a fun game to play."

Merri handed the ball to Danny. "It's your turn to hold it."

His face lit up. "Okay. Can we play now, Pipit?"

"Yes. Let's all go outside. Everyone can watch while I teach you how to play soccer."

~~~~~~~~~~~~

Claire and Linda sat at the table watching their sister make gravy for the potatoes which Matthew had just mashed. They were in awe. Neither felt adept enough to even offer help, other than setting the table. The children were still outside playing soccer, giggling and yelling.

Julia, who was seated by her husband on the couch, had opted not to help, unhappy that her daughter should have to work like this for a family that wasn't hers. However, they both watched Liz in amazement, for she seemed right at home in the kitchen. They scrutinized Matthew, who by now was also sitting at the table, noticing how he lit up whenever Liz spoke to him, but also noticing that he seemed a little less than relaxed.

~~~~~~~~~~~~

The dinner turned out far beyond Liz's expectation. Her sisters requested the recipe for the dressing Liz had made for the green salad. Her father remarked on the gravy and the tasty meat. Her mother was silent.

Her family had watched when Liz filled Matthew's plate and whispered to him where each item was. Sensing displeasure from Julia and Calvin that their daughter had to help him as if he were a child, Matthew felt self-conscious throughout the meal.

When it was time to put the children to bed, he was glad to escape the palpable disapproval he felt from Liz' parents. In small measure, he could understand their anxiety. If it were his own daughter, Merri, in Liz's position, he would be most unhappy, but he couldn't allow himself to dwell on this—he had his children, and at the moment that was all that mattered.

After Matthew had gone, Linda said, "I like Matthew, and the children are adorable."

"He's a very attractive man, Liz," Claire added, noticing her mother's look of displeasure, then spoke bluntly. "Linda and I could hardly believe your decision to marry him just to help him keep his children. How are you managing being married and yet not being married?"

"It feels about like it did before when I was caring for the children, except I have more control. I have my memory, a driver's license and a car. I can escape this house when I want to," she answered in a lighthearted manner, affecting a grin, hoping she could fool her family. "Come on," she said standing up, "and I'll show you a picture of Matthew's wife." She turned to her parents. "Would you like to come?"

"We've seen it," Julia replied through tight lips.

"All right." Liz led them to the front room. They both gasped when they saw the picture.

"She's beautiful!" Linda exclaimed.

"She is," Claire said. "Is it a good likeness?"

"Matthew says it is."

Claire studied her sister's face. "How is Matthew doing? Is he still visibly grieving over her death?"

"He holds it in well and doesn't inflict his grief on me or others. But just the other night, I left my door open so I could hear Merri if she had a bad dream. I didn't hear Merri, but I heard Matthew. He has recurring nightmares over the accident in which he lost Diane."

"How terrible," Linda said.

Scrutinizing Liz, Claire probed. "How do you feel about Matthew, Liz?"

"I care about him a great deal. He was so good to me in the cabin and I owe my life to him and his uncle Arthur."

"You've said that before, but how could you marry him just because you feel grateful?"

"Because, Claire, I love the children. What would we have done without *our* father? All three of us adore him. He's added something to our lives that we couldn't possibly have had without him. Matthew is a loving father like ours. Besides, I know Elinor Halstrom, his mother-in-law, and it would destroy them if she raised them...and it would destroy Matthew."

"If it would destroy the children, how come it didn't destroy Diane?"

"Diane was an amazing person. Everyone who knew her loved her. From what I've heard from the neighbors, and from Matthew, she sounds near perfect."

"That seems unlikely if her mother was the kind you indicate."

"She rose above it, Claire."

Claire looked skeptical, but Linda replied. "She must have been a good mother, Claire. Look at her sweet children."

"I suspect," said Claire, "Matthew had a lot to do with that...as well as our sister."

Liz, wanting to get her off the subject of Diane and Matthew, said what she'd been wanting to say to her sisters. "I want to thank you both for coming here with Mother and Dad. Last night, I felt so homesick I thought I couldn't make it. It means so much to me to have your support right now."

"You have our support," Claire responded, "but not our approval, Liz. We love you and want you to have a real marriage, not a marriage that will only be annulled in a few months."

"Do you think you and Matthew could ever fall in love with each other, Liz?" asked Linda.

"Matthew would not consider marrying anyone in his condition, and besides, he's in love with the memory of his wife, and I wouldn't consider marrying him under those circumstances."

"But you *are* married, Liz," retorted Claire.

"In my mind, I'm not."

Out in the family room, Matthew had returned to find that Liz and her sisters had gone into the other room. He was glad to have a moment alone with Liz's parents.

He seated himself in the chair after finding out that the Cabots were seated on the couch. "Mr. and Mrs. Cabot, I haven't told Liz this yet, but if my eyesight does not return in two more months, I'm sending her home."

"Why did you allow her to marry you in the first place, Matthew?" Calvin asked.

"Your daughter is your first concern as my children are mine. I can understand in some small measure how upset you must be for your daughter to marry under such circumstances, but if it weren't for Liz, I would have lost my children. Though I was very hesitant for Liz to do this, my children were my primary consideration."

"That is very little comfort to us, Mr. Melloy," Julia said.

"I know. However, I would like you to know, that in court, your daughter was magnificent on the stand."

Calvin's brows lowered. "I can't imagine how she did it without perjuring herself, and that is something Liz would never do."

"Of course not. She told only the truth, but she conferred with my attorney, requesting he ask her certain questions. She was clever, sincere and very credible. I'll be indebted to her the rest of my life."

Just then, Liz and her sisters returned to the room.

"Well, Liz," her father said, "we had better get to the hotel. Thank you for that most amazing meal you put on."

"Thank *you*, Dad."

"What would you like to do tomorrow and tomorrow night to celebrate your birthday, Liz?" her mother asked.

"Are you up to going to the zoo? The children have been begging to go again."

"The children? I...uh.."

"Mother, I would like the children to be around you and Dad. Their grandparents are no longer in their life and..."

"We are *not* their grandparents, Liz."

"No, but you could step in for a couple of days."

"Liz, we can get a babysitter for them tomorrow," Matthew said. "Your parents do not want them along."

"It's not that we don't want them, Matthew," Julia began, "it's just a difficult situation for us."

"I want them with us, Mother and Dad."

Julia sighed. "All right, Liz, it's your birthday."

Matthew quickly made a suggestion. "Since you want them with you tomorrow, Liz, I'll take care of them tomorrow night while you go out to dinner with your family."

Liz was about to protest, but thought better of it. It was obvious that Matthew felt uncomfortable around her parents and he preferred to stay with the children. "All right, Matthew."

After saying goodnight to her family at the door, Liz returned to find Matthew leaning over, his head in his hands. "What is it, Matthew?"

He straightened up instantly. "Oh, nothing. I'm just a little tired, I guess."

"I'm grateful my family could bring themselves to come, even though they made it quite clear they are still less than happy about our marriage."

"Can you blame them?"

"No."

"Liz..." Matthew began, "the way you wanted your sisters to meet the children, wanting to take them to the zoo...I...uh..." He cleared his throat, but in spite of it, his voice broke. "Thank you for loving my children."

Chapter Forty-Eight

In spite of her resistance to having the children around, Julia found herself more and more drawn to them as they all enjoyed the animals at the zoo. Against her will, and to her discomfort, she felt sad that they had lost their mother, and even sadder that they would also lose their 'Pipit' one of these days. She tried unsuccessfully to push these thoughts from her mind.

Claire and Linda, also, were taken with Merri and Danny, who in turn insisted on taking turns holding their hands.

Calvin watched it all, surprised at the changes in his family. Mostly, he was astounded at how Liz handled the children, but then Liz had always amazed him through every stage of her life.

Late afternoon, as pre-arranged with Matthew, they dropped the children off at Matthew's Phoenix store so Liz could go on to dinner with her family.

Liz insisted that they all come in and see the store. As they walked in, they saw Matthew sitting at a piano speaking with a customer. Liz put a finger to her lips and smiled which told the children that they were going to surprise their daddy again. As they drew near, he began singing a song for the customer. Julia and her daughters were mesmerized, and Calvin was impressed. When the customer left with sheet music in her hand, the children pounced on him. "Surprise!" they yelled.

And it was a surprise. He laughed and gathered them up in his arms. "Who's here with you?"

"All of us," Merri replied.

"Did you both have a good time at the zoo?"

"Yes!" Danny exclaimed launching into a recital of everything they saw, with Merri chiming in.

"We're going to the park again for a picnic tomorrow, Daddy," Merri said. "Can you come with us?"

Matthew's face sobered. "Liz?"

"Yes, Matthew."

"You need to be alone with your family."

"It was my family's idea, not mine. They're right here."

"Mr. and Mrs. Cabot, Linda, Claire, thank you, but...."
"Will you come on the picnic with us?" Linda asked.
"Well...I.."
"We really want you to join us," Claire added.
"Mrs. Cabot?"
"Yes, Calvin and I would like you to join us as well."
"Thank you," he said quietly. "I think I can manage it."

~~~~~~~~~~~~

Going to the zoo had been the turning point for her family, giving them an opportunity to get to know the children in a way they wouldn't have otherwise. When she mentioned having a picnic the next day, her mother didn't resist, in fact, she had even agreed with Linda and Claire that Matthew should also be there for the children's sake.

It felt good to be seated around the table in the restaurant with her family, and she voiced her feelings to them.

"It's good to be with you too, Liz, and find out that you're all right in spite of the situation," Claire said.

Calvin soon turned the conversation to Matthew's store. "It looks like it's successful by the amount of help he had, and the number of customers who came in while we were there."

"I think it is, Dad. He has another store in Scottsdale."

"Is that right? Where did he get the money to finance them?"

This gave Liz the opportunity to tell Matthew's story— the tornado that destroyed the peach orchards and killed his parents when he was fifteen, of his finding the family Bible and how Randy felt about Matthew, ending the story with him graduating from college and selling the land to finance the Phoenix store and eventually the Scottsdale store. Everyone was quiet after this poignant account of his life.

It was Linda who broke the silence. "I love Matthew's voice."

This gave Liz another opportunity to tell her family more about him. "Apparently, many people do because when they want to know how a piece of music or an arrangement sounds, not only do they ask Matthew to play it, they also want him to sing along if the piece has words to it. He plays by ear and has a great memory so he can still do this for his customers. Also, he can play almost any instrument that a customer might want to hear. As I told you, his voice is what led me in the direction of the cabin and saved my life."

Calvin wondered if Julia noticed what he did; Liz's whole demeanor became animated when she talked about Matthew. Either it was pure admiration or his daughter had deeper feelings for Matthew than she'd let on. He hoped with all his heart that his daughter would not get hurt again!

~~~~~~~~~~~

The next day after lunch, Liz and the children left home to meet her family at the park. Mike was going to drive Matthew there, and afterward, she would drive home while her parents and sisters went to the motel. They were leaving early the next morning.

Liz was grateful that her parents and sisters were warming up to the children and Matthew. Though they still were concerned about her, they would be more likely to understand why she did what she did.

If Merri and Danny hadn't been buckled in, they would be bouncing all over the car they were so excited about going to the park with their daddy and her family. The only time she'd seen them this excited was when they got to go play with their cousins. Liz felt almost as excited, for her mother had arranged for a caterer to bring the picnic, and a day without cooking was a real vacation!

When they arrived, her family was already there waiting as they said they would be. The minute Liz opened the car door, Merri and Danny unbuckled themselves and ran headlong toward Linda and Claire, throwing their arms around them. And to Liz's amazement, they then ran over to her parents throwing their arms around *them*! She watched her parents' expressions and knew that the children had, with this show of affection, finished winning them over completely.

Liz greeted her family with a smile. "The kids almost stumbled over each other trying to get out of the car to reach you."

"They seem to be very affectionate children," Julia said, smiling. "Where's Matthew?"

"Mike, his manager, is bringing him over as soon as Matthew can get away."

Linda said to the children, "Okay, you guys, can you climb that big contraption over there?"

With great exuberance, they claimed they could.

"Will you and Claire come and watch us?" Danny asked.

"We certainly will," Claire answered.

Liz and her parents followed and found a bench close by to sit down and watch. However, Liz had a hard time concentrating on the children; she kept looking in the direction of the parking lot for Matthew's arrival. Forty-five minutes later, she spied him getting out of Mike's car.

She got up and ran over to him, noticing how his casual shirt and jeans worn to work so he could go to the picnic, showed off his build—his broad shoulders, his thick chest, narrowing down to his hips. "Hi!" she greeted breathlessly.

"Hi, yourself."

Liz waved at Mike, took Matthew's hand, which sent a touch of excitement through her, and led him over to the bench where her parents were sitting.

"Hello, Matthew," Calvin said. "Glad you could make it."

"Thank you. Glad I could, too. Where are the children?"

"They're over there with Linda and Claire, climbing on a big wooden structure," Calvin answered.

He smiled. "Oh."

"Let's go over closer, Matthew," Liz suggested.

"Lead away."

Julia and Calvin watched with mixed feelings. Soon the children tired of climbing, wanted to go down the slide, then they ran to the swings. They followed them, finding another bench on which to sit and watch, but unknown to each other, they mostly watched Liz and Matthew.

After some time had passed, Julia let out a tremulous breath. "Oh, Cal, have you noticed what I have?"

"I probably have, what?"

"What a kind and loving woman our Liz has turned out to be. She's Matthew's eyes; she relates to him everything that is going on. But the animation on her face, the way they laugh together over what she tells him disturbs me."

"I can guess, but why?"

"Because I've never seen Liz this way with any man. I'm afraid she feels more for Matthew than she's telling us."

~~~~~~~~~~~~

The picnic food arrived at 5:00, and it turned out to be a feast. There were several kinds of fruit, potato salad, large fried shrimp, fried chicken, a platter of crisp vegetables, olives, cookies, cake, water, and lemonade. The children were so excited, both Liz and Matthew could hardly keep them from piling their plates with far more than they could eat. Diane had trained her children to like a variety of food.

No one could ever measure up to Diane, she thought. Despondency threatened to ruin her exceptional mood, but the fun and laughter issuing from her family and the children soon buoyed up her spirits.

There was a lot of food left, along with several Styrofoam cooler boxes in which to carry it home, pleasing Liz with the thought of no cooking for another day!

After they had digested the food, Calvin surprised the children. He went to the car and returned with a badminton set he and Julia had bought them this morning. Then he and Claire set it up. Merri and Danny were beside themselves with excitement. After they taught the children how to play, Claire and Danny played Linda and Merri. Matthew could hear Danny's yelling, Merri's squeals, and laughter from all four, and his heart was eased knowing that, at least, the Cabots had accepted his children.

When it came time to say goodbye, the children were tearful and begged Liz's family to stay longer. Julia, Calvin and their daughters shook Matthew's hand and hugged the children. When they hugged Liz, she thanked them profusely for coming.

"Liz," Claire began, "you are wonderful with the children. Who would have guessed it?" She laughed. "And you know what it has done for me?"

"No, what, Claire?"

"It has made me hungry for children."

"Me too," Linda confessed.

"It's about time," Liz said grinning.

The Cabots moved to their car, and waved at the forlorn and tearful children as they drove off.

Matthew whispered in Liz's ear. "I'm sorry, Liz, for comparing your parents to Elinor and Wayne Halstrom. They are nothing alike."

Chapter Forty-Nine

Her family had lifted Liz's spirits, making the rest of the week easier to get through, along with the fact that Merri's behavior was getting better each day. She and Matthew were amazed at how good Merri was during the Cabot's visit.

Matthew, continuing to respect Liz's wishes, held his affectionate nature at bay, only holding hands by necessity. He was feeling more and more discontented with the agreement, because in addition to that, Liz still kept herself so busy, there was never time to enjoy her company.

After four days of swimming, badminton, walks into the desert to find wild flowers and to look for, in particular, a little pocket mouse, Liz felt that the children needed other children to play with. They needed their cousins. She issued a long overdue invitation to Arthur, Mamie and Randy and his family to come to an early dinner the next day, Sunday, hoping it would turn out as good as the meal she had fed her family.

Saturday evening early, Matthew took his irritable children by the hand, insisting it was bedtime. After playing and swimming all day, they were overly tired. Quickly finishing the dishes, Liz stepped out of the front door, leaving it ajar so she could hear Matthew, and sat down on the step of the porch to enjoy the pleasant evening.

A fragment of a cloud moved slowly to the east, and a huge bee droned by alighting on yellow desert poppy. Perched in a palo verde tree a family of ash-throated flycatchers were engaging in subdued throaty chatter before tumbling out of the tree one by one to alight in a nearby jojoba. Liz breathed in deeper, trying to allay the growing fear that she wouldn't be able to resist Matthew any longer—that one day soon, she'd go against her own edict and ask him to give her one of those comforting 'bear hugs.'

She heard Matthew calling. "I'm out on the front porch, Matthew!" she yelled.

"What are you doing, Liz?" he asked, standing at the door.

"Just sitting here, enjoying the desert."

"Can I come and sit beside you?"

"Uh...I need to go in and put in a wash and..."

"Please, Liz, don't leave. I need your company. I've missed it."

She caught her breath. "You have? Why?"

"Because you've kept yourself so busy."

That isn't the answer I wanted to hear, she thought, *but then*, she chastised herself, *how can I expect any other?* She stood up and took his hand and led him to the edge of the porch where they both sat down.

"Ah, nice evening. We need to enjoy it while we can because it won't be long before the evenings will be too warm to be pleasant."

"Oh, Matthew, there's a little pocket mouse! We've looked all week for one and Danny is asleep."

"Liz, you are doing for the children things children love to do. Thank you."

"You're welcome, but you see, I love to do the same things. I'm really an outdoor girl. I've hiked the desert hills and valleys of California. My sisters are just the opposite. They like in-town living where they don't get sand in their shoes and can enjoy all the amenities and luxuries."

"I prefer outdoor girls, but I do like your sisters."

"I'm glad," she said, her mind still on the first thing he said, 'I prefer outdoor girls.' *Diane certainly wasn't an outdoor girl. Could that mean...* Quickly squelching the thought, she focused on the evenings subtle change. It was turning into that rare twilight when the sun paints the earth saffron gold, then all too soon, slowly withdraws its magic, returning the earth as it was—until sunset. "It's one of those golden twilights, Matthew."

"It *feels* golden." He smiled, wanting to tell her that it was because her company made it feel that way; instead he said, "My father used to compare these kinds of twilight with the brief moments of joy which come now and then in family relationships. The kind that keep us going, that give us hope during our struggles until the next moment of joy."

"What a nice thought."

A two-toned gray and white bird lit in the same palo verde in which the ash-throated flycatchers had chattered together. It began to sing a rich melodic song.

"Sounds like a mockingbird, Liz."

"It is."

"They're usually fond of singing on moonlit nights, but he must be enjoying this special evening with us."

~~~~~~~~~~~~

Sunday, the meal over, Arthur, Mamie, Liz and Matthew sat on the porch and watched Randy and Joan referee the badminton game between the cousins. They were comical to watch, and Liz drew a word picture for Matthew. They couldn't help but laugh together as the game progressed.

"Matthew," Mamie said, "you are looking good and acting more like your old self."

"I guess it's because I don't have Elinor breathing down my back—thanks to Liz."

"I feel rather sorry for Elinor," Liz murmured. "Do you think she would respond if we took the children to see her and Wayne or invited them over here?"

"No," Matthew stated firmly. "She holds grudges. I'm afraid it will be a long time before we can do that."

When evening came and they had fed the children again, Joan asked Matthew if she and Randy could take Merri and Danny home for a couple of days. "Becky and Johnny need someone to play with. Several of their friends are out of town, and they don't know what to do with themselves."

"I think that would be nice for them. Do you think you can stand a little vacation, Liz?"

The thought of being here alone with Matthew unnerved her, nevertheless, she agreed, "I think I could use a vacation. I'll go pack a little bag for each."

When they were ready to leave, the children excitedly gave their dad and Liz a quick hug and dashed out the door with their cousins.

"Well, Pip ol' girl, you are turning into quite a cook and nanny—a far cry from that 'spoiled rich kid' we knew up there in the cabin."

"Gee, thanks 'Uncle' Arthur," she smirked.

Mamie gave her a warm hug. "Have a good rest, and thank you for that wonderful meal...and for everything."

Liz closed the door and took Matthew's hand as they walked back into the family room, wondering if Matthew felt the sweet intimacy of their hand-holding, especially now that they were alone.

All he said was, "Yes, thank you for everything, Liz."

"Do you know how you can thank me?" she asked a little too brightly, "You can play and sing for me."

He smiled and moved over to the piano. "What would you like to hear?"

"Old songs, modern songs, it doesn't matter."

He began with a George M. Cohan song, *Give My Regards To Broadway,* making her smile, then on to *when My Sugar Walks down the Street,* and *Get Me To the Church On Time.* Next, he switched to one from the musical *Les Miserables, Bring Him Home.* Its beautiful melody cried out all that was in her heart. How was she going to keep her feelings from Matthew? Tonight, for a while, she could keep him busy singing songs, but what would tomorrow bring?

Chapter Fifty

While showering, Matthew wondered what Liz would do with herself all day without the children. She certainly didn't need to stay here and work, she could do whatever she wished; determining right then that he would suggest this to her.

He whistled as he combed his hair, deciding that this morning he could pick out his own clothes, mismatched or not. It must be getting tiresome for Liz to have to do this for him every morning...and all the other things she did for him.

The aroma of breakfast cooking reached his nose and he followed it. "Liz?"

"Good morning, Matthew. I'm over here by the stove thinking what a beautiful morning it is."

He smiled and found his way to the open back door and smelled the fresh spring air. He stepped over to the table and sang with gusto, "*Oh what a beautiful morning, oh what a beautiful day, I have a wonderful feeling everything's goin' my way.*"

She was smiling when it happened. Like the morning sun, it was the first thing he saw...then the blue of her eyes.

Liz gazed at the odd expression on his face. "What is it, Matthew?"

His expression changed to one of awe, his voice barely audible. "Your eyes are blue."

"I know." Slowly, her smile disappeared, her eyes widening with astonishment. "Matthew! Can...can you see?" she asked, holding her breath, gazing intently into his earth-green eyes, finding the blankness gone.

"I can see. I can see!" He picked her up and swung her around. When he set her down, tears were running down both their cheeks. They laughed, they cried. Looking around, he satiated his eyes with everything he could see, the room, the backyard—but mostly the woman he held.

The doorbell rang, interrupting their glorious moment of joy. An expression of regret crossed Matthew's face. "I forgot, Liz.

I asked Mike to pick me up early. I have an appointment with my accountant and another one with my business attorney."

He started for the door, stopped and turned to Liz with an expression of wonder. "I can drive my own car!"

She laughed and followed him.

Matthew, grinning wide, opened the door. "You're fired, Mike!"

"Wh...what?" he asked, shocked.

"You're fired...as my chauffeur!"

It took a moment for it to sink in and when it did, Mike let out a whoop that could have awakened the whole neighborhood. He laughed and shook Matthew's hand exuberantly. "I'm happy for you, Matthew! And for me. Thanks for firing me. I'm not much of a chauffeur."

"You're welcome." The smile never leaving his face, Matthew turned to Liz. "I don't have time to eat breakfast, but I'll come home as early as I can this evening, then we can go to Mamie's and Arthur's and tell them the good news...and then the children!"

Turning back to Mike, "I'm going to go get my keys and I want you to follow me down. Though I've started my car periodically, I want to make sure it will get me there after sitting in the garage for so long."

Liz watched him run to his bedroom to retrieve his keys and return, barely having time to do anything but smile and wave at her. Her heart full of happiness for Matthew, she watched from the door as he backed out of the garage and drove off, giving her another smile and wave.

She stood at the door long after he left, feeling as though a miracle had occurred. It had been approximately eleven months since Matthew lost his sight.

Slowly, she closed the door and walked back into the kitchen, fixed herself a plate of breakfast and sat down to eat, disappointed that he had to leave so quickly. She ate automatically, still in a state of euphoria, her mind flitting from one thing to the other. *Won't the children be thrilled to have their daddy back whole!* she thought. She could hardly wait to see their faces. And Mamie's and Arthur's....and Randy's... Now Matthew can join them in their desert walks! They can watch a movie together—then reality struck her in the face.

This was the time she and Matthew had agreed that she should leave—when they would get an annulment—when she could get on with her life. What life? Without Matthew she had no life! She covered her face. "What am I going to do?" The last thing she wanted to do was leave! Getting up, she quickly stepped out onto the porch to take some deep breaths in hopes she could calm her rising anxiety.

But she couldn't leave now! She wanted to be with Matthew when he revealed to his children, to Arthur, Mamie, Randy and Joan the wonderful miracle God had granted him! She would stay for a few days, or until they could find someone to take her place, then they could part in a deliberate, composed manner just as they had when they decided to marry. Composed? Matthew had been composed. Inside, she had been far from it.

An uncomfortable memory forced itself upon her mind. When she had to leave Matthew and the children before, she had become almost hysterical! "But this was just because of the head injury and amnesia. Surely, I can control myself this time," she reasoned aloud. A knot rose up in her chest just *thinking* about saying goodbye to Merri and Danny. However, as her thoughts switched to saying goodbye to Matthew, she could no longer hold in the tears, for the knot had turned into an intense heartache. Stepping back inside, the sobs became so convulsive she had to sit down.

When finally she had worn herself out with grief, she knew she had to face the awful truth. She had to leave *now*, this morning or as soon as she could pack! Her emotional nature would be her undoing if she stayed. When it came time to say goodbye to Matthew, she would blubber like an idiot, and Matthew would *know* how she felt. He was too kind and sensitive. She couldn't put that burden of guilt upon him.

Scooting back from the table, she began cleaning up rapidly. Suddenly, she realized she didn't really know how Matthew felt about *her*. Seeds of hope planted themselves. It had all happened so quickly—his sight returning and then his having to dash out the door for an appointment. There had hardly been time for either of them to totally react to the momentous occasion, let alone, time to think things through and talk about the future!

First of all, she reminded herself, Matthew had wanted her company last night, and even said he'd missed it. If he did feel something for her, he never would have said anything because of his condition—unless his sight returned. But—did he feel anything for her? How in the world could she tell between his *need* for her to be his eyes, his need for her to care for Merri and Danny, and his possible feelings for her?

Then she remembered the odd expression on his face. Apparently, she was the first thing he saw for he mentioned the color of her eyes. Why the odd look? Did he compare her face to Diane's beautiful face? Her heart sank. Of course he would! He was still hanging onto her memory. Didn't he just talk about her with such tenderness the other night? The fragile seeds of hope withered. Though it would be hard for Matthew to find a replacement for her, in the long run it would be easier on him if she left today, leaving him a note to start the annulment proceedings.

How fortunate that the children were with Randy and Joan. She wouldn't have to face saying goodbye to them. It was 'runaway time' again—something she was good at!

At least she was leaving everything in good shape. All the cleaning and washing she'd done in order to avoid being alone with Matthew had paid off. There was even food in the cupboards and refrigerator.

Getting down her suitcases, she began packing as quickly as she could, trying not to think. Her parents were certainly going to be surprised. When she was through packing and putting everything in the car, she cleaned her bathroom, changed her sheets and remade the bed. Grabbing her purse, she went into the kitchen to write a note to Matthew and one to the children, dreading it because she didn't know what she was going to say to make it easier on Merri and Danny...or Matthew. The briefer, the better she decided.

With that done, she locked up the house and got into her car, backed out, drove to the street and stopped. Glancing at her watch, she saw that it was 11:30. She wished she could say goodbye to Flo and Margo, but how could she explain to them her leaving so abruptly?

Before driving on, she took one last look at the desert she and the children had explored. A deep sadness settled over her.

Chapter Fifty-One

Liz drove into her parents driveway a little after 4:00 PM. Parking in the back, she entered through the kitchen to find Mabel preparing dinner. The good smells reminded her that she hadn't even taken time out for lunch. "Hello, Mabel," she said.

"Miss Liz! You're home! Are you here to stay?"

"I think so, Mabel. Is Mother here?"

She is. I believe she's talking on the phone. It just rang."

"Thank you, Mabel."

Liz suddenly felt exhausted and weak. She found her mother speaking on the phone in the family room. Her mother looked up. "Liz! Cal, it's Liz. She's home! You will?....Good. See you soon." She hung up. "Your dad will be here as quickly as he can get away."

Julia got up and hugged her daughter, then looked into her face. "You look tired, Liz."

"I am. I drove straight through without stopping for lunch."

"Why are you here, darling?" She paused. "Matthew's sight has come back!"

Liz smiled. "It did, Mother. It just happened this morning when he came out for breakfast. It happened spontaneously as the doctors said it might. He said, 'your eyes are blue.' It took a moment for it to sink in. It was so wonderful, Mother."

"I'm so happy for him...and for you...and to have you home. Would you like a snack before dinner?"

"No, thank you. I think I'll just go freshen up and eat with you and Dad."

Calvin arrived home at 4:45 eager to see his daughter. Julia, who had been watching for him, met him as he was entering from the garage. "Hi, darling," he smiled. "Where's Liz?"

"She's in her room. I need to talk with you before you see her."

"Is anything wrong, Julia?" he asked following her into the family room.

"I don't know. She looks very unhappy."

"Why is she here? Did Matthew's sight come back?"

"Yes, it did."

Calvin let out sigh of relief. "I'm so grateful...mainly for Liz, but also for him."

"Me too, Calvin, but you need to find out what's wrong. She's more likely to answer your questions than mine."

"I'll try, but you know Liz. She keeps things to herself."

~~~~~~~~~~~~

Matthew wasn't able to leave work until 4:30. He could hardly contain his excitement while driving home, wondering what Liz had done with herself all day. Never would he take his sight for granted again! Gazing at everything, it felt like the world was new. Smiling, he thought of how his employees had reacted to his good news—getting last minute refreshments, they turned it into an all-day celebration. However, it was with his family he wanted share this miracle, especially Merri and Danny.

Turning into his driveway, he saw that Liz's car was gone. Disappointment deflated him. He'd told her he would try to come home early. Surely, she'll be back soon.

This thought buoyed up his spirits as he drove into the garage and went into the house.

Quickly walking into his bedroom to change, he was struck by the sight of it, how it looked like Diane. Though he'd run in briefly this morning, he hadn't seen it since the accident. Stepping over to her closet, he turned on the light and gazed at her clothes, her perfume lingering. It felt as though his heart almost stopped, the pain was so excruciating. Stumbling out, he sat on the bed, sobs racking his body.

Ten minutes later, he slowly got up, went into his closet and changed into a casual shirt and jeans, realizing once more how much more devastating it was to lose Diane than his sight. He would gladly trade his sight if only he could have her back! Just then, a question came into his mind, one he'd never thought to ask himself until now. *How would Diane have handled his blindness if she had lived? Would she take his hand, be his eyes, and be there for him day and night...always?*

The question confounded him; he couldn't answer it. The next thought unsettled him. *Where was Liz? Maybe she left a note for him to meet her someplace.* Entering the kitchen, he was relieved to see a note—two of them—on the bar. He picked up the one to him.

Dear Matthew,

It is very difficult for me to leave right now and not see the reaction of Merri and Danny when they learn that you can see again...and to see Mamie's and Arthur's, and Randy's and Joan's reaction. But as we agreed, I would leave when your sight returned. I'm sure you'll want to start proceedings for an annulment.

The other thing I regret is that we hadn't started looking for a good woman to come in and look after the children. We didn't expect your sight to return so soon, did we? Good luck in finding someone. I'm so very happy for you, Matthew.

Love,

Liz

Matthew was dumbstruck. He read and reread the note. "Why did she leave so soon?! So abruptly!" He felt angry. The least she could do was say goodbye! How could she do this to him, to the children? He picked up the note to the children.

Dear Merri and Danny,

I'm so happy that your daddy can see again. Now, he'll be able to go on desert walks with you, watch a favorite video with you and read to you. I'm going home to my parents because you won't need me anymore. I'll miss our times together. Be good to your daddy and always obey him.

I love you,

Pipit

"So brief! Why didn't she wait and discuss her leaving with me?" Why?! Why didn't she know that leaving like this would take some of the thrill out of his seeing again? He wanted to share it with her! This morning, their sharing had been cut short—he didn't get to tell her how it happened. It wasn't like Liz! Or was it? She had run away before without telling her family where she was. Maybe he really didn't know her. Storming out to his car, he headed for Chandler.

~~~~~~~~~~~~

Julia knocked on Liz's door. Liz opened it. "Is Dad here?"

"Yes. He's waiting to see you."

When they entered the family room, her father smiled and went to her, his arms wrapping around her affectionately. "It's quite a surprise to have you home so soon after we left. I hear Matthew has regained his sight."

"Yes," she murmured against his shoulder.

"Let's sit down so you can tell us all the details."

Liz smiled. "It was all quite amazing, Dad." She told them both every detail, which didn't take long, Mike had come too soon.

Calvin studied his daughter. "Why didn't you at least go with him to tell his aunt and uncle and the children? Didn't you want to see their reaction and enjoy it with all of them?"

"I thought you and Mother wanted me to come home as soon as possible, Dad."

"You know we did, but a day or two wouldn't have made that much difference. Are you going to answer my question?"

"What good would it do to prolong our parting?"

"Liz, you are avoiding answering my question, why?"

Exasperated, Liz got up and looked out the window, trying to think how to answer. "I would have liked to see the reaction of his family, but...but it would have been hard to say goodbye to...the children. I'm good at running away, remember?"

"Liz, turn around and look at me," her father requested.

She sighed and turned around, her lips pursed together tightly, a response her parents knew well.

"Would it have been hard to say goodbye to Matthew, too?" her father queried.

"You know it would. I've told you I care about Matthew."

"How much do you care about him, Liz?" her mother carefully asked.

"As much as one can care about someone who has saved one's life."

"You are very adept at sidestepping our questions, Liz. You've done that far too often in your life. Please be honest with us. It's obvious to your mother and me that you aren't happy."

Liz looked down, her chin trembling. When she gained control, she spoke slowly. "You didn't want me to even go see Matthew, remember?"

"We remember," Calvin answered.

"You were right. I shouldn't have gone. But I'm glad I did because Matthew and his children are together. Even if Elinor hears that I've left, now that his sight is back, she won't be able to take them from him."

"You have accomplished your mission...so why were we right?"

"Dad, please don't interrogate me."

"Why?"

"Oh Dad..." She couldn't go on, for she had to press her lips together and blink back tears.

"Why, Liz?"

"I don't want to tell you because you could say, 'we told you so.' You'll know just why I shouldn't have gone to see Matthew against your wishes."

"We already feel we know what it is, Liz. We just want to hear it from your lips."

Her brows rose in surprise. "You do? Is it that obvious?"

They both nodded. "It was very obvious at the picnic," her mother informed her.

Still Liz hesitated.

"Liz?" her father asked more insistently.

"It...uh kind of snuck up on me. I didn't recognize it, or wouldn't allow myself to, but about eleven days ago, two days before you arrived, I realized that I...I loved Matthew, that I was in love with him. I didn't want it to happen because..." She sucked in her breath trying to hold in a flood of emotion.

"Why didn't you want it to happen?" The tone in her father's voice brooked no more holding back.

"Because it's hopeless! He's in love with the memory of his beautiful, perfect wife."

Her parents were silent for some time before her mother answered. "No one is perfect, Liz. Diane wasn't perfect."

"From what I've learned, she's close to it. I feel Matthew thinks she is. The odd expression on his face that I mentioned, could have been because it was very apparent to him that I wasn't beautiful like Diane."

This both shocked and dismayed her parents. "How...how could you possibly interpret his odd expression like that?" her mother asked, incredulous.

Her father reiterated the same, "Do you really believe that Matthew had time in that first moment when his sight came back, to think of *that*?"

"I...I guess not. It's just that I don't feel secure...I..." her voice trailed off.

Julia stood up, went over to her daughter, and held her close. "I've felt the same way in my life, darling."

"*You* have felt insecure?" Liz asked in amazement.

"Yes, Liz. I've told you that when I was in high school we lived where most of our neighbors, and many of my friends belonged to the country club. I always felt on the outside looking in. It wasn't until I met your father that I began to feel secure."

"You've told me about your neighbors and friends belonging to the country club, and how much fun it was when they invited you to some of their activities, but you never told me about your feelings of insecurity. Why?"

"I tend to keep things to myself, Liz. I guess you and I are alike in that."

Liz regretted that her mother hadn't revealed this about herself. She could have understood her better...been kinder to her. Her mother broke into her thoughts.

"When you love someone as much as you apparently love Matthew, it's only natural to feel insecure because you don't know how *he* feels. That's the key...you don't really *know* what Matthew is feeling." Releasing Liz, Julia gazed into her face. "He may not know himself. Give it some time. Time will give you answers."

Liz gave her mother a small grateful smile. "Thank you, Mother, that helped." Almost as she said it, her face clouded up. "Now that you've helped me take my thoughts off myself, and though I know it's best for Matthew that I left as I did, I'm concerned it may have hurt him. And that thought hurts even more."

~~~~~~~~~~~~

All the way to Chandler, Matthew tried to figure out why Liz would leave so abruptly. Again, he told himself it wasn't like her. Thinking back over several days, he tried to remember if something happened that would have upset her enough to leave without telling him. He couldn't come up with anything. His anger flared up again. Here he was, unable to enjoy his newly regained sight because of worry over Liz's actions!

Arriving at Arthur's and Mamie's, he remained in the car for a few moments, trying to calm down. As he did so, he remembered that he hadn't even taken time out for a prayer of thanks to the Almighty for His kindness and mercy, for blessing him to see again. He bowed his head in remorse, and silently thanked Him. His anger deflated, he got out of the car, feeling grateful that someone didn't have to lead him to the door. He smiled as he rang the doorbell.

Mamie answered it. "Matthew!" She looked around for Liz.

"I'm alone, Aunt Mamie," he said, stepping in.

"She dropped you off?"

"No." He grinned. "I like that green dress, Aunt Mamie."

"How...how did you know my dress is green?"

Matthew said nothing, only grinned.

"Matthew!" she screamed. "You can see!"

"Yes, I can," he said hugging her.

"Oh Matthew dear, I'm so happy for you," she said, tears sliding down her plump cheeks.

"Thank you, Aunt Mamie." He looked around. "Where's Uncle Arthur?"

"He's been out in the backyard. I think I hear him coming in now," she said, her eyes full of excitement, leading him into the kitchen.

Arthur looked up. "Matthew, this is a surprise. You didn't come to get Merri and Danny so soon did you?"

"Not exactly. What have you been doing, Uncle Arthur?"

"I've been putting some fertilizer on my citrus out in back."

Matthew went to the back window. "The trees are looking good," he said, grinning from ear to ear.

"Thanks. They should, I've worked....did you say they *looked* good?"

"I sure did, Uncle Arthur!"

Arthur walked over to him, searching his face. When he saw the long missing twinkle in Matthew's eyes, Arthur's own eyes brimmed with tears. "You can see," he said a little hoarsely.

Touched by his uncle's tears, Matthew smiled. "I can."

Arthur threw his arms around Matthew. "I'm so happy for you, son...so happy. Our prayers have been answered." Stepping back, he looked into Matthew's face. "How did it happen and when?"

Matthew related the few details surrounding it. "It's like the world is new. I can't see enough of it to suit me."

It was then that Arthur realized he hadn't seen Liz. "Where's Liz?"

Matthew's face clouded. "She left to go home. Didn't say a thing about going. I found a brief note to me and one to the children. She said I could go ahead with the annulment."

Arthur and Mamie glanced at each other, and Arthur asked, "Are you going to?"

"I have to take first things first. I've got to figure out what I'm going to do about the children...who I'm going to get to take care of them since Liz left in such a thoughtless manner."

"After all she's done for you, Matthew, how can you say that?" Mamie asked.

"Easy!"

"There has to be a reason she left like that, Matthew. Don't you have any idea what would cause her to do such a thing? It isn't like her."

"That's what I thought at first, Aunt Mamie. But then maybe it is. She ran away from her family and didn't tell them why."

"I still say she had to have a good reason to do something like that, Matthew."

"Not good enough to do that to her parents and sisters."

"And not good enough to do that to you either, I suppose."

"No."

"Humph!"

"Every time you do that, Aunt Mamie, you have something to tell me. What?"

"Do we have something to tell him, Arthur?"

"Not anything he can't find out for himself."

"What are you two getting at?"

"Nothing you can't find out for yourself," Arthur reiterated. "That is, when you get over being angry at her."

"I'm not angry."

Arthur raised a scraggly brow.

"Well...I got it under control for a few minutes...until I started talking about the way she left."

"Why are you angry, Matthew?" Arthur asked.

"It's obvious isn't it?"

"Not to me. Tell me."

Matthew knew from past experience that it wouldn't do any good to mention the 'obvious' reason to Arthur—he was wanting a different answer...what, he had no idea. "Hey, how about the three of us going over to Randy's and telling him and the children my great news!" Immediately, his spirits rose at the thoughts of being able to see his children's faces. How he had missed them!

~~~~~~~~~~~~~

Matthew drove home alone. Joan had wanted the children for about three days, but upon learning the news of Matthew's sight, and of Liz returning home, she offered to keep the children for a week or two until he could find someone to look after them. He was both relieved and sad, but decided it was best for them to stay, especially when he remembered he could go see them any day he wanted without having anyone drive him! Not yet used to the independence his sight gave him, he basked in its return.

Smiling, he recalled Randy's reaction to the miracle of his sight, and it touched Matthew greatly. Not only was Randy his first cousin, he was like a brother, a friend.

Still smiling, he thought about the children's reaction. They were happy, but took it in stride as if they'd expected it all along, prompting Matthew to realize that they hadn't really comprehended his blindness, nor did they comprehend the significance of recovering his sight.

What struck him the most was their reaction when they realized that Pipit wasn't with him. He'd hedged when they wanted an answer. They seemed more caught up with their disappointment over Liz not being there than their happiness over his returned sight. All this just emphasized the fact that it was with Liz he needed most to share his miracle!

Driving into his garage, he turned off the motor and sat there a moment dreading to go into the empty house. "Oh Liz, why did you leave? I needed to celebrate with you for a while, then you could go home." The protective anger had dissipated, leaving a hollow place inside him.

Making himself get out and walk into the dark house, he switched on the hall light and walked into the family room, almost wanting to call out as he used to, 'Liz?' hoping to hear her say, 'I'm here, Matthew.' But as he turned on the family room lights, all he could see was Diane, her touches, her colors, her taste.

Chapter Fifty-Two

Unable to go to sleep until 2:00 AM, Matthew awakened later than usual, blinking in disbelief at the morning light streaming through the window. For the briefest of moments, he thought he was dreaming, then the miracle that God had granted him came flooding back into his consciousness, filling him with such happiness, such gratitude, all he could do was lie there and marvel. Finally, slipping out of bed, he knelt and offered another heartfelt prayer of thanks.

With the light of day, Matthew's hopes soared. Perhaps he could solve the present dilemma of his children. After showering, he reveled in the simple pleasures of seeing whether or not he missed a spot while shaving rather than feeling for it, seeing how his hair looked after combing it, and picking out his own clothes.

As he stepped out of the closet, the subtle aroma of Diane's perfume turned his head toward her open closet door. Glancing in, he had the feeling that everything was suspended in time—as though waiting for Diane to return. He shook his head, as if to clear it. He thought of what Liz had said once about boxing some of them up for Merri one day and giving the rest away. The pain he'd felt the day before when he stepped into her closet, had been replaced by the *need* to do that very thing. He certainly couldn't keep her alive by leaving her clothes, her shoes, her jewelry just as they were before she died. Even though it would be somewhat of a closure for him, the thought of doing it was still painful.

Walking toward the kitchen for breakfast, Matthew looked into Danny's empty room, then Merri's, wishing they were there. He noticed that their beds were made and everything picked up. Smiling dolefully, he was struck by how well Liz had been training them. In the kitchen, he opened the refrigerator and saw that it was well stocked. Liz had certainly come a long way from the young woman he knew in the cabin.

He had been avoiding thoughts of Liz, and here she was all around him, from the empty hampers, to the clean clothes folded neatly in his drawers, to the well ordered family room! He thought of all that she had done for him, for the children, for their happiness. She had placed her happiness, her need to get on with her own life—on hold while she had served *them*. That was it—the words *service and sacrifice*—they epitomized Liz. Now she was gone, leaving a gaping hole in their lives, one he realized in a flash of understanding—was deepening.

~~~~~~~~~~~~

After work, Matthew drove to Chandler to see the children. But first, he stopped in to speak with Mamie.

"And to what do we owe the honor of this visit tonight, Matthew?" she asked, her smile making rosy apples of her plump cheeks. "We didn't expect you for a couple of days."

Matthew followed her into the kitchen where she was preparing dinner. "Something smells, good Aunt Mamie. Do you have enough for three?"

"Of course, you know me, I have a terrible time cooking for only two."

"Good! I came to ask you a great favor, Aunt Mamie."

"Ask away," she said, lifting a lid and poking a fork into some cooking vegetables.

"Could you help me go through Diane's clothes, shoes and jewelry? As Liz suggested, I need to save some of each for Merri one day...maybe even some jewelry for Danny to give to his wife someday, and then give the rest to charity."

Mamie tried to conceal the relief she felt. "Of course, Matthew dear, I'd be glad to do that with you. It will help you get on with your life."

He smiled lovingly at his aunt who had become a second mother to him. "Thank you. I've also begun to worry about living out so far. Leaving the children with someone makes me a little nervous. If anything happened, it would take me thirty minutes or more to get home, depending on the traffic. I've decided to sell the house and move to one as close as possible to one of the stores."

"I'm glad to hear that, Matthew. That isn't a neighborhood for children anyway."

"That's what Liz said. She said the children need other children to play with."

"She's right. Have you heard anything from her, Matthew?"

"No. And I don't expect to." He knew he sounded a little bitter, but it just came out that way.

"How do you know she got there safely?"

He'd been so caught up in the emotionality of her leaving, he hadn't thought of that. "How thoughtless of me! And after all she's done for us." A stab of fear ripped through him. "I need to call right now, may I?"

"Of course. Arthur has the Cabot's phone number right here," she said opening a drawer and pulling out an address book.

~~~~~~~~~~~~

Liz and her sisters had lunch at the club and spent the afternoon together. Driving home, she found herself puzzling over her sisters' reactions to her return. They said they were glad to have her home—yet, curiously, they displayed a definite lack of enthusiasm.

Linda, the most transparent one, actually looked disappointed when she learned that her sister hadn't stayed in Arizona long enough to see everyone's reaction to Matthew's regained sight. Despite Liz's repeated attempts to explain her reasons for leaving when she did, neither seemed to be convinced that they were valid.

"But," Linda had said, "you've always been good about hiding your feelings, Liz, why couldn't you have hidden them from Matthew?"

She had retorted, "Because, I didn't trust myself!"

She had enjoyed the outing, but it left her doubting the wisdom of her actions, just as the visit with her parents had.

~~~~~~~~~~~~

"Thanks," Matthew said, taking the small book from Mamie's hand, glad he didn't have to waste time calling information. He dialed the Cabots, his heart pounding with anxiety and nervousness.

"Cabot's residence," stated an unfamiliar voice.

"Is Miss Liz Cabot in?"

"Yes, she is. May I say who's calling?"

"Matthew Melloy," he said with relief.

"Just one moment please."

"Hello?" a voice answered reticently.

"Uh...hello, Liz. I was calling to see if you got home all right. And I see you did. I should have called last night, but..." he hesitated, then almost without volition added, "but I was so shocked you would leave like that after all we've been through together, that frankly, I was angry...and didn't think."

Liz hadn't expected this reaction and for a moment was silent.

"Don't you have anything to say?" he asked a little impatiently.

"I...I'm surprised that you were angry...maybe a little hurt, but mainly I thought you'd be relieved that you wouldn't have to deal with my leaving. Then you could go ahead and get the annulment."

"Hurt? Of course I was hurt! Why do you think I was angry? The least you could have done was wait so we could discuss your leaving and look for your replacement!" The minute he said this, he regretted it. "I'm sorry, Liz. I don't have the right to expect more of you than what you've already given. I was being selfish wanting you to stay. I guess I wanted you to share the joy of my seeing again."

I did hurt him! she thought. "I think my family wanted the same thing. They couldn't believe I left like I did."

This took Matthew by surprise. It was the last thing he had expected, but it certainly validated his feelings. "I'm surprised to hear that. I thought they would be overjoyed that you came home so soon."

"I did too," she said in a small voice.

Matthew laughed. "Sorry, Liz. But it's all a little strange...and yet amusing."

The tears were too close to see anything amusing about it, so she changed the subject. "Will you tell me how everyone reacted, Matthew?"

"I'm not a phone person, Liz. *That,* I'm afraid, I'd have to tell you face to face...but maybe not even then. You should have stayed if you wanted to know. Apparently, you didn't want to know that badly." Again, he couldn't believe what he heard himself saying.

And neither could Mamie. She had listened wide-eyed at the way Matthew was speaking to Liz.

Incensed, Liz replied, "I wrote on my note that it was the most difficult thing I'd ever done, Matthew, but apparently you didn't believe me."

"Actions speak louder that words, Liz."

"I had a good reason for leaving quickly, Matthew."

"Oh? What was that?" he asked, his tone belittling the reason.

"I guess I'm not a phone person either, Matthew. Goodbye!"

Matthew, left with only the dial tone in his ear, and an expression of shock on his face, slowly hung up the phone. "She hung up on me, Aunt Mamie."

"You mean, she didn't say goodbye?"

"She said goodbye all right, but it was definitely a hang-up!"

Mamie laughed. "Good for her."

"You're on her side?" he asked, looking a little betrayed.

She agreed, grinning. "I am, Matthew, I most certainly am."

~~~~~~~~~~~~~

After eating dinner with Mamie and Arthur, Matthew went over to Randy's to see the children. They were having so much fun with their cousins, they only had time for a quick hug from their dad, after which they ran off to play. When Matthew told Randy he was going to be moving, Randy gave him some flattened moving boxes he had in the garage. Putting them into his minivan, he left.

On the way home, he went over his conversation with Liz. Mamie had asked him why he'd spoken to Liz that way and all he could say was, "Because I was angry." He'd shaken his head in consternation. "I don't know why, Aunt Mamie. I'm just as baffled as you are, and a little ashamed over it." And yet—he didn't feel like retracting any of it or even apologizing to Liz. He thought he'd dealt with the hurt and anger, but apparently he hadn't.

Again, he found it hard to enter the house where he and Liz had shared so much. But when he walked into the family room, the emptiness Liz left behind became mixed up with the memories of Diane, intensified by the furnishings, the colors, the decor.

Until Mamie could come up and help him with Diane's clothes, he decided to go through some of their books and see if he wanted to keep them all.

Starting with the bottom shelf, he picked up his senior yearbook from Arizona State University. It was Diane's junior year. Memories came flooding back as he turned its pages. Involved as she was in school government and all the activities, Diane's pictures were all through it. His heart ached as he looked at the beautiful, vibrant girl he'd met at the beginning of that year. He often wondered if this popular beauty would have ever given him a second glance if he hadn't been student body president. After all, he was just a farm boy with an old Ford truck to drive to school and back. He hadn't sought the limelight. He guessed it was because he was gregarious and liked people that his many friends talked him into running for office. They had campaigned enthusiastically for him.

Also, he was tight on funds since he had to put himself through school. During the second half of that year he worked up the courage to ask Diane for a date. In order to take her out to dinner, the entertainment part of the evening had been a free campus concert. She had acted thrilled when he asked her for that first date, and later when they were engaged, he asked her why she had consented to go out with him.

Her answer was enigmatic. "Because you were the heartthrob of the campus."

He hadn't dated much the year he was student body president because he was so busy. When he asked her what she was talking about, she had answered, "Why were hoards of girls always in your office at school offering to help on this committee and on that project?"

"Because they wanted to be involved in school activities," he'd answered.

She had laughed. "That's what I liked about you Matthew Melloy, you aren't conceited like most of the boys I've dated."

The next yearbook was of Diane's senior year and it was also filled with pictures of her doing everything and of her in everything. He was slugging it out on his masters degree, but found time to organize a dance band which proved to be popular, so he had a few pictures in there also.

He couldn't date her as often as he had wanted because she kept herself so busy, and because she wanted to keep dating others. Finally, she agreed to go steady. They became engaged one month before the school year ended. Her parents tried to break it up, but Diane insisted that they were going to have a June wedding.

He got a job working with a music company, and rented a small apartment near the store. Elinor and Wayne Halstrom were incensed. Wayne tried to get him to go into business with him, and Elinor bought them a fancy condo, insisting he cancel the lease on the small apartment. He refused to work for Wayne, but Diane had insisted they accept the condo.

The memories were too heart-heavy, so placing the books back on the shelf, he got up and went outside, sitting on the front porch where he and Liz had shared a few golden moments two days before she left. He wished it were twilight as she had described, but it was dark—about like his spirits right now.

~~~~~~~~~~~~~

Liz, sitting on the patio, gazed up at the stars wishing she could enjoy the lovely evening, but all she could do was go over the conversation she had with Matthew. They had actually quarreled! She still smarted over Matthew's remarks. "Here I was, worrying over him being hurt." At least one thing his anger had done for her was dry up the tears which would have certainly given her away.

After an hour of fuming and talking to herself, all that was left was a terrible ache in her heart, and a debilitating loneliness. Never had she felt like this. Never had she loved like this.

Chapter Fifty-Three

The next week Matthew took off work to help Mamie go through Diane's things and pick out clothes, jewelry and even shoes for Merri to have one day, putting with them some beautiful jewelry for Danny's future wife. It was a painful task for Matthew, but Mamie's cheerful, happy personality, made it bearable.

In two days they were through and Mamie asked, "Do you want to keep all the furniture Diane picked out? Or," she asked pointedly, "can you live with it?"

Matthew hadn't thought about this, but as he did so, he realized he needed to get rid of all of it and only live with the memories inside him. "I would like to sell it."

"All right. We'll have a garage sale."

Matthew groaned. "I'd rather be strung up by my toes."

Mamie laughed. "All right then, you and Arthur can take care of all the children and I'll ask Joan to help me. I'll also con Randy into helping, too, since we may need some muscle."

"I guess we had better put the house on the market while the furniture is still here."

"Yes. It will sell better."

"I'll call a realtor tomorrow. No use in putting this off."

"When the house sells, Matthew, you and the children can move in with us until you find another home."

Matthew put his arms around her and kissed her. "What would I do without you, Aunt Mamie?"

~~~~~~~~~~~

A week had gone by and not a word from Matthew! Liz asked herself why she expected one, and answered aloud, "Because Matthew is the kindest man I've ever known, and a grateful one. He'll call and apologize." Immediately, the next thought unsettled her. *What good would that would do? The situation was the same—she was competing with the ghost of Diane, and Matthew's memories of their life together*! The tears she had cried since coming home could fill buckets!

Julia and Calvin watched helplessly, wishing they could do something to help.

Claire and Linda felt just as frustrated, wishing they could call Matthew and ask point-blank how he felt about their sister.

~~~~~~~~~~~~

The realtor, a friend of Matthew's who specialized in the Cave Creek/Carefree area had happily listed the house, and before the week was out, she had brought a number of clients through. By Saturday, she presented Matthew with two offers. He took the highest one, and they signed a contract. It had all happened so fast, Matthew hardly had any time to think, let alone, have any regrets. He also spent a lot of time at Randy's helping with the children and helping with bedtime, keeping his mind occupied for another week.

That weekend, the end of April, Mamie and Joan held a very successful garage sale. He had offered Joan and Randy some furniture, but they refused, so he gave them money toward something of their own choosing.

Taking time out to say goodbye to the Brodericks, Flo and Margo, he learned that they were all glad he planned to move into a neighborhood where there were other children. He told them he'd let them know their new address when he found a house.

Matthew called Elinor and asked her if she wanted Diane's white baby grand piano, and the car they'd bought for her. She'd hung up on him, so he had sold both of them. He boxed up Diane's picture and stored it, along with some other items, in a temperature controlled storage unit he'd rented.

The first day of May, after he and Randy had carried the last box to the small moving truck, he made his rounds of the house, and then stepped out onto the back porch. Memories of Liz besieged his weary mind and heart. Memories of their swimming together, her being his eyes, relating everything Merri and Danny were doing when they were playing on the lawn.

Going back in, he locked up the house and stepped out the front door deciding to look at the one thing he'd never seen—the sandbox Liz had him help with. Sauntering around the side of the house he smiled at the pathetic make-do sandbox and what was left of the funny looking castle he and Merri had made and all the roads Liz and Danny had made leading up to it. An unbearable loneliness for Liz descended upon him.

"I need to get away from here!" he muttered. He turned, and without another look back, he got into the driver's seat beside Randy and drove off.

~~~~~~~~~~~~

At first the children were excited about living with Uncle Arthur and Aunt Mamie so they could be closer to their cousins, but soon, they began to badger their father with questions about Pipit.

"When is Pipit coming back from visiting her mommy and daddy?" Merri asked.

"Yes, when, Daddy?" Danny echoed.

Even though Matthew knew this would happen, he found it emotionally harder to deal with than he had anticipated. Each time, he answered the same way. "I don't know, we have to be patient."

Arthur had heard this several times and pulled Matthew aside. "What's this 'we have to be patient' bit, Matthew? I thought you and Liz had decided on an annulment?"

"We did. I just don't know how to tell the children that their Pipit won't be coming back."

"Well, you must not be sure, Matthew, because you haven't even made a move toward getting that annulment."

"I know. It's just that I've been so busy with this move and getting adjusted to the new situation here."

"It's the eighth of May, you've had a whole week to get adjusted living with us. Come on, Matthew, there's something bothering you...something you're not telling me."

"I...uh...I thought that when I sold the house, sold all the furniture and moved out, I would get a little relief from the memories, but I'm more miserable than when I worked your damn cotton fields on those 105 degree days."

Arthur scrutinized his nephew. "I'll give you the same advice you gave your children. You have to be patient...time will lessen the pain of losing Diane."

Matthew shot a glance at Arthur. "It's not the memory of Diane that's making me miserable."

Arthur's brow rose. "Ohhh?"

Matthew paced the living room. "I miss Liz."

"How much?"

"So much, that I can't bring myself to start the annulment proceedings."

"Well...what are you going to do about it?"

"I don't know. She left so abruptly, I...I'm afraid she was happy to get away from me."

"Do you know that for sure?"

"No. I guess not."

"How do you *feel* about Liz?"

"Doggone it Uncle Arthur, I've asked myself that over and over. After all, it has only been a year since Diane..."

"You're not answering the question, Matt."

"You know you don't call me Matt unless you're annoyed with me?"

Arthur grinned. "I know, so answer the question."

"I've felt something for Liz from the time she dropped in at the cabin and greater affection when she came to care for us. When it began to change, I'm not sure, but I think that...I love Liz."

"Love...as in love?"

"Yes, doggone it! I'm so crazy in love with her I don't know what to do with myself."

"What's holding up the egg gathering then?"

"Fear, I guess. What if she's had enough of us...me and just had to leave? She's been pulling away from me for some time."

"How?"

"You are a persistent cuss, Arthur. I don't think I know how to answer."

"Or don't want to answer," Mamie stated, walking into the room. "The children are outside playing soccer so I can be in on the conversation."

"Tell her, Arthur. I can't." He left the room quickly. He needed to think. Voicing it to Arthur had cleared up at least one thing in his mind—he was going to go see Liz! Retreating to his old room, he closed the door, his heart pounding with excitement at the thought of it.

All week, as he'd agonized over his newly recognized love for Liz, something his mother always said came to his mind over and over: *"We love those whom we serve."* If that were the case it meant that maybe Liz loved *him*! She certainly went the extra mile from the very beginning, taking him by the hand and leading him, and in the end offering to marry him because of the children. "But that was because she loved Merri and Danny," he argued. "No!" he contradicted himself. "She cared what I wore, she reassured me that I would see again, she kept up the house, the wash because *I* wanted it, not the children." As he spoke out loud, he thought of all she'd done for him.

He found Mamie and Arthur where he'd left them. "I'm going to take the children and go see Liz day after tomorrow, Wednesday."

Arthur grinned. "Atta boy! It's about time."

Tears gathered in Mamie's eyes. "I'm relieved to hear this, Matthew. But do you think you ought to take the children?"

"I think I'll have a better chance with Liz if they're along, Aunt Mamie."

That night, after the children were in bed, Matthew paced his bedroom floor, planning and re-planning his visit. *He had to do this right*, he thought. Not only did he hope to win Liz over, but also her family. Finally, he worked it out, but he had to have help from Julia and Calvin, and he hoped with all his heart they'd give it to him!

Slowly, he picked up the bedroom phone and dialed the Cabot's residence, hoping it wouldn't be Liz who answered.

"Hello?"

Relieved, Matthew said, "Hello, Julia. This is Matthew Melloy."

Julia hesitated a moment before speaking. "How are you, Matthew?"

"Frankly, not so good."

"Would you like to speak with Liz?"

"No. I called to talk with you and your husband. Would it be possible to speak with you both?"

"I'll get Calvin on. Just a moment."

"Hello, Matthew," Calvin said. "How are you?"

"As I told your wife, I'm not doing well. That's why I've called you. I know you haven't approved of my allowing Liz to marry me, so I don't know how you will take what I'm going to say." Matthew took a deep breath and went on. "I was shocked when Liz left like she did. It upset me more than I can say. I needed her here to share with me the joy of my being able to see. I know I was selfish in wanting this, but I don't quite understand why she left. I know I'm rambling...so I'll just come out and say it. I have missed Liz so much I've been miserable. I've always had great affection for Liz, but I find that it's more than that. I'm in love with her. I have no idea how Liz feels about me, and frankly I'm terrified that the reason she left is because she wanted to get away from me.

"I know it isn't usual for a man to ask for the hand of the woman he loves from both parents, but that's what I want to do. May I ask her to marry me?"

"You're already married," Calvin said.

"But I want her to have that white dress she has always wanted...and to be able to walk down the aisle of a church."

Julia choked up, suddenly consumed with an overwhelming feeling of gratitude to Matthew for his sensitivity to her daughter.

Calvin himself had to swallow a couple of times. "You certainly have my permission, Matthew."

"Thank you sir! And you, Julia?"

"You have mine, Matthew," she managed to say, holding back the tears. "And, Matthew, we're so happy about your sight."

"Thank you, Julia, thank you on both counts," he said softly, feeling as though he had just succeeded in climbing Mt. Everest! "Now, I need your help...."

Chapter Fifty-Four

Unenthusiastically, Liz styled her freshly washed hair, applied her makeup and stepped into one of her favorite blue dresses. At 2:00, Claire and Linda were going to pick her and her mother up for an art show which her sisters were sponsering. They had both pleaded and begged her to go with them until she had reluctantly given in. She'd tried the social scene hoping to get her mind off Matthew, but it had only heightened her loneliness. Only because of her sisters had she given in.

Stepping out into the hall, she headed for her mother's bedroom. She knocked and stuck her head in. "Mother, are you ready?"

"Just about," she said from her dressing room. "I'll meet you in the foyer. Your sisters should be here any moment. They have to be there early."

Liz walked slowly to the front entry and waited in the library, aimlessly looking at the books, wishing she could even make herself read. The doorbell rang. She walked to the door expecting one of her sisters to walk on in. She opened the door, "You have a key...." She stopped in mid-sentence, her eyes wide with astonishment.

"M...Matthew!"

"Hello, Liz." His eyes devoured the face he'd seen so briefly. "You look lovely."

"Wh...what are you doing here?" she asked, seeing a *twinkle* in his eyes which had been so noticeably absent from the moment she'd met him.

"I've come to see the princess...you know the one who magically dropped in at the mountain cabin, who so graciously took care of the blind prince and his children and then ran away the minute he got his sight back?"

Liz swallowed the lump which lodged in her throat. "Come in, Matthew."

"Thank you."

"Would you like to sit down?"

"I sure would," he said, smiling.

With the new and irresistible twinkle in his eyes, his heart-stopping smile caused Liz's heart to thump so hard, she wondered if she could even catch her breath long enough to speak. She led him into the living room and sat down in an armchair. Matthew sat down on the sofa next to it.

"You're all dressed up. Are you going out?"

Pausing to breathe in and out several times, she replied, "Yes, I am. I'm sorry. I have to go to an art show my sisters are sponsoring. You're welcome to come and admire all the paintings...now that you can see," she added softly.

"I think I would rather stay here and admire *you*. You see, for weeks I imagined what you looked like, and the moment I actually got the opportunity, poof! you were gone."

"But, I have to go. I promised my sisters..."

"No, you don't have to go, Liz," her mother said, smiling as she entered. "There is no art show. Hello, Matthew. It's good to see you when you can see me."

Matthew stood up. "It's literally good to *see* you, Julia, and see how beautiful Liz's mother is."

"Thank you."

Liz stared from one to the other, shocked. "You...you and Matthew arranged this?"

"No. Matthew arranged it, and I knew you would want to look nice, so your sisters and I made up a reason for you to dress up."

Liz could only stare at her mother, her mouth ajar. "You and my sisters...."

"Yes, Liz. You and Matthew need to go on into the family room where it's more private."

"Thank you, Julia," Matthew said. "Lead the way, Liz."

Dumbfounded that her mother would be a party to this charade, Liz led the way to the family room and closed the door.

Matthew looked around. "This is a beautiful home, Liz."

"It is, isn't it? I told you I was a spoiled rich kid."

Still not used to seeing expression in Matthew's eyes, they almost melted her when he responded.

"I wouldn't call you a spoiled rich kid—I would call you an angel of mercy."

"Why are you here, Matthew?" she asked quickly.

"I came to find out why you ran away."

She stepped over to the window and looked out, trying to keep her emotional equilibrium. *What can I tell him?* she asked herself.

"Please, Liz. I have to know."

"Why?" she asked, her back still to him.

"Because my life depends on it. If you ran away because you wanted to get away from me, I'll leave right now. But if there is another reason, maybe..."

Slowly, she turned and faced him. "It was because I *had* to get away from you."

Liz watched the expression of hope leave his face. "All right...I'll leave," he said making no move to do so.

"I told you I had a good reason, Matthew," she said, her heart missing a beat, noticing how good he looked in the jade green shirt and light tan pants—how arresting his looks were...how handsome.

He stepped closer to her. "I need to hear the reason," he stated emphatically, his eyes pleading.

A masculine scent of cologne he hadn't worn before, unsettled her. "Why are you so insistent on knowing the reason? It will just put a guilt trip on you," she blurted out. "I couldn't do that to you, Matthew."

"Guilt trip?" Relief flooded across his face, then promptly changed to confusion. "Why would it put a guilt trip on me?"

"Remember when your sight returned?"

"How could I forget?"

"I didn't think about it at first, Matthew, but you had such an odd look on your face, I thought maybe you were...what were you thinking?"

His earth-green eyes gazed at her with such warmth, his smile so compelling, Liz could hardly breathe. Then he answered. "You were smiling when it happened. Like the morning sun, it was the first thing I saw...then the blue of your eyes. I thought I'd never seen such a beautiful sight."

"That's...that's what you really thought?" she asked, incredulous.

"Yes. And then it hit me that I wasn't dreaming, I was really seeing. All I can remember after that was the joy of seeing, and you sharing that moment with me."

How foolish I've been, she thought, turning to the window again.

"Please look at me, Liz." She reluctantly faced him. Matthew gazed at her. "I find myself savoring every move you make, every expression on your face, your beautiful eyes, your golden hair. I can't get enough of the sight of you, Liz. I've waited so long to see you. You are an enchanting woman."

She was speechless. No man had ever talked to her like that. Trying not to make too much of it, she asked, "You feel that way because you were curious about my appearance when you couldn't see?"

"No. I feel that way because you've become such a part of me. I can't imagine my life without you. I don't know exactly when it happened, but your leaving like you did, brought my whole life into focus."

Liz held her breath, almost afraid her ears were deceiving her.

"I love you, Liz. I've tried to think when it began. I have my thoughts about that, but I've been absolutely miserable without you."

Her breathing was so shallow, her voice came out in a whisper. "What about Diane?"

"I'll always love Diane, Liz. But so much has happened in such a short time. Mamie helped me box up Diane's clothes and things and helped me choose the ones I should keep for Merri as you suggested."

"Really?" she asked, still not daring to believe he could take his mind off Diane.

"Yes, and I sold the house. Merri, Danny and I are staying with Arthur and Mamie until I find a home near one of the stores."

Liz never dreamed that this would happen. She shook her head, amazed that Matthew had made these decisions, and had put them into action in such a short time! "How are Merri and Danny taking all these changes?" she asked.

"They were excited to move in with their uncle and aunt because they could be by their cousins...but lately, they've worn me out with questions about you—wanting to know when you were coming back."

"You haven't told them I wasn't, then?" she asked, still cautious.

"No." He stepped a little closer, his eyes searching hers. "Now, Liz, I have bared my soul, the least you can do is tell me why you ran away."

Her heart soared past her fears of Matthew's memories of Diane, past her forebodings of the power of those memories. She smiled at him through glistening eyes. "I ran away because I knew I wouldn't be able to hide my feelings from you anymore. I...I felt that it would put a terrible burden of guilt upon you if you knew that I had fallen in love with you."

It took a moment to sink in. Matthew just stood gazing at her, a mixture of incredulity and tentative happiness on his face as he slowly rephrased what she'd told him. "You...ran away from me...because you had fallen in love with me?"

She nodded, unable to speak, but her tear-filled eyes spoke volumes to Matthew.

He pulled her into his arms. "Oh my darling Pipit, my darling Liz, what a wonderful reason to run away. I'm sorry I was angry with you, but I needed you so badly." He drew back, his eyes studying every inch of her face, relishing the sight. Slowly he bent down and gently touched her lips with his, stirring within him a passion he couldn't remember feeling. Crushing his lips against hers, his arms pulled her tightly to him while her arms wrapped around him, returning his kiss with such ardor, it filled his aching, empty heart.

When they released each other, he gazed at her. "I love you. I love everything about you, Liz—the way you wear your hair," he kissed her hair, "your forehead," he kissed her forehead, "your brows, your cheeks, your nose," kissing each, he ended up with her lips, lingering there.

Letting her go, Matthew looked into Liz's dazed face. "My lovely Liz, will you please excuse me for a few moments?"

Surprised at the sudden change, all she could do was nod. She watched him leave the room. Finally coming to, she followed, only to see him go outside, shutting the door behind him. As she was standing there wondering, Julia came out of the library.

"Where's Matthew?"

"I don't know, Mother. He just said excuse me for a few moments and left."

"How did your visit go, Liz?"

She smiled at her mother, her eyes luminous orbs of blue. "He *loves* me, Mother!"

The doorbell rang. "It's probably Matthew," Liz said, smiling.

She opened the door. Her eyes widened in astonishment, for there before her stood Matthew with Merri in one hand and Danny in the other.

Before Liz could say anything, Danny, a wide smile on his face, spoke up. "Will you marry us, Pipit?"

"Yes. Will you marry us?" Merri asked, her eager little face full of smiles.

"Yes, *will* you marry us?" Matthew asked softly, his eyes twinkling.

Liz laughed and cried at the same time, hugging Danny, then Merri. "Yes! Yes I will marry you." Last but most important, she gazed into Matthew's eyes. "Yes, Matthew, I'll marry you."

"Yippee!" the children yelled in unison.

"Yippee, too," Matthew said, as he reached for all three. "How about a group hug?" So there on the front porch of the Cabot home, they hugged.

Claire and Linda, who had had the task of entertaining the children, stepped out from behind the foliage, raising a chorus of congratulations.

"Yes, congratulations," her mother said stepping outside, followed by Calvin who earlier had slipped in the back way.

Liz's mouth dropped open. "This was a conspiracy," she stated, accusingly.

"It was Matthew's conspiracy, Liz," her father said, smiling. "He planned it all and asked if we would help. But before that, he asked your mother and I for your hand."

Puzzled, Liz looked at Matthew, then back at her parents. "But...we are already..." she stopped for the children were all ears.

"Come on in everyone," Julia said. "How about a snack before dinner? Then Mabel can take Merri and Danny and show them around our big yard, while we adults listen to Matthew's plans."

Chapter Fifty-Five

After snacks, the children were delighted to go outside with Mabel to see the swimming pool and go find the 'secret arbor,' while the adults assembled themselves in the family room.

Before Matthew could say anything, Calvin said to Julia and his two younger daughters, "Maybe we also need to leave and give Matthew and Liz some privacy while they discuss their plans." Julia, pursing her lips, shot her husband a disapproving look.

Matthew noticed and smiled. "I would like all of you to stay, if you will."

An expression of relief passed over Julia's face. "Thank you, Matthew."

Calvin smiled at his wife and winked. "Yes, thank you, Matthew."

Liz assumed the plans Matthew was thinking about were where were they going to live. Matthew let go of Liz's hand and put his arm around her, pulling her close and wondered if he could get through this without becoming emotional. "Remember on the stand in the courtroom when the prosecutor asked you if you minded getting married in such a crass way...no wedding gown, no reception?"

Surprised, she nodded, "Yes."

Julia and Calvin and their two younger daughters were on the edge of their seats.

"Remember you answered yes, saying you had always wanted a church wedding and a white dress?" Matthew swallowed the same emotion he'd felt back then.

She looked down and nodded.

"I want you to have that."

Deeply touched, Liz thought about it for a few moments, then she gazed up into Matthew's tender and eager eyes. "You know, Matthew, I have fond memories of that small ceremony room with all of its special touches. I have fond memories of that lovely, brave woman, Pat Murphy who married us. And I remember the vows we took, even though they were distressful to us at the time. I'm willing to forego a formal church wedding and the white gown because...your pledge of love to me today makes that marriage ceremony special."

Matthew leaned over and kissed her forehead. "You're wonderful, my snow angel, but I want you to have that white dress...and a church wedding."

The silence in the room was electric. Julia, her heart filled with appreciation for her newly accepted son-in-law, held her breath—anxious and nervous over how Liz would answer. When Liz smiled and nodded her consent Julia released a breath of joyous relief.

Liz caressed Matthew's cheek. "Thank you, Matthew."

He gave her a quick, tender kiss on the lips. "You're welcome. Now, the question is when? I think you and your mother need to have some time to plan."

"Did you have a big fancy wedding with Diane?"

The question was so unexpected, Matthew didn't have time to hide his expression of apprehension. "Yes."

Liz, keeping a straight face, stated, "I'll bet the Cabot family can surpass it."

He wasn't quite sure how to react until Liz broke out laughing. Smiling uneasily, he answered, "I want you to have the wedding you've always dreamed of having, Liz."

"That won't be much, Matthew," Claire said, grinning. Calvin and Linda laughed. Julia smiled indulgently.

"That's right, Matthew, it won't be much. I've always wanted a simple wedding with only our closest friends and family, and a small celebration after."

Matthew's grin spread so wide they all laughed, all except Julia, who still hoped she could somehow make the small celebration as large and elaborate as she had for her other daughters, feeling that Liz deserved the same.

In spite of his relief, Matthew had observed Julia's reactions. So grateful to have her as a mother-in-law, rather than Elinor, he felt magnanimous. "Hold on everybody. I'll make a deal with you, Julia. If Liz is willing, I'm willing to go along with any elaborate wedding you want to put on—if you can do it in a short amount of time. I'm desperately anxious to have that honeymoon we haven't had."

This so surprised everyone, it took a moment for anyone to react, except Julia, who quickly replied. "It's a deal, Matthew! Liz, are you willing?"

Liz bit her tongue, holding back her first reaction. Then she remembered the promise to her parents that someday she would make them happy. Knowing that this not only would please her mother and sisters, she knew that what made her mother happy, made her father happy, also. She smiled. "It's a deal, Mother."

Julia clapped her hands together and beamed, "Wonderful! How long is a 'short amount of time,' Matthew?"

Matthew looked at Liz questioningly. "Is three weeks too short?"

Liz passed the question on to her mother with a quizzical look. Julia thought about it. "That is, almost." She got up and looked at the small calendar on the desk. "How about a compromise and make it three-and-half weeks? That would make the wedding fall on June 3rd."

"Does Liz have to be here during the planning stages?" Matthew asked. "If not, she can come with us back to Arizona and we can look for a house and furniture together."

"You sold all of your furniture, too, Matthew?" Liz asked.

"Yes. I have the memories. I don't need the tangible reminders."

Her heart relieved of that particular concern, Liz gave Matthew a look of gratitude, then turned to her mother. "June the 3rd is wonderful. I can tell you what I would like and you, Linda and Claire can do what you want from there."

At first Julia was disappointed. She wanted Liz planning it with her all the way, then she realized it would be easier with her not there. She knew her daughter. "I think we can work it that way, but what about your wedding dress?"

"Even before I was engaged, Mother, you insisted I be measured for it and choose the style and material, remember?"

"Oh yes, that's right. We'll get it made right away."

Frowning, Matthew said, "I keep forgetting that you were engaged, Liz. I guess it's something I don't want to remember. The wedding dress...I don't know..." he couldn't finish.

Liz smiled. "Matthew, if I hadn't chosen the style before, I would choose the very same style today. It didn't have anything to do with Kirk."

He grimaced. "I feel a little foolish that I was jealous."

"I don't mind that you were jealous."

"Good," Matthew said, grinning. "Can you be packed and ready to go with me tomorrow morning, Liz?"

She smiled up at him, her eyes shining. "I'm a very fast packer."

"Will you and the children stay with us tonight, Matthew?" asked Julia.

"We would like that very much. And I thank all of you for helping me today. It not only helped me surprise Liz, but your willingness to help gave me courage and hope that I had a chance with her. I knew if the children asked her first, she would at least consider it, if not today maybe in the future. I knew she loved the children, but I can hardly believe my good fortune—that Liz actually loves *me*, too...enough to marry me."

He quickly changed the subject to dislodge the lump in his throat. "You've done a great job with your daughter, Calvin and Julia. I can only hope that with Liz's help, maybe Merri can become the woman Liz is."

~~~~~~~~~~~~

That evening, Linda and Claire and their husbands came over and they had dinner together to celebrate Liz and Matthew's 'engagement.' Merri and Danny, who had to sit by Liz, ate up all the attention that the family directed toward them. It was an evening none of them would forget, especially Liz and Matthew.

Liz helped Matthew put the children to bed in the guest quarters, then they went outside. Hand in hand, they walked along the path together under the starlit sky, their hearts so full, neither could speak for a while. They were used to holding hands. They had done that from the beginning. But tonight, the sweet familiarity of it sent a thrill through both of them, sending them into each other's arms as soon as they were out of sight of the patio.

After some moments, Liz looked up into Matthew's face. "Thank you, Matthew, for insisting I have my white dress. You've won my mother's heart."

"It was as much for me as it was for you, Liz. It kind of relieves some of the guilt and pain I went through hearing the tears in your voice when you answered Hawkins' questions about the way we got married. And I prayed that you wouldn't think of it as your 'first' marriage, or a real marriage."

"But, Matthew, it *was* a real marriage. You sealed it with that kiss. It stirred emotions in me I didn't know were there."

"It did?" She nodded. He hugged her and grinned. "Me too, Liz! I was only going to give you a quick token kiss, but when my lips touched yours, I was a goner. It totally surprised me. I didn't know it then, but I was in love with you at that time. I don't know for certain when I fell, because my love for you was all mixed up with my grief over Diane, my anxiety over my blindness, and my worry over the children.

"When Arthur told me about the men finding your car, and of your parents call to him, he told me you were engaged. I couldn't accept it, you felt like my responsibility. The truth I didn't recognize then was—I felt that you were *mine*.

"I did something impulsive, Liz. Do you remember when I brought my suitcase to you before you left with your parents?"

"Yes, I do. You had a strange look on your face and I asked what was wrong. I've been meaning to ask what you meant when you said: 'You'll find out. I promise you.'"

"Well, at the time, I felt a little foolish for doing what I did, but I scribbled a note to you and placed it in a pocket of the suitcase I lent you, hoping you'd find it. When you left with your parents, I felt such a loss, I wondered how I could go on."

"What did you write on the note, Matthew?" she asked eagerly.

"When you came back, I thought you must have found it and read it...I was hoping anyway. But when you left so abruptly after my sight came back, I was sure you hadn't. I looked into the suitcase and found that I was right."

"What did it say, Matthew?"

"I don't know why I saved it...hope, I guess. I brought it with me." He reached into his pocket and pulled out the small piece of paper, and handed it to her.

The moonlight shone down upon the four words, making them clear as she read them out loud. *Come back to us, Pipit. Matthew.* There was a pause before a sob erupted from deep down inside Liz. Still gripping the note, her arms wound about him, she laid her face against his chest and cried—cried for all that Matthew had gone through, for the fearful obstacles that could have kept them apart, but mostly for overcoming them and finding their present happiness.

Chapter Fifty-Six

It was a happy goodbye for Julia and Calvin as they waved to Liz, Matthew and the children. They watched the children wave back until the car was out of sight, then hand in hand, they stepped up on the porch. Calvin led Julia over to one of wrought iron benches and they sat down. He put his arm around her.

She laid her head on his shoulder and sighed. "I never dreamed we would have two instant grandchildren, Cal."

He chuckled. "They're a couple of winners aren't they?"

"Yes." She smiled. "They're precious." She sighed again. "I've had certain dreams for our children, however, this isn't what I visualized or thought I wanted for Liz. As you know she's been the greatest challenge to me. I've invested a lot of effort and worry over her, and the more I invested, the more I wanted to have some control over her decisions." She threw her husband a side-glance. "And you know how that backfired."

Calvin smiled and nodded. "Do I."

"But the ordeal of Liz's disappearance, and everything that happened thereafter has had an effect upon me. I don't feel like I'm the same person, Cal. I've changed some of my ideas. I've learned from Liz."

Calvin gave his wife a squeeze. "I've learned from her also. I think we can finally put our fears to rest concerning her. Matthew's a good man. I approve of him heartily."

"I do too. He's an honorable young man—putting off the honeymoon until Liz has a proper wedding is rather amazing."

"It'll take some doing on his part," Calvin said, shaking his head. "Here they are...engaged to be married, so to speak, and yet they're married."

"Liz always said she wanted to marry a man of strength like her dad. And I believe she has, almost. But no one can measure up to you Calvin Cabot. I love you." She pulled his face down and kissed him.

"And I love you, Julia. You're the one who keeps my world turning."

She gave him an appreciative smile. "Oh, Cal, life is good right now, isn't it?" He nodded and she laid her head back down on his shoulder. "But you know, every now and then I think of Kirk and wonder how he is. I hope he can find some happiness."

"I do too, Julia. I always liked Kirk, but never felt he was up to Liz. I hope he finds a good woman. That's what completes a man...what *makes* a man."

They sat there for a while longer, each engrossed in thought.

Suddenly, Julia sat up straight. "I hope I can pull this off in three and a half weeks, Cal."

"You can, my dear. You are the most organized and efficient woman I've ever known."

"Thank you." She smiled. "It helps to have the money to do it with. First, I have to call your parents and mine and tell them the date of the wedding, ask them to call the rest of the relatives. I'll have to check on the caterer, the seamstress, the florist, the minister. Oh, my goodness, there are the invitations! I need to go write a list right now." She got up and walked briskly into the house.

Calvin followed her in, smiling. "Old habits die hard," he said.

She turned to him, her hands on her hips. "I said, I've changed *some* of my ideas, Calvin Cabot, not all of them."

~~~~~~~~~~~~

Merri and Danny sensed the change in the relationship between their father and Pipit, but all they knew was something felt good, and Pipit was with them. Their happiness bubbled over into chattering and laughing together in the backseat while they played with the toys Claire and Linda had given them.

Liz looked over at Matthew and gazed at the way his thick brown hair lay nicely against his neck. She studied his attractive profile. His full lips were turned up at the corners more than usual, slightly curious and amused at her perusal. Her eyes traveled to the rolled up shirt sleeves which revealed part of his strong looking forearms, then on to his wonderful hands, the hands which made such sublime music, and which were now gripping the steering wheel lightly. Her heart beat a little faster.

"Matthew," she said softly.

"Yes, Liz," he responded, his lips turning up into a full smile.

"We're in love. We are married. We are a family!"

"Yes. Isn't it wonderful? I never thought I would be happy again, Liz. Never thought I could marry again."

"We *are* married, Matthew. We don't have to wait until we have that symbolic marriage to...to go on a honeymoon."

Matthew exhaled heavily. "Elizabeth, don't think that hasn't crossed my mind more that once."

"Well?"

"Well, my enchanting princess, by implication, I promised your mother that we'd wait, remember?"

"When?"

"When I made a deal with her that she could put on any kind of lavish affair if she could do it in three and a half weeks—so we could start on that honeymoon."

Liz sighed in resignation, but her heart swelled with admiration. He was a man of honor, a man of moral strength, and wasn't this what made him so attractive, so desirable to her? "Well, then, Matthew, I guess we'll just have to concentrate on the next best thing." Her wide smile crinkled her eyes.

Matthew's heart skipped a beat. "To be the recipient of such a smile, it must be good."

"It is. We get to look for our home."

Matthew picked up her hand and kissed it. "We do, and I can't wait to live in it with you—really live in it—where you don't go to your room and I don't go to mine, but we go to *ours*."

" How sweet the *anticipation*," she whispered. "It's worth all the times I've refused the temptation—been unavailable to all the men I've dated in order to have this very moment, Matthew, to have these special three-and-a-half weeks to look forward to the wonderful promise that will be ours at the end of that time."

Deeply touched at her disclosure, Matthew gazed at her face illuminated by the sunlight streaming through the car window, certain that she really was sent to him from heaven on that wintry night. He caressed her cheek. "Thank you for making it easier for me to wait. Thank you for what you are, Liz. I pray that I'll be worthy of you someday."

~~~~~~~~~~~~~

Matthew called Arthur and told him he was bringing Liz back with him and told him approximately when they would arrive. When they drove into Arthur's driveway, they found Randy's car there also.

Upon entering the house, they found Randy and Joan and the children waiting with Arthur and Mamie, smiling, expectant.

Matthew grinned and was about to tell them the good news when Danny spoke up.

"Pipit said she would marry us!"

"She did!" Merri cried.

This brought a round of laughter.

"I'm glad you finally came to your senses, Matt," Randy said, grinning.

"It took me awhile, but I did. I think all of you realized how I felt about Liz before I did."

"We did for a fact," Arthur said.

Mamie's eyes sparkled with happiness. "This calls for a celebration and a half! Let's barbeque some hotdogs and hamburgers."

The four children agreed vociferously, then ran outside to play.

"We'll let the children eat outside and we'll eat inside while you and Liz tell us how you 'proposed,' Matthew," Joan said with excitement. "Especially," she grinned, "since you're already married."

Liz, holding Matthew's hand, looked up into his face beaming. "We'd love to tell you everything."

~~~~~~~~~~~~~

Because Mamie and Arthur had only two extra bedrooms, Randy and Joan insisted that the children sleep over at their house so that Matthew and Liz could each have a bedroom, teasing them about their unique situation.

Matthew and Liz went over, put the children to bed and visited with Randy and Joan until the children were asleep.

"Feel free to leave the children with us while you look for a house," Joan said.

"Thanks, Joan," Matthew replied, "we owe you big time."

"When you and Randy want to go on vacation without the children, you know where to leave Becky and Johnny," Liz added.

"Sounds great," Randy said.

Matthew stood up and took Liz's hand. "I guess we better say goodnight. Tomorrow, we'll need to plan out the next few weeks carefully. We have a lot to accomplish."

In the car headed for Arthur's, Matthew murmured, "Such an odd set of circumstances."

"What, Matthew?"

"Here we are, married and going to look for a house, and we haven't had any real time alone. We haven't dated. It struck me when we got in the car after leaving Randy's because it felt good to be alone with you."

"I guess it's going to be our lot. I'm marrying—I've married a man with two children."

"Well, my snow angel, these three weeks are not only going to give us time to find a home and buy furniture, it will give me time to court my fiancé/wife."

Liz laughed with pure joy and amusement. "Sounds wonderful, Matthew. I hadn't thought about it before because things have happened so fast, but I, too, feel a need for us to have some time alone. Now that we've admitted our love for each other, our relationship has progressed to a whole new dimension; one that we haven't fully experienced yet."

Matthew pulled into Arthur's driveway and turned off the ignition. Pushing the seat back, he picked up her left hand and kissed it. "What about these wedding bands we're wearing? How about an engagement ring and a new..."

"No," Liz interrupted. "I don't want an engagement ring and certainly not a new wedding band. I feel very sentimental about *these* wedding bands."

Matthew pulled Liz over. Wrapping his arms around her, he held her tightly. Finally, he said in a hoarse whisper, "Thank you, Liz. I was hoping you'd feel that way. These rings are special to me because they...they represent the sacrifice you made for me and my children—which led to this very moment, to our love."

He bent over and kissed her tenderly. "I love you so much, Liz, it almost scares me. I couldn't bear it if I lost you. I lost my mother...I lost Diane...I..."

Liz covered his lips with hers and kissed him with such passionate ardor, he forgot his fears.

Chapter Fifty-Seven

The plans Matthew and Liz made the night before, were going to be put into effect immediately. Matthew would go on to work and Liz would call a realtor Arthur had recommended.

They had decided to look for an already existing home, new or nearly new, located in between the two stores if possible and, when Liz found several she liked, then Matthew would look at them.

In the foyer before Matthew left for work, he took Liz's face in his hands and studied every inch of it, still feeling awe over his newly recovered sight. "I will never take my eyesight for granted again, Liz. I love the sight of your face. I love the way you smile with your eyes, the way they crease when you smile or laugh. How in the world could you ever think you were homely?"

Liz smiled up at him. 'I guess you are still blind—love is blind."

The admiration in Matthew's eyes intensified, as he continued to feast upon her face. "No, Liz. My recovery has brought back my sight in every sense of the word—and I find you lovely and enchanting."

Her eyes moist, she put her arms around his chest and murmured, "Thank you, Matthew, you make it impossible to think of myself as homely anymore."

He bent down and kissed her long and fervently. They clung to each other not wanting to be separated for an hour, let alone for a day.

"May I have a date for dinner and dancing tonight?"

"I'd love that, Matthew!"

~~~~~~~~~~~~

The day had not been fruitful. None of the areas, none of the homes the realtor had shown Liz were to her liking at all. But during it all, her excitement over going out with Matthew kept her spirits buoyed up.

All day during work, Matthew's employees noticed the change in him and remarked on it. He wanted to shout to the world his love for Liz, but he couldn't. As far as any of them knew, he had been happily married for some time.

Work had piled up, but his mind kept wandering to Liz, looking forward to the evening with her.

~~~~~~~~~~~~

Before driving to Arthur's, Matthew stopped at the florist and picked up one yellow rose. When he entered the house with it in his hand, Mamie clapped her hands in glee.

"How sweet and romantic, Matthew."

Arthur grinned. "I'd forgotten you two haven't had time to court, Matthew."

Just then, Liz entered the room dressed in a linen dress the very color of lemon and sun-streaked daisies. The short-sleeved jacket lavished with rosettes of lacy crochet, covered a tank dress with a full, sweeping skirt. The rays of sunlight from the kitchen window bounced off her shiny blonde hair, producing a halo of luster, and her eyes shone with happiness.

Matthew sucked in his breath at the captivating scene. He handed her the rose. "I picked out a yellow rose...because it signifies the sunshine you've brought into my life, Liz."

She stepped over to him and threw her arms around him. "Thank you, Matthew," she murmured, beaming. Finally letting him go, she said, "What a coincidence that I would wear a dress the same color."

Arthur and Mamie both smiled as they watched the two, freed from worry over Matthew for the first time in many years.

Driving to the restaurant, they savored each other's presence in silence.

Suddenly Liz laughed.

"What was that about?" Matthew asked responding to her contagious laugh.

"We're married, and this is our first date."

Matthew chuckled. "Our whole story is just as unique as you are, Elizabeth Melloy."

Driving into the parking lot of Avanti's, Matthew parked. Leaning over, he kissed her lips lightly and got out.

Sitting across from each other at an out-of-the-way table, which Matthew had requested when he made the reservation, they gazed at each other. In the background, the orchestra was playing a lovely tune.

After a delicious meal of authentic Italian food, and relaxed conversation, Matthew asked, "May I have this dance, Mrs. Melloy?"

Out on the dance floor, Liz stepped into Matthew arms and he laid his cheek upon hers, and danced to the music. Liz wondered how she could possibly feel any happier than she was at the moment.

And Matthew wondered why in the world he made that bargain with Julia. Three- and-a-half weeks was a long time—especially since Liz already *belonged* to him.

The feeling of Liz so close to him as they moved across the dance floor in perfect unison brought back a forgotten memory. Once, during a discussion at the dinner table, his mother had said to him, "*Matthew, I want you to remember this. When a couple gets engaged, their whole relationship changes. They feel like they belong to each other, so it's very easy to make a mistake. It isn't a good idea to have a long engagement. It's important for a couple to go into marriage pure. They owe that to each other.*"

He certainly needed that advice now, for just those thoughts were on his mind. Because Liz already belonged to him, the temptation to cross that line was certainly there! He was going to have to be more careful than he'd ever been!

He pulled her closer, kissed her hair and breathed in its fragrance.

~~~~~~~~~~~~

The next morning before Liz left her room, she knelt beside her bed and asked the Lord for help in finding just the right house in the right neighborhood. She knew how important this was for the children.

Matthew left for work early and Liz borrowed Mamie's car to go over and see the children, and to tell Joan that she was going to take everyone out to dinner that night to ease the load.

Another day went by with no luck, but the evening out with everyone was enjoyable.

Afterward, when Liz and Matthew were alone, Matthew asked, "How about a date to see a musical tomorrow night, Liz, if we can get tickets?"

"I'd love it. But could we make it the following evening? Let's take the children for a walk in the desert and show them all the desert flowers which are in bloom right now."

Matthew held her close. It seemed incredible that she would want to include the children in their dating.

~~~~~~~~~~~~

The fourth day, the realtor found several houses that Liz liked well enough to show Matthew. He got off work early so they could look at them together.

After looking at them, they went out to dinner and then went to the musical feeling undecided about the houses they'd seen. Matthew reached for Liz's hand, and they put all concerns behind them while they listened and laughed during the program, renewing themselves for the next day of searching.

The next day the realtor showed Liz another home in the McCormick Ranch region in the popular Sands Scottsdale area. It was a family neighborhood with basketball hoops in front of the garages, bikes and tricycles left out, and glimpses of swing sets in several backyards. This was not the in-between-stores location they had wanted, nevertheless, the area felt good to Liz. The realtor turned into a driveway of a home near the end of the cul-de-sac, explaining that this was a little older home than they had requested, but thought she'd like to look at it anyway.

"The owners have already moved out of state and are anxious to sell," the realtor said.

Liz studied it carefully. It was white stucco with a rose tile roof. A three-car garage faced the street. An attractive courtyard, surrounded by a low, white painted brick wall, led to double front doors inset with glass. Outside the courtyard, a large beautifully trimmed olive tree stood in front of two large front windows under which were several kinds of bushes. A tall palm tree planted inside the courtyard towered above the roof. Both trees almost hid the two second story windows. A green carpet of lawn spanned the length of the drive and width of the house.

Liz hoped she liked the inside as well as she liked the outside. The realtor opened the door to a nice sized foyer. The flooring was a light ceramic tile. To the right was the living room, and directly ahead was the side view of a white painted banister with an oak balustrade.

"Those stairs lead up to two bedrooms and one bath," the realtor said. Leading Liz, past the stairs she pointed to a hall on the left. "There are three bedrooms on the main floor including the master bedroom. The master has a large private bath and there is another bath between the other two bedrooms. There's a half bath off the laundry and close to a large play room. We'll start in the kitchen area."

Liz liked the large kitchen with the island bar, and connecting family room. When she saw the huge playroom across from the laundry room, she gasped in delight. The flooring and the carpet throughout the house were a neutral beige, the paint off white. The backyard had an already existing swing set and a fenced swimming pool.

Hardly able to contain her excitement, Liz said, "I need to call my husband and see if he can come over to look at the house right now."

Pleased, the realtor let Liz use her cell phone. *How lucky that Matthew is over at the Scottsdale store today*, she thought as she dialed it.

While waiting for Matthew, Liz went through the house again and then went outside to wait for him. She felt a little uneasy since she hadn't even asked the realtor the price of the house. If it were more than what Matthew wanted to pay, would he let her use her funds to help?

Matthew smiled at her as he parked in the driveway of the house. Breathlessly, she stepped over to him. "Hi."

"Hi, my glowing bride-to-be."

"Sssh. The realtor won't know what to think if you call me that in front of her. I told her you were my husband."

He chuckled. "I feel like confusing a realtor or two...unless I like the house. I like the outside of it, at least," he said studying it.

"Matthew, we haven't discussed having our own children."

He blinked, surprised. "Well, that was out-of-the-blue. What brought that on?"

"I'm serious, Matthew."

He gazed at her with such warmth in his eyes, she felt like jelly inside. A slow grin spread across his face. "I want children of our own, Liz. How about you?"

"When you see how many bedrooms there are in the house, you'll know I want them."

"Uh-oh. It's larger than it looks then."

"Matthew, uh...how would you feel if I used some of my funds to help..."

"If we need them, Liz, we'll use some. I want you to have the house you want."

Liz's eyes sparkled with happiness. She pulled his face down and gave him a quick kiss. "Oh, thank you!"

Hand in hand, they entered the house together.

Chapter Fifty-Eight

The next day, Matthew and Liz made an offer on the house with the request that the owner be contacted that very day and give them an answer. After several counter offers, a deal was struck with the provision that they could move into the house no later than June 7.

Matthew went on to work and Liz excitedly called her mother, informing her that they had bought a house and that they were ready to go looking for furniture.

"I'm so glad to hear that, Liz. And everything seems to be falling into place with the wedding plans here, except I have to get Merri's and Danny's measurements so the seamstress can make their clothes. They will walk down the aisle behind you."

"That's a wonderful idea, Mother. I think Joan sews. I'll have her measure them and call you."

"Good. Oh, by the way, your sisters and I want you to leave Merri and Danny with us when you go on your honeymoon."

Tears sprung to Liz's eyes. "That would mean a lot to me, Mother. Thank you! It will certainly give Joan and Mamie a break."

Her mother was so busy, the conversation was short. The minute Liz hung up, she asked Mamie if she'd like to go shopping for furniture with her.

"I'd love to, Liz. Let's go!"

~~~~~~~~~~~~

Fifteen days later, May 30th, Matthew lay in bed musing over everything. They were all packed and ready to leave for Palm Springs early tomorrow morning. The rest of the family would leave the next day. In three days, the wedding would take place.

He and Liz had accomplished everything they had hoped to. Liz and Mamie first picked out the furniture they needed just to get by: beds, bedding, dressers, and chests of drawers, a couch for the family room, and a kitchen table. After that, they chose several other pieces which had to be ordered. They had decided that the rest could wait until they had more time. In every case, Liz had insisted that Matthew look at the furniture, also. "I refuse to buy it, unless you like it and approve," she had said. This was a new experience for Matthew. Diane had such definite ideas, he had let her decorate the house as she wanted.

On alternating nights, he and Liz had gone out alone, then they did something with the children, including taking them to see the house. The swing set was all it took to get the children's excited approval. During all this, watching Merri turn into a more consistently happy child was a joyful experience for Matthew. But why hadn't Merri been happy before she lost her mother?

Pushing the troubling question far back into his mind, his thoughts returned to Liz. It didn't matter what they did, where they went with the children, Liz held his hand. When the children fought to be in between them, Liz had explained, "One of you can hold your dad's hand the other one mine, but I *always* have to hold your dad's hand." No matter where they sat, Liz stayed by his side, explaining the same thing to the children, and they had been perfectly happy about it. Matthew swallowed back the sudden constriction in his throat as he thought about Liz's love for him. Then it slipped in—the familiar gnawing feeling of guilt, and like the air seeping out of a balloon, so did his happiness. Finally, he fell into a fitful sleep.

~~~~~~~~~~~~

By morning, Matthew had forgotten his brooding thoughts of the night before. When he walked into the kitchen, Liz's smile, her embrace, sent his spirits soaring. After a big breakfast prepared by both Mamie and Liz, they said goodbye and went over to Randy's to pick up their excited children.

"See you tomorrow night," Randy said, as Matthew put the car into gear.

"Yes, and thanks for everything," Matthew said.

The four children grinned and waved at each other until they were out of sight. Once on the way, Merri and Danny settled down with their new toys purchased for the trip, and Liz fingered

Matthew's hair. "Only two days, and we can leave for our honey-moon."

He turned and gave her one of his heart melting smiles. "It still feels like two days too long."

When Matthew had asked where she wanted to go on their honeymoon, Liz answered immediately. "To the cabin. To that magical cabin I was led to by your beautiful voice."

"But do you want to cook?"

She paused. "No, but I guess I'll have to because I do want to see the cabin in the summertime."

Matthew decided to surprise her and take her to eat their meals at the ski resort not too far from the cabin.

He had reserved a honeymoon suite at the Marriot in Palm Springs for the first night. Their next two nights would be in the cabin. His heart beat faster as he thought about it. The cabin had always been a special place to him growing up, and now he was certain that it was the place God had arranged for them to meet.

Chapter Fifty-Nine

The large church was filled by 9:50 A.M. Matthew, dressed in a tuxedo, waited for his bride up front near the minister. Beside him stood his best man, Randy, with both 'already-worn' wedding bands in his pocket.

Finally, the organ began playing, and Matthew's eyes watched anxiously. At last Calvin Cabot appeared with Liz on his arm. Slowly, they paced themselves up the aisle. Liz's golden hair, under the simple veil, enhanced by the bouquet of yellow and white flowers in one hand, matched her radiant smile. Matthew's eyes blurred for a moment as he gazed at Liz in the *white dress* she had mentioned with tears in her voice while on the stand in the courtroom.

Merri and Danny, their eyes wide, their smiles shy, walked slowly behind their Pipit. Danny, in a small white suit with a yellow rose in his lapel, Merri, her long dark hair falling over the shoulders of her delicate white dress, holding one yellow rose, caused many a gasp from the guests as they passed by.

Calvin left his daughter beside the groom, and moved to his seat beside Julia, taking the children with him. Claire and Linda, with their husbands, sat behind the Cabots. All the relatives on both sides of the aisle sat up front.

The ceremony began, and Julia's eyes filled with tears. Her dream for her oldest daughter was actually happening! No bride could be lovelier, she thought, no groom more handsome. And the children were beautiful! Her heart swelling with happiness, she reached for her husband's hand.

Across the aisle, Mamie was wiping tears away, and Arthur was beaming. Next to them was their daughter, Elaine, and her husband, Richard who flew in the night before from Seattle. Seated behind them were Joan and her children.

When it came time for the rings, Randy handed Matthew the one for Liz. Matthew smiled and winked at Liz as he slipped it on. She winked at him when she slipped his on, then the groom kissed the bride.

~~~~~~~~~~~~

Immediately after, a combined reception and buffet luncheon was held at the country club from 11:00-2:00. The line consisted of Calvin and Julia, the bride and groom, and Arthur and Mamie.

The most important guests to Matthew, were Elaine and Richard. It was a tearful reunion, for Elaine had only seen Matthew once since Diane's funeral and not since he'd regained his sight. Matthew was thrilled to introduce them to Liz, and Elaine was equally thrilled to meet the woman who, according to her parents, 'made Matthew happier than they'd ever seen him.'

Liz, was delighted to meet Arthur's oldest. "Thank you, Elaine, for the loan of your clothes. They were a lifesaver for me at the cabin." She gave Elaine a hug. "And thank you for everything you and your parents have done for Matthew."

Elaine smiled at her new cousin-in-law, thoroughly agreeing with her parents that Elizabeth Cabot was the best thing that ever happened to Matthew.

Liz happily greeted her grandparents on both sides and many other relatives, introducing them all to her handsome husband, then to Mamie and Arthur. They expressed their happiness for Liz and, she noted, they seemed to be very impressed with Matthew and his children.

When there was a lull, Liz turned to her parents. "Thank you both for this lovely reception and luncheon. You were right, Mother. It was important to have it. I didn't realize, but I needed to share this with you as much as you needed to share it with me. Besides," she smiled, "how else could everyone meet Matthew and the children?"

Julia smiled at her daughter. "Thank you, dear, for appreciating it."

The guests kept trickling in and congratulating them. Matthew noticed the tall, good looking man greeting Julia and Calvin, but was taken aback when Liz threw her arms around him. A twinge of jealousy pricked at him, and as he was wondering who the man was, Liz introduced him.

"Matthew, I would like you to meet Kirk Morgan. Kirk, this is Matthew Melloy."

Kirk reached out his hand and shook Matthew's firmly. "I'm glad to meet you, Matthew. I sensed Liz felt something more for you than she said. Congratulations."

"Thank you, Kirk...uh.."

"I'm the one who lost her. I was her fiancé. You are one lucky guy. Take good care of her for me, will you?"

Before Matthew could respond, Kirk turned and left. Matthew looked over at Liz and saw tears in her eyes. His brows drew together, feeling a deeper stab of jealousy, but before he could say anything to Liz, more guests arrived in a never-ending stream.

Finally, at 1:15, Liz and Matthew were able to sit down and eat. Claire and Linda and their husbands joined them. They had seen to it that the children ate right at noon and had looked after them during the reception. Now, Julia and Calvin had them in tow.

At 2:00, the bride and groom started for the door, and the crowd followed. Claire, Linda and the children had slipped out a little earlier, along with the rest of the relatives. Julia and Calvin, Mamie and Arthur, Randy and Joan and Elaine and Richard remained, following close behind Liz and Matthew. Liz threw her bouquet, and a young woman squealed as she caught it.

The moment the bride and groom stepped out the door, Merri, Danny, Becky and Johnny bombarded them with bubbles, giggling as the smiling couple pretended to dodge them. Relatives lined both sides of the walkway filling the air with bubbles. Smiling and waving at everyone, the couple got into their waiting car and drove off.

Returning to the Cabot home, they quickly changed into something casual, grabbed their suitcases and left for the Marriott Resort.

~~~~~~~~~~~~

Matthew stood at the large window overlooking the beautiful grounds of the resort, brooding over the man that Liz had hugged, over the tears he saw in her eyes.

Liz looking around the suite, murmured, "Matthew, you shouldn't have reserved such an expensive suite. But it's beautiful."

She walked over to him, her excitement causing her heart to pound so hard she felt it pulsing in her throat. As she reached for his hand, he pulled it away, turning to her, his eyes troubled.

Shocked, Liz asked, "What's the matter, Matthew?"

"Why haven't you told me more about Kirk Morgan, and your relationship with him?"

Speechless for a moment, she studied his pensive face. "You never asked."

"He still loves you, Liz. And...you must feel something for him. You had tears in your eyes when he left."

This shocked Liz even more. "Why, Matthew, you can't be jealous of him. I married *you*."

Matthew's jaw rippled. "Why did you hug him? Why did you have tears in your eyes?"

Liz smiled, and reached her arms around his neck. He firmly removed them. The smile left Liz's face, a sliver of fear went through her. She had never seen this side of Matthew.

"Don't pull away from me, Matthew," she said.

"Tell me about Kirk Morgan."

"Matthew, this is our honeymoon night. I don't want to talk about Kirk, I..."

His face, a mask of stone, he repeated, "Tell me about Kirk."

"No, Matthew. Not when you are in this kind of a mood."

"All right, if that's the way you want it, Liz." He stepped back to the window, turning his back on her.

Liz stared at his back, realizing that she didn't really know Matthew as well as she thought she did. Something more was bothering him than his foolish jealousy of Kirk. Her first impulse was to say: *you may annul the marriage if you like. I won't put up with this kind of attitude,* but something stopped her. Instead, she turned and went into the bathroom, and feeling shy, changed into one of the beautiful, but modest nightgowns she had purchased for this very occasion.

I have been saving myself, and looking forward to this time for many years, she thought, *and I'm not going to let my knight-in-shining-armor ruin it for me!*

Her excitement returned as she left the bathroom and moved toward Matthew, who was still standing at the window. "I love you,

Matthew Melloy," she said softly to his back. "When I took that wrong turn up in the mountains which landed me on your doorstep, I already had, in my mind, emotionally broken off my engagement to Kirk. He wasn't the man I was supposed to marry, the man I wanted to marry, so the wrong turn up there—was really the *right* turn. It led me to a man so wonderful, I'm still pinching myself."

Slowly, Matthew turned around, the troubled expression beginning to recede. When he saw her dressed as she was, his face softened, and the expression in his eyes made her knees feel like rubber. He stepped over to her, took her into his arms, groaned and covered her face with kisses, then his lips covered hers. The world outside disappeared as theirs soared into the magical regions of their love.

Chapter Sixty

Driving through the high country of Arizona, they reached Eager and turned south on highway 180. As they drove the winding roads, Liz paid rapt attention to the mountain area where she'd had that fateful accident.

"Here we are," Matthew said, smiling. "This is the turn-off leading to the cabin, the small road you followed." He stopped the car for a moment. "There is the place they found your car, and not too far from it—right there," he grinned, "is where I think you stepped into the snow chest-deep trying to find it that day—where, blind as I was, I rescued you from your folly."

Liz laughed. "You're my hero."

"Thanks," he said, taking the turn-off. He parked in the driveway beside the cabin and opened the door for Liz.

Looking around, she said, "How different it looks in the summertime, Matthew. Not frightening at all."

Carrying the suitcases, Matthew led his bride up the steps to the front door. Setting down his load, he unlocked the door, picked her up and carried her over the threshold. "This isn't our home, but it will be our vacation home." He bent down and kissed her. "I hear that Princess Pipit lived here for a short time."

"She did. From what I hear tell, she fell in love with the handsome prince who saved her life."

"Is that right? The lucky dog."

"You can put me down now if you like."

"Oh, am I still holding you?" he grinned. "You're so light, so slender, I was hardly aware." He set her down, picked up their luggage and closed the door.

Liz looked around the room. Tender memories flooded back. "God has been good to us, Matthew."

"He has. He's the one who led you to me," he said quietly.

She nodded, her eyes moist.

"Which bedroom shall we sleep in?"

"Mine, of course," she said, walking into it. "This is where you awakened me with your music."

"And where Arthur and I shook in our boots as we clumsily tried to nurse you back to consciousness."

Liz gazed lovingly up into Matthew's face, "I have often thought what a frightening responsibility that was for both of you."

Matthew took her hand and kissed it. "But look at my reward." Still holding her hand he led her back into the front room to the piano bench. "Sit down beside me, my sweet bride. I'm going to sing a couple of love songs to you."

She sighed. "You know, Matthew, love songs make me feel very romantic."

"That's the plan," he grinned.

He began with *La Vie En Rose,* looking over at her every now and then, his eyes expressing every word he sang to her. Next, he sang *Devotion*, ending with the song *Embraceable You.*

Slightly breathless, she whispered, "Thank you, Matthew."

"My pleasure. Have I ever told you how much it means to me that you like to hear me sing and play?"

"No, you never have. You never let on."

"That's because I didn't dare dwell on the fact," he said, remembering it had been Diane's feeling that he needed voice lessons. Shaking away the memory, he looked at his watch, noting it was it was 3:20. "Let's go for a walk before it gets chilly," he said holding out his hand, "then we'll go to dinner."

"To dinner? I thought we were going to cook here."

"No. I have reservations at a restaurant up at the ski resort."

"Thank you, Matthew!" she said throwing her arms around him and kissing him.

"Hmm, nice. You're welcome."

Hand in hand they went for a hike, breathing in the sweet smell of pine and listening to the birds, basking in the joy of their companionship.

Suddenly, Matthew stopped. "Ssh. Look! There's a pipit over there on the ground."

Delighted, Liz watched the little brownish-gray bird walking leisurely, wagging it's tail continually, now and then pecking at an insect. Abruptly, it took flight, its call, a sharp *pit-pit,* echoed through the trees.

Liz clapped her hands. "At last I've seen the bird I was named after!"

~~~~~~~~~~~~~

After showering, Liz and Matthew changed their comfortable jeans to nicer casual clothes for their dinner date at the mountain resort. Matthew, in tan pants and a blue knit shirt and Liz, in a linen shirt dress the color of wild violets, got into the car and headed for their destination.

The six o'clock sun cast shadows of the tall ponderosa pines across the road, and the fresh smelling, rapidly cooling air blew through the open windows, exhilarating their spirits.

"We always went to the beach for our vacations, but I believe I like the mountains just as well, Matthew."

"I'm glad because it's my idea of a getaway in the heat of the summer. I used to bird-watch with Uncle Arthur. Would you like to do that with me?"

"I bird-watch too!"

"I can't believe my good luck," he said reaching over and picking up her hand, giving it a squeeze. He remembered he'd had to quit bird watching because Diane didn't care for outdoor activities.

By the time they reached the restaurant and ordered, they were both starved; the hike and the mountain air had increased their appetites tremendously. During the satisfying meal of fried chicken, mashed potatoes and gravy, they visited intimately, having eyes for no one but each other.

On their way out of the resort, they saw a small market still open. "Matthew, let's buy a few things for breakfast and lunch so we don't have to leave the cabin until evening for dinner."

"Hey, I like that idea, Liz. The more time I have you all to myself, the better."

The night air had turned cold and Liz shivered as they walked out of the market and got into the car.

"We'll build a fire in the fireplace," Matthew said, buzzing up the car windows.

"Mmm, that sounds wonderful," Liz replied, remembering how safe she'd felt at the cabin while sitting in front of the fireplace during the blizzard.

When they arrived at the cabin, they put the food away and Matthew built a fire. Liz curled up on the couch beside her husband, feeling a contentment far beyond that which she'd felt at any time in her life.

"Here we are, Matthew, right where we were thrown together— where I began loving you."

In response, Matthew's arms wound around her, holding her tightly against his chest. Liz felt swallowed up in his love, and the thrill of his touch.

They watched the cheerful crackling fire for some moments before Matthew spoke. "My Pipit," he began tenderly, "I haven't told you, but caring for you up here with Uncle Arthur filled my mind to such an extent, I didn't have any room to think of my own predicament. And when you awakened, your presence brought me peace—your hand brought me comfort. I marveled at it then, but now I understand. My mother devoured the scriptures, and she used to say, '*we love whom we serve.*' While caring for you that short time, holding you in my arms while Arthur fed you, I grew to love you. That's why..." He turned silent.

"Go on, Matthew," Liz urged, thrilled to hear that he'd held her in his arms. "We still have so much to discover—so much we need to learn about each other. Our time together has been so short we've never really told each other all our thoughts and feelings."

"You're right, Liz. I was sorting out some things in my mind. I guess it all boils down to the fact that *I needed you.* When we left the cabin, my need seemed to increase each day. That's why I asked you to stay with me and the children in the evenings. I became lonely and unsettled when you began working non-stop, making it impossible for us to be together in the evenings with or without the children present."

A smile of great satisfaction spread across Liz's face. "I'm happy to hear that it bothered you when I began finding ways not to be with you, Matthew, for I was suffering desperately. I had discovered I loved you, so I had to find a way not to be alone with you. I felt too vulnerable."

Matthew gazed at her in astonishment. "That's why you began to work constantly in the evenings? You...you had discovered you loved me?"

She gave him a woeful glance and nodded.

"Tell me when and how you made this discovery."

Liz relished telling him every tiny detail, and Matthew relished hearing it all.

When she was through, Matthew's face reflected amazement. "I was blind in more ways than one, but there is one question I've been wanting to ask you. How could you fall for me in my condition?"

"Though I missed seeing expression in your beautiful eyes, Matthew, your character, your strength, your wonderful personality still came through...so it was very easy." She pulled his face down and kissed him thoroughly.

The fire crackled and popped, as if to add emphasis to her kiss. They stayed in each other's arms for a long time—until the fire turned to embers.

Chapter Sixty-One

The next two days were glorious for the honeymooners. Matthew had packed two binoculars in his suitcase—his and Arthur's, hoping Liz would want to go bird watching. Liz had squealed in delight, so part of both days were spent in this activity.

On day one, Liz was the first to see a Western Flycatcher with its striking yellow belly. They stood entranced as they watched the little bird and listened to its call, *whee-seet,* the second note higher. Matthew discovered the beautiful little Mountain Chickadee with it's black cap and white eyebrows, light gray underbelly and darker gray wings. They listened to its hoarse call...*chick-adee-adee.*

On day two, Matthew spotted a Red-breasted Nuthatch and together they watched it glean small branches, and outer twigs for insects. They spotted many different birds both days, thrilled to have found a mutual love they could share with each other.

The third day, the 6th of June, they packed up and left for Palm Springs. They had decided not to take a longer honeymoon because of the children and the need to make preparations to move into their new home.

This time when they left the cabin, Liz wasn't frightened to face the world outside, nor the future. Instead, she looked forward to spending that future with her husband and, hopefully, more than the two children they now had.

The hours driving to Palm Springs were used to get further acquainted, both asking questions about each other's lives before they met. Liz only asked questions of Matthew's life before he married, not wanting to think about his life with Diane. It was almost as if he hadn't had a life with her; only when Merri seriously misbehaved did it come to her attention, and Merri hadn't done so for some time.

Matthew called on his cell phone, telling Julia when they would arrive. As they drove up to the front door, the children raced out of it with Julia following.

The children pounced on them as they stepped out of the car, greeting them joyously. Liz hadn't realized she'd missed them until then. They looked happy and well cared for. She hugged her mother, and noticed that she also looked happy.

"Did you enjoy being up in the mountain cabin?" her mother asked her.

"It was wonderful. Matthew took me to dinner every night at the ski resort."

Julia smiled at Matthew. "That sounds much better than cooking on your honeymoon."

"Daddy, Aunt Claire and Aunt Linda took us up high on the..." Merri looked over at Julia who prompted her, "Aeri..al...Tram..way ride," she repeated triumphantly. "At first we were scared, then we weren't."

"It was so fun, Daddy!" Danny exclaimed.

Before Matthew could respond, Merri expounded further. "Gramma and Grandpa Cabot took us on a carriage ride behind a horse!"

"And they took us on a boat ride," Danny said. "And we saw some pink flamingos and all kinds a birds."

Matthew looked questioningly at Julia who explained. "We took them for a gondola ride on the canal that meanders through the golf courses at Marriott's Desert Springs Resort."

"Oh. Thank you, Mother," Liz said. "And I'm touched that you have told them to call you..."

Julia raised her hand and interrupted. "It was their idea, and your father and I are delighted that they consider us grandparents. All we did was change the names from the more formal grandmother and grandfather to the other."

"Thank you, Julia," Matthew said. "Since my parents aren't living, that means a lot to me."

"My thanks is seeing my daughter so happy, Matthew. Come on into the house. It shouldn't be too long before Calvin gets home. Also Claire and Kelley and Linda and Bruce are coming over. We're all going to have dinner together tonight."

"Great!" Matthew said enthusiastically. "I'll get our suitcases. Go on in."

~~~~~~~~~~~~

The family had an enjoyable evening together. Liz thanked her sisters for helping with the children, and it was then that Claire made an announcement.

"I'm pregnant."

"What does that mean?" Merri asked.

Everyone laughed, and Claire explained. Liz clapped her hands as exuberantly as Merri. "We're so happy for you and Kelley."

"Thanks to you, Liz," Kelley said, "we're starting our family earlier than we'd planned. But I'm a little put out that you are already two ahead of us."

"And we're trying," Linda stated plaintively.

"I'm so glad. Our children can play together. They'll be close in age," Liz stated eagerly.

Everyone raised their brows, including Matthew. "Do you have something to tell us, Liz?" her father asked, smiling.

"Not that I know of, but I'm hoping."

Matthew laughed, leaned over and kissed her. "I'm hoping, too."

~~~~~~~~~~~~

The next morning, Julia began reading to the children while Matthew and Liz went into the bedroom to pack all her belongings. Liz found that her mother had boxes and tape ready for the project. Also, her father had hired a truck and driver to haul the wedding gifts and all her belongings to their new home.

Before they began packing, Liz threw her arms around Matthew and kissed him. "I'm so happy, I could burst. Moving all my things from home makes the fact that we're going to start our life together as a family, a reality."

Matthew held her close. "It's a reality that still seems unreal—too good to be true." It was afternoon before they finished and were walking out to their car. Claire, Linda and their husbands had said goodbye the night before and Calvin had hugged the children, kissed his daughter goodbye and shook Matthew's hand that morning.

Merri and Danny clung to Julia. "Can't you come with us?" Merri asked.

Touched, Julia explained that she and grandpa would come and see them in their new home. Satisfied with this, they climbed into the car.

Liz hugged and kissed her mother. "Thank you for everything. I love you."

"I love you, too, Liz. We'll miss all of you."

Matthew was the last to say goodbye. As he gazed down into Julia's beautiful face, his eyes misted. "I'm grateful to you for raising such a wonderful daughter, and for accepting me and my children as you have." He put his arms around her and hugged her, then kissed her cheek.

Julia's eyes also glistened. "Calvin and I are also grateful for the kind of man you are, and we're pleased over your marriage."

He smiled at her, appreciation in his eyes. "Thank you." He turned, walked around to the driver's side and got in.

They waved at each other, and Julia watched them drive out of sight, her heart full. When she walked back into the house, it seemed so empty, she had to go call her husband. When she heard his voice, the love she felt for him overwhelmed her. "I love you, Cal."

There was silence on the phone a moment. "They've gone," he said.

"Yes."

"And I love you, my dear."

Chapter Sixty-Two

The truck, full of Liz's belongings and the wedding gifts, was parked in the driveway of Liz and Matthew's new home. The children watched wide-eyed as the husky young man moved quickly, unloading Liz's belongings as she directed, placing all the gifts into the large playroom. The day before, Matthew had rented a truck and a helper to move all of his and the children's things in, along with the piano.

When the driver left, Liz promised the children they could help open the gifts after dinner. They let out squeals of excitement, and promptly began playing tag throughout the empty house, ending up outside on the swing set.

It was mid-afternoon when Matthew drove into the garage from work. Inside the house he glanced into the playroom and stared in amazement at the number of gifts that had been so generously given them by the Cabot's friends and family.

Liz's eyes lit up when she saw him. "I'm so glad you're here, Matthew. You know what I just discovered?" she asked, hugging him around the waist and squeezing him.

"No, what?" he asked, kissing the top of her head.

"I was planning to run to the store for cleaning supplies even though the house looks so clean. I just wanted to wipe out the cupboards myself. I was standing in the kitchen thinking about this when I spied a note on the counter kind of pushed into the corner. It was signed by Mamie and Arthur, Randy and Joan. Come into the kitchen and read it."

Matthew picked up the note and read: "Matthew and Liz, we were stumped over what to get you for a wedding gift, so as your gift we wiped out all the kitchen shelves, lined them with paper, cleaned the bathrooms and had the carpets shampooed. Congratulations!"

Matthew grinned. "Now that's a gift of love if you ask me."

"Isn't it?" The smile never left her face. "Now, we can open our gifts and decide where to put things! I'm so excited, Matthew. And look what I found in my purse!"

Matthew took the check and whistled.

"It came in an envelope with a note enclosed. It's a wedding gift from my parents stipulating that it has to go toward furnishing the house."

"How generous of them. You have your work cut out for you."

"Me? Us, Matthew. I want your taste in the house, not just mine."

"Thank you, Liz. Even though you insisted I help pick out some of the furniture before, I thought that would be the end of it. Maybe it's the artist in me, but I'd like to continue helping you choose the furniture and all the accessories." He kissed her.

"You're welcome." she smiled. "I'm glad you want to. Both my sisters' husbands don't like to shop for furniture." She clapped her hands. "This afternoon the stores are delivering everything we purchased before we left, including the beds. We get to sleep in our own home tonight, Matthew. I think I just might burst with happiness."

Matthew laughed. "Me too, my sweet Pipit."

~~~~~~~~~~~~~

The deliveries had now all arrived and Liz, Matthew and the children were finally alone, sitting around their new kitchen table. Matthew had picked up fried chicken and all the trimmings. Merri and Danny could hardly sit still long enough to eat, they were so excited about their new home, and the promise of opening all the presents that were piled high in the other room.

Matthew's eyes traveled from his children's happy faces, to his wife's, wondering how his heart could hold all the joy he felt.

When they were through eating, the children sat on the floor in the playroom, eagerly waiting to be handed a present to open.

"Merri and Danny, as we've told you, these are not the kind of presents we open at Christmas," Matthew emphasized. "They will be things to eat with, cook with and pretty things."

"We know, Daddy," Merri said, her eyes alight with excitement.

Danny nodded his agreement.

Matthew had seen extravagant wedding gifts before when he and Diane had opened theirs, so he wasn't surprised to see what he and Liz received. A far cry from the kind of gifts he could afford to give. Nevertheless, he enjoyed Liz's enthusiasm over them. Liz squealed when she opened Claire and Kelley's gift of a large set of cookware, and again when they opened a set of everyday dishes and a set of china from Linda and Bruce.

Remembering Liz's first days in the kitchen, Matthew chuckled to himself. Then aloud, he said with a broad grin, "You've come a long way, baby."

Liz, pretending a pique she didn't really feel, tapped him on the knee. "Oh, you!"

Around 7:00 PM, both children had begun to yawn, so Matthew and Liz quickly opened the sheets they had purchased and made their beds. Because of their hard play and all their excitement, both children fell asleep almost as their heads hit the pillow, giving Liz and Matthew time to open the rest of the gifts, recording the names of the givers as they went.

~~~~~~~~~~~~~

A week later, everything was put away, and the kitchen totally organized. Liz had located the grocery store, and gone shopping. Neighbors came by welcoming Liz and Matthew to the neighborhood, and they all had children of varying ages. Several close by had children Merri's and Danny's ages and they soon became acquainted and began playing together everyday.

Every evening at work when it was closing time, Matthew's heart beat a little faster as he thought of going home to Liz. And thanks to her, when the children saw him, they ran and greeted him as if they hadn't seen him in a week. And her reaction to his coming home filled every empty crack in his heart.

After they'd been in their new home for two weeks, Liz invited Flo, the Brodericks and Margo and Phil over for ice cream and cake. They included Arthur, Mamie, Randy and Joan and children. It had turned out to be a special evening for everyone, especially Liz. Seeing Flo and Margo felt like seeing relatives.

Liz was happy to start repaying Joan by taking care of her children when she needed it. Weekly calls were made to her parents and sisters, or they called her, updating each other on everything.

Merri was a different child, happy and loving most of the time. Danny was beside himself to have boys to play with every day instead of just a sister.

And Liz wondered how life could get any better.

At the end of the third week in the house, Matthew and Liz began looking for more furniture, working with a decorator. Matthew took off work as often as he could, and afterward they went out to eat, leaving the children with a reliable teenager from the neighborhood. Liz looked forward to these times when she could be alone with her husband.

To Liz's surprise and delight, Matthew played the piano and sang often. Why couldn't he have done this in the home where he and Diane lived? Liz was puzzled over this as well as over Merri's previous behavior. *Why should it matter?* she asked herself. But for some reason she felt it did—and the thought disturbed her.

Chapter Sixty-Three

The end of the first week in July on a blistering hot Saturday afternoon, Liz and Matthew were swimming with the children. After playing games for some time, Matthew got out, sat under the table umbrella near the pool and watched. He found great joy in watching Liz with the children.

He especially liked watching Liz. Still grateful for his sight, he watched Liz's' slim, firm body move gracefully in and out of the pool. No matter what she did, her movements were delightful to see, her face enchanting...and, he reassured himself, she was his.

She got out, grabbed a towel and rubbed the excess water from her hair, while walking toward him. "Hi," she said, sitting next to him. "You tired?"

"No," he said. "I just like watching you and the children together."

"I like watching *you* with the children," she said, grinning. "It makes me love you more when I see what a good father you are."

He took Liz's hand and kissed it, and just as he did so, a man's head appeared above the gate next to the house.

"Mr. Melloy?"

"Oh, that's my delivery," he said, jumping up.

"Your delivery?" she asked puzzled. "What are you having delivered?"

He gave her a mysterious smile. "Wait and see. It's a special surprise."

Liz waited anxiously. Soon, Matthew led the two men through the gate of the yard. They were carrying something. It was a saguaro cactus about five feet tall! That was the last thing she expected. *Why would Matthew think that this was a special surprise?* she wondered. The children scrambled out of the pool and ran over to their father, watching curiously. Liz went over to the patio and sat down to watch.

Matthew instructed the men to plant the saguaro in a corner of the yard that rose slightly and would face the morning sun. When they were through, Matthew paid them, took the children by the hand and walked over to where Liz was sitting.

Noting her puzzled look, he smiled. Pulling two chairs up for the children so that they were in a close circle, he said to them, "Listen carefully to what I'm going to tell Pipit. Don't ask questions. I'll explain what you don't understand after I'm through."

He took her hand. "Liz, I bought this saguaro cactus because to me it symbolizes our love. In the desert when the summer heat drains all life, and the air crackles with dryness, the brittle brush and the burro bushes shed all or part of their foliage and enter into a state of dormancy; they appear dead. But the mighty saguaro continues to grow during the heat, despite dust storms, and even during the long months or years of drought. It remains tall and strong, giving and succoring—it becomes a bird sanctuary. The woodpeckers make holes in the saguaro and build nests in it. When they leave, other birds live in those nests and drink of the saguaro's life-giving moisture." He smiled at his children who were sitting still, listening intently.

He returned his gaze to Liz. "Like this sturdy saguaro," he said, gesturing to the plant, "our love will endure—even through the heat of the trials that may come our way.

"Like the life-giving moisture in the saguaro, our love will continue to sustain and nurture our children and grandchildren through the heat and drought of *their* trials. This saguaro, a symbol of our love, growing slowly and steadily will someday stand tall as a monument—an example for our posterity long after we are gone."

"Oh Matthew," breathed Liz, her face alight with an inner glow and sense of wonder. "We have to preserve those words. Right now, before we forget, let's write them down. Then we'll have them engraved on a plaque that we can put right in front of the saguaro so Merri and Danny, and all those who come after can read and draw strength from them."

The tears that spilled from her eyes were tears of joy, and as Matthew bent over to kiss her, his tears mingled with hers.

~~~~~~~~~~~~

July 14 Danny turned five, and Liz had a neighborhood birthday party for him. In the evening he was treated to a family birthday party with his Uncle Arthur and Aunt Mamie, and of course his cousins Johnny and Becky and their parents.

That night on the way home, Arthur and Mamie commented to each other once more how happy Matthew and the children were, and marveled that Liz and Matthew didn't seem to be having any real adjustments.

A couple of days later, something happened that Liz and Matthew had been expecting, though not in the manner it did. Merri and Danny, who had been playing out in the backyard with some neighborhood children, came into the house, both in tears.

"Whatever is the matter, you two?" Liz asked, squatting down to their level.

"Our friends called us rude!" Merri exclaimed indignantly.

"They have been such nice friends. Why would they say such a thing?"

"They said we shouldn't call our mommy by her first name," Merri explained.

"I told them you were Pipit, not our mommy," Danny said.

She and Matthew had discussed beforehand what the children should call her when the time was right. And now seemed to be the right time. "Come over to the couch and let me explain something to you both."

When the children had seated themselves on the couch, Liz knelt before them. "Remember, I married your father." They nodded. "That makes me your mother...not your real mother who went to heaven, but what people call a stepmother. You are lucky that you have two mothers. Not every child has that. I am your mother, now, children, and you may call me Pipit or Mommy, whichever you choose."

"You are our mother, really?" Danny asked, looking a little incredulous.

"Yes."

"I want to call you Mommy, then," he said, smiling from ear to ear.

"I do too," added Merri, the tears vanishing.

Liz hugged them both. "I'm so glad because I love you as if you were my very own children. Now, let's go out and explain all this to your friends outside." Relief flooded their faces.

That night, they greeted their father with, "We get to call Pipit, Mommy, Daddy!"

"Did you know she's our mother?" Danny asked.

His surprise lasted only a moment, then a broad smile spread across his face. "I sure did, Danny." He looked questioningly at Liz.

She told him what had happened.

"Well, now, I think this calls for a celebration. After dinner, let's all go get an ice cream cone."

"Goody...goody!" The children yelled, jumping up and down.

Matthew smiled at Liz, and hugged her. "Great, huh?"

"More than great, Matthew. It's super great."

Chapter Sixty-Four

The next four weeks passed quickly. Liz and Matthew met the parents of a number of the children's friends. The Cargills, three doors away, turned out to be long-time customers of Melloy Music Center. On two occasions, they got together for a backyard barbeque.

Matthew endured some good-natured ribbing from his employees because his present behavior contrasted so sharply with that of his past. Now, he could barely wait to leave the store—to rush home to Liz and the children.

In between trips to the library, a couple of overnight stays by Becky and Johnny, and a trip to the museum, Liz and the children found time to polish up their kidnaping techniques on Matthew.

Merri and Danny blossomed, adjusting to the give-and-take of children's play, but their favorite activity was an evening spent playing games with Matthew and Liz. Their current favorite was a game called 'spoons.'

Liz felt a deep contentment. Merri was continuing to grow into a normal, well-adjusted child, responding to their love as well as the consistent discipline they tried to apply.

Matthew's business was growing and he had mentioned the possibility of a third store. To her, life offered unlimited opportunities to move forward and grow, certain that she would soon have children of her own.

~~~~~~~~~~~~

One Sunday evening, after they had put the children to bed, Matthew pulled Liz onto the couch beside him. "I've been thinking, Liz. I don't know why I'm feeling confused, but it seems that we should be doing more than just reading the Bible with the children. There's no way parents can raise children today without having strong religious principles and beliefs."

"I agree, Matthew. Now that the children are no longer isolated and are playing with other children, and will soon be going to school, I've felt a little uneasy. Do you think we need to begin looking for a church we both can feel good about affiliating with?"

"Maybe we should, Liz. I was raised with the idea that attending church weekly was very important for a family."

"I wasn't raised that way because both my parent became disenchanted with several churches we attended. Instead, my dad instigated daily Bible reading. What church did you attend when you were a boy?"

"I don't really know. Maybe it was Baptist. Anyway, my parents liked the minister." He put his arm around her and pulled her close. They were silent for some time—neither as hopeful about finding the church as they wanted to be.

~~~~~~~~~~~~

It was on a day near the middle of August that Matthew had arrived home early and was preparing to join Liz and the children who were already in the pool, when the doorbell rang. He answered the door to find Margo standing there, a sack in one hand, and mouth open.

"Matthew! What are you doing here at this time of day?"

"Margo!" He laughed. "I might ask you the same thing. Come in. It's good to see you. Liz and the kids are out in the pool." He stood aside for her to enter.

As they walked through the house, Margo looked around. "Oh, you have some of the furniture you ordered. I love the bright cheerful colors. Liz told me you picked it out together."

"Yes. It was a new experience for me, but I really enjoyed it."

"Well, it's certainly more homey and enjoyable than the 'whited sepulchre' you had before." She looked over at Matthew, checking to see how her statement affected him. He seemed contemplative as he followed her gaze over the furnishings.

Out on the patio, Matthew hailed Liz and motioned for her to come over.

Liz flew across the lawn, looking to Margo like a beautiful water sprite. Margo glanced at Matthew. A wide grin split his features; his eyes were alight as she had never before seen them—he was looking at the approaching figure of his wife with something akin to awe.

"Margo!" exclaimed Liz, "It's wonderful to see you." Forgetting her watery state, she threw her arms around her visitor, then drew back in alarm. "Oh, Margo, I'm sorry. I was so happy to see you I forgot I was all wet."

"Phil often says I'm all wet, so I feel right at home. You look wonderful, Liz, and so does he," she said, gesturing toward the still smiling Matthew. "You must agree with him. I was on my way to the Fashion Square Mall, but first I wanted to drop off these chocolate chip cookies for the kids."

"How thoughtful of you. You wait right here while I'll go get them out of the pool They'll want to see you, and, I'm sure, gobble down some cookies." She turned and walked quickly back to the pool.

Margo looked at Matthew, then snapped her fingers to get his attention. She laughed. "Hey boy—over here. Quit gawking at your wife."

Matthew gave a slightly embarrassed laugh, as a slow pink color overran the tan on his face.

"Matthew, I meant what I said to Liz. I used to be concerned about you, and Merri too—but not any longer."

Just then, the children, followed by Liz, arrived to greet Margo and claim her attention. She missed the sudden change in Matthew, as a shuttered expression settled over his face.

Chapter Sixty-Five

It was after Margo's visit, and a time when the August heat seemed to have evaporated every hint of moisture from the desert, when the days were unbearably hot and the evenings smothering warm that Liz first noticed a change take place in Matthew. He seemed withdrawn, preoccupied. When she asked him how things were at work, he had told her that business was good and that both managers were doing a good job. Assuming it would pass, she ignored it for a few days.

Finally, she asked, "What is wrong, Matthew? You don't seem yourself."

His brows rose. "Not a thing, Liz."

"But Matthew, you seem far away much of the time lately."

"I do? I'm sorry, I don't mean to do that. Maybe I'm thinking more about work than I thought. I know I haven't been sleeping as well as I should." What he didn't want to tell Liz is that the night after Margo's visit, the nightmares about the wreck had started up again, only with a different twist. His thoughts about Diane were disturbing, and the guilt he'd been feeling about neglecting her returned with increased intensity. All this came on the heels of Merri's transformation. *Why wasn't she happy and secure before Diane was killed?* he asked himself again. *How was it all connected?* He still didn't know the answer.

One night, Matthew cried out during one of his nightmares, "No! It's Diane! No!"

Liz was shocked. She neither moved nor spoke to him; she just waited until it was over. She lay awake for a long time wondering what this meant. He had been so happy...until lately. Maybe she hadn't yet filled the empty place Diane left. Pushing this thought out of her mind, she decided to just wait, feeling sure that time would take care of it.

A week passed and she could see no improvement in Matthew's spirits. Also, she had begun to feel very tired in the afternoons. This and the feeling that Matthew was pulling away from her became a time of hanging on, enduring, letting the days pass.

One evening, after the children were in bed, Matthew studied Liz. "You look tired. Don't you feel well?"

"I feel just fine," she said tersely.

"We're kind of short on groceries and I was wondering..."

"So I'm not keeping up like I should." Tears sprang to her eyes. "If you don't like the way I'm doing things, you can just do them yourself." She ran from the room into the bedroom and slammed the door.

Shocked, Matthew stared after her, then followed her. Opening the door, he saw her curled up on the bed crying. He went over and sat down on the edge. "Hey, you interrupted me. I felt that maybe you've been working too hard. I was going to offer to go grocery shopping for you to relieve you."

"You were?" she asked in a small voice. "How would I know? You've pulled away from me, Matthew."

"Pulled away? If anything, it's the opposite. That's the way I feel, anyway."

"You have a strange way of showing it."

"I'm sorry, Liz. Be patient with me. I'm trying to grapple with something."

She slid off the bed on the opposite side and stepped away from Matthew. "Well, I'm trying to grapple with your grappling!" The tears started again.

"Please come here, angel." His nickname 'snow angel' had recently been shortened.

When he called her that Liz softened and she stepped around the bed to him. He pulled her down beside him and he took her hands in his.

"Tell me something. Have you been tired lately?"

"Yes. I never nap in the daytime, but every afternoon lately I feel such a need to. I just drag and by dinner time, I can hardly get dinner." More tears sprang to her eyes.

"Your tiredness, your emotionality...maybe...maybe you're pregnant, Liz."

"Pregnant?"

"Yes," he said smiling.

She thought about it. "Yes, maybe...I...I think I might be! Oh, Matthew." She threw her arms around him. "I hope so!"

He took her in his arms. "I hope so too. You need to see a doctor."

~~~~~~~~~~~~

The doctor confirmed their suspicions. That evening, Liz nearly jumped into Matthew's arms. "It's true, Matthew, I'm going to have a baby!"

He laughed, picked her up and swung her around. "I thought I would never have another child, Liz. Thank you...thank you." He covered her face with kisses.

She laughed. "It feels like Christmas, doesn't it, Matthew? When shall we tell the children?"

"Whenever you want to."

"Maybe we ought to wait a while so it won't seem so long to them before it's born."

"Maybe so. How about we go out this weekend for dinner?"

"That sounds wonderful, Matthew." She kissed him. "We haven't been out alone for a while have we?"

"No, and we need to remedy that."

Merri and Danny came running in from the play room. "Daddy, Daddy you're home!"

At the moment, the troubling emotions Matthew had been feeling seemed far away, and life felt good.

~~~~~~~~~~~~

Liz began napping every afternoon at the insistence of Matthew. He'd promised the children he would rent a good movie for them if they stayed inside and played quietly or watched one of their videos quietly so their mother could take a nap on the couch by them.

The knowledge of the life growing inside her, and Matthew's return to his old self were like twin joys—to be taken out and examined a dozen times a day. The hot days of August no longer sapped her strength. She awakened each morning feeling like she was carrying a miracle inside her...a miracle that only happened to other women...not her. Yet...it was really happening to *her*!

The first of September, Liz enrolled the children in the nearby grade school. Her babies were going to go to school! Danny in kindergarten and Merri in first grade. She walked with each of them to their classrooms, kissed them and told them she'd be there to pick them up. Their excitement overrode their shyness, and they walked into their classrooms by themselves.

Liz entered the empty house, wondering what she was going to do with herself all day, then she remembered with excitement that she and Matthew needed to go shopping for a baby bed. She could fix up the baby's room!

~~~~~~~~~~~~

It was only a week later that Matthew began to withdraw again. This time, it had a devastating affect on Liz. She found herself staring out the window at the saguaro, remembering Matthew's words, hoping to keep her spirits up for the sake of the baby.

She wandered through her partially furnished house trying to put her mind on ideas for the special touches of decor that make a house a home, but without Matthew, she found her interest waning. Entering the kitchen/family room area, she looked around hoping for inspiration. This was the most important place to start adding special touches. The only thought that came to her was her usual feeling of gladness that she could see the swimming pool from the window above the sink and the swing set from the far left window of the family room. At all times she could keep an eye on the children while they played outside.

Already she felt tired, so she went to her bedroom. This was the other room that was important for her to decorate, but so far they had only the necessities...a lovely wide alder wood chest of drawers stained a light wheat color with matching night stands. A small couch was on order for this room where she and Matthew could sit together in the evenings.

The made bed looked inviting to her tired body and spirits—a lullaby to the senses.

Her taste and Matthew's blended just as the bed ensemble they had picked out did. It was an aristocratic melding of understated neutrals and a rich pattern in a soft cotton matelasse. Like a fine tapestry, the intricate acanthus-and-rose pattern in tone-on-tone taupe and cream swirls over the duvet cover with a tailored bed skirt, standard shams and sheeting of pure mocha colored pima cotton, looked stunning against the rich alder wood headboard.

She lay on top of the spread, curled up trying to rest, but the tears which lately were so close to the surface, flowed. Pulling a tissue from her shorts, she kept drying them until she drifted off to sleep.

Matthew had left for work that morning unhappy because Liz's pale drawn face had disturbed him. He felt helpless to make her feel better, for he was still struggling with the nightmares and guilt. She was far too intuitive. He couldn't fake it.

On impulse, he decided to go home and check on her. Entering the quiet house, he walked through looking for her, finding her curled up on the bed asleep. Stepping over to her, he saw the tissue in her hand, and the vestige of a tear on her cheek. His heart ached.

He couldn't stand to see her unhappy. He watched her as he had night after night after each nightmare to make sure she was still there, loving her beyond that which he thought possible, wondering if he was worthy of her, hoping and praying God would not let anything happen to *her*.

Chapter Sixty-Six

By the middle of September, Matthew was beside himself over Liz's unhappiness. She refused to even call her family to tell them about their baby. Her malaise was concerning him. The doctor had told her everything was fine. Even though Matthew knew emotions could affect a baby in the womb, he was more concerned about Liz and his inability to make her happy.

No matter how he prayed, how he mentally searched for an answer to his dreams and the disturbing emotions that came with them, he was not finding the answers, nor was he getting any better. Today he couldn't concentrate on work so he left and headed for Arthur's and Mamie's hoping they could help him. He'd always been private. It would be hard to divulge his problems and the problem of their marriage, but—did he have any choice?

He had called ahead so they were waiting for him. When they saw him, they were both concerned.

"Whatever is the matter, Matthew?" Mamie asked, studying his troubled face.

"I wish I knew. Thank you for being willing to talk with me."

Arthur clapped him on the shoulder. "We love you, Matthew. We're here to help...if we can. Tell us what's on your mind."

Matthew told them about the nightmares he'd had before he married Liz, and the strange twist to them since. He explained the feelings of guilt he couldn't shake, guilt over working six days a week, and at times in the evenings, neglecting Diane and the children.

"And the question that accompanies all this, and which plagues me for some reason is why was Merri, as you put it, Aunt Mamie, an unhappy and insecure child? Her behavior was bad long before I started working so many hours."

Arthur and Mamie glanced at each other knowing exactly what the other one was thinking. It was Arthur who spoke. "Matthew, your Aunt Mamie has told you more than once that you needed to become more introspective. We men are bad about this, especially you and I. Randy happens to be a little better at it. It was Mamie that had to gently prod me to look at things now and then. Sometimes I listened, but most of the time I resisted. Now...I listen all the time. It takes a long time for us men to grow up."

Matthew smiled at his crusty old uncle, touched at his disclosure. "I know I've avoided looking too closely, but I'm willing, now, to face anything painful if I can make Liz happy. So how do I go about this introspection?"

"Look at your marriage with Diane for starters," Mamie said, bluntly.

"I already have. I just told you about it."

"*Why* did you begin working so many hours, Matthew?" she asked pointedly.

He thought a moment, shook his head. "I don't know, but somehow I think you know. Do you?"

"Yes...it's..."

Arthur put his hand on Mamie's arm and gave her a look. "I think we know. Mamie is sure that we know. We have discussed it more than once, Matthew, and we decided that it would be best for you to find out the problem for yourself."

Mamie sighed. "It is, Matthew. But I do so want to make it easier for you."

"Why is it better for me to find out for myself?" Matthew asked, frustrated.

"If we told you that," Arthur said, "we'd have to tell you part of what we think the problem is, and believe me, you wouldn't appreciate it. In fact, you'd get upset with us."

"I can't believe that."

"You better believe it, Matthew. We know you," Arthur replied.

Matthew left feeling disgruntled and discouraged. He decided that he couldn't go back to work, his desire to find an answer had escalated to such a point, he couldn't think of anything else. While driving, he voiced another prayer. Suddenly, the thought came into his mind that he should go see Diane's father, Wayne Halstrom. This struck him as so odd, he had to find a place to pull over and think about it for a few minutes.

Wayne Halstrom was the last person he wanted to see! He was the last person he thought he could talk to about his problem, yet, the feeling that he should was overwhelming. Reluctantly, he pulled out his cellular and called the number he still had memorized—Wayne's office number.

Betty, his long-time secretary answered.

"Betty, this is Matthew Melloy."

She was silent for a moment, then with a cold and formal tone of voice she said, "What may I do for you?"

"I would like to speak to Wayne. Is he there?"

"He's busy, Matthew."

"Betty, I know how you must feel, but it's terribly important that I speak with him."

"All right," she replied hesitantly, "but you had better not upset him more than he already has been."

Wayne's voice had an element of surprise in it. "Matthew, I didn't expect to hear from you again. What can I do for you?"

"I'm having a problem, Wayne. It's not getting any better, if anything it's worse. For some reason, the thought that I needed to talk with you came very strongly into my mind. I have no idea why. I'm just following a feeling, and I'm so desperate I worked up the courage to call you."

Wayne was silent for a few moments. "All right, Matthew. Why don't we meet over at the club and find an out-of-the-way alcove and you can tell me what's on your mind."

Matthew breathed a sigh of relief, started the car and drove toward the country club. Twenty minutes later, they met each other walking in.

Wayne stopped and looked at Matthew, incredulous. "You can see!"

"Yes."

"When did this happen?"

"The 10th of April to be exact."

"I'm happy for you, Matthew...happy for my grandchildren."

"Thank you."

"How are they, Matthew?" he asked anxiously as he began walking toward the entrance of the club.

"They are doing so well, Wayne. Merri is a different child. She's in first grade now and Danny is in kindergarten. You're welcome to come and see them anytime. In fact, quite some time ago, Liz wanted to invite both you and Elinor over."

"She did?" For the first time since he'd known Wayne, he saw tears surface in his eyes.

"Yes. Would you come over?"

Wayne didn't answer immediately. He led Matthew to a quiet spot and they sat across from each other in small overstuffed chairs.

"I want to see Merri and Danny, but Elinor wouldn't even consider it. Down the road, if she doesn't change her attitude, I certainly will take you up on your offer. Thank you, Matthew, it means a lot to me that you would invite me under the circumstances."

"The children need their grandfather, Wayne."

He nodded, his eyes heavy with sadness. "What is it you want to talk to me about, Matthew?"

"Frankly, Wayne, I don't know. Maybe you can help me figure out why I had a feeling to come and talk with you. Maybe you can help me figure out what's causing my problems."

"I can't even solve my own, Matthew, but go on."

Matthew thought a moment and began telling him of the nightmares that occurred after the wreck and how they had started up again, not telling him of the change in them, however. He told him of the feelings of guilt which had sent him into the depression, making it necessary for Arthur and Mamie to step in and help him.

The last information shocked Wayne. "Your feelings of guilt caused the depression?" Matthew nodded. Wayne's face looked troubled, but all he said was, "That's too bad. Go on, Matthew."

"I'm sure you're aware that Merri has been a difficult child since she was a toddler. Long before I began neglecting Diane and the children. The question that won't go away, Wayne, is why was Merri that way? She's a happy secure child now. What caused it, and why is that tied so closely to my feelings of guilt? My wife, Liz, is pregnant and I'm making her unhappy...and soon the children will be."

There was pain on Wayne's face. "You can't figure it out? You have no idea?"

"I'm totally clueless."

"I thought you might recognize the truth at the end of the court hearing. That's when I finally accepted it myself."

"You know?" Matthew asked incredulous, hopeful.

"I only figured out about Merri at the end of the trial. I had no idea about your guilt feelings, Matthew."

"Do you have any idea why they are tied closely together for me?"

Wayne nodded slowly. He struggled with his emotions for a moment, then he began. "You see, Matthew, *I first* neglected Diane. I didn't realize how much until she...she died. I was always so proud of her. In spite of her mother's inability to show affection to her, she turned out to be a wonderful mother."

"She did, Wayne. I was always amazed at it."

Wayne smiled sadly. "Thank you. At the end of the trial, when I saw how the children reacted to Elizabeth, I was relieved, but the thing that stood out more than anything was Elizabeth Cabot's *love* for *you*. I knew right then and there that that, more than anything, would *heal* Merri. The fact that Elizabeth loved them and they loved her was a bonus, almost as important, but not quite."

Matthew's brows drew together, puzzled. "I don't understand, Wayne."

"I see that the problem is still too painful for you to acknowledge, Matthew. I can relate. I, too, have closed my eyes to painful things and as a result I have suffered much more in the long run, and so has my family."

Wayne took a deep breath and said, "Now, what I'm going to say is very hard for me to say, Matthew. It was Diane who neglected *you,* not the other way around."

Matthew was stunned. Not only the idea, but the fact that it was coming from Diane's father was unbelievable. "I don't...uh see that, Wayne."

"Of course you don't. You see...Diane didn't love you."

"What? You're wrong, Wayne!" Matthew exclaimed.

"No. I'm not, Matthew," he said quietly. "She wasn't capable of loving a man. She'd never had an example of that. Her mother didn't and doesn't love me. Elinor was raised by a cold and cruel mother who didn't love her husband. It's multi-generational. If only I had realized it sooner, maybe I could have helped Elinor. Maybe I could have helped Diane...I..."

"But Wayne, Diane acted like she loved me."

"She cared for you as much as she was capable. I saw her inability to love too late. You see, Matthew, Elinor berated me continually in front of Diane as she was growing up. When Diane was a senior in high school, she began pulling away from her mother somewhat, but after you and Diane were married, Elinor regained some control of her. I'm afraid Diane never quite got over hoping for her mother's approval, her love.

"Merri is such a sensitive child. She adored you, her father, yet, she *felt* her mother's lack of love for you...and she heard Elinor's criticalness of you. I'm no psychologist, Matthew, but from my perspective, it looks as though Diane was transferring Elinor's feelings toward me to you. It seems as though Merri was transferring her mother's feelings or lack thereof, and her grandmother's criticalness of you—to Danny."

Still agonizing over what he'd just learned, he couldn't think. "I...I'm sorry, Wayne, but I don't quite understand."

"I don't know whether I can clear it up for you, Matthew, but I'll try. In my desire to get my employees to perform, I've studied human nature. I've watched them, friends and neighbors go through a lot of trials and I've learned some things. If only I had watched my own family as closely, maybe I could have..."

His chest heaved in an anguished sigh. "When I said Diane didn't love you, I mean that since Elinor was her role model, Diane didn't learn that love means serving the one you love and doing whatever is necessary to make him or her happy. Diane, like her mother, put her charities, projects and other people first. She didn't make time for her husband, her children's father, her thoughts were not on him. What I observed was, she didn't *serve* him...you. Elinor's criticalness of you along with me burying myself in work to escape, severely added to the problem.

"From my point of view, Matthew, though Merri didn't understand, she saw and felt all this and it confused her—made her feel insecure. She couldn't transfer what she felt to her other caregiver, you, so she transferred her confusion and anger to the other male in the family, Danny. I saw all the signs in my little granddaughter, but I didn't understand them until it was too late. All this turned Merri into one mixed up and unhappy child."

It was beginning to make sense to Matthew. He placed his elbows on his thighs and covered his face. What Wayne had disclosed hurt—he had loved Diane so deeply it was almost too difficult to accept that she didn't love *him* in the same way, yet, something inside him told him it was true. Apparently, Arthur and Mamie could see it, but he had refused to see it, he had closed his eyes to the bitter fact. It was a few minutes before he could speak.

"I know that hurt you, Matthew. I'm sorry."

"Thank you, Wayne. And thank you for having the courage to tell me. I'm sorry that you've been hurt by Elinor, also. That I could see, of course, but I was too blind to see my own situation. I ran from it."

"Matthew, if Merri's happy and secure now, it's because of the amazing love that Elizabeth portrayed for you in the courtroom, and apparently is still showing you."

"She does love me. She didn't even know it when she offered to marry me to keep custody of the children. She sacrificed herself to do so because she loved Merri and Danny and because Arthur and I had saved her life up on that mountain. We were going to annul the marriage the minute I got my sight back."

"That's quite amazing, Matthew."

"But I feel, Wayne, that if Diane had lived, she could have *learned* to love if she could have had some counseling. She had already overcome so much. She was such a special person, so kind, so good..."

"But would we have opened our eyes in time to save her and Merri, Matthew?"

Matthew swallowed back an avalanche of emotion. "I have to think that we would, Wayne. It's too tragic to think any other way. God loved her. We have to believe He would have guided us, that He would have humbled us enough, somehow. I know this, I will never stick my head in the sand again."

They sat there for some time, each feeling his own pain as well as the other's. The two men with a commonality of pain and tragedy had bonded, had closed the gap of estrangement.

Finally, Matthew said, "I don't know what I would have done if you hadn't had the charity to share with me what you did. Thank you. Would you come over and see the children soon?" Wayne nodded. "We want you to come over as often as possible. The children need you. I owe you a lot, Wayne. The goodness and kindness that was in Diane was enhanced and brought out by your love for her. You gave her much more than you realize, Wayne." He stood up.

The two men shook hands and clapped each other on the back, feeling great affection for each other as they parted, knowing that it wouldn't be long before they would be brought together again by their mutual love for the children.

Chapter Sixty-Seven

Matthew sat in his car thinking. Parked under a tree, he had rolled down the windows. The still very warm September air was at least cooler than inside the car. Glancing at his watch, he saw that it was 3:30. Picking up his cellular, he called work and told them he wouldn't be back today. He had some serious thinking to do before he faced Liz, but his concern for her was such that he had to do something right now. He dialed his home. Liz's voice came over tired and flat.

"Hi, Angel, I just called to see if I could take you and the children to dinner tonight."

The silence on the phone troubled him. Finally, she responded. "The children will love that."

It was apparent that she didn't feel the same as the children. But could he blame her? He had unintentionally been distant with her. "What time shall we go?" he asked.

"I'll have to shower and wash my hair, Matthew, and I'm not moving very fast today, so let's make it 6:00. I'll feed the children a snack to hold them until then."

"All right!" he said with more exuberant cheerfulness than he felt. "I love you, Liz. See you about a quarter to six."

With that taken care of, his mind went back to what Wayne had told him. The words, *"Diane didn't love you,"* rang in his ears, in his heart. "How could I love her so deeply and she not return it?" he asked aloud. Shoving the seat far back, he struggled with his emotions, but they won out. Quiet sobs racked his body. The grief for himself soon turned into grief over his *real* blindness. If he hadn't refused to face the unhappy fact, maybe he could have helped Diane!

When the grief played out, he left the car, went through the club and out to the beautiful grounds surrounding it. He paced, thinking about what could have been, what might have been if he hadn't refused to face what was *his responsibility to face*. After flagellating himself unmercifully, he prayed for forgiveness, swallowing back the overwhelming emotion which that brought to his heart.

Exhausted, he found a bench and sat down. Now that he knew the facts, he understood what he had done. He had worked long hours six days a week as an escape! Unconsciously, he felt Diane's lack of feeling for him. She said all the right words, but her interest was only in the children, in all her activities, and in those people she looked after and sponsored such as Flo—not him.

Finally, his thoughts were able to go where they needed to be now, to his beloved wife, Liz. His mother's words which she'd said over and over, as if she knew she wouldn't be around long to teach him, came to his mind. *"The greatest gift you can give your children someday, Matthew, is loving God and His Son Jesus Christ, and secondly, loving their mother. The greatest gift your wife can give your children is loving God and His Son Jesus Christ, and secondly, loving you, their father."*

"Thank you, Mom," he said quietly, as he blinked back tears. "Liz has given our children this gift and healed them. Her love has healed me."

He got up and walked slowly through the club and out to his car. Heading toward his home—his family, he said a prayer of thanks to God, who had so mercifully answered his prayers.

~~~~~~~~~~~

Liz couldn't help herself. She tried to look as nice for Matthew as possible. She put on a peach colored component which consisted of a textured cotton shirt slightly vee'd neck, with a casual cotton skirt. Underneath she wore a while tee. She wore this because the skirt had a stretch band which fit her thickening waist.

When Matthew called, she could tell that his cheerfulness was a bit forced, so she wasn't hopeful that he was any different. Nevertheless, she was glad that she didn't have to cook tonight, she felt so tired.

Calling the children in from play, she cleaned them up and had them change to clean clothes. They could hardly stand still, they were so excited, *a little too much so,* she thought. Had they been feeling her anxiety? Their father's preoccupation?

~~~~~~~~~~~

Sitting around the table in the restaurant, the children were hyper and talkative. After they had ordered, Matthew studied Liz. She was trying to put on a good front for the children. Her cheeks slightly flushed, made her face even more lovely and alluring against the peach color of her outfit. But he did miss the sparkle usually present in her eyes.

At one point, Liz had to get firm with Danny, he was talking and giggling so loudly. His face fell.

"Don't take it so hard, Danny," Matthew said, "you were being too loud. There are other people in the restaurant too, and we have to be considerate of them." Still, Danny looked downcast. "What's the matter, Danny?"

"Mommy doesn't smile anymore."

Shocked, Liz stared at him, then glanced at Matthew. She was right, the children were feeling their stress. "Uh...Matthew, I think it's time to tell Danny and Merri about our surprise."

Matthew looked puzzled until Liz discreetly patted her stomach. "Oh! Yes, we have a super surprise."

Danny's face brightened, and they both begged to know what it was.

Matthew looked over at Liz and she said, "You tell them, Matthew."

"The reason Mommy doesn't smile as much as she did is because she's feeling very tired right now. She's going to have a baby. You're going to have a baby brother or sister."

They stared at their daddy, then looked over at Liz, trying to take it in, then they both squealed and yelled so loud, it startled the people at the next table.

Matthew laughed. "Sssh, not so loud."

"When...when, Daddy?" asked Merri.

"When we get home, we'll get a calendar down and show you when. Now, go hug Mommy and tell her you'll help her so she won't feel so tired."

Danny was the first out of his chair, then Merri, both promising to help her. Liz returned their hugs, kissing each of them. "I'm sorry for not smiling more. I'll feel better soon."

Yes, you will, Liz, Matthew promised silently.

~~~~~~~~~~~

Immediately upon arriving home, the children begged to look at the calendar. Though not comprehending time, it still looked to them like a lot of days before they would see their baby brother or sister.

After tucking Merri in, Matthew went to Danny's room, but stopped at the entrance. The sight he saw and heard held him mesmerized. Liz was sitting on the bed, holding Danny in her arms, rocking him back and forth.

He heard her say, "Danny, I love you. I'm sorry I haven't smiled very much lately. I'm so happy you're my little boy. I promise to smile more—because I love you." He could see Danny's smile as he soaked up Liz's outpouring of love.

When the children were settled down for sleep, Liz went into the bedroom and changed to a nightgown, washed her face and was just about ready to climb into bed when Matthew entered. He strode over to her and took her in his arms, holding her tightly, his heart bursting with such love for her he couldn't speak for some time.

"I love you, Liz. I'm sorry I've been so distant. I'm sorry that I've caused you unhappiness, but it's over. I promise you. The problem I was grappling with is solved."

She pulled back and gazed into his face. She felt deeply gratified when she saw the intense love in his eyes. Still, there was uncertainty. There was the nightmare—his call for Diane. "I love you, Matthew," she managed to say, "but I'm so tired, I need to go to bed."

He was disappointed; he'd wanted to talk with her, especially since he noted the uncertainty in her eyes, but she did look tired, so reluctantly he encouraged her to do so.

The lights off, Liz turned her back to him, but Matthew put his arm around her waist and pulled her close. Though exhausted after his emotional day, he was sleepless. Unknown to him so was Liz, but after awhile, they both drifted off—so a part of each other—yet feeling apart.

Chapter Sixty-Eight

The music drew her up and out of the darkness, reaching deep inside to a longing, a partially fulfilled dream. Flat on her back, she stared at the familiar ceiling of her own home. The clock on the night stand glowed 3:00 A.M. She felt for Matthew. He was gone! The music was coming from *him*. She heard his wonderful mellow voice singing an unfamiliar song—a hauntingly beautiful melody.

She got up, and stepped into her house slippers. As she slowly walked toward the music, it brought back the memory of another awakening. Matthew's back was to her as he sat at the piano. The lamp beside it reflected light upon his hands as they moved across the keys. Totally entranced, she stood quietly a few feet behind him. Though having not heard all of them, the words were speaking of her...to her! When he finished, he sat there for a few moments.

Without turning around, he questioned, "Pipit?"

"I'm here, Matthew," she answered softly.

His shoulders shook with a heavy shuddering sigh. Still without turning, he said, "Come and sit beside me, my sweet Pipit."

She did so.

He looked over at her. "You were too tired to hear what I needed to say last night. Maybe that's why I woke up with these words and melody running through my mind. I hope they'll tell you the things I wanted to express."

She stared at the title above his penciled notes..."Pipit's Song." She swallowed the lump in her throat and listened as he sang the song to her.

PIPIT'S SONG

I called to you, you came to me,
In my grieving time of need.
It echoed through the tall dark trees
You came, my heart to feed.

My cry for help, were songs I sang
Echoing through the trees
Your path was cold and full of pain
But yet you came to me

You held my hand, my eyes to be
By you my path was lighted
Through you my eyes could clearly see
My floundering ship was righted

Our Pipit, our Pipit, your love you spread
Like rays of shining sun
The children's broken hearts you fed
Their hearts you quickly won

My Pipit, My Pipit, you paid the price
You chose to be my wife
My love, you chose not once but twice
With this you gave me life

When the song ended, Liz was in such a state of euphoria she could only sit and gaze at these penciled notes and words written down in the wee hours of the morning by the man she loved.

Matthew watched her, waiting.

Slowly, she turned to him. He saw the dancing lamplight mirrored in her tears. Through them, he saw her awe, her admiration, her love.

"The song, the words are beautiful. I can hardly believe you wrote them for me—and in the middle of the night. I...I didn't know you could write like this, compose like this."

"This is my first. You inspired it, Liz."

"How can I live up to those words?"

Matthew scooted from the bench, and rose, taking her hand, he gently pulled her up. He took her in his arms and murmured, "You already live those words. They're *you*, Pipit." He bent down and kissed her tenderly.

She clung tightly to him long afterward. "Thank you, Matthew. Thank you."

He turned the lamp off and led her to the bedroom, thinking that now they were ready for sleep, totally one in heart and soul. Instead, she reached for the lamp on her nightstand, flipped on the light, and turned to him, her face troubled.

Shocked and dismayed, he asked. "What...what's the matter, Liz?"

"I...I have something to tell you."

Fear sliced through him. "What?"

I know you've been having nightmares again, Matthew, nightmares about the wreck. You cried out one night."

"I did?"

"Yes. You cried out 'No! It's Diane. No!' I know you love me, Matthew. That song expressed it so beautifully, but I realize, now, that Diane will never leave your heart enough for us to build our love, our marriage the way I had hoped and dreamed we would. I know that's why you pulled away from me. I love you so much, Matthew, I'm willing to accept it, but I needed to let you know...that I knew."

Shocked, Liz watched a smile slowly come across his face. "Matthew!" she exclaimed indignantly. "This isn't anything to smile about...for me it certainly isn't."

"My precious wife, come with me into the family room," he said taking her hand. "We can't go to sleep just yet, I see. We need to sit down while I tell you something."

He led her to the couch where they seated themselves. Sitting slightly sideways so he could see her face, yet touch her, he smiled at her pursed lips which belied her curious eyes.

"First, my angel, I'll begin with the nightmares. They did start up again, but this time there was a startling change in them. When you heard me cry out, 'no, it's Diane, no,' it was because I dreamed that after the wreck I went to bed expecting to find you and found Diane there, alive, instead of you. In my dreams each time, I yelled 'no!, it's Diane. no!' I felt bereft, grief-stricken. I wanted it to be you there, not Diane."

He watched the change come over her face, the gambit of emotions take place. First, total surprise, then almost disbelief, and finally, ultimate surrender which comes only with unequivocal knowledge, and acceptance of the truth.

She reached for him, hugging him fiercely. "Oh, Matthew, Matthew, I'm so relieved, so happy. You wanted to tell me this last night?" He nodded. "Thank you for loving me like that." A new freshet of tears wet her face.

Matthew smiled, blinking a little fast himself, feeling joy at her happiness, hoping he could always make her happy, hoping he could make her as happy as she had him." Suddenly, she stopped crying and said, "You said you solved your problem. What problem? How?"

"I was wondering when you were going to ask that. Hadn't we better go to bed and talk tomorrow? You've been so tired."

"I don't feel a bit tired, Matthew."

He laughed. "Just as I suspected, part of your tiredness has been emotional."

"I think you're right. So tell me."

Matthew told her everything—the guilt, how puzzling it was to him that it seemed to be tied to Merri's behavior, his trip to Arthur's, and finally, he told her of his talk with Wayne Halstrom, relating everything Wayne had disclosed. Her expression was one of deep shock. When he was through, Liz was sobbed quietly. Matthew put his arm around her.

Finally able to control the flood of her emotions, she said, "I feel hurt for you, Matthew, for what you suffered during your marriage. But mostly, I feel sad for Diane. I can tell by Merri and Danny what kind of a person she was. They are such sweet, kind children. But I knew there had to be an answer to Merri's behavior."

"You did, and I was too stubborn to listen. And as Wayne said, he knew *your love for me* would heal Merri, and it has."

"I can't take all the credit, Matthew. Some of it goes to the example of my loving mother. At this moment, I appreciate her more than I ever have in my life. I'm going to call and tell her that, as well as give her and Dad our good news."

Matthew kissed her. "Good. Now—since we're telling all, I think I deserve to hear about Kirk Morgan."

"You do." Liz began with the first three proposals she'd had and what she'd discovered about the motives of these suitors. Then, she told him all about Kirk. As she did so, she watched Matthew's face reveal shock, then anger, and at last, sympathy for Kirk.

"No wonder you ran up into the mountains to me." He held her close. "Well, now it's my turn to feel sorry for Kirk. The poor guy...losing you. Lucky me for getting you." He paused. "You know, I think I realize why I felt jealous of him on our wedding night. I believe I felt insecure. I realize, now, that subconsciously, I didn't feel secure in Diane's love—so it must have carried over to you momentarily."

"Thank you for helping me understand, Matthew. Your actions on our wedding night were so unlike you."

"But you handled it beautifully, Liz." He smiled, remembering that unforgettable evening.

"I feel I must have had some help," she murmured, voicing a silent prayer of thanks that she hadn't followed her first impulse. She glanced toward the brightening window. "How beautiful, the sun is coming up." The first soft, lucent light filtered into the room.

They got up and went over to the window. Matthew opened it, and let the deliciously cool morning air in, refreshing the room from the stale refrigerated air.

It felt good to Liz and Matthew, it felt like fall...a new season for them...for their love.

"Matthew look!" she said pointing. "Our saguaro!"

They watched as the sun bathed the king of desert plants with its golden morning rays. "How magnificent it looks," she added, "even though it hasn't grown any arms yet."

"As you know, Liz, it takes a long time for the arms to grow, but next May beautiful waxy-white, funnel-shaped blossoms will crown the top, opening at night and remaining open till around mid-day, feeding the birds and animals. And every May after that. When it grows arms, blossoms will crown *them*, just as our love will grow and blossom as the seasons come and go."

Cradled in Matthew's arms, Liz leaned her head against his chest and sighed. "Oh, yes, Matthew, it will, because we'll *work* at it."

"You bet we will. I'm committed to it," he said kissing the top of her head. "Look, Liz, there's a little cactus wren perched on top of our saguaro. He's looking around as if he were surveying a glorious new world."

"Just as we are, Matthew, just as *we* are."

Epilogue

On March 31st Liz gave birth to a 6 pound, 7 ounce blue-eyed, blonde-haired baby girl. Merri was beside herself with excitement over her new sister. Danny's disappointment at not getting a brother soon dissipated when he held his baby sister for the first time. The protectiveness he'd always shown Merri was now focused on the tiny helpless bundle that had come to live with them.

Matthew was thinking of the miracle that brought him Elizabeth and now little Pipit Elizabeth.

Liz could hardly *believe* the miracle she held in her arms. "Don't you think," she said, smiling at Matthew, "that as soon as possible, little 'Lizzy' needs another sibling—one that is closer in age?"

"Yes," Matthew said, "and while we're at it, I'd like to order another girl—and two more boys."

Two days later, after Matthew brought Liz home from the hospital, the doorbell rang. Matthew answered it. It was Margo with an armful of gifts, and a wide smile on her face.

"Margo! Come in."

"You bet I will. I've come to see that new baby girl."

He led her into the family room where Liz, rocking the baby in the new rocker, was trying to put her to sleep while four little hands rubbed the baby's head, and played with her tiny fingers.

When the children spied Margo, they ran over and hugged her, their eyes wide at the presents in her arms.

"How are my two favorite children?" she asked.

"We have a baby sister, Mrs. Stillman!" Merri exclaimed.

"Come 'n see," added Danny, grinning wide.

"Hi, Margo," Liz said, happy to see their dear friend. "How sweet of you to come by."

Margo studied the baby carefully. "Well, Matthew, little Lizzy looks like her mother."

Matthew laughed. "Only a woman could possibly know that at this stage. Anyway, I sure hope you're right."

"I'm always right, Matthew," she stated. Turning to the children, she smiled. "I've brought little Lizzy a present and one for each of you. Here are yours," she said handing one to each.

Eagerly, they took their presents and tore them open. A tiny baby doll for Merri and small dump truck for Danny. Each, thrilled with their gifts, gave her a hug and a thank you.

"Let's open Lizzy's present now," Merri insisted.

"Here, Matthew, your hands are free," Margo said giving it to him to unwrap.

He opened it and gingerly lifted out the most beautiful white baby dress Liz had ever seen. All she could do was stare with her mouth open. Matthew handed it to her.

"Oh Margo, how beautiful. Thank you!"

"Yes. Thank you, Margo," Matthew added.

Entranced, Merri fingered its delicate lace. "Can we put it on her right now, Mommy?"

"It's too big for her now, Merri, but not for long. It's a small size." She looked up at Matthew. "In a couple of weeks, we'll take her to church in it."

"To church?" Margo asked.

"Yes. Matthew and I have decided to find a church we both feel good about and attend as a family."

"Well...talk about a coincidence," she quipped to hide her sudden emotion. Then pausing to regain control, she said quietly, "I have one more gift—one for all of you." She pulled out a beautifully wrapped package from her purse. "This is the most prized gift I could give you. I've been waiting a *long* time for the right moment," she said, handing it to Matthew, "and I feel this is it."

Liz noticed that their no-nonsense friend was blinking rapidly over moist eyes.

To hide the tears, Margo turned abruptly, and walked in the direction of the foyer. Over her shoulder, she said, "Phil and I will be back to talk to you about it."

Hearing the front door close, Matthew and Liz looked at each other.

"What a strange thing for Margo to do," Liz said. "Open it now, Matthew."

"Yes, open it now," the children chimed in.

Matthew knelt beside the rocker and undid the wrapping. To their surprise, it was a book. Matthew slowly read the title. *"The Book of Mormon...Another Testament of Jesus Christ."*

They all gazed at it for a moment, then Matthew lifted the cover. "There's a note here from Margo."

Danny reached out and touched Matthew's arm. "What's it say, Daddy?"

Matthew began to read:

>Dear Matthew, Liz and Children,
>Phil and I are members of the Church of Jesus
>Christ of Latter-Day Saints. We believe that this
>book was revealed by God as a witness that Jesus
>is the Christ. It is a record of Christ's visit to the
>Americas. It goes hand in hand with the Bible.
>I have a testimony that this is a true record
>delivered by the hand of God in these latter days,
>and translated by divine revelation.
>Matthew and Liz, read it prayerfully so you
>can find out for yourselves that it's a true record, that
>it is another Testament of Jesus Christ.
>>With Love,
>>Margo

Liz and Matthew's eyes met.

"Matthew, could...could this our answer?"

"I feel *something*, Liz, something I can't define," Matthew said, his eyes penetrating hers.

The children, though not understanding Margo's note nor what it might mean, fell silent. Merri clung to her mother and Danny to his father knowing instinctively that whatever it was, it must be important.

Palpable joy surrounded Liz. With her free arm, she pulled Merri closer, smiled at her, then Danny.

Matthew, still holding the book tightly in his hand, put his arm around Danny and with the other one he gripped his wife's arm— the one that was holding little Lizzy. He too smiled at Danny and Merri, then at his wife, feeling a sweet love and closeness he'd never felt before.

The small family remained this way for moments only, but for them the moments seemed suspended in time as a special spirit filled the room.

Finally, Matthew looked into his wife's face and spoke softly, "I don't know, Angel, if Margo's church is the one we should attend, but we're sure going to find out."